ENCHANTING
BEAUTIES

Mr. & Mrs Borter,
You were so special
to me growing up. that
I love that
you instilled a
love of music in
my life.
love,
Hannah

HANNAH R. HORCH

PAGE PUBLISHING, INC.
New York, NY

First originally published by Page Publishing, Inc. 2019

ISBN 978-1-64350-559-6 (Paperback)
ISBN 978-1-64350-561-9 (Digital)

Printed in the United States of America

For Eula Kate and Miss Elizabeth

To photograph is to appropriate the thing photographed. It means putting oneself into a certain relation to a world that feels like knowledge, and therefore, power.

—Susan Sontag on photography

CHAPTER ONE

1932

The noisy rumblings of her father's 1929 Dodge summoned Henryetta Dixon. Stepping out from her makeshift darkroom at the back of the garage, she caught just the butt end of her father's car as it barreled down the drive, gravel crunching beneath the fat tires, leaving clouds of dust suspended over the yard. Through the haze, his red taillights flickered long enough for the car to come to a rolling stop and then forcefully peel off. Had Henryetta known this would be the last time to see her father alive, she might have at least waved, but how could she know?

Shrugging off her father's dramatic exit as typical, Henryetta returned to her darkroom—her haven, her sanctuary where she was free from the heavy constraints she sometimes felt. No prissy mother fussing over her hair that was "out of style" or hollering at her to "wear stockings" even if it was a hundred degrees and she was only going to the mailbox. Her mother sought to control the tiniest of things when it came to Henryetta.

Then there were the nosy busybodies she could not escape. Henryetta was a natural beauty—statuesque, blonde, twenty-two, and born into wealth. By Brownsville's standards, she was almost past marrying age. Most of her high school classmates married at eighteen and now carried children on their hips. She often wondered if they felt caged. Henryetta cringed at the thought of wifedom, fussy babies, washing soiled diapers, and endless cooking and cleaning. What Henryetta craved most was freedom—freedom to roam the world with her best companion, her camera. Photographing heads of state, exotic peoples, chiseled canyons of rust colored rock and grass carpeted savannahs dotted with grazing animals lived in her dreams. She had traveled with her parents. There was more out there beyond this small cotton town of West Tennessee. Just beyond the city limits, a whole world of roads waited to take her to so many places she had read about in school.

Still, it did not stop the town gossips. Spinsterhood troubled everyone *but* Henryetta. At the market, at church functions, anywhere really, gossips attempted to weasel just an inkling that Henryetta Dixon had a beau. Why was everyone so eager to marry her off anyway? In here, under the red bulb Henryetta could be her truest self.

In here, *she* was the master. A deep satisfaction, like a soul getting its wings, settled over her as she developed the images she had captured. Field hands, gin employees, ladies at the market, children playing hopscotch—just daily lives at work and play were her favorite photographs. Henryetta grinned as she watched the image come to life on the photo paper. Of all the labels, people out there had given her, *that lady photographer* was the one she relished. She knew she was a novelty, a local character that stood out like Marvel Dotson or Harry Segal. Marvel was a crazy, little Negro man who wandered up and down Main Street carrying on conversations with people who didn't exist. Harry was the most talented painter around. Storefronts, walls, murals, family portraits—he was your man, except everyone whispered Harry really wanted to be a woman. Whether or not it was the truth, that's what stuck. Henryetta was one of *those* people, but because *she was a Dixon*, it was all right that she was a little peculiar.

And so what? Maybe she was strange, not wanting the things that most young women wanted, but *really*, what else was there for women to want? Why couldn't she dream a bigger life for herself than what everyone else was? After all, Amelia Earhart was flying wasn't she? Henryetta's photography was certainly as good as any man's. If it wasn't, why were people from three counties over hiring her to take their portraits? Maybe the novelty got her hired at first, but now, professionally, she was one the best photographers around.

However, since the Depression started, her business had dwindled to almost nothing. On this particular morning, she was developing a set of family reunion photos. It was her first job in two months. Five generations, some smiling, some straight faced, gathered around the matriarch who celebrated ninety years of living. She had worked and worked to get an image where the youngest of the clan was not a blur of squirming.

It was early morning, but already, the sun pounded the tin roof of the garage. She worked mostly after dark or before sunrise so she could leave the door propped open allowing in a breeze. She had all but put away her developing solutions and tools when her father left abruptly. As Henryetta tidied up, she looked forward to the rest of her day.

Her family's former housemaid, Minnie, was teaching Henryetta how to make her famous three-layer jam cake. At sun up yesterday, Henryetta had driven them out to her grandparents' farm, where she and Minnie filled a five-gallon bucket three-fourths full of luscious purple blackberries before nine. The rest of the morning, they spent in the Dixon kitchen, canning jar after jar of blackberry jam. Henryetta's mouth began to water imagining the sensation of taking that first bite of velvety soft cake, covered in rich, grainy brown sugar icing. Negro or not, Minnie was one of the best bakers in all of West Tennessee. Everyone knew that the ribbons Henryetta's mother took home from the county fair were really Minnie's. Lucille Dixon had not cooked so much as a cup of coffee her entire life. Daughters of cotton barons didn't do such things.

Earlier that year when Henryetta's father's opera house burned to the ground, the Dixons had to let Minnie go. The Depression had lingered and for the first time ever, the Dixons had to tighten their belts. Letting the help go was only the beginning. Still, Minnie was a sharp entrepreneur and an even better saver. So, she used part of her savings to start a baking business. People might have not been able to afford a whole cake, but a slice here and there with pennies pooled together kept Minnie busy baking.

Lost in thought of jam cake, Henryetta's hand jerked involuntarily, clinking two bottles together when a disturbing lone gunshot rang out and hovered in the sky just outside. Gooseflesh swept over her arms, and a deep foreboding flooded Henryetta's senses. As much as she wanted to push that sound from her brain, she could not. Her instincts told her who pulled the trigger long before the man ran up on the porch calling out for the Dixons to "come quickly". In *this* moment, though, her brain tried to play it off as a blown tire. After all, tires blew out all the time, but if that were true, why were her hands shaking when the sound of police car sirens erupted?

She listened as blaring sirens erupted in the direction of the police station. They were on the move. The noise was getting louder and coming closer to the center of town. As Henryetta stepped outside, the sirens died down, just like that. Suddenly, all was quiet. The chirping birds fell silent. The children's voices from next door disappeared. The breeze stopped. The only thing Henryetta could hear and feel was her own heartbeat. Gooseflesh covered her arms. As she gazed at the sky in the distance, the sunrays poured through the clouds. Since she was small, she believed those rays were pulling souls to heaven. Then a singular word came to her. *Daddy*. Her father was dead.

Like the colorful geometric bits of a kaleidoscope that are juxtaposed and jumbled, ever evolving into figures with each turn, so it is with memories. Over time, bits of reality and pieces of imagination turn over and over in the brain until a new memory emerges and becomes a person's truth. Although Henryetta did not see the moments before her father's death, she often imagined them from what she knew about her father and from an eyewitness report. Together, they became her truth.

How many times had she seen her father reach for the small wooden case inside the right-hand drawer of his desk? Nestled inside of it, sleeping in poinsettia red velvet was Thomas Dixon's prized Colt .45 pistol. Did he gaze upon his beloved pistol one last time before he loaded it with a single bullet? How did he get to the place where he would turn his gun on himself?

The day Thomas shot himself, an older Negro man shuffled along the street. In her imagination, the blurred figure of her father came into focus slowly. Standing there, among the piles of charred wooden beams, metal rubble, and ash where his opera house once stood, the midmorning sun beat down on her father, turning his face crimson. Stinging sweat trickled into his eyes and down his cheeks. He removed his suit coat to reveal random sweat stains under his arms and across his chest. The breeze cooled his face as he closed his eyes, leaned his head up toward heaven, praying for forgiveness. Then, he took his Colt .45 into his mouth. His yellowed teeth nervously tip-tapped on the barrel until he had the nerve to bite down. He tried to will his tongue to stay away from the barrel, but he lost, and swallowed the taste of the metal and the bitter slickness of the gun oil. The end of the barrel poked at the flesh in the roof of his mouth. His eyes closed for the last time as he steadied his hand. Then, ever so slowly, he pulled the trigger back. The gunshot echoed as her father collapsed to the ground, blood pooling beneath his head.

CHAPTER TWO

*T*he Dixon family dining room table was littered with an excess of sympathy casseroles, fried chicken, three bowls of ambrosia, and an odd assortment of food they couldn't possibly begin to eat in three months' time. Upstairs, Henryetta's mother, Lucille was bedridden with grief.

Her mother was down at First Methodist working the soup kitchen with the UMW when she first learned her husband had taken his own life. She went into high-pitched hysterics for twenty minutes before Pastor Ferrell and his wife could calm her down enough to drive her home. Her mama had held up long enough to tell Henryetta how to make funeral arrangements. Then she disappeared into her room. Henryetta's older brother, Thom Jr., had gone fishing that morning. He had no idea his daddy was dead.

Just as the sun was setting, Thom Jr. nonchalantly waltzed into the living room where Henryetta rested in her father's chair.

"What is it? Where are Mama and Daddy?"

"You really don't know?"

"Know what, Henry?" Thom Jr.'s heart began to pound. "Know what? What's the matter?"

"Where have you been all day, Thom?"

"I told you I was going fishing. For the last time, what's going on?"

"Daddy's dead," Henryetta mumbled.

"What do you mean *Daddy's dead?*

"I *mean* he's dead . . . he shot himself this morning down at the opera house . . . right in the middle of where the stage used to be."

As much as she wanted to break down, and as much as she wanted to scold Thom for being gone all day and making her endure this day alone, Henryetta did not have the energy. Her eyes void of emotion, stared blankly at Thom, looking right through him. He too, just stood, dumbstruck and immobile.

"Where's Mama?"

"I can't get her to come out of her room."

At the words, Thom ran for the stairs.

"It's locked!" she called out too low for Thom to hear her.

After several attempts to get their Mama to respond, Thom Jr. dragged out the ladder, propped it up against house, and climbed in through the open window of their mother's bedroom. The last rays of purple and orange light illuminated the sleeping figure of his mother. She lay atop of the brocade bedding, still in her day dress and pumps. Clutched to her chest was her wedding photo. On the bedside table was an emptied bottle of his father's forbidden scotch. Even though she had probably passed out, his mother looked peaceful, so Thom Jr. quietly tiptoed over to the door, twisted the key to the left to unlock it, pulled the key out, and placed it in his right trouser pocket. He slowly turned the doorknob to find Henryetta standing just outside the door with her hand held out to take immediate possession of the key.

Thank God for Minnie showing up the morning of the funeral. Lucille still had made no effort to come out of her room. If it were not for Minnie, Lucille would not have attended her husband's funeral at all. She reminded Henryetta of a rag doll with a blank stare. Lucille would not respond to any amount of her daughter's coaxing to bathe or eat. It was Minnie who gently led Lucille to the bathtub, all the while humming soothing hymns as she bathed her long-time employer. Lucille only allowed Minnie to dress her. At the church, Lucille sat frozen in the front pew. When Lucille would not rise to follow the casket out, Henryetta looked up at the pastor who understood and motioned for the congregation to exit, leaving just the two them in the sanctuary. Outside, Minnie waited at the bottom of the church steps. Soon Henryetta appeared. Together, she and Minnie took Lucille by the arms and led her to Thomas's grave.

After the funeral, Henryetta soon grew weary of hearing the doorbell chime. It meant more stories and awkward expressions of sympathy. Henryetta wanted to believe they were truly concerned, but the visitors began to frazzle her nerves. Thomas Dixon's suicide was big news for a small cotton town in West Tennessee. He was well known. For three straight days, complete strangers who had never set foot in her house, probably not even the edge of her property, now stood in their foyer feigning concern. Meanwhile, their eyes ogled the Dixon mansion. Their eyes darted from the expansive living room outfitted with rosy velvet sofas and lounge chairs to the oriental carpet on the foyer floor then to the china cabinet filled with an assortment of silver serving dishes and crystal goblets. Henryetta wanted to shove the meddlesome strangers right back out the front door, but her mother had taught her to be gracious. On and on, people asked questions she could not even begin to answer. Didn't they know how awkward it felt having to face people in light of her father's death? Minnie could see the mounting frustration on Henryetta's face. When Minnie caught her eye, she motioned for Henryetta to chin up and be strong.

With Minnie's encouragement, Henryetta smiled as she thanked friends and strangers alike for their concern and quickly ushered them to the dining room table where she invited them to help themselves to a plate of food.

At one point, out of the corner of her eye, Henryetta saw Minnie at the backdoor accepting condolences from her family's former employees. As Negros, they knew better than to come to the front door. "The last shall go first," popped into her brain as Henryetta half smiled and raised her hand to wave to them. Both, with hats in their hands, nodded back to Henryetta out of respect. Secretly, she longed to invite them into to join her front door guests in dining room. Employees or not, Henryetta had grown up with them. To her, they *were* family. Seeing the exchange, one of the mourners, a stranger, shot Henryetta a disapproving glance. Henryetta, at her wit's end already, forgot decorum, and challenged the stranger.

"Minnie! Please tell Moses and Clarence to come on in. Fix them a plate. They are welcome to eat at the kitchen table." The room fell silent at her words. If they did not like it, *they* could leave. This was her home.

By four o'clock, Henryetta grew desperately tired.

"Miss Henry. You don't have to answer the do' no mo'. Go on up and check on yo' mama. I's down here. I can tell folks you's don't want to be disturbed. What can dey say?"

Henryetta shrugged her shoulders. She wanted to lock the front door, but she knew what her mama expected of her, so she stayed on greeting folks, but when a lull came, she ran up the stairs to knock at her mother's door, hoping she would take over downstairs, but no response came from within. Even hours later, after the house finally emptied out of visitors and Minnie had gone home, Henryetta tried again to rouse her mother, only to be answered by more silence.

There were still piles of dishes to wash, but Henryetta told Minnie not to fret. They would be there tomorrow. When Minnie insisted on staying to finish up, Henryetta overruled, reminding her of the danger she risked being out alone after dark.

As Henryetta walked back downstairs to carry the last of the plates and tea glasses to the kitchen, it felt sinful letting all that left-over food go to waste when people were lined up for a meager bowl of watery potato soup. Thom sat at the kitchen table eating two plates full before telling her not to wait up for him. He was going out, and just like that, he disappeared again, leaving her with the mess. Walking to the dining room, she stared at the leftovers, watching the flies land and light, land and light.

Why didn't people come and offer to clean up and cook basic meals instead? Was it that having to figure out what to do with all the food and clean-up after the hordes of people was supposed to take her mind off losing her father? Henryetta felt it was as if death was another excuse to have a social event. Disgusted with the waste-fulness, yet too exhausted to do anything about it, she left it for the flies, pushed the light switch button, and headed upstairs for sleep.

About half way up the stairs there was a faint knock at the front door. Then it grew louder and staccato. Henryetta paused. The last thing she wanted to do was deal with one more visitor. It was too late for someone to be calling, so she started back up the stairs, but insistent knocks turned to pounding. Thinking maybe Thom had come back home without his house key, Henryetta turned to shuffle back down to the door. Before opening it, she peeked out the sidelight window, but was surprised to see a disheveled woman around her same age. As Henryetta peeked through the glass, the stranger's weary eyes begged for her help. The woman reminded her of a conversation she overheard at the grocer's that past Saturday.

Filthy hoboes—boldly knocking on doors for food, money, or work. Shameless! I tell you.

While Henryetta did not like the holier-than-thou comments, she let this exchange float out her mind so easily. Thank God, she was a Dixon. She was safe from the Depression. She never expected to be confronted by beggars, but now in front of her stood a hungry soul.

Dark shoulder-length curls peeked out from under the woman's camel colored, felt hat that was pulled down tightly on her forehead. The woman was wearing a raincoat over a mauve, cotton day-dress. In normal circumstances, Henryetta imagined the woman would be quite pretty.

"What do you want?" Henryetta asked through the glass.

"Food. Do you have any food to spare?" the woman pleaded. Henryetta just looked at her. She was torn. She had enough food to feed the town, but she wondered if she fed the woman, would she be opening Pandora's Box? Would she have a beggar on her porch every time she turned around? She knew how charity spread like wildfire through the poor. Her mother would have disapproved instantly and told the beggar woman to get on her way, but Henryetta was not her mother. Lucille Dixon served Hoover Stew down at the church for show, not so much for the real reason.

"Wait here," Henryetta said, holding her hand up. Her first notion was to fix the stranger a plate and tell her to leave it on the front porch when she was finished eating. As Henryetta walked past the dining table full of food, her dead father's words from her childhood echoed in her tired brain.

16

"There is nothing more painful than for a robust man, capable of hard work, to take a handout."

Why wouldn't this be true of a woman? Henryetta, living a life of privilege, never imagined the possibility of not having enough, at least not until her father passed. Even then, though, she shrugged it off. She was a Dixon. That meant there would always be enough and then some, but looking into the stranger's longing eyes, something clicked, changed over. Henryetta imagined herself on a stranger's porch, feeling gnawing hunger. She was not sure she knew what it really even felt like. Was there a difference between feeling hungry at suppertime and only having pride to swallow for days on end? There had to be.

With that, Henryetta turned on her heel and went for the front door. When she opened it, she found the woman, turned partly toward the front yard with her finger to her mouth to hush what Henryetta saw to be a toddler trying to break free of his small sister's grasp. Startled by the door opening, the woman whirled around to avoid being caught, but she knew Henryetta had seen, and now could hear the child whimpering as he struggled to get to his mother. The woman looked scared as if Henryetta would be angry with her for her deception.

"You have children," Henryetta said.

"Yes, ma'am. Two," the woman replied quietly, not looking away from Henryetta's gaze.

"I will feed you and the children, but you have to work for it. I don't give handouts," Henryetta said, attempting to sound firm like her mother would have.

"Thank you, kindly. We would be most grateful," she said.

"Call your children, and then come in," Henryetta commanded.

The woman turned and signaled for the children to come to her. They both began to run to their mother who met them on the bottom porch step. The toddler bounded into his mother's arms. Together, they walked up the steps and past Henryetta who held the door and closed it behind them.

"Is this a palace, Mama?" the little girl asked her mother. Henryetta smiled at the question as she passed and motioned for them to follow her into the kitchen.

"No, my love. This is just a very nice home," she replied as she took her hand and followed Henryetta to the kitchen. Henryetta noticed right off that the woman was not from around Brownsville. Her accent had more of a twang than the typical West Tennessee drawl.

"You can eat first. Then, I need you to clean up the kitchen. Can you do that?" Henryetta spoke, wondering how much older the woman was. The children looked to be five and two. Henryetta did not ask. She had her own calamity to think about.

"There are all sorts of foods on the dining room table and more in the icebox. Help yourself. You can eat here in the kitchen, but wash up first. There's a bathroom around the corner, just there," Henryetta said pointing to the help's half-bath.

"Thank you, miss," the woman said, herding her children to the bathroom. From the icebox, where Henryetta pulled out a plate of fried chicken and a red-velvet cake, she heard the sounds of water running and small voices. Soon the family emerged, their faces, hands, and arms much cleaner. Henryetta could not help but notice the long purplish-green bruise on the woman's right forearm. When the woman became aware of Henryetta's gaze on her arm, she self-consciously rolled her sleeve down to cover it.

Feeling awkward for staring, Henryetta gestured toward the dining room. The woman smiled, nodded, and grabbed three plates. As the woman fixed plates of food, Henryetta studied her more. How different they were, she thought. Henryetta towered over the woman at a statuesque five feet nine. This woman was no taller than five foot and some inches. Henryetta still wore her flaxen blonde hair in a longer bob, even though long hair was coming back in fashion. She liked the ease of it. She could wash it, let it air dry, and go on with life as opposed to sleeping in curlers, spending an hour brushing, pinning, and spraying it in place. Henryetta was never one to fuss over her appearance. As the woman made her way back into the kitchen, she looked at Henryetta's bare feet and wrinkled funeral dress. In ordinary circumstances, Henryetta might have apologized for her disheveled appearance, but her azure eyes revealed exhaustion. The woman's sympathetic grin felt like a gift.

As they ate, Henryetta filled a glass with lemonade and stood at the counter by the sink. This woman was quite ordinary. The woman's faded, handmade dress and worn leather pumps said she was maybe just a little bit above poor or maybe just country. Everything about the stranger was plain, yet the more Henryetta studied her features, the more she saw this woman was naturally beautiful. She still had an hourglass figure, even after two children. Henryetta's mother always complained that she was "too lanky, too tall, and too gawky" for society. Henryetta's mother fretted that her daughter did not inherit her curves. The stranger's little girl had her mother's dark wavy hair and large, almond-shaped brown eyes. All three of them had sun-tanned skin. Henryetta wondered how long they had wandered outside. At least she could help them in a small way.

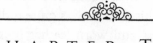

CHAPTER THREE

The woman reminded her children to slow down as they ate the Dixon's funeral leftovers even though she gobbled her own food and had gone back for seconds.

Henryetta covered the rest of the food on the dining room table with a sheet her mother kept in the buffet. At least these strangers were a distraction from her own pain. She smiled at the irony of the phrase, "Misery loves company." Here they were together in her kitchen-four miserable souls just trying to finish this day. How Henryetta longed for her soft bed and sinking beneath its covers that she would pull over her head to shield her from this world. Just to sleep and to not have to think.

"Do you have a place to sleep tonight?" The woman hesitated.

"No, not really," the woman said, looking at her almost-empty plate.

"You will sleep here then." Wasn't the preacher always talking about taking care of widows and orphans? She could argue with herself, but not with God.

Feeling satisfied with full bellies, the tired mother bathed her children and tucked them into the four-post bed in the guest bedroom upstairs. Soon after, she returned back down to the kitchen where she and Henryetta began to wash and dry all the stacks of dirty dishes left from the mourners who had come to pay their respects that evening. At first, neither woman spoke a word, but after the fifth glass was dried Henryetta could no longer stand the silence.

"My name is Henryetta Dixon," she said, extending her hand to the woman who had just laid a plate on the counter for Henryetta to dry. The woman shook the water from her hand and rather than a full handshake, she latched on to Henryetta's fingers and shook them like a woman attempting to comfort another woman.

"Florence Bell. I, we, are blessed to know you, Henryetta," she introduced with deep sincerity and surprising strength.

Henryetta could not explain it, but in that simple handshake she felt more genuine comfort than she felt shaking dozens of people's hands that she had known all her life. Neither woman smiled, but Florence's small gesture knitted a bond of kinship between them.

With the silence erased, small talk quickly led to Florence confiding in Henryetta about her family's unfortunate circumstances. For days, Florence had talked to no one about her predicament. She was a complete stranger to this town. One never volunteered private business anyway. Besides that, she had to be strong for her children, Junny and Marjorie. When Henryetta asked what her story was it was a great relief to unpack all her troubles.

Back home, deep in the mountains of Eastern Kentucky, Florence Bell had been a schoolteacher. That surprised Henryetta. Most schoolteachers were unmarried and sent home after nuptials. In Florence's case, the county made an exception. Her pupils put up such a fuss when the school system tried to send home their beloved teacher, that their parents protested the tradition. Florence worked in a little one-room, backwoods schoolhouse just a holler over from the small farm where she and Walter were raising their children, but her time as a teacher did not last long. Early on in the Depression, the county closed her school for an extra two months beyond the summer. The county offered to allow her students to go to a school in town, but most did not because of the long, strenuous walk back and forth through the hollers. Most of her pupils were very poor. Some did not even own a pair of shoes *before* the Depression began.

Her school opened up again, but by winter, the county shut it down for another seven months. The Great Depression only worsened, so the county had no choice but to lay off Florence and all the county teachers for good in early '31. Her county ran out of money.

No work meant no taxes, and no taxes meant no school. The mayor meant well when he promised her she would be back teaching soon, but it just did not happen.

Despite the closures, Florence took it upon herself to hold reading classes twice a week at the school without pay. Her students' parents would send a jar of canned peaches here, or a jar of apple butter there just to thank their beloved Missus Bell for teaching their children. But all that halted the day Missus Bell's lesson was interrupted by the doors bursting open and Superintendent Brown calling out to her, "Y'all can't be here!" She and her pupils sat stunned for a moment, but then Florence gave him her best look of disdain. That face had stopped many a child who thought to misbehave. If Florence, aka Missus Bell gave *the look*, all the children knew she would not bother with *the look* the second time. She would send the troublemaker outside to pick his switch off the closest tree, and wait for her. Now, it was very rare that Missus Bell had to resort to whipping a child with a switch. In fact, she may have only whipped one child in all the years she had been teaching. It only took one to scare the daylights out of the rest. The whipping became legend. You did not test Missus Bell.

Superintendent Brown backed off his bulldog stance without even blinking twice. He suffered *the look* quite often from his wife. He knew better.

"We're not hurting a soul, Superintendent Brown. I do not see why we cannot just meet here. I am not asking for any pay. These children need to learn how to read and do sums. Surely, you agree?"

"Aw, now Missus Bell, you know I do," he said even removing his hat.

"Missus Bell, you know most folks can't find work. Businesses are failing left and right. There ain't no taxes to be collected. The mayor says I have to lock the doors. Please, Missus Bell. Don't make this any harder than it has to be."

Florence looked around at her schoolhouse and sighed deeply.

"All right, then. I see we have no choice. Children, gather your things."

Out in the schoolyard, Florence and her pupils watched with tear-stained faces as Superintendent Brown chained and locked the doors forever. Their beloved little school would be no more. Without giving the grieving group a second glance, the superintendent put the key in his pocket, mounted his quarter horse that he tied to a nearby maple tree, and rode off down the hill. Once he was out of sight, Florence embraced each student telling them it would be all right, even though all of them knew it was not. Florence remembered thinking in that moment how grateful she was that Walter had a good job in the coalmines, even if it was dangerous.

Every evening Walter dragged in, weary and covered in filthy black coal dust with a nagging, often hacking cough that could never seem to expel the coal from his lungs, but then this changed. Appalachia was far from the hustle and bustle of bigger cities and out of the range of radio reception, but as outsiders wandered into their neck of the woods looking for work, they brought with them news of workers up north unionizing. Factory workers were striking for better pay and reasonable working conditions, so it did not take long for these ideas to catch fire in the coal miners' minds.

Walter quickly organized a group of likeminded miners who sought to unionize. For weeks, in the dead of night, fellow miners would hike through the hollers to meet in the Bell's barn to argue how to push for better working conditions and equitable pay. Florence feared Walter's zeal would get him into trouble, but she said nothing. He was her husband. She would just have to trust him; however, one of ten men betrayed the group. Fearful he might lose his job, the miner went to the bosses and revealed that Walter was leading the miners to unionize. So on a rainy Wednesday afternoon, the day before the men were all set to persuade the miners to strike, Walter emerged from a day's labor in the mine, joking and talking with others when he noticed the crew boss's displeased gaze. Suddenly, the boss stepped right out in front of Walter, stopping him cold.

"Bell, you're fired."

The boss handed Walter his wages for that week and quitting papers. Stunned, Walter searched the boss's face for a trace of mercy. Other miners stopped to watch the exchange.

"Ain't no union coming here!" the boss bellowed to the crowd. Some miners bowed their heads in shame. Others shrugged their shoulders, unconcerned and wandered off. Walter's closest companions stood firm beside him. One put his hand on Walter's shoulder in solidarity. The boss turned back to Walter, glaring at him while inhaling the last of his cigarette. Walter clenched his fist, restraining his anger. Then, Walter moved in close to the boss's face and in a deep, steely tone told him that he was flat out wrong.

"And you know it, boss."

The boss nonchalantly blew stale cigarette smoke in Walter's face.

"Well, you won't be around to find out about it, now will you, Bell?" He tossed the cigarette butt to the ground and squashed it with his foot.

"Any of you others want to lose your jobs? Go ahead! Just try organizing! There are ten hungry men just waiting to take your spots!" The defeated miners fell silent as the boss walked off.

As Henryetta and Florence washed plate after plate, Florence continued her story. It felt good to tell it to someone after all this time. It was as if someone opened a floodgate and Florence could not stop talking. Henryetta did not mind. It kept her own thoughts at bay and the work was moving along quickly.

"At first, we didn't worry. Walter was a good saver. We had plenty of preserves, chickens, several hogs, and a milk cow. Walter always loved hunting, and the mountains had plenty of deer, wild turkeys, and squirrels, so we always had meat." Florence paused.

"It got hard though. The preserves went faster than what I ever thought. You can vegetables and fruit all summer to get you through the winter, but when you do not have cash on hand to buy the little things at the store . . . Well, you eat what you have. Even the wild game became hard to find. Walter's hunting trips started taking longer because he had to walk miles and miles to track game. I remember being outside hanging the wash out to dry and hearing shots off in distant hollers in different directions. Everyone was hunting to survive, you see. When it came down to it, we knew we were going to lose the farm if we did not pay our note. We had no choice other than to dip into our savings. Walter called it his 'rainy day' savings, and Lord, it was pouring, and it just kept coming down.

"It got so bad, and I hated it, but I let Walter sell my horse. I know it sounds silly, but Philippa was not just any horse, she was a thoroughbred mare . . . she came from champion racers. She was a gift from my grandfather. He was a horse trader and quite the poker player according to my mother. He never could have afforded Philippa on his own. She was worth thousands. Granddaddy always said she could have run in the Derby. The story goes he won her in a poker game. Anyway, he gave her to me when I was twelve years old. She was just weaned from her mother. We grew up together— Philippa and me. She could run like the wind." Florence smiled. Nothing was better than the nudging of Philippa's muzzle against her neck, the earthy smell of the hay barn, the feel of her horse's warm, smooth coat as she lovingly groomed her.

"It liked to kill me the day that Walter took her to the stock-yards. She was not worth thousands anymore. By that time, she was thirteen, and nothing was worth the same money. I cannot imagine whatever happened to her. I felt like I betrayed her. Philippa was my family, just as much as Walter or the children. I could not handle it, so I took the children blackberry picking early that morning. I could not be there when Walter rode Philippa to town. I'll never forget that day."

Florence thought about the moment she returned home from blackberry picking. The horse pen stood empty.

"I dropped the whole metal pail of blackberries to the ground, spilling them into the dust. The funny thing was that I did not even know I did it. Something broke in me. It was like there was this hole in my chest. I could feel it. It really felt like my heart was actually broken. I cried. I cried so hard."

Florence's grief was so deep she detached from the family and sat despondently in her front porch rocker for days. When the children whined for her and tugged at her dress, Walter would come over, pick them up, and whisper to them to let their mama be.

"I just sat there in that rocker staring out at Philippa's empty pen. I could not make myself get up. After a few days, though,

Marjorie did something that just snapped me right out of it. She was drawing stick figures out in the dust when she started singing 'This Little Light of Mine.' I don't know, but it was as if God was telling me to stop wallowing and count my blessings. Philippa was saving us from losing the farm. When I realized that, I felt humbled. Here God put this horse in my life when I was a little girl, knowing that she would someday serve to save my family and me. Once I understood that, I wiped my tears, went in the house, put on my apron, and got back to my chores.

"Still, it only got worse. After we sold Philippa, thieves started stealing off our livestock while we were at church. First, it was a just a chicken. Walter said, 'God bless them. They need the chicken more than we do.' But when a second chicken and a hog disappeared the next Sunday, Walter changed his tune. He stayed behind from church, waiting just inside the barn with his rifle, loaded, ready to shoot, but nobody ever came. Whoever it was, they must have been watching us.

"Our Holstein cow, Tilda, was the last to disappear. Stubborn old thing. She never wandered too far from her feed trough. I always wondered if the thieves had tried to steal her before, but she made such a huge racket that they gave up. Walter used to say she was the best guard dog we ever had because she would get to bawling every time someone or something came up on our property. Tilda never let you forget to feed her either. Loudest cow I ever saw. She woke us up early every morning to feed her. That is how we knew somebody stole her. We woke up to silence. Not hearing her, we ran out to the barn.

"'We're finished,' Walter whispered to me as we stared at the empty stalls in the barn. There had been talk in town about there being farmwork out in California, but Walter kept saying that was our last resort. With our animals, he thought we had enough in savings to outlast the Depression. Fresh eggs and milk, hogs . . . we would be fine, but when we lost Tilda, desperation took hold of Walter. I could see it all over him. I tried to remain steady and hopeful.

"That night, after we tucked the children in bed, Walter went up to the hayloft, opened a secret panel, and got out our Mason jar where he hid our cash. Together, we sat at the kitchen table and counted out our life savings. We debated whether to risk taking our family out to California. His parents lived some counties over in a wide valley. They made their living off fruit trees, corn, and tobacco. With the Depression, though, they were not that much better off than us. Besides, Walter was a prideful man. Since I met him, he was always trying to prove himself to his daddy. Asking them to take us in was out of the question.

"In the end, Walter said it was better we try do something rather than do nothing. I did not question him. I knew poverty. Day in and day out, hungry, raggedy, barefooted coal miners' children came to the schoolhouse. People in Appalachia know hunger for sure.

"So, not long after, we walked down to town. While I was waiting on Walter, I found an abandoned newspaper on a street bench. While the children played on a patch of grass, I read about how there was no relief in sight. Everyone was blaming President Hoover. I remember there was this photograph of a Hooverville on the outskirts of Chicago. It's like a shantytown. Really, it is just shacks made out of whatever people could find. They reminded me of the houses Marjorie makes out of playing cards or a moonshiner's tarpaper shack I used to see deep in the woods when I went trail riding. Anyway, all those poor souls. At least we hadn't been pushed that far . . . yet. Then Walter came driving up in a Dodge Six he bought for almost nothing from a widow woman who said she had no need of the car since she had never driven one and never intended to. Walter made it clear we were going out to California to get work.

"We packed as much as we could carry by strapping it on the running boards and roof of the car. Walter had no idea how far California would be or how much money it would take to fill the gas tank, but he believed we had enough. We just took off blindly. I guess we thought we could outrun hunger. Fools. We were fools.

"We got as far as west Tennessee when Junny began whining and crying, nonstop. I thought that maybe he was just tired of being in the car. Finally, when Walter could not stand the fussing a minute longer, he pulled off just in time for me to get poor Junny out of the car to vomit everywhere. It was awful, because he got diarrhea too.

It was all over his pants and down his legs. Marjorie got out the car and came over to where I held Junny, who had collapsed in my lap. I told her to go back to the car. I was afraid she would catch it. It was so frightening."

"Flo?" called out Walter from the front seat. "Is everything all right?"

"Little June bug is sick. He just soiled his pants. Can you find me clean undershorts and a pair of pants for him? Bring a towel too. They are in the smallest suitcase." Walter threw his half-finished cigarette out the car window. He opened the door and smashed it with his foot. He walked around to the side of the car where he had strapped on the suitcase.

"Daddy, you know which suitcase?" asked Marjorie.

"I think so, Miss Busybody. If I get the wrong one, will you show me?" Walter teased as he smiled at Marjorie. She smiled and nodded as he unstrapped the suitcase.

"Does it matter which ones, Flo?" he called to her who was stripping off all of Junny's clothes.

"Any, Walter, and bring the canteen. I need to wash him off. He's a mess." Walter brought her the clothes and the canteen.

"Shoo-ee. That boy stinks!" Walter said, grimacing as he handed her the canteen.

"Walter, I don't know if we can go on right now. He is really sick." Junny was lying in his mother's lap whimpering, listless.

"Come on, Junny. Up you go. Mama has to wash you off." As Junny stood up, he vomited again, followed by diarrhea, this time just foul water.

"Lands sake, Flo!"

Florence did not take her eyes from Junny.

"Don't just stand there, Walter! Help me wash him. You hold on to him, and I will get him clean," Florence commanded as she began to pour water from the canteen over his bottom and legs. After she dried off Junny, he collapsed naked into his father's arms.

"Junny, June bug is as naked as a jaybird," Marjorie sang, thinking this might make Junny smile. He only slept.

"Florence, it looks like there is a stream just down over the hill. Do you want me to wash his clothes out?" suggested Walter.

"No, I'm a mess. Let me go. I need to change my dress, too." So Florence walked down to the stream and washed out Junny's clothes.

"Mama, Daddy said to give you this soap," Marjorie called out as she walked down the hill.

"Thank you, love. Can you ask Daddy to send my green dress down the hill to me?"

Now in a clean dress, Flo climbed back up the hill. She was worrying about her baby, but began to worry for all of them. Was it something they ate? What if all of them caught it?

When she reached the car, she saw that Walter had spread out a blanket under an oak tree. Still naked, but covered with a towel, Little Junny slept. Florence went over to Junny and felt his forehead. His skin burned to the touch.

"Walter, we have to get him to a doctor. He's burning with fever," Florence stated with urgency. With that, she picked up Junny, blanket and all, and got into the car while Walter placed Junny's wet clothes in a small metal pail he had packed in the back seat. Within the hour, they saw a water tower that read "Brownsville: A Good Place to Live." Walter pulled over at the first filling station he saw to get directions to the town's doctor.

"And that's how we came to be here," Florence said as she handed Henryetta the twentieth plate they had washed that night.

"Where's Walter now?" Henryetta asked.

"Gone."

"Gone? What do you mean gone?"

"Well, Junny getting sick took most of our money. He ended up in the hospital for a few days. Then there was the motel bill and meals at the diner. Walter thought we had just enough money to ride the train out to California if he was able to sell the car. The trouble was no one in Brownsville wanted to buy it. When I woke up the third day we were here, Walter was not in the room. I guessed he had gone for coffee for us, but I found a note on the table by the door. He said he had gone to Memphis to sell the car. He would wire us money to catch the train to meet him there."

Florence stopped speaking and leaned over the sink on her elbows. Her body began to shake with sobs. Henryetta put her hand on Florence's shoulder.

"He never wired the money," she said softly. "My horse . . . my home . . . and now my husband. Everything has been taken from me. Everything, but my children. I won't lose my children too." Florence stood upright, took a deep breath, and faced Henryetta.

"I'd been praying and praying for God to send us a miracle. This is the God's honest truth. As I was wandering down the streets, I was praying. Then I saw all of the cars in your driveway and people dressed all in black. When I saw all the ladies carrying food to your house, I knew you would have food to spare. So I waited until dark, knowing everyone left. That is when I knocked on your door. You're our miracle."

Henryetta sighed deeply.

"You did right. I would have done the same thing, and to tell you the truth, I am not sure what is going to become of my own family before all of this is over."

Florence turned to see the sorrow in Henryetta's eyes but did not want to pry.

"I reckon Walter hopped a train to California without us. Without a single word. I have no idea what has happened to him."

"He didn't leave you with any money at all?"

"Not really, I had a dollar of the cash that was left. I found the train station hoping Walter would arrive on the train from Memphis, but he did not. I waited and waited at the station, but he never showed. So I went back to the motel to see if Walter had wired us money, but nothing. Once the owner of the motel knew our predicament, he was good enough to take us in for one night for free, but after that, he kicked us out."

"Where have you and the children been sleeping?"

"The first night we came across a wagon with a tarp over it. We climbed in it and slept. The next night we found an empty garage. When I knocked on your door, I had not eaten in two days. The children ate some old bread and fruit I found in the bin outside the grocer's."

Henryetta fought hard not to grimace at the thought of digging in the trash for food.

"And your arm? What happened to it? I noticed it was bruised."

"A fight at the bin. I was fighting off a crazy little Negro man who was trying to grab the bread right out of my hands. He said I was stealing from him."

"I know the man—Crazy Joe. He wanders up and down Main Street begging for work. It used to be he was the only one. Now there are a whole slew of them, young and old, Negros . . . whites. So many men have lost their jobs. They just hang out in front of the barbershop waiting for a farmer or somebody to pick them up to go do a day's worth of work. Every now and then, we will even see a bunch of hoboes hop off the train to eat at the Methodist soup kitchen. Did you find it, the soup kitchen?" asked Henryetta.

"No. I didn't know."

"Well, you found me. Lord knows we *can't* eat all this food. You are welcome to stay here as long as you need. Let's go to bed. I am ready for this day to be over."

"Thank you, Henryetta. I am much obliged to you for taking us in like this. We will be out of your hair as soon as Walter sends for us. It should be any day now."

Henryetta smiled and pushed the light switch off as they left the kitchen for bed.

CHAPTER FOUR

R estless, Henryetta could not get Flo's story out of her head. Try
as she might, Henryetta struggled to fall asleep. Flo's story inter-
mingled with her father's suicide replayed repeatedly. Finally, around
three, Henryetta had just dozed off for the first time when she heard
her brother, Thom Jr., cuss as he stumbled into the hall table. He was
probably drunk, but that was nothing new. Thom's carousing had
worsened in the past three months, causing a frequent raucous in her
home. She found it ironic that Prohibition was supposed to prevent
this kind of thing, but it seemed to make drinking worse as far as she
could tell. The preacher sure said so.

Her parents were fit to be tied with Thom's latest antics. He
had never behaved this way in his life. He was always sensible, but
over the past year and a half, Thom changed. Before, he was introspective. He enjoyed walking in the woods and helping his grandfather with his gardening. He was fine to be solitary, but loved a good
story—the kind of stories his grandfather and father loved to tell.
Then, his moods suddenly began to change like the weather. One
day he was sunny and fun to be with. The next, he was sullen or
angry like dark thunderstorm clouds threatening to pour down. He
lashed out at his father for the smallest of things. Henryetta soon
dreaded dinnertime, wondering what argument might crop up next.
The Dixons soon found it better not to talk at all at the dinner table.
They shrugged it off as "I'm just tired," or "Nothing really happened
today worth talking about." At best, they only spoke when it was
absolutely necessary.

Before Thom's drinking began, around when he was twenty, he and his best friend Sy McGhee discovered the "drinking shack" as the locals called it. One late morning, they were walking out of the bottoms from where they had been cat fishing since before dawn in the Big Hatchie River. The drinking shack was a sad, weathered clapboard house. Abandoned decades ago, it sat in silence among a grove of pecan and hundred-year-old oak trees. Thom and Sy had walked past it a thousand times and never really paid any attention to it. When they were younger, they dared one another to peek in the windows. Both swore up and down the boogeyman lived there. They went on and on about the time Sy supposedly saw him sleeping on a mat by the fireplace. Thom was never so lucky. Sy reasoned the boogeyman simply vanished before Thom could get a good look at him. After all, that is what the boogeyman did. Repeatedly, the boys tried to catch boogey at home, but never saw him again. "Base" was an oak tree that sat twenty feet from the front corner of the house. One boy would dart to the window to peek in and then dash like lightning back to the tree.

On this particular morning, two mud-splashed flivvers sat parked under the grandest oak tree in the side yard. Two men made several trips, back and forth from the flivvers into the shack, carrying wooden crates through the front door. As they came closer, they recognized one of the men to be Amos Lytle, a boy who graduated two years ahead of them. Thom motioned for Sy to stop and move behind some brush to continue spying. When the two cars drove off, Thom and Sy walked into the unlocked shack and discovered a makeshift bar.

Wobbly, four-top tables, flanked by a hodgepodge of mismatched chairs were scattered in each room. The floors squeaked and groaned with every footstep. The dank smell of mold floated in the heavy air. The floor and the walls bowed in some places giving the feeling that the whole shack would cave in at any moment. The floral wallpaper peeled up in several places behind a dusty piano in the corner of what used to be a parlor. Sy, grinning mischievously, went over to the piano and gently tapped two notes breaking the silence. Surprisingly, the piano was tuned.

Sy followed Thom into the kitchen. A multitude of small, over-turned glass jelly jars lay lined up for drying beside the sink. Brown bottles with cork plugs peeked out from the slats of several wooden crates, stacked in the corner of the kitchen. Someone had pried off the lid of the top crate and a single bottle rested beside the jelly glasses. Thom went over, removed the cork, and inhaled the strong aroma of bootlegged moonshine. He took two swigs from the bottle, feeling the warm liquid travel down his chest. Thom handed the bot-tle to Sy who eagerly guzzled it, leaving only a quarter of the spirits in the bottle.

"That'll do it," Sy smiled, wiping his chin, waiting for drunk-enness to kick in.

In town, Thom and Sy asked friends what they knew about it. It turned out, the police turned a blind eye to the shack on account of the fact that the Chief himself was known to partake of "just a nip" every now and again. About once a month, though, an angry wife would ride her moral high horse over to the police station and insist the shutdown of that "den of iniquity" for good. This typically happened when a husband came home reeking of moonshine and cheap perfume. The shutdowns only lasted a few days. Thom grew especially irritable then.

However, the night of the worst row between Thom Jr. and their father, the shack was open. It was the middle of the night, just three days before her father shot himself. Henryetta had been asleep, so she did not hear or even know the first part of the argument started down in the cellar of their Victorian mansion. Henryetta woke to her father's name-calling once he and Thom reached the second floor landing.

"Shiftless drunkard!" her father screamed angrily, and then both of their bedroom doors slammed shut. Silence again.

Henryetta and Thom shared a wall between their bedrooms. Thom's window squeaked and groaned as Thom worked to open it wider to step out on front porch roof. She debated whether to go out and talk to Thom. Since they were little, they had spent many a night sitting out on the roof stargazing, telling stories, or just talking. Lately, though, a curtain of awkward silence hung between them.

Thom Jr. knew his sister had heard the rumors in town about him—how he spent his nights drunk, and his days hung-over. It was true. If anyone needed Thom Jr. all one had to do was drive the main street. They'd find him either shuffling aimlessly down a sidewalk, sitting on a bench at Court Square, or shooting the breeze with other bums, just outside the barbershop doors. Rumor had it that Thom Jr. had turned into a no-good philanderer. Henryetta believed her brother to be a good person and did not want to pay attention to petty gossip, but still, she worried about the changes she was seeing in her brother.

For most of his life, Thom had been so quiet at school; his classmates mistook his shyness for arrogance. After all, his daddy was Thomas Dixon, one of the richest men in Brownsville. Thom Jr.'s classmates perceived him as "too good," but Henryetta knew they just did not know the real Thom. Thom Jr.'s irresistible natural good looks only added to their jealousy. Well over six feet tall with thick golden hair that he left long in the front and trimmed tightly at the sides and back, Thom inherited his mother's light green eyes and refined air. Henryetta always smiled when her girlfriends plotted to win her brother's heart, because she knew he would be totally dense to their advances.

From his father, he inherited a profound love of the outdoors. He loved the tranquility of the woods, the call of the wood duck, and the quiet gurgles of the stream. At school, Thom sat silently as his classmates complained about their supposed sweethearts. Ball and chain was more like it. It seemed to Thom they spent more time squabbling than loving. Thom wanted no part of the drama having a sweetheart would bring to his life. Mother Nature was enough of a woman for him.

What Henryetta did not know was how Thom transformed after the first time he had a drink or two of moonshine. His body warmed, his teeth numbed, and his muscles relaxed. Suddenly, the boisterous laughter, the ragtime piano, and the curve of a pretty woman's hip sucked him in and he would not let go of any of them. Thom willingly reveled in the sensations of the moment. He did not think about consequences. He let go of everything he was and opened himself up to this new man the moonshine coaxed him to be.

It only took two visits to the drinking shack before people cheered on Thom as he entered the shack. Suddenly, Thom was never without a woman hanging on his shoulder whispering lusty promises if he would only be hers. It was then he became aware of his warped power of attraction. The moth's flame, a luring magnet, the well in the desert—Thom proudly likened himself to all these. The moonshine's physical sensations, the women, and comradery of the shack allowed Thom to emerge easily out of his more reserved self. Even deeper though, buried in the recesses of Thom's broken heart was the real reason he had embraced the drink.

If Thom was drunk, he found he could cope. A few months earlier, Thom Jr. discovered his father had a dark secret, one that could destroy their family. Twisted up inside, Thom Jr. was a mess of fear, loathing, betrayal, and aloneness. The longer he carried *it*, the worse *it* was for Thom Jr. So in a moment of grief, Thom Jr. gave into Sy's badgering. For the longest time, Sy had tried and tried to convince Thom Jr. to go out to the drinking shack with him. Confessing his father's wrongdoing to Sy felt so good after three shots of moonshine. Drunk, Thom Jr. boldly claimed he didn't care what his daddy did, but when the moonshine's warmth left his numbed brain, Thom Jr. grew tight lipped and even more somber.

Since that first night, Thom Jr. turned into the worst kind of womanizer. On top of the hood of a car, against the wall of the shack or in the backseat of Sy's Ford, it did not matter where. Time and time again as Thom crashed deeply into a woman's inner body, he felt reckless hate for what those women allowed his father, and now him to do to them. He longed to be unshackled from this loathing and sought to free himself in climax—a freedom that never came. When Thom Jr. finished with a woman, he somberly, without a word, a thank you, or a kiss walked away, never to talk to her again. It was in those moments Thom never felt emptier in his life.

Now a notorious heartbreaker, his cast-offs warned other women to steer clear of him. His popularity at the drinking shack soon dried up and Thom found himself back where he started, singular and quiet with an even heavier amount of remorse hanging around his neck.

By the time Thom and Henryetta's parents got wind of Thom's behavior, he was drinking almost every night. Thomas and Lucille sat in constant fear that a random woman would show up on their doorstep claiming Thom to be the father of some bastard child. This was nasty business for the president of the United Methodist Women and Businessman of the Year. It was true. Thom and Henryetta's father had been the prestigious owner and operator of the Brownsville Opera House before it tragically burned only six months earlier. Henryetta knew her parents would not swallow Thom's behavior easily. Little did she know there was a nasty secret egging on Thom Jr.

The night of the argument between her father and Thom Jr., the smell of Thom's cigarette floated in Henryetta's window and lingered above her. Henryetta threw back the covers, wrapped an afghan over her shoulders, and went to the window. Thom was lying on his back, taking a deep drag, angry tears streaming down his cheeks.

"Thom."

"Leave me alone, Henry. I don't want to hear it," he said between drags.

She stared at him until he looked her way.

"What?" he half yelled at her.

"He didn't mean it," she comforted.

"Not this time, Hen." He turned to look at Henryetta.

She averted her eyes to the sleeping front lawn and then back to him. She knew her father meant it. Her father was not one to mince words. Thom knew he was on the road to ruin. He just did not know a better way to cope with his father's dirty lies. Fights like these with his father, tempted Thom to expose their father to Henryetta, but he knew the deep disappointment she too would harbor. Thom couldn't do that to Henryetta. Instead, Thom suffered disappointment alone.

Across the hall, Thomas Sr. stared at the ceiling, still riled up from the argument with his son, but it wasn't really Thom with whom he was angry. Thomas Sr. loathed himself. The opera house was gone. His investments were gone. The money in the bank was gone, too. His debts only kept mounting. Failure waited for him on the corner, out in the car, down in the kitchen. It was everywhere, and to conceal his failed finances, Thomas Dixon had desperately turned his former hobby, photography, into risky business. This business that if discovered, would steal away everything that really mattered, his good name, his wife's love, his family's well-being, his freedom, all of it. However, he had to maintain appearances for Lucille's sake. She was accustomed to a high society life style. He could not fail her, so he risked everything rather than admit failure.

Thomas Sr. carried guilt and an even greater fear that Thom Jr. would out him to Lucille and Henryetta. He *could* tolerate losing material possessions. It was losing Thom Jr.'s love and respect that drove him to first conjure his own death. He knew if Lucille and Henryetta ever discovered what he was doing to keep them afloat, he could never forgive himself. He could not live the rest of his life with them knowing the truth.

"He's right. I've turned into a drunk," admitted Thom Jr., putting out the stub of his cigarette on the roof.

"So stop, Thom."

"That's just it, Hen. I have tried. God knows I've tried, but I can't."

"Why not?"

"I don't know." Thom lied.

"There's nothing else to do in this godforsaken town." More lies.

"You could get a job . . . and keep it," Henryetta suggested sheepishly.

"Oh yeah. Easy for you to say. Like what? Picking cotton, working at the gin? Working like some poor nigra-man?"

"Then go to college," she suggested.

"I am not for college Hen, and you know it. I barely could stand high school."

"Sounds like you don't want to do anything, Thom, except what you are already doing."

"Thanks a lot. You are as bad as he is. Just go back to bed, why don't you, Hen?"

"Thom, you'll find it. I know you will."

"Yep. I'll find it at the bottom of a bottle," he said turning on his side away from her.

Henryetta sighed deeply and then backed away from the window and pulled it down.

Since that particular night, she and Thom had not a full conversation, even when they discovered their father shot himself. What bothered her most was Thom's flippant lack of grief. Here it was the night of their father's funeral and Thom Jr. was so drunk he could not even walk straight down the hallway. She heaved a heavy sigh and then prayed for sleep.

CHAPTER FIVE

*D*awn spilled through Henryetta's windows, calling her to wake. Still groggy, her mind wandered to her former life out of habit. She completely forgot her father lay stone cold in the ground with mounds and mounds of dark soil piled atop of his coffin. Her mother who slumbered alone next door did not cross her mind.

Instead, Henryetta began to think of her work. Who would she meet with today? Was it a couple about to be married? Someone's birthday? A church social? She had a solid reputation for quality work, especially here in a small town. Memphis was fifty miles south, but times being hard, photographs were not a necessity, but more so a luxury. Every now and then people would pool their pennies and call Henryetta to photograph them in their Sunday best for nothing more than simple pleasure. There was no money to go anywhere, so why not? It took their minds off the times. It was something to while away the hours of lonely sameness.

When Henryetta's photography dwindled to nothing, she lowered her prices. Then, she even began to barter for a new dress or vegetables from someone's garden. The truth be told, she loved photography, just for the sake of photography. It was not work. It was her passion. She did not care that bartering and lowering her prices were not in her best interest. In Henryetta's mind, the Depression would not last forever. People would remember her character first, and later, choose her over other photographers.

Then, suddenly, her thoughts were yanked abruptly back into the present by the sounds of small feet pitter-pattering from the bathroom to the guest room. It was funny how quickly one night turned into weeks. Florence, Junny, and Marjorie were now a part of Henryetta's life. On Sundays, in church, Henryetta regularly thanked God for them, especially the children. Their antics and questions diverted her from worrying about her mother who was now a recluse. Their zeal for the smallest of things reminded her of her own childhood. Their wonder and amazement helped her cope when her mother refused to come out of her room, refused to bathe, or even eat. If Henryetta's mother knew they had houseguests, she did not let on. Lucille just continued passing through the upstairs as if she were a living ghost. Getting her to bathe, getting her to speak, or getting her to eat became such a battle that Henryetta was faced with calling Dr. Castellaw to their home after several days of what Florence termed "nonsense."

"She's depressed," stated Dr. Castellaw.

"The whole world is depressed, Doctor. What can I do?"

"Give her time. These things tend to improve. She is grieving," Dr. Castellaw said as he closed up his doctor's bag and excused himself out their front door.

Henryetta stood very still, wondering when *she* would have time to grieve. When could *she* shut herself off from the world and just cease to exist like her mother, or maybe she would join Thom and his pals at the drinking shack. She could drink to forget what she had just passed through and what she now faced.

Shortly after Dr. Castellaw left, the telephone rang. It was her father's lawyer again. Four times, he had called the Dixons, telling them it was time to read the will, and four times her mother just gazed at Henryetta despondently, blankly, as if what Henryetta was telling her was not remotely intelligible. When Henryetta tried to persuade Thom Jr. to go down to the office with her, he protested saying they needed their mama to go. This was the fifth time. Surely, she could coax her mother out of her bed today. They needed to get on with life. After all, all this sadness had to end sometime, didn't it?

Henryetta tiptoed up the steps and opened her mother's door just a crack. Without looking into her mother's room, she called out to her mama.

"Mr. McBride rang us again, Mama. He says we need to come down to the office to read Daddy's will . . . Mama? Mama? Did you hear me? We've got to go down to the lawyer's office." Nothing. Henryetta pushed the door open to find the room empty.

"Mama? Mama? Where are you?" Henryetta went around the other side of her mother's bed to find the space empty.

"Mama! Where are you?" No answer. Puzzled, Henryetta opened her father's closet. The scent of pipe tobacco lingered on his dress coats, pinstripe trousers, and white button downs. As she closed the door, she noticed her mother's closet open just a hair. As Henryetta opened the door wide, there in the dark, sat her mother, clinging to her knees, hidden by her nightdress. Henryetta sat down next to her mother and gently patted her mother's upper arm.

"Oh, Mama. Please come out of there. This is not helping. It is time to move on. That is what Daddy would have wanted. He does not want you spending the rest of your life in this closet, crying your eyes out every day. Please, Mama. Do it for us. We need you."

Her mother simply shook her head and buried her face into her knees. For four weeks, her mother had not uttered a single word. Henryetta sighed deeply at her mother's sorrow. She did not know how to help, how to get through to her. After a few moments, Henryetta got up to leave. Her mother reached for the closet door and closed herself in the dark. Henryetta realized it was up to her to take charge of the family business. Thom Jr. was not eager to step up, and her mother was clearly incapable. She telephoned Rufus McBride to let him know it would be her alone representing the family. At first, McBride resisted. She was the daughter. It was not her place to take care of family affairs.

"Don't you think we might ought to wait for your brother at least?"

"Mr. McBride, if Thom Jr. was remotely interested, don't you think we would have taken care of this weeks ago?"

"Well, all right, but this goes against my better judgement. I just feel it would be better . . ."

"I understand, but someone has to step up, and I'm the only one willing to do it. I'll be there at one o'clock if it is all the same to you."

"Fine. One o'clock then."

"Yes, sir."

As Henryetta walked to lawyer's office on the perimeter of the court square, she could only imagine how much money she would be required to manage. What if she made mistakes and cost them their fortune? Surely, she would not have to do much. Her mother had been worth millions. She imagined herself writing checks at her father's desk as she had seen him do many times over the years. Curiously enough, even though it was her mother's fortune that funded her father's success, her mother never had any interest in their bank accounts. When she wanted money, Thomas Sr. handed it to her with a smile.

Lucille came from generations of cotton money and in her younger days had many wanton suitors, some just plain predators, drooling at the prospect of inheriting her father's fortune. Lucille told stories of how she had so many suitors she had to "beat them away with a stick." Henryetta laughed and laughed at this trying to imagine her mama even picking up a stick. When Lucille came out into society, there were plenty of other rich, white heiresses to cotton fortunes, but none as handsome and accomplished as Lucille. Lucille had inherited an abundant head of waist-length, jet-black hair, a tiny stature, and a curvaceous bosom. Her skin was the color of alabaster, with lips and cheeks the color light pink roses.

There were all sorts of wild tales about Lucille's possible ancestry. First, there was her great-great grandfather's clandestine affair with a Cherokee woman who died giving birth to their child. Others said somewhere in the family tree there must have been a secret love child. Perhaps the child was born from a mulatto lover. That had to be who gave her those thick black ringlets. Henryetta's grandmother scoffed at all the outlandish stories and insisted Lucille's green eyes were proof that she was nothing other than an Irish lass—end of story. While Lucille relished being at the center of people's conversations, these rumors fueled Lucille's behavior to be above reproach at all times. Cherokee, mulatto, or Irish, it made no difference. Lucille was a lady.

To Thomas Sr., the genes she inherited made no difference to him. The moment he laid eyes on Lucille, he knew she was to be his. Lucille's wealth was only an added benefit, especially for a poor actor, but one with a head for business. For several years, Thomas dreamed of owning his own company of actors, even his own theater, so quite soon after they married, Thomas Sr. invested Lucille's dowry in the stock market and tripled their money almost instantly. Smart investments allowed Thomas to build Brownsville's Opera House.

There was not much else to do other than church, social clubs, and work in West Tennessee, so the draw for entertainment brought crowds from town, neighboring counties, and even Memphis as her father was quite good at advertising his talent. The opera house was extremely lucrative and afforded them the Dixon's Victorian home. Her father beamed as he read, "It is quite remarkable that such a small town could boast such lively entertainment," from the Memphis newspaper. Twice, the town awarded Thomas Sr. Businessman of the Year because of the money the opera house brought to town. Another tycoon built a motel, and a late night diner opened up for after-production meals. Thomas Dixon was a hometown hero.

For Henryetta's whole life, the Dixon family never wanted for anything. Often, after a satisfying meal, her father would lean back, unbutton his suit coat, and declare, "Now, that's living high on the hog." Several times a year, Thomas traveled north in search of actors and plays for the opera house, taking his family with him. Whenever they traveled, Henryetta marveled at how her mother could adjust her demeanor to any social situation. In Brownsville, she was the epitome of the "good Christian woman." She was humble and gracious, but in New York, her color changed from purest angel white to glitzy gold. Her mother relished every moment of buying the newest dress fashions, eating dinner in gourmet restaurants, and schmoozing with other wealthy wives, "real society," as she liked to call it.

Lucille was even quick to change her accent from a Memphis drawl to a plainer Midwestern one, unless of course her accent made her more charming. Some circles adored her elongated vowels and begged her to talk some more. She basked in the attention. Perhaps, Henryetta thought it was her mother's ability to perform for whatever crowd that had attracted her father to her in the first place.

Thomas worshipped talented actors, and her mother was one. Either place, either woman, she was in the center of society, right where she wanted to be. Now, Henryetta wondered if the shell of a woman who seemed barely to exist upstairs was an act or the real woman that had been hiding just below the surface for years. Henryetta felt more than a tinge of resentment that her family left her alone to deal with her father's business. She pondered how quickly her father's suicide turned her life upside down.

Just a week and a half ago, Henryetta had counted the money she had been saving to travel solo up to New York to see her mentor and photography instructor, Ezra Rubenstein. Since she was a small girl, there had never been a trip to New York without spending time in Ezra's camera shop and later gallery.

Henryetta's earliest love of photography came from her father. Thomas had always been fascinated with cameras and photography. Thomas loved photographing people, and rarely, was he seen without a camera close by. However, her mother grew outdone with Thomas's hobby very quickly. She tired of constantly posing for photos. She wanted to get on with things instead of waiting for him to get his camera, but two days ago, Henryetta charged up the stairs when she heard an enormous sob expelled from her mother's mouth. When she flung open her mother's bedroom door, there was Lucille, sitting cross-legged on her unmade bed next to an emptied, upside-down strongbox and dozens of photographs just sobbing.

Typically, reminiscing their lives through albums of her father's photographs was something they enjoyed doing around the Christmas holidays. This time though, the depth of her mother's sorrow would not draw her in. Henryetta had too many responsibilities. When her mother did not acknowledge her presence at the door, Henryetta quietly backed out of the room and left Lucille to her grief.

Before Thom Jr. and Henryetta were born, their father installed a darkroom at the back of the garage. When Henryetta was old enough, she began to spend time with their father, learning how to

HANNAH R. HORCH

develop photos. As she grew older and developed her own talents, Thomas Sr. made it clear that he wanted to be alone in the darkroom. He also said that she no longer needed his help. At first, her father's change upset Henryetta, but later, she came to relish the hours alone in the darkroom. A few years later, when Henryetta developed her own portrait business, her father moved his supplies to their cellar. She was a professional, but her father was a hobbyist. She clearly needed more space and time to work.

Over the years, Thomas had collected quite a number of cameras as they evolved, all bought, and paid for at Ezra's. He housed them lovingly in a large, glass paned curio case just at the base of the front stairs. He often stopped and admired his collection, but Lucille could not stand looking at them. She felt they were awkward and did not fit the décor of her "majestic home." Lucille plotted for just the right moment to make him move them to the attic. Once after a huge blunder on Thomas's part, Lucille had punished him by not speaking to him for several days. He begged and begged Lucille for forgiveness. He promised he would do anything to get her to forgive him. Well, Lucille pretended to think and think, and then, it came to her.

"Get those unsightly contraptions out of my grandmother's curio cabinet!" she commanded. Thomas's face fell. "And only one camera out at a time, and I don't want to see it lying around. Put it away. I have had enough of your photography business!" And that was that. Thomas's photography had gone underground.

The summer after Henryetta graduated from high school, she and her mother spent the second half of the year in New York City in order for her to study photography with Ezra. It was that October of 1929 that men hurled themselves from buildings upon learning the stock market took a nosedive. What Henryetta didn't know was how that day changed her family's lives forever, setting off a series of events that now caused her to be walking to the lawyer's office for the reading of her father's will.

"I'm afraid the news is rather grim, Miss Dixon."

This was not at all what she had expected to hear. Rufus McBride was not her father's friend, but he knew all of Thomas's business.

46

"There are things you don't know about your father, Miss Dixon, things your father attempted to keep from your family, but in this situation, I'm sure you are looking for answers."

Henryetta did not respond, but only waited for Rufus McBride to continue.

"The truth is, Miss Dixon . . . your father was flat broke. The home has been left to your mother and then Thom, in the event of her death, and last, to you in the event of his death. It *is* paid for, but, my dear, the cash is gone. This Depression has wiped him out."

"I don't understand. I know we had to cut back to one car, and let the help go, but Daddy, he . . . Well, he never let on that it was this serious." Henryetta felt her heart drop to her knees and just stay there sullen, broken, and silent.

"And why would he? He didn't want to worry the family. Perhaps it became too much?" The lawyer's voice trailed off. The whole town was trying to explain away her father's suicide. Henryetta, puzzled, shook her head.

"Mr. McBride, do you know what happened? Anything at all?"

"I think it started with the Crash of 1929."

Thomas was back home in Brownsville preparing for the upcoming Brownsville Christmas Pageant, hosted every year since he had owned the opera house. It had become one of the most beloved town traditions. Unexpected news from New York arrived by telegram early in the morning. Thomas's broker advised him to sell his shares as the market was acting very strange. He returned word to his broker to sell, but by the time his broker got the message, it was too late. The market crashed and Thomas lost ninety percent of his money. What little was left, he had wired to their local bank. At least he could get his hands on it if he needed it.

Only Rufus McBride knew how Thomas fretted his losses. Lucille suspected nothing. Thomas was not even certain she was aware of the financial crash at the time it happened. Lucille was not one to keep up with current events. Thomas found comfort that his substantial savings in his opera house account at the local bank made life appear unchanged for the Dixons, but in 1930, people panicked and made a run on the banks. There simply was not enough cash to pay Thomas what his accounts said he had on paper. He walked out of the bank with a mere twenty percent of his savings in cash where he hid it in the gun safe in his study. Thomas had always operated on credit and was good for it, so local merchants did not think a thing of it when Thomas's debts went unpaid at first. When the merchants first approached Thomas about owing them money, he begged favors, promising to pay them soon, but it did not happen. The opera house debts were heavily outweighing his profits as more and more people were giving up entertainment to put food on the table.

To make matters worse, a loud banging at the front door came in the middle of the night, in the dead of winter. "The opera house is burning to the ground!" a voice cried out.

Thankfully, Thomas had insured the opera house, but even that money was late in coming. When it did arrive, Thomas used it to pay off his debts, leaving very little money on which to survive.

"He almost told your mother how grave their predicament was, but in the end, he didn't want her to worry. He told me he would find a way to keep you afloat, and I suppose he did. He *was* able to pay off all his debts."

"It makes sense now. Daddy said we had to tighten our belts, but we thought it was to save money so he could rebuild the opera house. We let go of Minnie, Moses, and Clarence. None of us wanted to see them go, but we understood that frivolities were bygones. We had to make sacrifices."

What little money Henryetta made from her photography business, she used to buy food or help pay the light bill. She learned how to clean the house and on several occasions spent an afternoon with Minnie learning how to cook her family's favorite dishes. Often, Henryetta drove her mother to the church, the grocer, or the beauty shop in her father's car which later they would sell to make ends meet, leaving only Thom's car for the four of them to share. Henryetta became somewhat of a taxi service, but enjoyed the talks with her family, running them from place to place.

Thom had odd jobs that did not last, often because he did not show up, or he showed up reeking of bootlegged whiskey. When Thom was on a straight streak, he helped with expenses and the yard work. The only one who did not work was Lucille. She was too busy with her own schedule— United Methodist Women on Mondays, bridge on Tuesday, soup kitchen on Wednesday and Thursday, the beauty shop on Friday, and the grocer's on Saturday. For Lucille, life went on as usual, and Thomas wanted it that way. He recognized her for who she was—a surface person, but still, he loved her. Lucille motivated him to be the better man, but in the end, ensuring her comfort is what drove him to take his own life.

Henryetta's eyes trailed to the brass letter opener on McBride's desk. She did not want to think about what was going to happen to her family. In the distance, she heard the train's whistle as it approached the depot just a few blocks away.

"Miss Dixon?" Rufus McBride said quietly noticing Henryetta in a deep stare. "Miss Dixon?" he repeated, but Henryetta did not respond. Instead, she envisioned herself as a silent movie heroine trapped on a railroad, shackled with a ball and chain, a steaming locomotive approaching her at break neck speed. Just as the train was about to plow over her, she came to. She was back in McBride's office. She shook her head and refocused on McBride's face.

"Yes, sorry. This is a bit much. I am not sure what to do, Mr. McBride. I mean, my photography . . . it's barely enough to pay the lights."

"I understand," McBride hesitated but thought it might be better to speak in truthful terms rather than try to placate Henryetta with comforting words, but he wanted her to arrive at her own understanding of what he was trying to say.

"Have you thought of selling your parents' home?" McBride suggested.

"Who could afford to buy it? No one in this town has any money," she doubted.

"I understand, Miss Dixon. Times are hard. Many folks are pawning off things they don't necessarily need anymore. There is a peddler man from Memphis who comes through town once a week with a big cotton truck. He parks down on court square. They say if you tell him what you've got to sell, he'll drive out and pick it up from you at the house."

"Yes, but I've heard he's a crook. He buys at a fraction of what folks paid," she retorted.

"Beggars can't be choosers, Miss Dixon," McBride said, realizing immediately at how crass he sounded.

Henryetta picked up on his embarrassment and shot him a look of contempt.

"Hmm. Thank you, Mr. McBride. I will make the best of it," Henryetta said, excusing herself from the chair in front of his desk.

"Surely. If you need help, Miss Dixon, please don't hesitate," he said, trailing her backside to the office door. He expected her to respond.

Henryetta appeared not to acknowledge him, but Rufus McBride could have sworn he heard Henryetta call him an "ass" under her breath as she passed into the hall.

CHAPTER SIX

*H*enryetta stepped out of the lawyer's office on to the sidewalk, momentarily blinded by the mid afternoon sun as it reflected and bounced off empty store windows. Noisy yelling a block down to her left caught her attention. It appeared to be a group of hoboes, fresh off the train. It was common to see them from time to time. What amazed Henryetta was how young they were. Mostly they were boys a bit younger than her or men her own age, but today, she saw one smaller, almost feminine-looking character in the middle of the pack. As they passed her, Henryetta felt a pang of fear, but it quickly disappeared as the motley group greeted her cheerfully as if on a great adventure of sorts. Henryetta focused on the feminine figure clad in boy's overalls to see that in fact it was a young girl, maybe just two or three years younger than herself.

Henryetta marveled at the girl's freedom. She appeared to be a major force in the group. She talked as an equal, if not as a leader. She was a sort of Wendy with her pack of tattered Lost Boys, but then Henryetta wondered what cost this young woman had paid or continued to pay just to stay alive. Life was not a fairy tale, after all. It was anything but. Henryetta had heard stories of women who sold their bodies to stave off starvation. She wondered if Florence had not knocked at her door, if she too would have resorted to that life to feed her children. Henryetta then questioned if she would do that to stay alive herself. The whole idea had never crossed her mind until this bleak moment of discovering her family was completely broke.

Shaking the mere idea of it out of her head, she watched the gang gallivant aimlessly down the court square sidewalk, the opposite direction of the Methodist soup kitchen. She turned away from them to begin walking toward her home just a few blocks away, not aware of a lone hobo who was quickly approaching her at a jogging pace. Just as he was about to dodge Henryetta, she turned directly into him, colliding forehead into forehead, startling both of them.

"Oww!" she cried out in pain and shock, reaching for her forehead, not looking at who she had bumped into. Opening her eyes, the stranger's shoes were worn and dusty. His pungent body odor reminded her of a hay barn.

"So sorry, miss!" he said, reaching out to touch her shoulder.

"Don't touch me!" she yelled at him, causing him to jump back.

"I'm sorry, miss. Really I am. I didn't mean to run into you like that. I was in a hurry to catch the gang. They are going . . ."

"The wrong way!" she interrupted, rubbing her forehead. Looking up at the stranger, a young man maybe the same age as herself stood before her. His kind eyes struck her immediately. He looked more intelligent than indigent.

"The wrong way," she said more calmly, straightening up. "The soup kitchen is back the other way. I imagine that is what they are looking for, right?"

"Yes. I'm the lead goose," he said.

"Pardon?" she asked.

"You know the lead goose? I am the scout—the one that finds the food, the safe water to land. Well, I found it."

"Oh yes," Henryetta replied, smiling at his metaphor as it reminded her of her father. Henryetta understood the lead goose. Since she was little, her father caught "fowl fever" from September until the end of January. Memories haunted her. Branded into her ears was the sound of her father's goose call. Clearly silhouetted images of geese changing their flight pattern at sunset to circle and land on her grandparents' lake popped into her head. Over the years, her father had tricked many a tasty goose by playing the lead goose himself. Her smile then faded to irritation. She wondered if everything would connect her to her father's memory. If only she could just bring her memories back to life. Memories were all she had of her father now, but they were doing her no good.

Seeing her smile change to a frown, the hobo looked away from her, but he could not help notice how beautiful she was and turned back for another gander. She was taller than most women, probably too tall really, but she pulled it off well. He wondered if her blond curls that rested around her face and neck were natural or if, she like most women spent hours with curlers drying in their hair on Saturdays. She wore minimal make-up, but like most well to do women her eyebrows were perfectly shaped and her lips stained crimson. Yes, he decided it was his lucky day. She was a real beauty, but a scent of sorrow surrounded her now down-turned smile.

"Aw, gee. I am sorry, miss. No harm done?" he said in a friendly tone.

"No," she said quietly and smiled. "I suppose you'd better catch your friends. They'll have left you by now." With that, the hobo tipped his hat at her and ran off, calling out random names.

"The lead goose indeed," she thought and walked toward her home, shaking her head at the chance exchange of words with this stranger. She paused for a moment thinking perhaps her Daddy was playing with her from the great beyond. She had been her father's daughter, and several times since his death, she felt his presence. People did not talk of these things, but she felt he was not far from her and somehow felt comforted.

CHAPTER SEVEN

*T*he telephone rang five times before Marjorie picked it up and yelled for Henryetta. This had been a new game for Marjorie, answering the phone. Henryetta had put her in charge of it to give her something to feel useful when she was not tending to two small stray kittens that had appeared on their front walk. It helped because she and Florence were in the process of cleaning out closets and the attic—a chore that the family had never done since Thomas and Lucille moved in back in 1905.

At first, Henryetta set to cleaning to take her mind off her brother's drunken tirades and the possibility of having to turn off the electricity for good. She found herself happier cleaning than trying to rouse her catatonic mother out of her chair. Since Henryetta was a small girl, she had trusted Minnie and considered Minnie her best friend. Ten years Henryetta's senior, Minnie could make sense of life and of things that really mattered, like matters of the heart. Her own mother, Miss Lucille, was too caught up in her own self—her socials, and her circles of friends—to take notice of Henry's life, her questions, or her ideas. Minnie figured that never taking a good look at life was what put Miss Lucille to sitting up in her chair wasting away. Miss Lucille had a lot of thinking to make-up for.

The truth be told, Henryetta was dead set against doing anything Rufus McBride suggested. It was Minnie who actually convinced Henryetta to go along with his advice. Now, Minnie believed in confirmation from God, and not two Sundays before, Minnie believed God had spoken. When she heard Rufus McBride's advice,

Minnie knew this was confirmation that she was meant to be a dress broker. It made it all the more easy for Minnie to approach Henryetta about selling her mother's cast offs. In the end, the two women split the profits fifty-fifty.

Divinity sparked an idea in Minnie's brain that Sunday through her church sisters' complaints about having to wear the same dresses for years on end. Why, how many times had she helped Miss Lucille unpack a trunk full of new dresses from New York City? Every spring, since she started working for the Dixon's, Minnie took to carrying old dresses out of Miss Lucille's closet and wardrobe up to the attic to make room for her "latest fashions." Last season's cast-offs were nothing more than dust collectors up in the attic. Miss Lucille had not given those dresses the time of day in years.

"Ladies, I knows what we's gonna do! We's gonna have us some fancy dresses fo' next to nothin'!" Minnie explained she would start selling rich white ladies' cast-offs. Before she knew it, she and her church sisters brainstormed the names of over ten ladies just like Lucille who had clothes to sell. Minnie's business was born.

"Thank you, Father, God," Minnie said in earnest, reaching her hand up toward the church rafters. Her church sisters followed in suit saying, "Amen, sister."

Cleaning out gave Henryetta a purpose other than grieving, and for that she was grateful. She and Florence had moved to cleaning out the closet under the front hall stairs. It wasn't much money, but selling their belongings to the peddler man always gave them just enough to get by. The attic was too hot now that it was late August and a thick, oppressive, hazy air had settled over Brownsville. At best, they would have to clean it out after dark when the blistering heat broke.

As if the never-ending heat and humidity were not aggravating enough, there was still no word from Walter. Florence wrote to Walter's parents, still back in Kentucky, with news of where they were and if Walter was to write to them, to send him Henryetta's phone number and address. Marjorie knew this and every time the phone rang, she ran to it just hoping it was her father. Each time, she moved to the phone just a little bit slower, but Henry convinced

Marjorie that she was her own personal secretary and she needed her help. Soon, the telephone would be a luxury, not a necessity. Henryetta knew there would not be enough money to pay the bill next month. What little she had saved and the few pennies she was earning would pay for food. The thought of giving up bigger items like her mother's jewels, china, and even their furnishings didn't sit well with Henryetta.

"Dixon residence. Marjorie speaking."

"Marjorie, darling, may I speak to Henryetta? This is Pastor Ferrell's wife, Mrs. Ferrell." Marjorie knew she was Junny's Sunday school teacher. Marjorie held the phone to her chest and called out for Henryetta.

"Coming!" she called from deep in the closet under the stairs.

"She will be right with you, ma'am." Marjorie gently placed the phone on the table like Henryetta had taught her to do.

"Hello."

"Henryetta, can I ask a favor of you? I'm at the soup line, and there is a big group of well . . ." she paused thinking of how to put the situation delicately.

"Hoboes, Mrs. Ferrell?"

"Well, yes, dear. They are here eating now, but Henryetta, they are *so filthy*. I've seen them before. They were here about a month ago. We just don't have any place for them to get cleaned up."

"You want them to come here? To bathe?"

This meant Henryetta would have to stop what she was doing and take care of this mess. "Stick to the plan," she could hear her mother saying in her head. The thought of that riffraff coming into her house worried Henryetta. She imagined those hooligans stuffing silver spoons in their dirty trousers as they ran out the door, thanking her for her hospitality.

"I don't know, Mrs. Ferrell. That's an awful lot to ask, even for a Christian."

"Why, Henryetta Dixon! Your mama would have your hide."

"Mrs. Ferrell, no offense, but why don't you just have them bathe at your house?"

A pause of silence answered her question.

"Henryetta, we couldn't afford to pay the water and light bill, so . . ." Her voice trailed off. "People can't afford to tithe much. We've been taking sponge baths ourselves using water from the old well."

Henryetta did not know how to respond. She heard rumors that city water might disappear altogether because so few people could afford it. Many of the houses in Brownsville had just been wired for electricity, but many folks did not have the money to buy electric stoves and these new *refrigerators*, so they still had the wood burning stoves and ovens. The ice company had not gone out of business yet, but without city water, there would be no ice. It was all so troubling.

"Henryetta, they are good young people. They are just down on their luck, like everyone else. They have sort of a boss man, a nice young man, rather well educated, I expect. He asked me where they could find a hot bath and clean clothes. He said they are willing to pay. They work on and off when they can find work. Apparently, in some of the bigger cities, they have shelters of some sort that allow hoboes to eat a few meals, rest, and get cleaned up. I know you took in Florence and her two children, and the word is, you have clothes to sell."

"My, my. How news travels."

Small-town gossip miffed Henryetta, but she remembered her encounter with *Lead Goose* about a month ago. *Was this him?* She remembered feeling a bit scared when she first noticed the hoboes. *Would they mob her and pester her for money?* As they passed by her, though, they appeared more like a group of friends who might have been on their way to the fair or a matinee picture show. They did not pay any attention to her at all.

Over the past month, she had caught herself thinking about Lead Goose, wondering where he was and what he might be doing. She fantasized about meeting him again and what she might say to him. She sometimes imagined hopping on a train and just riding away from her troubles. She told herself, these daydreams were "non-sense" and nothing more than a diversion to keep her entertained, but thinking of meeting Lead Goose again caused her heart to race.

"All right, but I will have rules they have to follow, and if they don't, they have to go. I want to do what is Christian, but I don't want a bunch of hoodlums stealing from me. Times are hard, Mrs. Ferrell, and I know you understand."

"I do, Henryetta. You are going to earn crowns in heaven for this dear. I just know it. I will send them over."

"Goodbye, Mrs. Ferrell."

Henry placed the receiver back on the hook. Marjorie stood on the hallway rug where the phone table sat.

"Well?" said Marjorie. "Is she sending hoboes to us? I don't like hoboes. Mama says they are dangerous."

"And don't forget dirty!" hollered Florence from the other room, who had been eavesdropping too.

"Henryetta, are you out of your mind? You don't know these people! What about the children?"

"You were strangers, too, once. Y'all turned out all right."

"Yes, but we were different. God knows where they are from or what diseases or bad habits they are carrying with them. I just don't want that riffraff around my children!"

"Well, take them out to Minnie's for the afternoon. There are several dresses I need to carry out to her anyway."

"But, Mama!" cried Marjorie. "I've never met a real live hobo! Please, Mama, don't take us out to Minnie's. This is most exciting thing that has happened. Besides, Mama, maybe they know where Daddy is," Marjorie said just above a whisper, not looking at her mother.

Henryetta quickly looked at Florence's face for a reaction to Marjorie's words. Though Florence appeared tough, there had been moments when Henry had seen Florence crying out in the swing in the backyard while the children were napping in the afternoon. Henryetta knew Marjorie had touched a tender spot and not even Florence would leave the house. As Henry looked at Florence, she noticed her patting her front apron pocket. She had never noticed this before, but she could make out the faint outlines of what seemed to be a wallet-sized photo, probably of Walter.

"Oh, all right, I suppose, but don't you get near them. You hear me? They could have lice or worse!"

"Yes, ma'am. Can't I talk to them through the screen door?" she asked while Henryetta tried to hide a smile from them.

"We'll see," said Flo, heading toward the closet under the stairs.

Within the hour, Marjorie cried out from her post at the screen door, "I can hear them! Here they come, Mama! Look!" Flo stopped what she was doing and walked over to look out the door.

Sure enough, a group of what looked like ragamuffins paraded up the sidewalk and paused at the mailbox. Flo could tell they were looking for this address. She opened the door and stepped out on to the porch. As she did, the troop noticed her and turned en masse up the sidewalk that cut through the middle of the front yard.

"Miss Dixon?" A male voice called out from the middle.

About that time, Henryetta emerged from the house, letting the screen door slam shut. Florence remembered how Henryetta had been quite formidable and stern when she herself first appeared at Henryetta's doorstep. Flo almost smiled, remembering the front Henryetta put on, only to quickly fade into generosity and kindness.

Henryetta was gritty and independent for sure, but there was also a softer side Flo recognized in her. Henry was one of those loud thunderclaps, threatening a storm, but then quickly blew over, back to sunny skies. Flo wondered if many people saw this side of her. Henryetta was wound tightly and was better at asking questions of others than talking about herself.

Henryetta stepped forward to stand side by side with Florence at the edge of the front porch steps. Her face was unsmiling and her hands were on her hips. She was sizing up the lot of about five hoboes. They were loud, tattered, but jovial almost, just like the first band of hoboes she had encountered. The hoboes silenced themselves as they approached while gazing at the two women both with stony eyes. They paused at the bottom step.

Henryetta was almost sure it was the same group as before. There were stories of these young hoboes who just took off and rode the rails from city to city looking for work, trying to escape poverty. As she scanned their faces, her eyes stopped at the young man positioned front and center of the group.

It was Lead Goose.

Her heart began to race wildly again, like it would explode out of her chest.

"Miss Dixon?" he said, smiling up at Henryetta.

She could tell he remembered her by his genuine, almost-triumphant smile. It was as if *he had found her*. There was just something about him, something electric, but something comforting in seeing his face. Maybe it was the possibility he embodied—the possibility of freedom, hope, maybe even love. Whatever it was, she did not want to show it.

"Lead Goose, you've landed back on our pond, I see."

Henryetta tried to play cool, but her stomach quivered, and a sensation of wanting him, all of him, shot up from her womanly parts up to her neck. Suddenly, the word "lust" screamed in her head, sounding a lot like her preacher's pulpit voice. *Was this lust?* Her neck and face flushed a rosy scarlet.

"You know him?" Flo asked, looking at Henryetta with surprise.

"Not really, Flo. We just had a chance encounter the day I went to the lawyer's office."

Lead Goose quickly removed his cap and held out his hand to Florence.

"My name's Gus, ma'am."

Florence nodded back at him, disgusted by the filth lodged beneath his fingernails. His smile did not waver as he looked to Henryetta with his outstretched hand. How she wanted to touch him, but she didn't dare. She was convinced her desire would surely burn him.

"Miss Dixon, I'm Gus. Mrs. Ferrell sent us here to get cleaned up. We would be much obliged. Did she tell you we could pay? Because we can."

Gus lowered his hand down awkwardly, seeing she did not intend to shake it.

"Yes, but did she tell you I have some rules? I don't know y'all, and I don't want you taking advantage. I have to take care of what I have too. You understand?"

"Yes, ma'am. We won't cause you any harm. I promise. We're just looking to get clean and put on some fresh clothes, if you have them, ma'am."

He looked at the others, signaling them to nod. Henryetta noticed they could not be any older than she was. A couple of them looked no older than fifteen. They were all thin, for sure, but not totally wasted away or sickly like some of the men who loitered outside of the barbershop.

"You can bathe one at a time while the rest of you wait here on the porch. Any of y 'all have lice?"

Henryetta's frank question startled the group. The faces looked at one another, but all heads shook their heads no.

"Flo, you stay out here with them while I walk the first one up."

Henryetta gestured to the smallest hobo as she opened the screen door. Marjorie backed away, quickly holding her brother's hand.

"Hello there, cutie pie," a feminine voice said to the children, causing Henryetta to turn around.

A girl?

The hobo smiled at her and winked. Henryetta climbed the stairs with the girl hobo following closely behind her.

"What's your name?"

"Gertie."

"Well, Gertie, the bath is five cents, and for another fifteen cents, I'll outfit you in clean clothes. Take it or leave it," Henryetta said.

"Do you have any clean rags?"

This took Henryetta aback. Gertie pulled off her cap to reveal shoulder length hair the color of black coffee. She was a tiny little thing, not more than five feet tall.

"That's the hardest part so far. You know? When Sarah pays a visit? It is so embarrassing to have to take care of women's business around a bunch of boys, but I am safe with them. I guess that I am used to it now. I need some more rags if you can spare them. I lost mine a few weeks ago when the railroad police got after us. I lost my knapsack running from them."

Henryetta pondered the girl's plight, imagining surviving alone. She was lucky if that was the worst she had to worry about.

"I'll see what I can find," Henryetta said, moving to the linen closet to retrieve an old towel for the girl. It was hard not to be curious about this girl and her life. Henryetta kept telling herself not to ask questions because then she would be involved. Look what that had done for her. She had a house full.

"The tub is in there. There are a lot of y'all. Don't go filling it up more than a few inches, and wash it out when you are through. I will bring you some clean clothes and put them right outside the door. That's twenty cents," Henryetta said, holding out her arm to the girl. She began to dig into a trouser pocket to pull out a dime and a nickel.

"I don't have it. All's I got is fifteen cents to my name."

Henryetta had to decide quickly. If she took all of Gertie's money, what would the girl have to do to replace it? Perhaps she would make Gertie work off the extra five cents just like she had Florence.

"How about a bath, some rags, and a few pairs of panties for five cents?" the girl haggled seeing Henryetta perplexed about what to do with her.

"Done."

The girl turned and closed the bathroom door behind her, leaving Henryetta alone in the hall. It was that moment she heard a loud crash come from her mother's bedroom.

CHAPTER EIGHT

*T*he first crash was followed by an ear-bursting wail from Henryetta's mother and the shattering of glass. Henryetta quickly moved to fling open her mother's door to find the bedside table facedown and her mother's silver-handled hairbrush at her feet. The room reeked of her mother's perfume that had pooled and now was gently, slowly gliding down the floorboards away from the dresser. Shards of glass from her mother's mirror and perfume bottle twinkled in the afternoon sun that crept into the room from behind the blind, but her mother was hidden from sight.

"Mama?" she asked quietly as she tiptoed into the room.

"Mama," she asked, this time a little louder. Then she saw her mother sitting in the floor on the other side of the bed, her back against the bed and her forehead resting on her knees. Lucille's body heaved up and down in silent sobs. Henryetta froze in place at the end of the bed.

"Mama?" she whispered once more. Her mother began shaking her head no and then looked up at Henryetta with a tear-stained face of desperation. Henryetta's mother was almost unrecognizable to her. Black circles framed her grief-possessed eyes. She looked touched for sure. Lucille's normally perfectly coiffed hair was tied at the base of her neck with a blue velvet ribbon, but unruly strands hung over her sunken cheeks from weeks of refusing food. It was as if she were looking at Henryetta, but not seeing her. Lucille was looking beyond into a dark place, maybe even hell itself.

"Mama, what is it?" Henryetta dared to ask, inching toward her mother and crouching down to be eye-level with her. Henryetta tentatively reached out to tuck her mother's bangs behind her ear, but her mother caught Henryetta's arm with her forearm, flinging Henryetta's hand against the mattress, stunning her.

"Get out," her mother mumbled, her head hanging down. Henryetta reached out to touch her mother's shoulder. .

"I . . . said . . . get . . . out!" Lucille's voice rose one word at a time into a shriek, but Henryetta refused to move, believing she could comfort her mother. These were the first words Lucille had spoken since the funeral. This gave Henryetta hope that her mother was ready to face her father's death. If Lucille would only talk to her, they could get through this together, and move forward and away from despair.

Before Henryetta could react, Lucille, unexpectedly and quickly moved to all fours and crawled toward a large shard of her mirror, gripping it so hard that it cut her hand between her thumb and pointer finger. Lucille sat back on her ankles, her back blocking Henryetta from seeing her slash the inside of her left wrist, allowing blood to stream onto her night gown, quickly soaking through the light fabric to her legs. Henryetta imagined the cut as she saw her mother's arm moving in a cutting action.

"Mama!" Henryetta fearfully cried out, shifting to her knees and then reaching for her mother's arm that held the shard. Panic riddled every space in Henryetta's mind and body as her mother jumped up and ran. Henryetta's fingertips brushed her mother's arm, causing her to topple over. Balancing herself, Henryetta hurriedly hopped to a standing position to face her mother who stood half-stooped over, blood dripping from the jagged cut on her wrist. Lucille's eyes, wildly demonic and insane, frightened Henryetta. What would her mother do next? Henryetta stood petrified debating how best to get the shard from her mother's hand.

"Mama, stop!" she cried out, attempting to sound forceful rather than hysterical. At Henryetta's words, her mother's shoulders slumped, her eyes closed, and her head hung limply. Then, a single, blood-curdling wail erupted from her mother's mouth. Lucille dropped the shard and then collapsed to her knees, head down, again. Henryetta ran to her mother's door and called out for help to Florence. Then, she ran to her father's closet and pulled one of his shirts from the hanger. Henryetta took the sleeve and bound it tightly over her mother's open wound. As Henryetta held the end of her dress to the cut on her mother's hand, she applied pressure to stop the bleeding. Florence and Gus soon rushed into the room.

"Oh, Henry," gasped Florence at the sight of Lucille who had crumpled over to a fetal position, catatonic once again.

"What am I going to do, Flo?" Henry asked her as tears began to flood her eyes.

Florence shook her head in quiet sadness. She had heard gossip tell of people who had lost their minds and ended up in the looney bin, but everyone knew they were vile places. Too vile for the likes of Lucille Dixon. She felt deep sympathy for Henryetta-losing her father, and now her mother.

Gus spoke up. "You have got to call a doctor or take her to a hospital. This is serious."

Henryetta looked at Gus, half embarrassed by her reality and yet grateful for a sensible man's calm now. She stood on the precipice of hysteria, but something in Gus's eyes eased her back and assured her that everything was going to be all right, maybe not what she wanted, but all right.

"Yes," Henryetta said, getting up and rushing downstairs toward the phone to call Dr. Castellaw.

"What's the matter, Henry?" asked Marjorie as Henryetta dialed the operator.

Henryetta half-smiled at Marjorie as she put her fingers to her lips to signal for Marjorie to be quiet.

"Dr. Castellaw, please," Henryetta said, trying to sound calm even though her body pulsed of adrenaline. She thought her heart might pop out of her chest.

"Marjorie, go watch your brother," she said, waiting for the operator to connect her to Dr. Castellaw's office.

"Dr. Castellaw? I need you to come quickly. Mama has hurt her-self . . . Yes, it is serious," Henryetta spoke quietly into the receiver, not wanting the children or the hoboes on the porch to hear her conversation.

"She cut her wrist with a broken mirror . . . She is lying on her bedroom floor now. I wrapped it up tightly with one of Daddy's old shirts . . . Yes, Florence is with her now . . . Yes, I understand. Yes, Dr. Castellaw."

Henryetta placed the receiver on the hook and ran back upstairs to find her mother's head resting in Florence's lap. Florence lightly caressed her mother's temple like Henryetta had seen Florence do to Junny's when he was tired and about to sleep. Gus stood, looking out the front bay window.

"Dr. Castellaw wants us to take her to the mental hospital in Bolivar," said Henryetta.

"Oh, Henryetta, are you sure? I've heard they can be terrible places. You don't want that for your mama, do you?" Florence replied.

"What else can I do for her, Flo? She's not right, and I can't do anything for her. I don't have any choice, really," said Henryetta, downtrodden. She shook her head and then looked at Gus who didn't give any indication of support or lack of.

"What if she tries to hurt herself again, or me, or you? Flo, I can't have her being this way with your children here. They shouldn't see such things," Henryetta continued.

"Gus, will you help me take my mother to the car?" she asked. He nodded.

"Flo take the children next door while we move her to the car. I don't want them seeing Mama this way. See if you can find out where Thom is, then tell him what has happened. Gus, please tell your friends they have to move along now. I'm sorry," directed Henryetta.

Florence gently moved out from under Lucille's head and proceeded downstairs, with Gus following behind her. The bathroom door opened and closed quietly. Henryetta heard light footsteps traveling down the stairs. With that, she grabbed her mother's housecoat to hide her blood-stained nightgown.

She worried about the neighbors' gossip if they saw her carrying her mother to the car covered in blood. Brownsville was a small place with big tales to tell. Nothing was private and nobody was ever exempt from the storytelling game. There was nothing more pleasing than relishing a bit of scandalous news while sipping sweet tea out on the porch. It broke up the monotony of the heat and endless sea of cotton. Every manner of sin was covered with the blood of Jesus if the gossiper uttered these three words, "Bless her heart."

As she wrestled to put the overcoat on her mother, Henryetta wished Minnie was there. She would know what to do and speak sense to Henryetta, but she was not. Henryetta felt entirely alone. She sighed heavily, shaking her head at the misery that kept after her, endlessly trying to pull her into the dark place—the one her father traversed, her mother toyed with and her brother tried to drink away. The anguish was magnetic and wanted to attach itself to Henryetta and probably would have if Gus had not reappeared at her mother's bedroom door.

"Miss Dixon? Let's get your mother to the car," Gus said, breaking sorrow's grip on Henryetta's thoughts.

"Yes, Gus. Thank you."

Her mother was deadweight. They tried to carry Lucille between them, propping her arms around their shoulders, but her legs were limp and her feet dragged the floor.

"Wait," said Gus, twisting to face Lucille. With one quick movement, he hoisted her over his shoulder like she weighed no more than a sack of potatoes. Henryetta marveled at Gus's strength. He appeared wiry and not as strong as he actually was. His ill-fitting, baggy hobo clothes deceptively hid years of calisthenics, swimming and football. Gus placed Lucille in the back seat in a resting position and then closed her door. He moved around the car to the driver's side door.

"You ride in the back with your mother," he said, motioning for Henryetta to get into the back as he opened the passenger door. Henryetta looked at him for a moment, not expecting any more from Gus, but so grateful he was there. She then got in and rested her mother's head in her lap. Gus revved up the car and began to back out the long drive toward the main street.

"Which way is Bolivar?" he asked, stopping just short of the street in the drive.

"East," Henryetta said, looking at Gus's eyes in the rearview mirror. Seeing only his eyes as the late afternoon sun hit them, she noticed golden flecks around his pupils, reminding her of a photograph she had once taken of sunflowers against a blue sky. Had she not felt exhausted from the trauma she now faced, she might have smiled at Gus. Instead, she just gazed at him and then looked away down the sidewalk watching the hoboes round the street corner out of sight.

CHAPTER NINE

*A*s Gus drove back from Bolivar to Brownsville he found himself in a predicament with Henryetta. What he imagined to be a simple stop for a meal, a bath, and perhaps a place to lay his head if he was lucky, had turned into a rescue of sorts. It had been months since he had driven a car. He hopped on a fast train or as the hoboes called it a "cannonball" back in Chicago just this past Tuesday, like he had a month back. He remembered this particular stop because of the water tower that read, "Brownsville: A Good Place to Live." He ventured to say that it was because everyone seemed friendly and eager to help. They were certainly kinder than the railroad bulls chasing after them with Billy clubs as they emerged from the train cars at certain stops.

Life riding the rails in search of work and adventure had certainly not been as footloose and fancy free as he had imagined. It was even traumatic at times, and today was a day he would not easily forget. He glanced over at Henryetta who rested her forehead on the edge of the passenger window, feeling the cool surface of the metal, if only for a moment. He thought it peculiar how lives of complete strangers could intersect so easily, so suddenly. Sometimes the lives remained intertwined forever. Other times they simply intersected, served a purpose, and then moved apart. Gus wondered why fate had crisscrossed his life with Henryetta's. Would they be intertwined or just a momentary connection stored away as a memory?

Henryetta was in the frame of mind where she thought she might collapse of sheer exhaustion, run away from it all, or just die.

She wondered how long the sting of leaving her mother in the insane asylum would haunt her broken heart. She felt so tired, like she wanted the day to end, but heartlessly, it was still going.

She started talking to God, asking him to help her hang on, to give her strength to finish out the day, and for her mama. Then doubt whispered in her ear and told her to stop believing. She was alone. Naked she came into this world. Naked she would go out. It just was not soon enough. Not after this day. Just when Henryetta thought her suffering could not get any worse, it always did. How could God do this to her? Why would God do this to her? She racked her brain trying to make sense of it. Not believing in anything would be so much easier than not having to try to understand why God would let these terrible things continue to happen.

"You all right?" Gus asked glancing from the road to Henryetta.

She could not even respond to that question. Instead, she looked away and out of the window at the hazy twilight than hung in and around the freshly cut pastures. Gus said nothing but drove on toward Brownsville.

Several miles down the road, Gus noticed the gas edging toward empty. The skies had turned flamingo pink with deep blood orange hues sinking into the horizon. It was late and he doubted any filling station would be open.

"Miss Dixon, I hate to trouble you, but your car is almost out of gas, and I doubt there's a filling station open or even around here. What would you like me to do ma'am?" he asked her.

Henry neither moved nor said anything.

"I'm going to pull off at the next farm and see if they have any gas I can buy."

"Fine," Henry finally muttered. "But we're only a few miles from town anyway. There's a little drinking shack just up ahead, down the next road, to the left. Someone might have some extra gas for us," she said pointing ahead.

Gus wondered how she knew where such a place was, but he didn't let on. She did not strike him as the type of woman who frequented makeshift bars out in the woods. Instead, he drove on with no change in expression. If he had learned anything about getting a person's real story, it was by not showing any signs of judgment. Gus turned on to a dirt road that wound around through an uncleared patch of forest. In the distance, a small beacon of light appeared.

"See that twinkle of light?" Henryetta asked. "That's it."

They continued on, the car bouncing them up and down as it traversed the potholes that had formed during the rainy season. With each dip, the windows and metal parts rattled. Soon a line of parked cars in a large clearing came into view. Henryetta scanned for Sy McGhee's car. Sy was her brother, Thom's, oldest friend and worst influence. If Sy was here, Thom probably was too. Gus pulled the car closer, in behind a Ford. Henryetta opened her door to step out catching Gus in a half jog around the front the car to open her door for her. Even though she showed no signs of being nervous, her heart was racing out of fear. She had never been here, but had heard stories of what went on—the trashy women, the gambling, the fights, typical stories. The thought of what she might see scared her.

"I could have gotten that for you," Gus said, slowing to a stop as she walked toward him. Henryetta looked at him for a split second, but then started for the shack, as she scanned the cars for strapped-on gas cans.

"I know, Gus. Just help me look for gas cans," she replied just as she spotted an old jalopy truck with a wooden sign that read "Oregon or Bust" outfitted with boxes, tins, mattresses, suitcases, and a rusty, red gas can.

"There," she said, pointing right at the jalopy. "Now, we have to find the owner."

"Let me go in. Go wait out in the car," Gus said, gesturing for her to stop.

"Always the lead goose. I'm going in with you. My brother is probably in there. He probably knows whose it is," she said moving forward to see her brother and a group of men she did not recognize other than Sy leaning up against a car, laughing and drinking bottles of bootlegged corn whiskey. Thom looked not to be too drunk yet.

"Thom!" she called out to him.

Startled to hear Henryetta's voice, he looked up at her in surprise.

"Thom!" she called out again.

This time the men chided and teased him about her. He muttered that she was his sister and to watch their tongues. Within a few steps, they met.

"What are you doing here?" he spat at her. "You need to go on home, Henry. And who is he?" Thom said, giving Gus the once-over. Thom was clearly just drunk enough to be a bit forthright in an overbearing tone. Thom reminded Gus of a bully he had known when he was younger.

"I'm Gus," he interjected, stepping up to be not six inches away from sticking his hand out for shaking. Gus looked him square in the eye, but Thom did not take his hand, but rather scowled. The men stared at one another until Henryetta pulled Gus back and stood in front of him.

"Did Florence get ahold of you?" she asked.

"No. What are you doing here?"

"Mama tried to kill herself today. She's in the mental hospital in Bolivar. Gus, here, drove me, and we're almost out of gas."

Thom took a long drag off his cigarette then tossed the butt to the ground and stepped on it. As he looked up at Henry, the angry tears pooled. Then, without warning, he turned and angrily smashed his bottle into a nearby tree. He slumped down to his knees and covered his face. Clearly, Thom was very drunk. Her brother was not known for his dramatics, at least the brother she knew. Henryetta walked over to Thom and gently placed her hand on his shoulder.

"God, Hen," Thom said barely above a whisper.

Henryetta stood silently, waiting for the moment to pass. They had lost their father and now, today, their mother. Taking a deep breath, Thom stood up and wiped his face.

"All right then. I'll be home later."

"But, Thom, we need gas. Do you know who owns that jalopy over there? They have a gas can," she said motioning toward it.

"It belongs to one of those boys over there," he said, pointing to where he had stood when she first came upon him.

"I'll ask them if y'all can buy some gas off of them." Thom walked over to the group while Henry and Gus waited. Sy, who Henryetta called "Sly" behind his back, sauntered toward her, with a grin that turned her stomach. He had been after Henryetta since she was sixteen. At first, he had been doting and kind, but she was not interested in him. The sweetness Sy showered her with soon turned bitter and his words became cruel and taunting. Henryetta prided herself on not hating anyone, but her feelings for Sy were as close to hate as she would let them be.

"Hello, princess. Who's this? Your *new* lover maybe? Brought him for a little hanky-panky in the woods? Looks like a hobo to me. That's a little low for you, princess."

"Just shut up, Sy. Go back to drinking with the boys. You do that so well."

"What if I don't?" Sy said, challenging her, but looking at Gus.

"God, Sy. Just go away. Gus is not going to fight you. Just go on," she said, putting her hands on her hips.

Gus didn't move from Henry's side. Gus knew a man's bluffing and when his jealousy did the talking. He had seen it many times at college—usually at Greek mixers or pick-up football games on the lawn. Puffed up fraternity boys from different houses got testy with one another, usually over a pretty girl or sports. Sy did not faze him. Gus knew a coward when he saw one.

Sy leaned forward into Henryetta's face, grinning drunkenly. She did not flinch or avert her steel gaze. When Sy saw he could not get a rise out of her, he sighed and turned away from them. He slinked off as if nothing had happened. Henryetta stayed planted in place following him with her eyes in case he should turn for one last cheap shot, but Sy continued straight into the bar. As the door closed, Henry turned to Gus, shrugged, and nodded in disbelief.

"Yellow belly," Gus said, smiling at her.

For a moment, Henry forgot the events of what had been the second worst day of her life. Gus's smile reached into her and reminded her that not all days were like these and that small comforts stockpiled into large blessings. She returned his smile, conscious of how Gus suddenly felt like home. Then she realized that Minnie, Flo, and the children all felt like home, too. How was it that a stranger felt closer to her than anyone she had ever met? Minnie always said,

"Deys folks who come into our lives for a season, some for a reason, and others for a lifetime."

What was Gus? Surely just a reason—just to help her through this day.

"Henry! Come on over here!" Thom called to her from the car where he and one of the boys stood emptying gas into her tank. She and Gus walked over as the man was screwing her gas tank cover back on.

"I've worked out a deal with Bob, here. He needs a place to hang his hat for a few days. He's been traveling out to . . ." Thom paused, interrupted by Henryetta.

"Let me guess, Oregon?" Henryetta said, rolling her eyes and smiling.

Bob guffawed at her joke and nodded his head in a friendly way. Bob was extremely tall and lanky. His skin was tan and his clothes were wrinkled and looked as if he had not changed them in several days.

"As I was saying . . . Bob needs a place to rest a day or so before he heads back out on the road. We could oblige him, couldn't we, Hen?"

"I suppose," she responded matter-of-factly, the complete opposite of how she felt below the surface.

Then Thom pulled Henryetta aside again.

"Is Mama going to be all right?"

Thom had always been closer to his mother than his father. Lucille understood when Thom's father would not accept Thom for who he was. Henry was always their father's prized child, but Thom was too quiet, not smart enough, and now a drunk. Henry knew this and could not bring herself to say "No" aloud. She simply shook her head. The doctor said there was little hope at present. Their mama had suffered a serious mental break. Thom grabbed Henry's arms pulling her closer to embrace her. They both began to cry in each other's arms. They parted both wiping their eyes with identical gestures. From a short distance, Gus noted how alike these siblings looked in appearance as they rejoined Bob and Gus.

"Then it is all right if I stay a day or two? I won't be no trouble, ma'am. I am real handy so if you needed help around the house, you know fixing little things, I am your man. I don't want no money, just a place to light for a short spell," Bob explained. "Oh, and I won't drink around you or the house. I reckon you wouldn't like that too much and all."

"All right then," Henryetta agreed, straightening her skirt. "Thank you for the gas. We're leaving now. Are y'all coming on?"

"Yes, ma'am. Thom and I will come directly. I need to pay the tab and then we'll be on our way," said Bob. Henry smiled politely and then turned to walk back to the car where Gus opened her door. Henryetta paused and placed her hand on Gus's arm.

"Thank you, Gus, for everything. Really. I don't know how I would have gotten through this day without you." Gus grinned and tilted his hat at her. Then closed the door behind her. She was almost home now.

CHAPTER TEN

The next morning, the kitchen was alive with Florence clanking pots, men's chatter, and children's squeals and laughter. Henryetta slept later than she had in months. She wandered slowly down the stairs just listening to the foreign sounds coming from her kitchen. The happy banter reminded her of Christmas morning. Even Thom told jokes and did not give the appearance of a young man who had lost both of his parents. Instead of going in, she just sat down midway on the stairs, listening. The only voice missing was Gus's. She didn't normally attach to people quickly, but Gus was different. He was intoxicating.

"Well, if it isn't Sleeping Ugly," came a voice from the sitting room corner. Henryetta had not noticed Gus sitting in her father's chair writing in what looked like a diary. She smiled at him, truly glad he had not left yet.

"Good morning, Lead Goose. What are you scribbling?" Henry asked, not getting up from her sitting position.

"Just thoughts, notes, ideas, mostly," he said, smiling at her. "Did you sleep well?"

"Too well I think. What are your plans?" she asked right to the point.

"Thom mentioned you may put all of us to work today cleaning out the garage. He said you have been selling off clothes to the Negro woman and the peddler man from Memphis."

"Thom said all that?" Henry said, disbelieving Thom would be that involved in her affairs.

"Yes, well, Marjorie and Florence filled in some of the gaps," he revealed.

"That sounds about right. You are welcome to help if you like. Lord knows we have so many things we will never use. The garage is filled with props and costumes from the plays at my father's opera house before it burned."

"Is that . . . is that how your father died? In a fire?" he asked. Henryetta bowed her head.

"I'm sorry Henryetta, may I call you Henryetta? I shouldn't have . . ." Gus said rising from the chair.

"No Gus, he didn't die that way, and yes, you may call me Henryetta, or Henry if you like," she said, half smiling as he approached her, resting his hand on the mahogany banister.

"I'm sorry, Henry. Another time. Let's work on having a better day today," he said reaching out his hand to help her to her feet. She reached out and let him pull her up. It seemed he had been doing that ever since he walked into her life.

"Agreed."

CHAPTER ELEVEN

G oing up to the attic would not be a pleasant chore. It had been almost two months since Thom, Gus, and Bob had helped them organize the garage to gradually sell off its contents. Their work had kept food on the table and paid her mother's hospital bills. Sometimes Henryetta spared enough pennies to buy developer chemicals and film to take the occasional portrait, but mostly she spent her film taking pictures of the cotton fields, the growing Hoover Stew lines in town, and of Marjorie and Junny.

She found peace spending hours in the dark room practicing developing techniques she learned from Ezra in New York. When she drove out in the country to snap pictures, she would park in a grassy pasture that shared the railroad tracks. For hours, she would sit on the hood of her car waiting for a train to pass by. She fantasized spying Gus perched atop a passing boxcar waving to her. Sometimes, long freight trains passed by with packs of hoboes looking out boxcar doors or riding on the rooftops of the train as it traversed the countryside. Almost always, they waved at her, but none resembled Gus.

Sometimes, she would drive out into the county to watch the sunset because it reminded her of riding back from Bolivar with him. Inside, she ached for him—like a longing, maybe homesickness. Despite the horror of that day, Gus being there reassured her that goodness does exist. Every now and then flashes of seeing her mother on the bedroom floor tried to creep in and capture her thoughts, but she would fight them off by concentrating on Gus's face, Gus's voice, the way he laughed, the way he made her feel. *Was he a reason?* She hoped she would see him again.

One day in late August, a postcard with palm trees and the beach with "Key West" on the front arrived in the mail for Henryetta. Marjorie was on mailbox duty when she spotted what she called a "little card with funny trees" on it. Henryetta and Florence had been teaching Marjorie to read in the mornings. Every evening, after the children had their baths, they looked forward to listening to their favorite radio program "Little Orphan Annie." Often Marjorie pretended she was Annie on the path of solving some mystery. The arrival of this postcard could have been a "clue" she excitedly exclaimed. Marjorie, eager, begged to be the one who read it first. Henryetta smiled and allowed her to read it while they sat together on the front porch steps.

> Dear Henry and the Gang,
>
> Greetings from the sunny seashore in Key West, Florida. You would not believe this paradise. A hobo never goes hungry if he has a fishing pole. I have met some interesting characters down here on the southernmost tip. Look it up on an atlas.
>
> Your friend,
> Lead Goose "Gus"

"Do we have an atlas? What is an atlas anyway?" asked Marjorie.

"It is a big book filled with maps. We have one in the living room. Let's see where in the world Lead Goose has flown to," said Henryetta, taking Marjorie's hand and pulling her up to go inside the house. Henryetta felt herself smiling as she imagined Gus fishing-Gus sitting under a palm tree with a parrot on his shoulder-Gus lying on a beach soaking in the sun bare chested, tan in cut-off khaki pants.

"Why so happy, Hen?" Flo asked, looking up from playing with Junny on the living room rug. Blushing heat rose from Henryetta's heart straight up to her scalp causing her skin to turn crimson.

"Mr. Gus sent us a postcard from the beach and we are finding where he is on that . . . What is it called, Miss Hen?"

"An atlas. Gus is or was in Key West, Florida," Henryetta said smiling at Flo who smiled momentarily and then looked down in dismay. She had not heard a word from Walter. She feared the worst had happened to him. Flo pushed this thought from her head. She got up to look at the map with Marjorie and Henry.

"Where do we live?" asked Marjorie.

Henryetta pointed to the western corner of Tennessee.

"What about Mr. Gus? Where is he now?" she asked.

"Well, Mr. Gus was here in Key West, Florida."

Henryetta showed Marjorie, pointing to the atlas once more.

"And where was Mr. Bob going?" Marjorie asked tracing circles around the map with her small pointer finger. Henryetta covered Marjorie's small hand with her own and guided her finger to Oregon.

"Is that far from here?" asked Marjorie.

"Very."

"My daddy is in California. Is that on the map?"

"Yes. See if you can find it yourself. It starts with C . . . A . . . L," said Henryetta stepping back from the atlas, placing her hands behind her back. Marjorie began scanning the map for the letters, and within a few seconds, she found it. At first, she smiled triumphantly, but the smile downturned to a frown.

"What is it, Marjorie?" Henry inquired causing Florence to look up at her daughter.

"Daddy is very far away from us," she replied quietly.

"Yes," said Henry solemnly, but then remembered that Marjorie needed hopeful magic, not realism. "Yes, but I bet your daddy is working very hard to get you out there. See this valley on the map?" Henry pointed out. "This is where most of our vegetables come from. There is more work there than any of us can even imagine. You wait and see. Your daddy will be sending you good news any day now." Henry comforted Marjorie, patting her on the shoulder.

In early September, milk delivery stopped, Brownsville shut off city water, and the icehouse stopped delivering block ice. Henryetta was thankful for the electric icebox her mother insisted having when money still flowed like an eternal spring. The old well still pumped spring water from deep below the aquifer into the kitchen sink; however, there was no running water in the upstairs bathroom. At first, Marjorie and Junny thought it was fun to bathe in a horse trough, but soon, they tired of their kitchen bath and wished for the days they could just turn on the faucet and have a hot bath in the tub. They had the old outhouse cleaned out, but none of them liked heading out back to use the toilet. They simply had no choice.

Even though Thom was around, he really wasn't. Every day, he left the kitchen after breakfast to look for work that did not exist. Mostly, he just dawdled downtown outside of the barbershop with the other men out of work. Occasionally, he helped the peddler man load people's possessions on his truck to haul back to Memphis. They had built a rapport with one another from the peddler man's frequent stops.

In the evenings, like clockwork, the sun would go down, Sy would pull up, honk the horn, and Thom would skip down the stairs, let the screen door slam behind him, and ride off to the drinking shack. It was just Henry, Flo, and the children most of the time. They all looked forward to Minnie, who stopped in at least twice a week. Minnie would come in the back door as she had done for years and call out, "Whoo-hoo!"

"Minnie!" Marjorie and Junny squealed in delight. They dropped whatever held their attention and barreled toward Minnie, embracing her all at once.

"Have you got another story for us, Minnie?" was the first thing out of Marjorie's mouth every time Minnie showed up. She came from a long line of storytellers. Henryetta grinned at Marjorie and Junny who, like her, when she was little, would sit still, mouths agape, bedazzled as Minnie changed her voice and her gestures for each character. The children would laugh and clap, and then cry out, "Tell another one, Minnie!"

Henryetta considered Minnie the smartest person she knew. Minnie had natural ingenuity, and wisdom—the kind of wisdom that comes from struggle. Minnie always wanted to go to school, but when she was growing up there were only a few schools in the county, and the one closest to her was several miles away, too far for a little Negro girl to walk to alone. Besides, her great-grandmother needed tending while her parents worked for Henryetta's grandparents. Henryetta figured that is where Minnie must have learned all her stories.

What Minnie knew of reading, writing, and arithmetic came mostly from Henryetta. In the afternoons, Henryetta would sit at the kitchen table with Minnie and teach her what she had learned at school that day. Minnie would then practice reading her Bible at home and would write her favorite verses until she had perfected cursive writing. Henryetta was not a naturally inclined bookworm, but Minnie loved a good story, and once she got good at reading, she pestered Henryetta to check out books at the library. She knew Henryetta would lose interest and leave the book lying around. Henryetta went along with the charade because she knew the library doors were not open to Negros. Here the librarian thought Henryetta was a reading champion, when all the while, it was really Minnie.

They also loved Minnie's visits for her cooking. Flo and Henry would stand frowning at the pantry, not relishing the idea of opening another can of *whatever-was-there*, but Minnie could take the can of *whatever-was-there*, and somehow whip up a delicious meal that had them all smiling and smacking their lips. As much as Henryetta and Flo insisted Minnie did not have to cook for them, Minnie knew they appreciated it. It did not hurt that Minnie got a meal out of it, too.

All summer long, when Minnie came over, she braved the Dixon's attic heat to collect dresses she knew she could sell. It had been good business for both Minnie and Henryetta. Her mama's old dresses kept all of them fed, but by late September, Minnie had emptied the attic of Miss Lucille's castoffs. It was about the same time that Henryetta sold the last load out of the garage, other than a box of feather boas, costume jewelry, hats, canes and other odd accessories she thought might serve as good props for portraits. Their cash flow dwindled, the hospital bills eating up most of it.

Henryetta and Florence had been putting off cleaning out the attic for a cooler day when they could actually bear the heat. How Minnie had even set foot in that oven . . . In late October, the days and nights finally grew cooler. They decided to go up early in the morning when the air was still crisp and the sun's rays illuminated the attic from the eastern windows.

As they entered, sleepy cobwebs hung in corners and rust colored dust that had blown over from Oklahoma had settled in every nook and cranny. All summer they had fought the dust that lingered in the air. The radio called it the *dust bowl* and reported that railroad companies stopped eastbound and westbound trains to shovel dust off the tracks to keep them from derailing.

"What a mess," Flo said, taking in all the dusty boxes and trunks.

"Yes, but this mess is going to keep food in our stomachs. Let's get busy," replied Henryetta as she moved toward the first stack of boxes closest to the lighted area of the attic. She pulled off the lid of the box to find her mother's wedding dress, yellowed, but still incredibly stunning with the beaded bodice.

"Oh," gasped Flo as she looked at the dress. "I couldn't even dream of something that beautiful for my wedding."

"Minnie missed this, didn't she?" said Henry as she touched the silk sleeves adorned with brocade. She smiled imagining her mother's wedding day. She must have looked at her parents' wedding photo on their dresser a million times growing up, but since Bob and Gus left, Henryetta had not dared to open her mother's bedroom door. Suddenly, the memory of her mother bleeding, lying in the fetal position, flashed in her mind. Barricading her thoughts, she asked Florence, "What was your wedding like?"

"Simple, I guess. Walter's mother wanted a big wedding. She didn't get it. We eloped. The justice of the peace married us. I wore a red dress," Flo said looking sentimental.

"I loved that dress. That was a good day. I really loved Walter then."

"And now? Do you still love him?"

"Hmm. Yes, I suppose I love him as much as I can, seeing that he abandoned us and all."

"Oh, stop. He's going to send word any day now. You'll see."

"I don't know if I really want to hear word. What if Walter's life is not how he hoped? What if he is dead?" Flo paused and looked directly into Henry's eyes.

"Don't even think that, Flo. Walter is all right. This has hurt a lot of men. Walter is no different. He just can't face you. I was listening to the news the other day, and thousands of families are being abandoned by their husbands. You aren't the only one. At least Walter is alive."

Henryetta sighed deeply and looked away thinking back to the time before her father shot himself. Why didn't she see it—the changes? Had he been more melancholy, and she missed it? Had he dropped clues, hoping his family would find his masked sorrow, his masked shame? Never. Not one single clue.

"You know you can't sell your mama's wedding dress. Please tell me you won't even considerate it."

"It would bring a good price, but it is so outdated," Henry commented.

"Henry, why don't you ask her? She might want to keep it," Flo said, moving to the next box.

"Hmm. I do not know if it would do any good, Flo. Mama just sits in that chair looking blankly out the hospital window for hours on end. The doctors say she is wasting away. What can I do?"

"Hope. Pray. That's all any of us can do," replied Flo.

"That doesn't seem to be working very well for me," said Henry.

"Oh, Henry. You are just mad at God like the rest of us. It does not seem right he would do us like this, but my mother always said that God is closest to us when we are suffering. He carries us, Henry."

"All right, Pastor Flo."

Out of the corner of her eye, Henryetta glimpsed a rust-covered black metal strongbox. She stood up and walked over to the shelf where it rested. She imagined cash that would save them, but when she tried to open it, she found it locked. She scrounged around the shelf looking for a key to find only more dust. Stumped, she shrugged her shoulders, let it go, and moved on to other boxes and trunks. Within a few hours, Henry and Flo had dragged everything worth selling to the front lawn. Henryetta contracted with the peddler man to come directly to her house that afternoon to pick up what was left of her family's bygone treasures. As he drove off, Henryetta crinkled the cash in her hand. She wondered what they would do now. This cash would help them survive at least a month if nothing went wrong.

"I'm going for a drive, Flo," Henryetta said, handing her the cash, minus a dollar for gas and a much-deserved soda in her estimation. Before she left, Henryetta went to retrieve her camera from the darkroom in the back of the garage. She was determined never to sell any of her cameras or equipment that had become her livelihood. This space was her church—where she worked her magic, where she captured life in a millisecond.

She shoved open the door and flipped on the light to find her camera. She picked it up, and grabbed a canister of film. As she turned to leave, there, resting on nail beside the door, she noticed a small set of three keys—one tiny, and the other two, door keys. For all the hours she had spent in the darkroom, the keys had never registered. They were just part of the landscape, and did not matter until this moment.

Will the tiny one fit the strongbox in the attic? Tomorrow. I need to be outside now.

She flipped off the light and headed for the cotton fields that had blossomed like snowfall.

CHAPTER TWELVE

"Flo! Flo? Get up here! I need you!" The metal strongbox popped open effortlessly when Henryetta inserted the tiny key from the darkroom.

"Flo!" She screamed louder.

"Coming! For goodness sake! What is it, Henry? I was teaching Marjorie to subtract."

"I need you to see this!" Henryetta said excitedly, but nervously.

"What is it?" Flo said out of breath as she reached the attic.

"Just look," Henryetta said, pulling Flo to the floor where she had opened the strongbox. Florence looked at Henryetta and then tentatively opened the box. Henryetta looked anxiously at Florence as she slowly opened the strongbox lid. Before her were a pile of pictures that had been turned facedown in the box.

"Turn it over, Flo," said Henryetta. She turned over the eight by ten photo to reveal a nude woman with her nymph-like, curvaceous haunches to the camera. Her snakelike body writhed to her head where between her teeth rested a rose. Her deep cow eyes revealed wanton sexual desire. The photo appeared to be an antique. The paper the photo was printed on was thicker than anything Henry had used to develop her own photos. What props or costumes existed looked almost Victorian, maybe from their grandmothers' heyday. Flo looked at the photo not revealing any emotion while Henryetta looked at Flo with eyes wide open.

"Well, Flo?" asked Henryetta impatiently.

"Well what? This is complete trash! Burn them," responded Flo.

"Burn them? No! Look at the rest!" urged Henry.

"I most certainly will not!" cried Flo in protest.

"Why not? They are women, Flo. Just naked women. I think some of these photos are really old."

"Henryetta! What's gotten into you? I don't care how old they are. This is filth. Don't you understand what these are? What men use them for?" Flo slammed the top of the strongbox.

"What? What do they use them for?"

"God, Henry. You can't be that naive. Am I going to have to explain this to you? Didn't your mother ever tell you the facts of life?" Flo said strongly to her. Henryetta looked away because Lucille Dixon never talked about such "unladylike things." For all Henryetta knew, her future husband would place a seed in her milk that would plant a baby in her belly someday. Then Gus popped into her head and she remembered her longing for him to kiss her as they danced under the moon light the last night he was in Brownsville.

"Please, Flo."

"Henryetta, these are for a man to . . . Well, you know . . . pleasure himself."

Flo looked away from Henryetta, remembering her first time with Walter. Seeing him naked, hard, his eyes full of desire slowly peeling her red wedding dress from her shoulders. All of it came rushing back to her memory. She shook the memories out of her brain.

"Henryetta, men can desire a woman for two reasons. One is for love, and the other is for lust. When a man pleasures himself, it is lust. These photographs, well, they are what some men look at to . . . well, like I said, pleasure themselves. Surely, you know what the male sex looks like? Didn't you ever see one by accident? Maybe your brother's when you were little?"

Henryetta had caught a glimpse of her brother and his friends swimming naked in a pond one summer when she was twelve. They were spending a week out on their grandparents' farm, and her brother and some of the neighbor boys had slipped away to skinny-dip in a small pond at the back of the farm. That was the summer she was a perpetual pest. Henryetta constantly spied on and trailed the boys. Several times they had thrown rocks at her to make her leave them alone, but this time she had an idea that she would jump in the pond before they could protest, but she was stopped by the sight of them naked. They were not like her at all. Long and short appendages dangled between their legs. She cringed and grimaced as they grabbed them and had a peeing contest to see whose urine could fly out the farthest. Embarrassed, she wanted to run away, but she was too fascinated to get up and move from behind the pokeberry bushes.

"Yes. I know they are different from us. Can I tell you something, and you promise not to laugh at me, Flo?" Henryetta blushed.

"Anything," she said with a serious, nonjudgmental gaze.

"I . . . I really don't know anything about . . . you know . . . what happens between a man and a woman," Henryetta admitted. "Since you are married and all, maybe you could . . . educate me?"

Flo wanted to roll her eyes at strong, ignorant Henryetta, but remembered her own innocence until her wedding night with Walter. There had been kissing and arousal between them before marriage, but never sex. She recognized Henryetta's innocence as her own not so long ago.

"Henryetta, let's talk about this when there is a man in the picture. Right now, you have got to go down to the trash barrel and burn these," Flo said, gesturing to the attic stairs. "This is not right having this filth in your home!"

Then Henryetta started thinking money. They sold off almost every nonessential. Soon, she would be forced to sell off essentials and heirlooms that reminded her of her parents before the rug had been pulled out from under them. She may have not known a man herself, but from the burning sensation she felt thinking of Gus, she knew these photos could be of use to them.

"Flo? Could these bring in money?"

"Don't even say that! We will not sell these! Can you imagine if people got wind of this?"

"Who would know, Flo? Maybe the peddler man knows someone who buys this kind of thing?"

"Hush your mouth. Shame on you, Henryetta Dixon! Burn them!" Flo emphatically commanded. "I don't want to talk about this anymore. Burn them, this instant!" Flo turned on her heel and left Henryetta alone with the strongbox.

Instead of following Flo, Henryetta slowly overturned each picture one by one, looking at the parade of nude or scantily clothed sirens that beckoned to the viewer. Their allure was magnetic, calling her to explore each photo closely.

She marveled at all the different body sizes and types—some cushiony and soft with ample breasts with half-dollar-size nipples. She imagined the feeling of sinking into the woman in the photo felt like sinking into her father's easy chair. Henryetta touched her own waist, and found no soft tissue, but a tight abdomen. She recalled an odd comment Ezra Rubenstein made once after a large, but wealthy woman left the gallery. He mentioned that he loved hugging fat people because they felt soft, safe, and even comfortable. Why that stuck with her, she could not have told you, but some of those women's bodies reminded her of his words.

Other bodies were slender and lithe with tiny breasts that pointed at attention, which made her cup her own breasts in comparison. Henryetta had gazed at her own body, and knew it well, but now she had photos to judge her own physique. In the corner of the attic was an old mirror covered beneath a sheet that belonged to her great grandmother. Henryetta walked over to the mirror, pulling the sheet off it, flinging dust into the air.

As the dust calmed, Henryetta stared into her own blue eyes. She looked tired and her midneck length blonde bob suffered from sweat and flyaway strands. If the eyes were the window to the soul, hers appeared torn apart by sorrow. Her expression was not even close to the blanket expression of lust every one of those women in the photographs shared. She wondered if Gus had seen lust in her own eyes of which not even she was aware.

Henryetta pulled her day dress that she thought resembled a dirty potato sack over her head revealing only her brazier and panties. Then Henryetta slid out of her panties, and undid her bra and let it drop to the floor. The fall air on her exposed breasts felt cool and made her flesh tingle. She stood looking in the mirror at her tall nude stature, her slim, athletic limbs. She had thinned down since her father died and her mother was hospitalized. Her appetite had not been good and she felt compelled to keep herself busy to occupy her mind. She paid little attention to how her body had changed.

Footsteps on the second floor and the sound of Flo's door closing to put the children to bed woke Henryetta from her mirror gazing. She quickly put her clothes back on and went back over to continue looking at the more modern photographs of sacred body parts that were hidden by a feather, a tassel, or lace. She found them to be more enticing than the ones who bared all. Those photos left room for imagining the undressing of the woman. Some of the photos she found artful, beautiful, and even tasteful. When she got to the last photo, she noticed an envelope at the very bottom of the box. The return address was New York, New York. She carefully removed and opened the letter from the envelope.

> Dear Thomas,
>
> I trust this letter finds you in good health. I have found a client who very much desires to invest in your line of photography. He is looking to expand his business into this line of product. He was impressed with your work and is eager to talk with you about further ideas he has. Enclosed is a check for $50 for the sample photographs you so generously supplied earlier this month.
>
> If you are interested in expanding your business, please contact me at the following address below:
>
> Tommy Sylvester
> 829 Market Street
> New York, New York

Henryetta read the letter three times before she checked the envelope for the check, but it was empty. She soon folded the letter and put it back in the envelope. Now, she was equally intrigued and appalled by her father's clandestine dealings. Fifty dollars was nothing to scoff at. Questions rattled around in her head.

Did her mother know about his underground business? Were these the photos her mother was looking at the day she cried out?

Henry studied the pictures again looking for familiar faces, when after three pictures she remembered one of the women to be an actress in one of her father's productions from when she was a small child. She kept searching only to recognize some of the props in the photos as some of those they had recently pawned to the peddler man. Had he really photographed these actresses right here in Brownsville? Her father did keep strange hours and was away quite often on theater business. Then the third key on the ring called her attention away from the photos.

It was a door key, but to what door?

Suddenly, it was all too much to take in. This was the one loose string her father neglected to tie before he left this earth.

Did he want them to find out about his secret dealings—this other life he led? And do these photos have anything to do with his suicide?

Henryetta closed and locked the box, placed it back on the shelf, and decided to hide the keys in her dresser downstairs. She would have to think about this when they were almost out of money. Her tattered soul could not bear one more tear.

CHAPTER THIRTEEN

*G*us, tanned and shirtless, his brown hair now highlighted golden from the sun and salt, napped under the shade of a palm tree on the grainy, gray sand of the Florida Keys in the midafternoon sun. Just off the beach, anchored, Patricio's fishing boat rested from a day's worth of fishing on somewhat choppy seas. The air had cooled considerably, and woke him. Gus knew the afternoon rains would soon arrive. He studied the billowy gray-green sea as white-capped waves began to pound the edge of land. Above, the mercurial sky was changing moods. Not too far out to sea, towers of storm clouds were stacking themselves up to unleash showers. Something about that sky made him think of Henryetta. He smiled thinking of her deep blue, angry eyes the first day they met. He had been with Henry on her worst day and even in her suffering, her eyes remained a blue that mirrored the depths of the ocean he now spent so many hours fishing. Out on Patricio's fishing boat, Gus spent many evenings staring at the sunset wondering what it must look like back in Tennessee. Some nights he imagined Henry emerging from her dark room to pause and take in the same moon he saw reflected in the evening tides that brushed against the sides of the boat.

Did she think of him as he thought of her?

Gus had been in the Keys for six weeks now. He simply could not bring himself to leave. He had ridden the rails between Miami and Key West several times. Miami would only permit hoboes one day within the city limits before the cops escorted them out of town. Yes, Miami granted the hobo a nice trip to the beach, a meal, and then a fare-thee-well or jail. Gus mostly rode a bit, but then just stepped off the trains on the different keys to explore. That is how he had met Patricio.

Many locals warned him he was exploring in hurricane season, but so far, the worst was the late afternoon rains. Gus found work on Patricio's fishing boat on Marathon Key. It started with him helping Patricio unload fish for a local grocer. He had hopped aboard for a ride to Key West and had never gotten off. Two months ago, Gus could not have told you a thing about tides, salt-water fish, nets, or fishing. Now, with the tutelage of an old Cuban fellow who sipped rum all day long, he felt like a foster son of the sea. Gus never grew tired of Patricio's need to teach him, or tell stories. Patricio gave more to Gus than his own father, a scientist, ever had. His father's time could not be wasted under any circumstances. Books, experiments and symposiums consumed his father. Patricio, however, was a simple man, born on an island and destined to die on an island or at the hands of his first love, the sea.

Staring out into the Gulf, Gus wished Henry could see this place. Everything was a photograph yet too immense to be captured on paper. People and moments were portrayed more truthfully than nature. Gus had never seen a photograph of nature that fully depicted its essence, beauty, or even the ferocity of Mother Nature who had a sincerely unforgiving, sinister side. No white borders of a photograph could contain the landscape before him. Henry would have to see it with her own eyes, breathe it in, and live this nature, so foreign from the cotton fields of West Tennessee.

Gus knew he would have to get back on the rails to continue his research on hoboes for his dissertation, but the Keys had been such a wide-open space to collect his thoughts and trace the patterns in his notes and journals. There was something about the salty breezes, the lush foliage, and the cries of the seagulls that calmed him and allowed him to think. The whole place teemed with life and it made him want to write. Fortunately, Gus gained access to a borrowed typewriter after sharing more than one drink with another writer at Captain Tony's Saloon. The fellow had entertained him and other patrons for hours with tales of Montana from where he had just returned. He lent Gus his typewriter for a few days while he and his wife were away on a fishing trip down in the Dry Tortugas.

For months, Gus had been posing as a hobo, riding the rails to study their lifestyles, their dreams, and their reasons for uprooting and moving on. It was a unique time in history, and their stories were his ticket to earning his doctorate in sociology. No publications such as he was writing existed. What intrigued him most was the age of the hoboes. Most were just kids and younger men. One thing held true, they were society's lepers, but not above pity. He had seen people who did not have a dime to spare put a few pennies in a hobo's hand or offer them a day's work.

Then there was Gertie, a girl who dressed and tried to act like a boy to ride the rails. Her story was the outlier, the one he was slowly working on getting. Gertie tended to run with his gang, but then would depart from the group on and off. He did not know where she went, but sooner or later she would show up again, happy-go-lucky, but tough. The boys in the gang protected her as if she were a sister. Gus wondered if she had been the victim of some sort of abuse to make her want to leave home, but people did not speak of these things. Asking her directly for her story would be rude. He wanted to earn her trust so that she would open up to him without asking.

His idea to study hoboes came from two experiences that seemed to happen one right after the other. After Sunday dinner at his Aunt's house, the family piled in the car to take a drive at her request. The Depression had not hit his Aunt Trudy and Uncle Ben because his uncle owned a food packaging plant close to the outskirts of Chicago. Business was good as far as Uncle Ben was concerned. Even if they did have to tighten their belts, they were not to worry. Aunt Trudy had more money than God. The Depression would not touch them.

Recently though, Uncle Ben and his partners had discovered a way to package peanuts and popcorn in small boxes that would keep them fresh. "Snacks" they were calling them. While thousands were lining up to be served thin soup and a bread crust, Aunt Trudy and Uncle Ben were buying lake property. It was their fortune that had paid for Gus's college degree and now his graduate studies. They had no children of their own, and when Aunt Trudy's sister, Gus's mother, died from tuberculosis, she had seen to it that Gus never wanted for anything. Gus and his father moved in with Aunt Trudy and Uncle Ben to make it easier for all of them. Aunt Trudy and Uncle Ben were more his parents than his own father.

On this particular Sunday, Aunt Trudy wanted to see what the fuss was about. The radio had been talking about the "Hoovervilles" that had sprung up outside of the city. They were deplorable shack cities with no plumbing, no fresh water, nothing, just shelter. So their family drove out just beyond the city limits. On that day, the air was crisp and cold. Uncle Ben drove the car up a hill that overlooked the makeshift neighborhood. Uncle Ben shut off the car. It was quiet in Hooverville. Only lonely gray smoke floated into the sky from makeshift stovepipes. As Gus's family peered down into Hooverville, the feeling of desperation that hung in, above, and around the hovels seeped into the car creating silence.

Then Gus noticed figures standing around a barrel of fire for warmth. He imagined them to be a family—a father, a mother, and two small children. As Uncle Ben drove closer, Gus tried not to lose sight of the silhouetted figures who, from a distance, looked shrouded in blankets. As they came closer, Gus found that the figures were all wearing remnants of a cut-up oriental carpet. Their shoes, wrapped up in newspaper, were bound with string. They were survivors he thought.

Who were these people before the Crash?

Gus realized that inside every hovel lived a story worth recording for his study, and yet this topic was almost too obvious. He did not completely dismiss the idea, but he thought there still might be another topic that no one had yet approached. Still, on his travels when Gus had moments of struggle he remembered that family and silently thanked God for his multitude of blessings. It could always be worse.

The second experience came quite soon after that afternoon drive to Hooverville. Gus's father was headed to Minneapolis to consult with another inventor by the name of Carothers who worked for the DuPont Company—something about a new substance that was going to revolutionize the clothing industry. He had driven his father to the train station to see him off. He always cherished these moments when he had his father's full attention.

When Gus was about fifteen Aunt Trudy heard him crying in his room late one night. It was not like Gus to cry, but his father had disappointed him again. All he asked was that his father watch him play football, but as Gus scanned the crowd, his father was absent again. When he returned home, his father was still working in his basement laboratory. For several moments, Gus stood silently at the bottom of the stairs watching his father. Gus figured his father would at least greet him, but he didn't even seem to notice Gus.

"Father."

"Oh, Gus. What brings you down here?"

"We won."

"Who won, son?" His father did not pause to look up at Gus.

"Forget it. Good night, Father."

Gus did not move, hoping his father would ask him what he was talking about, but he did not. Staying focused on his work, Gus's father, simply said, "Night."

Angry tears filled Gus's eyes and he clenched his fists as he turned to walk up the stairs to his room. It was the straw that broke the camel's back.

Why didn't his father care about him?

Aunt Trudy knew Gus better than anyone did. Seeing his rigid posture and clenched hands as he marched upstairs to bed, she knew something was not right. Aunt Trudy knocked at Gus's door. When she sat at the edge of his bed, Gus complained that his father barely knew he existed. Aunt Trudy tried to console Gus by explaining it was his father's way of coping with the loss of Gus's mother.

"You remind him of her," Aunt Trudy said. "Some men dive into the bottle, but your father dove into his work." Gus wondered if his father would ever climb out from under his grief back into Gus's life. Since that particular night, there had been fleeting, millisecond moments with his father—each one a treasure. Gus guessed that Aunt Trudy had given his father a tongue-lashing. She was good at that.

As Gus watched his father's train pull away, he saw his father swiping a square of white paper against the window glass. For years, his father had always done that to say goodbye. Gus raised his arm to wave goodbye and then let it drop as the passenger cars rounded the bend as the train sped up. As he watched, a commotion on his left moved toward him. From an open boxcar door, a group of young hoboes taunted a security guard who ran furiously, waving his Billy club in wild circles. The louder he shouted empty threats, the harder they guffawed and provoked the guard who soon ran out of sidewalk.

Gus noticed a lone hobo climbing down from the roof of a boxcar to slip inside, escaping the frigid Chicago wind. In that moment, he got the idea that he would take to the rails, outfitted as a hobo, and study their lives for his dissertation. Gus thought himself pretty ingenious at that moment, but after a few weeks of sleeping on cold boxcar floors, facing gnawing hunger, and some close calls with several unsavory characters, his ingenuity turned sour quickly. Life on the rails was not as glamorous and as carefree as he imagined.

After Gus's professors approved, even lauded his proposal, he presented his idea to his family, jokingly telling them he was "running away to join the circus." At first, they all thought his joke was funny. Who hadn't joked that they were running off to join the circus at some point? When Gus spelled out his plan to disguise himself as a hobo in the name of research, his Aunt gasped in disbelief. Even his father felt it was an unwise move and encouraged him to rethink his topic. Uncle Ben said nothing, which typically meant he did not approve either. Aunt Trudy's nagging became incessant.

"You're only twenty-four."

"You might get killed."

"What if you end up in jail?"

"What about the weather?"

And on and on. She would not drop it.

The more she nagged, the more he studied the train routes and planned where he wanted to go. As soon as it was warm enough to hop a train with just a knapsack and a jacket, Gus left a note on the hall table telling his family he would be in touch and not to worry.

The one thing he had to say for Aunt Trudy is that her worries made him think ahead of what could possibly happen to him and how he could troubleshoot his problems. His forethought often served him well. That is how he got his nickname "Lead Goose" but even so, reality and expectation were on opposite ends of the teeter-totter. It was a balancing act or life could crash down quickly. Gus found he needed a pack mentality to survive.

Gus had decided to take small trips down into Indiana, Ohio, and over to Michigan. He spent as much time on the ground watching the comings and goings of the hoboes as he did actually riding the rails because that was their pattern. He kept his distance, but had a particular group he had been following because of their jovial nature. In hindsight, they probably were not the best choice. Their clothes proved they were new at this like him. He would have been better off getting in with an older gang of hoboes who were a little worse for the wear, but they could be dangerous and territorial. Three times he had been threatened to move on, that he was on someone else's boxcar, and he was not welcome.

His ties to the gang that nicknamed him Lead Goose were knotted to the day that brutish guards murdered Li'l Randy. The gang had been staying at a local shelter, but had talked of moving along to some place down South where they could work tobacco. Some train stations turned their heads at hoboes. Desperate times caused the rules to bend, but at this particular station, this mentality did not exist. In fact, it was quite the opposite. The station guards had the authority to deal with the freeloaders who were stealing rides from the railroad accordingly. They dealt Li'l Randy blow after blow, accordingly.

Li'l Randy, a thirteen-year-old orphan, took to the rails six months prior. He eagerly showed the gang the ropes. He taught them how to hoist themselves into the moving boxcars, where to scavenge food behind grocers and restaurants. He knew which cities had shelters and soup. He found them day jobs that paid them enough to get a bite to eat here and there or even see a picture show on a cold or rainy day. On this particular day, Li'l Randy would show them what death on the rails looked like.

Gus had been hiding in an empty boxcar for several hours when he felt the train jolt into motion. Then one by one the gang helped one another up and into the boxcar minus Li'l Randy.

"Come on, Li'l Randy! You can catch her!" yelled Sal.

Li'l Randy latched onto the door handle when suddenly he fell out of sight. Gertie and the boys cried out in horror. Gus moved between the gang to peer out the door. The railroad bulls had caught up to Li'l Randy. The first blow sent the boy reeling to the pavement. By the time Gus peered out, blood pooled down the sidewalk from a boy who the guards continued to strike, even when it became clear his body was lifeless. The guards halted and turned toward Gus and the gang. They yelled something, but the locomotive's noise drowned the words. Stunned, the gang sank down into the shadows of the boxcar and traveled miles and miles in silence. Li'l Randy was gone.

It was not hard for Gus to blend in with the gang, even become its leader. The death of Li'l Randy had bonded them. Gus was older than the rest of them and educated in human behavior and leadership skills. Quick decisions and confidence were most of it. Gus found it easier for the gang to open up to him when he remained neutral and just listened to their stories. They never suspected him of being an incognito researcher from the University of Chicago. They teased him sometimes for writing in his "diary," but soon overlooked this peculiarity and chalked up this quirk to being "Gus."

They left him alone because Gus had common sense and grit. He had led them to food and a clean bed many a night. His calm and mannerly way of talking had saved them from being hauled off to jail by the railroad bulls more than once. Sometimes they asked him why he was riding the rails when he was smart enough to be making a living for himself. He always replied, "Adventure," and smiled in earnest.

Now he was here in paradise, not sure if he was ready to go back to riding the rails. Since Brownsville, he hadn't seen his gang because he opted to travel to Florida. They mostly stayed within five hundred miles of Chicago. He had been gone from home since mid-April. It was now late October and the weather only improved here, but the trees would be in full fall color back home. Riding the rails up north would present a challenge in the winter months. Patricio was easy come, easy go. He would find another Gus to help him on the boat. Gus also thought about the upcoming presidential election. He wanted Hoover out and FDR in, but he would have to return home to vote. He had enough money to buy a regular train ticket home. He could even have Aunt Trudy wire him the money, if he really wanted. But then, there was that last night in Brownsville with Henryetta. If he traveled north, could he stop himself from going back there to see her? How he wanted to see her again.

No matter how he fought himself, his thoughts always seemed to digress back to the week he spent with Henryetta, helping her empty the Dixon's garage of non-essentials. He grinned thinking of the greedy little peddler man who couldn't wait to hock their belongings in Memphis and Little Rock for a pretty penny. Those days had been hot and the work dull, dirty, and sweaty. He relished sitting in the horse trough of cool bathwater at the end of the day out in the backyard. The city water had been shut off during the first day of their work, so Gus and Thom drove out to a local farm and bought a used livestock trough. The men all took turns emptying and refilling the trough out of doors and hauling well water to the tub upstairs where the women and children bathed.

In the evenings, the men slept out on the back screened in porch and the women and children in the parlor with the front and side porch screen doors open letting in a slight breeze from the west. Flo and Henry traded her mother's crystal goblets for eight military cots the peddler man had on his truck. Thom agreed and decided the cots could come in handy if they should ever need or want to take in boarders. It was much cooler sleeping downstairs than upstairs in the August heat.

The evenings were indeed the best time of Gus's day. Bob and Thom headed out with Sy for drinking and cards. They invited him, but he declined politely. Florence busied herself with the children. Henryetta spent time in the darkroom developing film and Gus wrote in his journal. The night before Gus was heading back out, he finished writing and ventured toward the darkroom. He could hear music coming from an old Victrola inside. He rapped his knuckles on the wooden door.

"Henryetta, may I come in?" Gus called to her, but there was no answer.

"Henryetta, did you hear me? I want to come in. Is it all right?" When there was no response, he pushed open the door, only to startle her.

"Oh, Gus! You scared me!"

"Sorry. I knocked and called out to you," he said in a loud voice, trying to talk over the music.

"The music!" she shouted and moved to turn down the volume. "The music. I didn't hear you."

"What are you working on?" Gus asked.

"I am just practicing my developing techniques. Come in. I'll show you."

Gus followed her to a clothes line of photos that were drying.

"Look at these. They are all parts of one entire photograph I am trying to emphasize." One photo showed two hands clasped together. Another the man's face. A third one a woman's face. The fourth, four feet walking in step with one another.

"These are quite good. Where did you take them?" Gus said, gazing at each one thoughtfully.

"From my last trip to New York. That is where I studied photography. My father used to go to New York at least twice a year to locate talent for his opera house. My mother and I went with him. When I was sixteen, I began studying with Ezra Rubenstein."

"Is that what you want to be? A photographer?"

Henryetta smirked at his question.

"I *am* a photographer, Gus. I had a good little business going before there was a run on the banks. What about you? What did you do before you . . .," her voice trailed off, not knowing how to put it.

"Became a hobo?" he filled in, half laughing at her awkward question.

"I was a college boy. University of Chicago. Sociology major." Henryetta looked at him, puzzled.

"I don't understand. Why are you riding the rails then?" she asked.

"The circus wouldn't take me," Gus said, smiling at her mischievously.

She raised her eyebrows at him, but didn't lose eye contact and smiled as she tilted her head. In the week he had spent with her, Gus found Henryetta's smiles did not come easily.

"Adventure, I suppose. I wanted to see America before I settle down." That was his stock answer when people asked him why he was out there on the fringe, but for a millisecond, he considered telling Henryetta the truth.

"By settled down, do you mean you are engaged, then?" Henryetta asked him, bravely looking directly into his eyes.

"Me? No," Gus said, looking back at the drying photographs and then back to her questioning eyes. He smiled at her and continued, "Definitely not."

Henryetta smiled at this.

"What about you, Henry? Do you have a fella?"

She rolled her eyes and smiled. "Around here? No. I think I am doomed to be an old maid."

"Don't go selling yourself short," Gus flirtatiously cautioned. He moved over to the Victrola. "Listening to Louis Armstrong?" He wound up the crank and placed the needle on the record.

"Henryetta, would you dance with me?" Gus asked holding out his hand to her.

"Here? Now?" she said blushing.

Gus nodded toward the yard.

"Out on the lawn, if you prefer. It is much cooler out there."

"Well, yes," she said, reaching out to take his hand. Gus turned up the volume of the Victrola and then led her out onto the cool grass.

Barefoot himself with his pants rolled up to his knees, Gus suggested. "Take off your shoes. The grass is so cool," Henryetta slid out of her pumps feeling the cool tickle of the grass on her feet.

"You're right Gus," Henryetta said, looking into his eyes, smiling again. His left hand now rested on the curve of her back.

Together, they began to sway back and forth. She felt too far away, so Gus pulled her closer to him resting his chin against her forehead. Even though every cell in her body ignited with nervous energy, she did not resist. Since her mother's episode, Gus had felt compelled to take her in his arms and just hold her while she cried. He had not seen or heard her cry once. Within a few measures, Henryetta rested her head on his shoulder. Nothing separated them, but their clothes.

It had been such a long time since he had danced with a girl he actually wanted to dance with. In college there had been mixers and socials, but to dance with Henryetta here under the ancient oak tree with the moon overhead and cool night grass beneath them . . . This was not one of the adventures he expected to have out on the rails. Aunt Trudy never warned him about falling in love.

Holding her, feeling the heat exchange between their bodies made him dizzy with desire for her, not just her body, but *her*, all of her. He twirled the ends of her hair around his fingers as they swayed back and forth slowly. He wanted to kiss her in that moment. Gus backed away to look into her eyes. Henryetta smiled up at him in a beguiling way, her deep eyes reflecting the moonlight overhead. She had no idea how beautiful she was. That was what he admired most about her. She was a natural beauty, a strong woman with her own mind, and independent like him. She had no idea of her allure.

He leaned in close to almost touch her lips with his, but then the thought of leaving her, and possibly hurting her more when she was already so wounded stopped him. Finishing his dissertation quelled his desire. He knew he wanted get back to his research and kissing her would change everything. One kiss could lead to more, maybe even love. He wanted to be able to finish. With a thread's width between their lips, Gus put his forehead to hers and simply whispered her name.

"Henryetta," Gus said aloud under the palm tree as fat drops of rain and crack of tropical thunder broke Gus's memories of that night. He returned to the present to hear Patricio calling him to come to the boat, a storm was coming. They had to tie down the boat in the harbor. With that, he hopped up, ran for the water, dove in washing the sand from his body and Henryetta from his mind.

CHAPTER FOURTEEN

*F*lo woke in a panicked sweat, crying out for Walter. She had the tornado dream again. Always it spun black and fierce, and loud, always coming for her. It always started with Flo riding Philippa bareback through her grandfather's empty cornfield in her red wedding dress. In the distance, by the white washed fence, Walter and the children smile and wave to her, but then a train-like roar draws her attention to behind her. Soon the towering vortex of wind engulfs her and Philippa who whinnies in distress, but continues toward Walter and the children. *If only I can save them in time.* Flo sees Walter sucked up, in, and whirls away from her sight. In her dream she cries out, and wakes herself before the children are drawn in.

"Mama. You were dreaming again," comforted Marjorie.

Flo didn't move, but took several deep breaths to try to calm her racing heart.

"I'm sorry, darling. Did I wake you?" Flo turned to stroke Marjorie's forehead.

"It scares me when you have bad dreams, Mama."

"I know, my darling, but it was just a dream. Go back to sleep now."

Marjorie nodded and rolled away from her mother.

Flo lay there for a moment, still trying to shake the feeling that her skin was crawling. *Where was Walter?* She could not accept that he would just abandon them. That went against everything Walter had been to her and to the children. Walter was a good man, a reliable man. She couldn't even think of the alternative. She tried and tried to keep the words, "Walter is dead," from popping into her head, but before she could stop them, they were already there. Most times when this happened, she would swallow down the sob and clean something.

Thank God for Henryetta's generosity. Sometimes Flo wondered if circumstances would have been very different if Henryetta had not been as charitable. There were days Flo dared to wonder who was taking advantage of whom more. Flo often doubted Henryetta would be doing as well as she was had Florence and the children not happened upon Henryetta's father's funeral. She didn't come from the best of stock, after all. A daddy who shot himself, a crazy mama, a drunk for a brother, and now these sinful pictures. God knows where they even came from. Then Flo stopped herself from being judgmental. She could hear the backwoods revival preacher telling her to take the log from her eye. If Henry had not taken them in she and the children might have already starved. Even though she and Henryetta both kept company with misery, it seemed less painful with one another.

The next day, the telephone rang and Marjorie called out to Henryetta that it was the hospital. Flo paused washing the breakfast dishes to listen. She couldn't quite make out what Henry was saying, but she could tell it was just short replies of understanding. Soon, Henryetta appeared at the kitchen door.

"Mama died in the night," Henry said in a matter-of-fact tone.

"Poor Henry," thought Flo. *Two parents in six months.* Internally, Flo punished herself for her earlier thoughts and then told herself that we don't choose our blood relatives. Flo's granny used to say that sometimes our closest family members were *not* related to us by blood. Flo had never really understood what her granny meant until this exact moment. Henryetta was all the family she had right now and vice versa.

"I'm sorry, Hen. She's better off this way," Flo said, drying her hands and walking over to place her hand on Henryetta's shoulder. Henryetta made no move to respond. For a moment, Flo thought this might break Henry, but then she spoke.

"The hospital already sent her body to the funeral parlor."

"Yes," Flo said quietly and paused a moment, looking into Henry's forlorn eyes.

"What do you want me to do?" Flo asked.

Henryetta apathetically shrugged her shoulders and bit her lower lip as she stared at the linoleum floor. The way Henryetta was slumped over reminded Flo of a limp dish towel. Flo wasn't quite sure what was holding up Henryetta. She was lifeless and drained of energy.

"I'll tell you what. I am going to call down to the funeral parlor and find out what needs to be done. In the meantime, why don't you come and sit out on the porch for a while. When I'm off the phone, I'll make us some tea to sip on," comforted Flo.

CHAPTER FIFTEEN

*H*enryetta hadn't been in her parents' room since her mother hurt herself. Later in the evening after Miss Lucille's breakdown, Florence swept up the glass and put Lucille's things back on the dresser. Gus and Bob had righted the night stand. But Henryetta, she had not even opened the door since that day. As she walked toward the door to open it, Henryetta imagined her dead parents lying side by side in the bed as if in their coffins. This frightened her and she paused before touching the doorknob, but a bustling Florence cut in front of her and flung open the door as if it had been her own room the whole time.

A thick layer of red dust that had blown over from the Oklahoma dust bowl slept silently on the bed linens, drapes, hardwood floors, her mother's perfume flasks and silver handled hairbrush. The room smelled faintly of the perfume that had spilled and run down the floorboards during her mother's breakdown. In the other rooms, Henry and Flo had waged war on the dust all September and October. Once, it got so bad, they draped wet sheets over the windows to catch the dust before it could invade every crevice, but it was so sweltering hot, they gave up and let the dust in. Some nights they would cover the kitchen table with long sheets and sit under the table to eat. Marjorie and Junny loved it, thinking it was a game, but really it was to keep the food from tasting like gritty Oklahoma soil.

"Just pick one, Flo," Henryetta said from just outside the door, not daring to cross the threshold.

Flo opened Lucille's closet and looked for the prettiest Brownsville-appropriate dress she could find. Considering there were only two left, a day dress and one that would have rivaled some of the movie stars', it was an easy decision. Henryetta nodded in resignation.

"She would want to go out in style," Henryetta said in a tired tone. Florence pulled out the dress and closed the closet door without saying a word. She simply walked out, past Henryetta, and downstairs where Mr. Turner from the funeral parlor waited.

Henryetta took a long look and then closed the door and went downstairs to talk with the funeral broker.

"Miss Dixon," he began.

"Henryetta," she said.

"Henryetta," he said in an uncomfortable tone. "We must talk about the payment for your mother's funeral. There are some decisions you must make. Times being hard and all, I wasn't sure how you wanted to handle your mother's burial."

"What is it going to cost me?" she asked pointedly.

"Well, for a funeral and burial appropriate to her status you are looking at $345," he said plainly.

Henryetta looked at Flo, knowing they did not have that kind of money. Flo wanted to look away from Henryetta, but that is not what she needed or wanted.

"We don't have that kind of money, Mr. Turner," spoke up Flo.

"No, Mr. Turner, we don't. What is the cheapest funeral I can give my mama?" asked Henryetta.

"Miss Henryetta. There are payment plans," Mr. Turner offered.

"No. Mr. Turner. I don't know how much money there will be tomorrow, let alone in the future. What is the cheapest, please?"

"Well, let me think a moment. You have provided her clothing," he said, looking up at the ceiling and calculating fees. "Seventy-five dollars."

"What does that get me?"

"A graveside service in a pine box. If you want a preacher and an obituary on the radio and in the paper, that will be an extra twelve dollars."

Henryetta snorted and rolled her eyes as tears filled her eyes. "Well, Mama, you always got the best, and that is our best these days," she said, looking skyward.

"So that will be eighty-seven dollars?" he asked Henryetta.

She nodded, tears beginning to roll down her cheeks.

"The sooner we bury her body, the better. There will be no embalming. I suggest later today or tomorrow morning first thing. The grave diggers can be sent out to your family plot directly," said Mr. Turner.

"Yes. Today at sunset, please. I can't give her a fancy funeral, but God can give her a pretty sky," said Henryetta. "Plus, I need time to find my brother."

"Yes, ma'am. Now regarding the payment, I will need that now," he said, not trying to sound pushy.

Florence walked out of the room toward the secretary where she and Henryetta took care of paying bills. She opened the cash envelope they hid between the bills and pulled out the total cost. She quickly counted the fives and ones left. They had thirty dollars, about a week and half's salary, maybe two weeks if they stretched the money.

"Mr. Turner, your money," Florence said, handing him the cash.

"Thank you. Miss Henryetta, my sincerest condolences to your family," he said and then turned to go.

CHAPTER SIXTEEN

*E*xhausted from a day of stooped over pea-picking, Walter sat propped up under an oak tree, the same oak tree he sat under every afternoon. Everyone in the camp had their routines, and his was to sit under the tree and look at their family picture. He reached down into his threadbare pocket for his wallet. Once again he pulled out a wrinkled photo with frayed edges. He looked at Florence's smiling face. In her arms, she held Junny who was just a few months old. On her left stood Marjorie smiling, with her head tilted just to the left. Behind her stood Walter with his arm around Flo's shoulders. His heart ached to be with them, but how would Flo ever forgive him for abandoning them? He shuddered in self-disgust to think of their fate. The worry he caused her was a wall of shame he would never surmount.

This was the tail end of the pea-picking season and the energy around the camp was of constant worry. Earlier that year many pickers had gone on strike to protest the reduction in their wages from seventy-five cents a pack to fifty cents. Last winter, many of the pickers and their families barely survived. They turned to government relief, but were only awarded meager benefits. Two cents a day per person. This small gift was wiped out by the four-dollar rent charged by the landowner for them to camp on his land. Suffering was everywhere.

Walter's dreams of bringing his family out to California for a better life were dashed as he walked into the pea-picker camp that first day. He was greeted by what he called a parade of scarecrows, their clothes raggedy, their faces, hands, and legs caked with California dust. Their hollow faces looked as if they could not be filled with food, water, or hope. One afternoon during a break, Walter struck up conversation with a man he imagined to be in his forties to find out he was only a few years older than himself. Walter studied the man's graying temples and the deep wrinkles around his eyes. Like most pickers, the man's skin was tanned and leathered from the California sun. Walter listened as the man related his story. The stress of his failed farm, a journey of hardship from Oklahoma, the constant gnawing of hunger, the strain of picking peas from sunup to sundown had aged the man in a matter of months.

Seeing the man, Walter wondered how much he himself had aged. Walter hadn't looked in a mirror in months. Seeing the desperation that first day, Walter tried not to lose faith. He would work hard and save enough money to send for his family, but after a few nights sleeping out of doors, using a ditch as a toilet and bathing in a small stream at the back of the camp, he knew it would be months before he could send for them. But, then, why would he bring Florence, little June Bug, and Marjorie to this hellhole only to starve? Walter looked up at the sky and squeezed his eyes shut expelling lonesome tears that no one could stop.

He had thought to write to Florence to tell her of his whereabouts, but how could he? Walter had no idea where she and the children might be. He wondered if she had returned to Kentucky to live with his parents. Several times he started to pen a letter to them, but the shame he felt of leaving his family overpowered him. Three times he angrily crumpled the paper and tossed it away. Knowing what happened to them would be worse.

Sometimes when the camp was all bedded down and quiet, Walter would go out of his makeshift tent and walk down by the stream to listen to the soft gurgles of the water as it went on its way to the Pacific. Staring up at the universe, Walter found a moment's joy in the solitude. Sitting there, gazing up at the vast sea of stars he told himself that there were infinite possibilities. He could not fathom God abandoning his family. He surely would feel it if something had happened to them, if they were gone from this earth. He earnestly prayed for protection and comfort for his family. Then without realizing, he whispered the words, "Forgive me," out to the universe, hoping somehow Florence would hear him and feel his plea wherever she was.

CHAPTER SEVENTEEN

A majestic sunset splashed across the sky. Henryetta, the pastor's wife, Henryetta's neighbors, Flo, Marjorie, and Junny recited the Lord's Prayer as Thom Jr., Sy, and the grave diggers lowered her mama into her resting place. Henryetta had uprooted a bunch of mums to leave with the grave diggers to plant on her mother's grave. Her payment was two apple pies that had been brought over to her house by church members who served with her mother in the United Methodist Women.

As Thom drove them back into town from the cemetery, Gus's gang of hoboes walking slowly up the sidewalk caught Henryetta's eye. They were headed to what looked like her house. The thought of Gus shook her out of her sorrow. Could he really show up today? If only he could see her happy. She had been so happy once. In that moment she yearned for the past, but then knew it would do her no good. They were all getting out of the car when she heard Gertie's voice call out, "Helloooooooo! Remember me? It's me, Gertie!"

"And who is that?" asked Thom.

"They are hoboes," volunteered Marjorie, "and that's Gertie. She's a girl hobo, but she has to act like she's a boy so nobody will bother her."

"Is that so? And how do you know a bunch of hoboes, Marjorie?" Thom asked as he watched them approach.

"Mr. Gus. He brought them last summer. They paid to take a bath, but then Miss Lucille had her fit and they had to go." No one responded, but waited for the crew to make it up the drive.

"Hey there, Miss Henryetta. Y'all sure are dressed up. Been to church or something?" Gertie asked as the rest of the boys, took off their caps and nodded in greetings. Henryetta didn't even notice Thom telling Gertie they had just buried their mother. She scanned the filthy boys' faces for Gus, and when she didn't find him, she looked past them down at the end of the drive hoping to see him rounding the corner.

"I'm real sorry to hear that, Miss Henryetta," said Gertie.

"And Lead Goose? I mean Gus? Is he with you Gertie?"

"No, ma'am. We haven't seen Gus in a good little while. The last time we saw him was down in Miami, Florida. He said he liked it so much he was going to ride on down to Key West. We've been as far west as Texas, but the dust got so bad, they had to stop the train to clear it off the tracks. That was bad news for us, because the bulls searched the boxcars and threw us off. We spent a rough time of it in Texas. We were walking back this direction looking for another train station to hop a train and there was just miles and miles of nothing. We saw hundreds of jalopies packed to the hilt. Everybody in Oklahoma was headed for California."

"When was the last time you ate Gertie?" Flo spoke up.

"Truth? Two days ago, Miss Flo."

"Well, come on up, we have more than we can eat. Is that all right with you Henry? Thom?" Flo asked as she motioned toward the house. Henry and Thom nodded in exactly the same way at the same time, a family trait.

Soon, what had been a sad moment in the Dixon family history was turned around to *the night the hoboes came to stay* that would become legend in later years. Their guests' stories and cheerful moods of having a bite to eat lifted Henryetta's spirit despite her disappointment that Gus was no longer traveling with them. Uncharacteristically, Thom stayed around that evening talking late into night out on the front porch while each hobo took turns bathing in the makeshift tub back in the kitchen. By the time everyone had their turn, it was almost two in the morning.

The next day, Henryetta and Flo spent the day washing and mending the hoboes' clothes as much as they could. Thom gave two of them a few hand-me-downs, and two of their father's coats. Winter would be coming soon and the nights were already getting colder. The gang stayed until the extra food ran out.

To pass the time, they played checkers, danced to swing music on the radio in the now cleared-out dining room. While Henryetta had help, she asked the hoboes to carry chairs, the dining table, her mother's linens, crystal, and china out to the peddler man's cotton truck. It was not easy to watch her family's possessions that held her memories drive off in a hunter green flatbed Ford, but the money would keep them awhile. The funeral had all but wiped her out. They sacrificed meat some nights so they could save a few extra pennies to get Marjorie and Junny their favorite treat, Twinkies, or take them to a picture show. If it weren't for those little things, the monotony of doing nothing would have driven them to insanity.

Henryetta had also worked out a deal with the peddler man to keep her in film, developer, finisher, and photo papers. He liked Henryetta, and he liked the money her parents' possessions were making him at auction, so when she asked, he stopped off at a little photography shop in Memphis that she told him about. He knew the place since it was on his way to the auction house. He picked up what she needed and brought it to her. When Henryetta presented him with several photos of himself loading the truck, shaking hands with clients, driving down the road, he was touched. He had these reminders of his place in the world-who he was, what he did, and a reminder that he should be grateful in these times. He knew eventually, Henryetta would run out of linens, furniture, and jewelry. Soon, their paths would no longer need to cross. He worried for her, almost like he would for a daughter if he had ever been the marrying kind.

When the gang left for the rails, the house was quiet again. Gertie promised she'd return in a few weeks to spend Christmas with them. Henryetta, Flo, and the children had taken a special liking to her. They marveled at how different she looked when she stepped out of her stained overalls into one of Flo's clean dresses. Gertie was actually quite gifted at applying make-up and styling hair. The girls had spent more than one afternoon letting Gertie play "beauty shop" on their hair and faces. Using the barber shears Gertie carried with her at all times, she gave all the boys haircuts.

"Gertie, you should do this for a living," Thom Jr. told her as he sat waiting his turn for a haircut.

"I was in beauty school. Almost done, too, but Daddy's business went belly-up. There wasn't money for me to go to school anymore. I've made some money cutting hair here and there while I've been out on the rails. Most men don't like their hair being cut by a woman. They don't think it's proper, but down in the hobo jungles and sometimes in the shelters, they'll pay a few pennies to get the hair out of their eyes. Sometimes they want me to shave their faces, but I don't do that. I'm scared I might cut their jugulars. Then again, some of them would be better off. You have never seen the likes of some of those pitiful souls. Bags of bones in filthy rags. They act like dogs waiting outside the door for any scrap they can get. Then some of them are just plain 'flicted or dangerous. There's been more than one occasion my scissors have saved my neck," Gertie told plainly, not letting on that any of it bothered her. It was just a fact that America was starving, at least the America she lived in.

After a few days of life without a houseful of roustabouts, the postman's march up the front porch steps caused a ruckus in the household. In a time of monotony, mail was always exciting for Marjorie and Junny who would race to the front door at the sound of the mailman's knock. In unison with the mailman, they would all three cry out happily, "Mailman," causing an outburst of laughter every time no matter how many times they had said it before.

Two letters arrived, one of which would change their lives. The first letter came addressed to Flo. The postmark was from Kentucky. Flo had written to Walter's parents several times, but hadn't heard back from them which worried her. Marjorie had learned how to write in cursive over the past months, so she could read her mother's name on the envelope. She began to scream excitedly for her mother waving the letter in the air running into the kitchen.

"Marjorie," Flo said loudly over her.

"Mama! You got a letter! Can I open it? Can I? Please?"

"Calm down, please. Let me read it first," Flo said, taking the letter from Marjorie as Junny ran in circles and clapped happily. Flo began to read to herself.

"What is it? What does it say? Is it from Daddy?" Marjorie tugged at her mother's apron.

"Just a minute," Flo said, pulling loose of Marjorie's grip. Henryetta walked in the back door.

"What's the fuss?"

"Mama got a letter from Kentucky," said Marjorie.

"Hmm. That's news. Let your mama read. She'll tell us all about it," Henry said as she looked back forth between Marjorie and Junny making faces to distract them.

"It was from my mother-in-law," she said, rescanning it and then looking up at Henryetta.

"Good news?" Henryetta asked.

Flo crouched down and hugged both of her children and kissed them.

"Your daddy is in California. He is working very hard, and he loves you."

"Is that all that letter said, Mama? It sure took you a long time to read it," said Marjorie.

"Well, Me-maw and Pap-paw are fine. They say times are hard there too, but Me-maw has been selling the vegetables and fruits she canned this past summer. Your daddy got a letter to them just last week. He has been picking peas and is going to a different part of California to harvest nuts. He is saving money."

"Does he know we are all right?" asked Marjorie.

"I think he does," Flo said, patting her on the back.

"Can I write to Daddy?" Marjorie asked.

"Well, Me-maw said that when Daddy gets settled, he will write again with an address. Me-maw will send it to us. You will be able to write him then,"

"Yeah!" Marjorie cried out, twirling with her arms stretched toward the ceiling.

Junny really had no idea why Marjorie was dancing, but he clapped and jumped up and down. Henryetta felt herself smile and realized she felt genuinely relieved for Flo and even happy. She became aware that the physical sensation of the sorrow that weighed down her heart day after day lifted and allowed her momentary joy. Flo hugged the letter to her chest and silently thanked God for this small thing, this letter that assured her that everything was going to be all right.

When the children calmed, Henryetta noticed the second letter that sat on the kitchen table. As she picked it up, she noticed "New York" in the return address. At second glance, Henryetta noticed it was an address she knew.

"Who is it from?" Flo asked, noticing Henryetta staring at the envelope.

"Not sure. It's from New York. It may be . . ." Henry's voice trailed off as it dawned on her that the handwriting was the same as that on the letter she found in her father's strongbox that had not been touched since that day she and Flo had discovered the photos in the attic.

"What? What is it?" Flo asked, starting to reach for the letter.

Henryetta quickly whipped the letter out of her reach and turned her back to Flo and began to open it with her pointer finger.

"Henryetta Dixon!" Flo said, pulling on her shoulder to turn her around.

"Stop, Flo! Let me read." As Henryetta unfolded a letter, a one-hundred-dollar bill slipped out and floated to the floor, below the kitchen table. Flo stooped down and picked up the bill, her eyes wide with disbelief she gasped.

"Henryetta, look!" Henryetta turned to face Flo, who held the bill in two hands in front of her chest. Henryetta looked puzzled and then began to read aloud the letter.

November 28, 1932

Dear Thomas,

It has been many months that I have not heard from you. I have to assume you have rejected my offer, but I assure you that I have a client who is very committed to buying your unique product. He has found a niche market that he believes will be very lucrative for you, and him, of course. As a token of his confidence, he asked me to gift you with this small advance. He says there is much more to be had should you decide to enter into this business relationship. It is his hope you will reconsider his offer. Contact me for details using the return address.

Sincerely,
T. Sylvester

"Who is it from?" asked Flo.

"I didn't tell you, but I found a letter in with those photos in the strongbox. It was an offer from a man in New York. He said he had a buyer for my father's photographs. I have to think they were photos like the ones in the strongbox. I looked at them, Flo. I recognized some of the women. They were actresses in some of Daddy's plays." Flo shot Henryetta a look of disdain.

"Did you burn the photos like I told you to? You know we could get into a lot of trouble if anyone ever found that filth," Flo scolded. "Here. Take this dirty money, and send it back to that man in New York. Tell him you don't want any part of this sinful business."

"This money could keep us fed for a month or more if we are careful," Henryetta said hesitantly. "I wouldn't have to sell any more of my parents' things for a while. What's the harm in it, Flo? The man's not expecting his money back."

"I don't like this, Henryetta, not one bit. This man knows where we live. Suppose your father has gotten himself mixed up with the mob?"

"Oh, come now, Flo. That sounds like a picture show. It could be an editor for one of those gentlemen's magazines, for all we know. I am half tempted to—" Henryetta stopped midsentence, hiding her idea from Florence's obvious disapproval.

"What? Write the man? Burn it and the devil's money too. If someone comes asking, you don't know anything about it. Be done with this business."

Henryetta breathed in deeply, letting a long sigh escape. She knew Flo was right, but what if?

"All right. You are right, Flo," Henryetta lied.

In her mind, Henryetta was going to get rid of the photos, but not burn them. She hated to be deceitful, but she knew they were one day closer to going hungry. She was determined to not let that happen. Devil's money or not, she was going to do what it took to survive. Maybe the Depression would end soon now that Roosevelt had been elected President. Surely he could turn America back around. She had to hope that God would not punish her for trying to keep food on the table. From Gertie's and the boys' stories of riding the rails, she knew it could be so much worse.

The next morning Flo took the children to Sunday school, but Henryetta stayed behind. This was not altogether atypical for Henryetta. Since her father passed, she was less and less inclined to go to church now that her mother wasn't there to make her go. Plus, she hated people treating her like a fragile china plate. People seemed to say too little or too much. Either way, Henryetta wasn't in the mood for hypocritical niceties and manners. It also seemed the less time she spent worshipping, the more the devil seemed to leave her alone, and she needed him to get off her back.

She decided she'd rather not attend church since Minnie lost Maurice. Henryetta was fourteen at the time. She really couldn't do much except act huffy when her mother insisted she attend every Sunday.

"Like it or not, Henryetta, you are going to church with the family. And that is final!" her mother's strict, voice echoed in her memories.

Henryetta believed in God. She even loved God. When she said her prayers she imagined herself meeting Jesus who waited for her in his white robe under the old oak tree in their back yard. Henryetta recognized Jesus in the small gifts like finding two forgotten dollars in a pocket. She heard him more clearly through Minnie's words and actions than any preacher she had ever listened to. That's why she just couldn't understand how God could let such a terrible thing happen to Minnie.

After Maurice was lynched, going to church changed for Henryetta altogether. In town, she overheard God-fearing adults talking about Maurice after it happened. They boldly spouted, he was "an uppity nigger who forgot his place . . . a dirty nigger that got what he deserved." No, nothing ugly was kept secret in town. Everyone played along like they didn't know who was a part of the Klan, parading around in white hoods "stringing up niggers" in the middle of the night, but it was just a lie. Everyone knew who was a member of the Klan and who was a "dirty nigger-lover." There wasn't room for any other sides.

Henryetta grew so angry about Minnie losing her soul mate that she completely lost sight of any of the truly good souls who actually went to church to worship. Instead she sat stone-hearted, just plain seething because three of Maurice's killers, church deacons, no less, sat in that very same sanctuary as if they were the holiest of holies. Every Sunday since Henryetta was a little girl, she had counted the silver white hairs on Deacon Turner's bald spot, who sat on the pew directly in front of her. Exactly twelve. Across the aisle on the right and two rows up sat Deacon Cannon with his arm confidently resting on the back of the pew. Then there was Deacon Rucker who led the Lord's Prayer each Sunday. He sat in the front row on the right-hand side of the pulpit.

Sunday after Sunday, in her head, Henryetta replaced the preacher's sermon with her own rantings about the hypocrisy of it all. It got so bad, that one Sunday, Henryetta imagined all three of those deacons hanging from smoldering crosses in hell, the tips of flames licking their toes and ankles while they cried out in pain and remorse. She imagined Minnie and Maurice with countless others who had died at the hands of ruthless white men standing en masse, rejoicing while the devil leaped and frolicked at the base of the crosses, waving a white flag with the word *justice* written in the deacons' blood.

The next day, as Henryetta and Minnie sat outside on the backyard swing sipping ice tea, Henryetta revealed what she had imagined.

"And in church, child!" Minnie exclaimed, flashing disapproving smile.

"I know, Minnie, but I can't help it. They killed Maurice in cold blood, and nobody is standing up to them! Those men are getting away with murder. It's not right!"

"Yes, they are, but, Miss Henryetta, you gotta remember that God will take care of deys men. It's ain't up to us to be judgin' folks. Don't ya remember dat verse about takin' the log outa your own eye?"

A guilty frown formed on Henryetta's face. In her mind, Henryetta heard her Sunday school teacher reciting, "Judge not and ye shall not be judged."

"But, Minnie, how can you forgive those men for what they did to Maurice? It doesn't seem right that they are deacons in the church when they are the ones who lynched Maurice. I hate them!" Henryetta spat.

"Girl! You cain't let anger eat you up 'cuz den the devil's got a hold of ya, and dat's what he wants. Naw, you gotta let it go. I done forgave every one of 'em for what deys did to my Maurice, but dat don't mean I ain't never gonna forget it. Lissen to Minnie, I don't wanna spend the rest of my life hatin' dem men. Hatin' folks just makes a person flat-out mean. Plus it jis plum wear ya out. It didn't take me long to figure dat out. I was tired of hatin' dem men. It didn't leave me no room for lovin' folks. Ya wanna be mean, Miss Henryetta?" Henryetta shook her head no.

"Ya wanna be tired? Ya want folks to not wanna be around ya? 'Cuz if ya keep on hatin' dat's what'll happen to ya. God put us on dis earth to love one another, and I love you, Miss Henry." Henryetta looked at Minnie with fat tears itching to drop.

"Aw, come on now. Come 'ere." Minnie folded Henryetta into her arms while Henryetta cried silently. Minnie always smelled like rose water and cooking, and that always comforted Henryetta.

"Ya mean the world to me, Miss Henryetta," Minnie whispered as two tears trickled down her own cheeks.

"I love you too, Minnie. You're the best friend I ever had."

The moment Henryetta was sure Flo and the children were well on their way to church, Henryetta stole up the attic stairs with her father's key ring to take the photos out of the strongbox. As she pulled them out, the third key grabbed her attention. She wondered again what this key unlocked, and perhaps whatever it opened would answer her questions. She decided she would package the photos properly for the mail, but until then, she would stash them where none of them went, her parents' bedroom. As much as she feared going back into that space, Henryetta knew that Flo would not suspect the pictures to be there.

Henryetta paused at the door frame of her dead parents' bedroom and breathed in and out several times before her hand reached for the knob. Quietly and slowly, she opened her parents' door to see nothing different than it had ever been. The furnishings, the curtains, even the scent of her mother's perfume lingered with her father's tobacco in the curtains. Henryetta told herself she would sell everything in the house before she would sell her parents' bedroom suite. The closets were now emptied of Sunday suits, hats for various occasions, and shoes. She remembered her parents' voices as she ran her fingers over the silk bedspread.

"Nothing but the best," she whispered to their paintings that flanked either side of the cherry dresser.

Henryetta had not gone through the dressers yet. As a child, one of Henryetta's favorite past times was her mother allowing her to look at her jewelry box she kept in her bedside table. Though she had never seen her mother wear many of the pieces, she liked imagining her mother as a young girl, wearing the jewels to various social events. What intrigued Henryetta was that her mother had been someone before she was her mother. Her mother had lived a whole life before the life they now shared. To Henryetta, the jewels were magic, almost a promise that she too could live an extraordinary life, one worthy of jewels. Then she grew sad, knowing that life can end very tragically.

After placing the strongbox emptied of photos and the keys on a shelf in her parents' closet, Henryetta walked to the far side of the bed and lifted the mattress just a bit, to stash the envelope of pictures between it and the box springs. She promised herself that she would mail them only if things got desperate. As she slid the pictures under the mattress, the envelope hit something hard. Curious, Henryetta pulled out the envelope and looked beneath the mattress to find a small book. She gripped it and pulled it to her to see the word "Journal" embossed in gold lettering. At first, she thought it was her mother's, but realized this journal was on her father's side of the bed.

When she opened it, a photograph fell to the floor. Henryetta stooped to pick it up to find the words "Wedding Night 1904" written in pencil on the back. When she flipped it over, it was not at all what she expected. There lay her mother on her chaise lounge clad in nothing but a wedding veil and her beaded wedding shoes.

"Oh my," escaped from Henryetta's mouth.

Out of respect, she quickly tucked the photo in the very back of the journal. The inside journal cover was inscribed, "Happy Christmas 1907, my darling Thomas." This journal had been a gift for her father. Henryetta fanned the pages looking at the dates her father had written in the top right-hand corner of each entry. They spanned from that Christmas to the present. This was her chance to find answers. She quickly finished shoving the envelope of pictures under the mattress and then went downstairs to sit in the arm chair next to the fireplace to read.

CHAPTER EIGHTEEN

*H*enryetta had so many unanswered questions for which she wanted answers, so she began toward the end of the journal rather than at the beginning.

March 27, 1932

> I'm happy to report I have paid our debts, and as a fortunate twist of fate, my middle man found a permanent buyer for my photographs. This excites me, but I fear I will have to spend time away from the family "on business" because my pipeline of female subjects has all but dried up. Before the damned bottom fell out, I had actresses begging me to photograph them playing the part of the lusty siren. God, they were healthy and brazen, blind and deaf to the names good society had for them. Sometimes they wanted to pose for the sheer rebellion of it. But they always *wanted* to.

Henryetta had to pause reading for a moment. She had never considered a woman actually *wanting* to pose in the nude for pleasure, or even more puzzling, rebellion. Henryetta wondered why a girl would purposefully shame herself and her family. Did they know something she didn't? Then she recalled hearing Amelia Earhart on the radio earlier that year. She was daring to do what only men had done in the past. She was letting nothing stop her. Perhaps this was just another way a woman could say she was in charge of her life. Good or bad, every woman has a choice. She went back to reading.

It's not that I can't find a woman hungry enough to pose for my camera, it is where to find willing subjects that aren't starving or whose brokenness shines brighter in their eyes than yearning. Then there is the guilt. Will my drive to keep Lucille and our fine things overshadow the guilt I feel knowing my subject would never choose to pose for my camera if her children weren't starving? I have misgivings because they are creatures far different from my former models. They are someone's wife, mother, or daughter. How would I feel if Henryetta were reduced to a life like this?

Unthinkable. Still, posing for a camera is better than them selling their bodies for pennies. Yes, I am saving them from a worse humiliation . . . from diseases . . . or violation. At least with me, they can trust that they are safe. I make it clear I have no carnal appetite for their bodies.

Still, it isn't easy to convince them, journal. Over and over, I must persuade them that I am not looking at them as women that I want for my own pleasure. It is only the camera who sees them. I tell them I am an artist, like Michelangelo or Da Vinci, and I suppose, really, I am. But they are still troubled by the men who will eventually gaze at their bodies forever captured on photo paper. They always protest against baring their bodies to me for this reason.

"What if someone recognizes me?" they always ask. They are more scared of what would happen if they are discovered than undressing for the camera.

To them, I reply, "Nonsense. Strangers. They are men far away from this place. Men who will never even cross paths with you."

Then I always argue, "Wouldn't you rather pose for the camera where no man can touch you or use you up and then leave?" They all get that same faraway look in their eyes as if I had tapped some buried memory. The truth be told, most of them have already been abandoned by runaway husbands or lovers. They wouldn't give me the time of day otherwise.

"How much will I earn if I do this?" always comes quickly after, and then the deed is done. The truth be told, the money isn't great, but it will be now that Tommy has made connections with investors. Traveling back and forth to New York made transactions easy, but now I have no real reason to go north, not to mention, any money. Sending photos in the mail is always risky— theft, damages, or worse, discovery. Still, there is money to be made. That is why I will find a way.

The entry stopped there, and Henryetta thought for a moment. Would she pose for a camera if things became desperate enough? Even though men were out of work, the housewives were never laid off. Some took in washing. Some cooked meals. Some had taken in boarders, all these doable, but Brownsville was small. Most folks did their own washing and cooking. The pay would not even be close to one hundred dollars from the envelope that just fell to the floor like it was nothing. Henryetta wondered how much Walter made in a month and if Florence would ever make it out to California. Then she returned to her original question and half-whispered the words out loud to herself, "Would I pose?" She sat for a time envisioning it. "Would *I* ask a woman to pose?" She shook her head firmly. "No!" She slammed the book shut, feeling duped by her father. She couldn't read another word.

The man who wrote these words was not the father she knew. How could her father keep this part of himself hidden from her and the family? It was like he was two completely different people. Similar to her mother. Lucille was one way in Brownsville and a whole other person in New York. Then she wondered if her mother had found the journal and this caused her breakdown. But wouldn't she have known he was up to something? Was she really that ignorant about where the money came from? Didn't she ever suspect? A wife should be able to tell if her husband is up to something, right? All those nights her father professed to be working late at the opera house. He was working, all right. Could she believe he had never been with any of those wanton women? Her mother was cold and proper, but was there a side to her that Henryetta never knew? Did her mother put up with this secret life so she could maintain a lifestyle?

All these thoughts whirled and clashed thunderously in her head until she felt so disgusted, she had to get up from her chair and return the journal to its hiding place. Thankfully, she heard the kitchen screen door slam and the children's voices coming from the kitchen. She pondered telling Flo about her find, but in the end she decided not to say anything. Not yet at least. Not until she had read more. In the meantime, she decided the one hundred dollar bill would be best kept hidden in her father's journal and quickly pulled it from the secretary drawer before running up to her parents' room to stash the journal.

CHAPTER NINETEEN

*T*hey were down to their last twenty dollars and three days away from Christmas when Henryetta decided to risk mailing her father's photos to Tommy Sylvester. Since burying her mother, she and Flo found ways to pinch pennies as far as they would go. They had turned off the radiators in all the rooms except the living room where Henryetta, Flo, and the children spent both day and night. The first night that Flo and Henryetta set up the army cots, blankets and pillows, near the fireplace, it took Marjorie and Junny a long time to settle before falling asleep. Marjorie insisted that they pretend they were camping. Then she demanded campfire stories. After two stories, an exhausted Flo firmly told them "time to sleep," but Junny tooted causing infectious giggling. It took about a week of bedtime silliness before sleeping on the cots lost its novelty and just became bedtime again.

Thom was home more now that it had turned cold, but insisted on sleeping in his own room upstairs. It wasn't too terribly cold because it was above the living room and had its own fireplace. He often became restless, so to squelch boredom, Thom split wood out in the back yard. They had enough wood for three winters when he was finished. This gave him the idea go around asking folks if they needed wood split. He didn't earn much money, and usually spent it as fast as he earned it out at the drinking shack. Earlier in the month, he blew a week's worth of money on bullets for his duck gun to go hunting with Sy in Arkansas. At first Henryetta protested, but when he brought home ten ducks, she thanked him heartily at suppertime for having meat to go with the potatoes.

Knowing they were a week away from no money, Henryetta wrote a letter to Tommy Sylvester posing as her father. Stupid? Reckless? Naive? Hungry? Not far from it, Henryetta thought to herself as she began up the staircase. Even though she hated not being truthful with Flo, she was willing to risk Flo's anger and disapproval if it prevented the children from going hungry and the electricity from being shut off. She quietly entered her parents' bedroom and pulled out the envelope of her father's photos and Tommy Sylvester's letters and placed them on her parents' bed. She pulled the journal out from under the mattress and looked at her mother's picture one last time and then placed it in the strongbox in the closet. It deserved to be there. After all, it was the original sin. Then she tucked the one-hundred dollar bill into the journal, and then stashed it back under the mattress.

Henryetta remembered she had a small box out in the garage darkroom that she could use to post the photographs. Henryetta carefully placed the photos in her handbag, and dressed in her warmest coat because skies threatened ice or snow. Downstairs, she donned her hunter green beret and black velvet gloves. As she was going out the kitchen door, she called out to Flo that she was going to the darkroom for a bit and then was running to the market. Before Flo could respond, she had slammed the door and was halfway down the back stoop steps.

The lonely streets greeted her with silence. On her way to the post office, just a few blocks from her house, she noticed the absence of the men who had become accustomed to hanging out on the court square, in front of the barber shop, and by the market's front window. She wondered where they could all be. As she turned the corner of Main Street to head south to the post office, she heard Sy's car horn from the street. She looked over to see him rolling down the passenger side window to speak to her.

"Hey there! Want a lift?" he called out, smiling. *Sly at it again,* she thought. Would he ever give up? She tried not to roll her eyes to his face.

"No, thanks, Sy. I'm just going to the post office." She waved, looked straight ahead, and kept walking.

"Suit yourself!" he called back with a "See if I care" tone as he revved the engine and sped off. She watched Sy drive on down the street and turn right at the end of the block. *Thank God.* Sy had simply driven off and left her alone. He wasn't always that easy. Long ago, there were a few years when she and Sy were as close as siblings, once she understood where his meanness came from.

Since they were little, Sy was the type to unapologetically call names and make fun of anyone he found inferior or weak. He played dirty tricks, like breaking the erasers off of other pupil's new pencils. He laughed and laughed when his victim cried. As they got older, Sy grew to be an even more confident and cunning bully. He easily intimidated everyone. Even some of the school teachers didn't know what to do with him other than to whip him or put him in the corner, but it did no good. Most children tried to stay on Sy's good side to avoid being the brunt of his cruelty, except Thom. He was the only one who courageously stood up to Sy and got away with it. Thom was always a head taller than Sy, but that was just a small part of it.

At first, Thom and Sy were playmates at school, but their friendship was forever fixed after going on their first duck hunt with their fathers' hunting club. On the outside, it looked like they were bound by a love of the outdoors, but on this trip, Thom came to know the gentler, sensitive side of Sy that no one else knew. This made it easy for Thom to forgive Sy for his shortcomings.

Still, for a long time, Henryetta didn't understand Thom's loyalty to Sy because of his abominable behavior. Then one late summer night when she was twelve and Thom and Sy were fourteen, it became clear to her. It had been too hot to sleep, so she and Thom climbed out of their bedroom windows onto the front porch roof to talk. They hadn't been out there long when they saw a boyish figure running up the drive toward their home.

"Who is it, Thom?"

"Sy! Is that you?" Thom called out, but there was no answer.

The runner continued toward the house.

"Sy! Look up! On the roof!" Still no reply.

So Thom and Henryetta climbed back through her window and ran down to the front door and flung it open to find Sy on his knees curled into a small ball. Henryetta pushed the button to turn on the porch light.

"No!" Sy cried out. "Leave off the lights! Please." He was crying hard, rocking back and forth.

Thom kneeled down and put his hand on Sy's back to comfort him, but the second his hand made contact, Sy shirked away.

"Sy. What happened?" Thom asked.

"What's the matter, Sy? Do you want me to get our mama and daddy?" Henryetta offered.

"No! Please. No." His fetal body heaved up and down again and again as he cried. Thom sat back, Indian style on the porch floor by Sy when he saw that this would not pass quickly. Henryetta moved to the glider sofa that sat next to the front door looking at Sy then Thom then Sy. Finally, when Sy was spent, he sat up to look at Thom. The moon was full that night and its light shone brightly enough to illuminate the blood that covered Sy's nose and mouth.

"Oh, Sy. What happened? Henryetta, go get a towel with water on it."

"My daddy." Sy began to sob again.

Thom nodded that he understood and patted Sy on the shoulder. This was not the first time Sy had taken a beating from his father.

"You want to stay here with us?" Thom asked him.

Sy nodded.

That night as Henryetta lay in her bed trying to sleep, she felt betrayed by Mr. McGhee. He was so friendly at the drugstore. He always joked or had something quick-witted to say. She loved that he gave her a sucker each time she came into the drugstore. In fact, it had puzzled her how Sy could be such a rotten egg with such an amiable father. Mr. McGhee was one of the wealthier men with a lot of clout. He had a seat on the town council and was a deacon at the First Baptist Church. He was generous with his money. Everyone knew he spoiled Sy giving him anything he wanted, but times were good back then.

Henryetta now understood Mr. McGhee gave everything to Sy except what he really needed, love. He also gave Sy a lot of what he didn't deserve. Sy's twisted, silent rage had to come out somehow. She didn't justify Sy's evil actions, but she now understood the dark place from which they sprung. The next morning at breakfast in the dining room, after the boys had left the table to go fishing, she overheard her parents talking in the kitchen about what to do about Mr. McGhee hurting Sy.

"Don't you dare go to the police! You will shame his family. What will Dovie do without her husband? They'll starve!" her mother whispered adamantly to Thomas.

"This is not right, Lucille, and you know it. No man should hurt his own child. There's a whipping, but did you see the bruises on the boy's back and face? Why, I ought to . . ."

"No!" she interrupted Thomas. "Go talk some sense into him, Thomas. Threaten him with the police, if you have to, but see if he can work this out before you go embarrassing their family," Lucille argued.

"Who knows how long he's been walloping on Sy? What's the guarantee he won't do it again?"

"I'll call Dovie and tell her Sy is here. She is probably out of her mind with worry."

"Yes," Henryetta's father replied as she watched him pace back and forth across the kitchen floor.

"Yes," he said again, then without saying a word, her father walked out the back kitchen door, got into his car, and drove off.

As time went on, Sy spent more and more time at their house without any questions or complaining from Henryetta and Thom's parents. Thom's good nature rubbed off on Sy, and his bullying wasn't as frequent. Sy was as close to normal as he could get when he was around the Dixons. Henryetta came to see a softer, kinder side of Sy. She imagined if Sy had had been born into a different family, he might have turned out to be a very gentle and good man. She wondered if he would ever let go of his anger and learn to live at peace. At school, Thom halted Sy most of the time before his mouth got him in trouble, but every now and then, especially if he had spent a night back at home, Sy would sideswipe some innocent classmate.

As Henryetta walked on to the post office, she recalled the time Sy played a cruel trick on Clive Ogilvie, one of Sy's favorite targets. Clive suffered from an overprotective mother, a constant worrier, who was prone to coddle him. Clive was gullible, a well-known hypochondriac, and quite puny for his age. While most of their class-mates' bodies where changing and growing, at fifteen, Clive stayed as short as some twelve year olds.

In this particular episode, their teacher had everyone collecting bugs for a science project. Sy had collected three gargantuan roaches in a Mason jar that had holes he'd punched in the lid with a nail. At recess, Sy stayed inside to wash the blackboard, but really it was just a plot to get Clive good. Once Sy was sure the class was around back of the school playing, he pulled the Mason jar out of his satchel. He jiggled the Mason jar to see if the roaches were still alive. Then he began looking for Clive's red plaid lunch box. Once he found it and looked inside to see a peanut butter sandwich and an apple, Sy quickly dumped in the gargantuan roaches and slammed the lid shut quickly as their antennae flicked back and forth, trying to escape.

Later, at lunchtime, Sy perched himself on an outdoor table to get a clear view of Clive across the picnic area. Sy's right knee bounced nervously as he awaited Clive opening his lunch box. Suspense was killing him. Finally, poor Clive opened his lunch box and pitched it with a yelp. Sy laughed so hard he fell off of the table to the ground. Clive looked at Sy lying on his back kicking his feet, overcome with laughter. In that moment, Clive knew Sy was responsible for this unforgivable prank.

As their classmates rushed up and crowded around them to see what the raucous was, all eyes asked Clive what he was going to do about it. In that split second, Clive realized he had taken all he could take. He rushed Sy and kicked his groin with as much force as he could muster, screaming crazily, "I hate you, Sy McGhee!" Kick. "Take that, you worthless . . ." Kick to groin. "Piece . . ." Kick. "Of garbage!" Kick.

For a moment, Sy lay there, stunned. The physical pain in his groin radiated out to his stomach and legs, but Sy had taken much worse from his father. Clive knew he was asking for disaster, but he didn't care anymore. So he lashed out at Sy.

"Did you hear me, you ugly piece of no-good trash? I . . . hate . . . you! Everyone . . . hates . . . you!" Clive's fists were balled up, and his eyes leaked angry tears over his vengeful red cheeks. He was shaking. Sy started to get up to rush Clive. He would give Clive a beating like he had never known, but Thom jumped in between the boys to halt the fight.

"Out of my way, Thom. This little midget is going to get his!" Sy said, trying to move past Thom, who now had a strong hold on Sy's arms.

"No, Sy. Enough!" Sy still stared at Clive, who had not changed his expression.

Thom could see the angry, frenzied look in Sy's eyes. It was going to be difficult to reach him, to bring him back from the tortured place Sy went.

"Look at me, Sy," Thom commanded, but Sy continued to stare down Clive. Sy's eyes saw Clive, but his heart saw his father with a belt, saw his father's fists aiming for his face, and heard his mother's cries. Thom knew it, too.

"Sy. Don't be like him . . . don't be like your daddy," Thom whispered strongly into Sy's ear.

Instantly, Sy's mind shifted from avenger to victim. Sy hated himself, probably more than his father hated him, but someone still had to pay for his father's sins, and the list of sins would have trailed all the way to Memphis and back. Knowing what she did about Sy, Henryetta felt caught between pity and loathing. Even though she knew why evil pervaded every inch of his black heart, she could not bring herself to allow that to pardon *his* sins.

Henryetta's relationship with Sy soured the day she rejected him. Henryetta became aware she was Sy's love interest when she returned home from studying photography with Ezra Rubenstein in New York. In a matter of months, Henryetta had blossomed into a confident, poised young woman. Henryetta found her passion and her zeal was magnetic. Everyone wanted to talk to the girl photographer. She was a novelty in a small town of be-alikes, look-alikes, and do-alikes.

At first, Henryetta was fairly dense about Sy's advances. Holding the door for her, offering to give her rides wherever she needed to go, helping her load her camera equipment in the car. These were typical actions for a gentleman. He had never once been cruel to her, so she figured he was just being nice. However, she came to understand the depth of his affections very clearly one Sunday after church. The annual spring picnic had been that afternoon in the church yard and Henryetta stayed behind to help clean up. She told her parents she would catch a ride home with one of the church ladies. Remembering she still had her camera equipment set up out back in the yard where the picnic had been, she left the church to pack it up. There leaning against the back of his car in the shade of the oak trees that circled the church yard, stood Sy. He was smiling at Henryetta like the mischievous Cheshire Cat.

"Hey there, Henryetta," he greeted.

"Hey, Sy. What are you doing here? I figured you and Thom would be out somewhere fishing."

"Nah. I knew you needed a ride. I figured I'd carry you home." Sy walked right up to her and stood not three inches away from her, never losing eye contact, and never ceasing smiling. He stood there for a moment or two. Uncomfortable with this intimidating closeness, Henryetta smiled back, but it was an uneasy smile. *What was Sly up to?* She wondered. Sy moved a step back and then picked up her camera case and held it open for her while she inserted the camera into it.

"Thanks," she said quietly as she began to dismantle the tripod stand. Again, Sy came and stood behind her, very close. She almost bumped into him when she stood up straight from collapsing the tripod. From behind her he asked, "So are you finished up, Henryetta?"

She nodded at him without turning around. Something about Sy felt off.

Once they had loaded the car and were driving, Sy struck up a conversation with her.

"So your trip to New York was amazing, I hear."

"Yes." She looked out the window at the upcoming right turn onto Main Street, but Sy continued straight.

"Where are we going, Sy? I really am tired and would like to go home."

"I have something important I need to talk to you about."

"Can't we talk at home? It has been a long day. Really."

"Can't a guy take his favorite gal out for a ride?"

She turned to look at Sy who had put his right arm on the seat back. The tip of his middle finger just reached the edge of her collar where her skin was exposed. Sy grinned his best wolf grin, then lightly caressed her skin, sending chills down her back. Gooseflesh made the hairs on her arms stand on end. Sy noticed and smiled at her. Alarms went off in Henryetta's head. This was a Sy she had never encountered.

"Sy. Take me home," she protested, her eyes angry, and moved closer to the door, shrugging out of his reach.

"I will, but just give me a minute." He pulled over into the parking lot of the train depot, put the car in park, and shut off the engine.

"Henryetta, I really thought a lot about you while you were gone."

"Sy, just stop. Right now. I want to go home." She grabbed the door latch to get out.

"Hear me out at least, Hen. I have to get this out, or I am going to explode."

Henryetta sighed loudly, slumped her shoulders, and let go of the latch.

"Henryetta, I have loved you since we were kids." He paused and touched her forearm like a brother might do. Henryetta turned to face him.

"I've been hiding it for a long time, but while you were away, I decided I can't anymore. I won't hide it anymore because it's not doing me any good." Henryetta's face softened as she felt the blood rush her crimson cheeks. Her heart and mind raced. *To be loved.* To be wanted by a boy was something she had yearned for. At night, before she went to sleep, Henryetta fantasized being wooed with flowers and walking down the aisle to a smiling groom, like the heroines in picture shows. For a moment, Sy was hopeful as he read her face.

"You are always so kind to me, Henryetta. I think you love me too. Please say you love me."

His words ushered in a pang of guilt that choked this brief taste of romance. Henryetta could never return his affection. She didn't see Sy romantically. He was like a brother. The realization that to reject him, to cause him hurt, filled her with instant remorse. Hurting Sy was not something she ever wanted to do. Sy had had enough of rejection in his own family. *Why me?* She felt cursed. *Why did he pick me to be the one to break his heart?* As Henryetta's expression changed, so did his. Instantly, Sy realized he was mistaken. Dejected, he took his hand from her forearm and looked away and out the front car window.

"I do love you, Sy, but only like a brother. I'm so sorry," she whispered, looking at him. She remained in place as Sy sat quietly thinking for a moment. Unexpectedly, impulsively Sy turned to Henryetta and kissed her hard and full on the mouth as he gripped her forearms. Frightened by his forceful embrace, Henryetta struggled to lean back from him.

"Just give me a chance, Henryetta," Sy said forcefully, desperately to her as she turned her head away with her eyes shut tightly. "I know I can make you love me. I know I can. Let me prove it to you."

Henryetta opened her eyes and faced him. He leaned in so close to her face that their noses were almost touching. Henryetta looked into his pleading eyes.

"Sy. You're hurting me! Let go!"

With resignation, he released her and moved back behind the steering wheel. He pulled out a cigarette and lit it. They sat for a few moments in silence as he took several deep drags, letting the rejection flood his heart while the smoke flooded his lungs.

"Sy. Please. I don't want to hurt your feelings."

Sy shook his head. He had that same defeated look she had seen on his face the night when he came to them for help. She had devastated him.

"I'm so sorry, Sy. I would never hurt you on purpose. You *know* that."

Sy stared ahead, saying nothing to her. He had gone to the place where the only voices he could hear were his own. Placing the cigarette in his mouth, he started the car, put it in gear, and drove her home. Henryetta didn't see Sy for two weeks. But once he reappeared, the hazing began. She would pay. Someone always had to pay.

Yes. As Henryetta walked to the post office, she was so grateful to see his car round the block and out of her way. Having the gumption to mail her father's photos was taxing enough without having to fend off Sy too. Once in the post office, Henryetta took deep breaths and told herself to *act natural*. This wasn't the first time she had mailed photos. She mailed photos to Ezra on a regular basis to get feedback. She wondered if the post master would notice the address was not to an Ezra Rubenstein. She blocked out the worries that someone might open her package and she would be discovered.

"Miss Dixon, the return address?" Think. Think.

"Oh yes. How silly of me to forget," she pretended. "Just let me write it now." The post master looked at her blankly.

"Just in case it doesn't make it," Henryetta said, smiling, trying to hide her nerves. The postmaster didn't return her smile. He simply stamped it and tossed her package in a bin behind his chair. Relief. They were out of her hands.

"Thank you." She turned and walked out, silently praying for the pictures to make it to the right person in New York. Now to wait for a response.

CHAPTER TWENTY

1933

*C*hristmas came and went very uneventfully with the exception of one beautiful orange in each of the children's socks they had hung on the mantle. Gertie promised she would return for Christmas, but did not. Marjorie and Junny had been complaining about oatmeal for breakfast and beans for lunch and dinner. They hadn't had meat or fresh vegetables for weeks trying to make their last bit of cash last. The coal for the furnace that heated their radiators ran out. The wood pile they thought would last three winters dwindled a lot faster than they ever dreamed as they sat huddled in blankets close to the fireplace for warmth.

Wearing their overcoats and gloves with the fingers cut out became normal. There was no money for the electricity bill, and the car just sat in the garage. Henryetta and Flo didn't speak of these things, though they weighed heavy on their minds. Instead, they continued as if everything were normal. They played games, read stories, took walks on sunny days, and went to church to pray for an end to the Great Depression. After all, Roosevelt had just taken office and promised to end unemployment and hunger. That was something, after all, wasn't it?

Henryetta couldn't bring herself to spend the hundred dollars tucked safely in her father's journal. That was for when there was no other way to survive. Plus, she didn't want to reveal her wrongdoing to Flo. Disappointing her was the last thing Henryetta wanted to do. The Bells had come to mean so much to Henryetta. There were days she hoped they would never leave. So life went on, hard, but on.

Everything was normal until one afternoon Marjorie complained of a sore throat that quickly turned into a high fever and body aches. Florence peered into Marjorie's throat to see white speckles that dotted her inflamed tonsils. Florence knew this was serious. All her life, Marjorie had been prone to throat and ear infections. Their doctor in Kentucky had advised her and Walter to have Marjorie's tonsils removed.

"I'm a stupid woman," Flo berated herself quietly in the kitchen as she stirred a bit of salt into a cup of warm water.

"What's that?" Henryetta said, coming into the kitchen.

"I'm stupid and prideful," Flo said, not looking at Henryetta.

"Don't say that."

"No. It's true. The doctor told us we should have taken her tonsils out, but we didn't. A little boy we knew died from having a tonsillectomy. We were scared of losing her."

"You can't blame yourself for that, Flo."

"And now we don't have any money. She might die anyway. I've seen this before. It can go right into scarlet fever. She needs a doctor and medicine."

"She'll be all right." Flo shook her head in disagreement. She put the spoon in the sink, and without looking Henryetta in the eye, Flo walked past her with the salt water gargle and loudly whispered, "I wish I'd never told you to burn that dirty money. Then we wouldn't be in this mess."

Henryetta didn't follow her into the living room where Marjorie rested on the sofa. Henryetta knew this day would come. Sinful money would save them. She was about to head up to her parents' bedroom to retrieve the money when she heard the drop of letters in their mailbox next to the front door. Florence was tending to Marjorie and Junny was napping on a cot.

They hadn't had any mail in weeks. So a letter could mean welcome news. She rushed to the front door, quickly enough to speak to the mail carrier as he walked down the porch steps. Pulling out a single letter, her eye caught that familiar handwriting. Happy terror ran through her veins seeing Tommy Sylvester's name and address on the outside of the envelope. It was addressed to her father. She closed the front door and started for the kitchen to open the letter.

"Who is it from?" Flo asked, looking at Henryetta, but she chose to ignore Flo.

Instead she sat down at the kitchen table, opened the envelope, and pulled out the letter. As she unfolded it, a fifty, a twenty, and a five caught her attention first. Flo saw the money as Henryetta placed it behind the letter.

"Is it from Walter? Has he sent money for us?" she asked, desperately excited.

"No, Flo," Henryetta murmured as she began to read Tommy Sylvester's words out loud to Flo.

Dear Thomas,

I was pleased, as were my contacts, to see that you are receptive to our business venture. Enclosed you will find seventy-five dollars for the product you supplied. While my partners and I request that you continue to produce your unique photos, we have found the more creative the photo appears, the better it sells. We are willing to pay up to ten dollars per photo depending on its exceptionality and ability to sell. We would, however, like to change our arrangement to ask you to only send negatives. This decreases our risk and enhances our ability to mass produce your photos. If this goes well, your potential earnings will be greater per photo. We look forward to your next shipment.

Sincerely,
Tommy Sylvester

Henryetta folded the letter and put it back in the envelope. She looked up at Florence, who was speechless.

"I'm sorry, Flo. I lied about the pictures. I couldn't burn them. I was afraid—"

Flo raised her hand to signal for Henryetta to stop speaking. Henryetta stood silently, waiting for Florence to punish her with a morality lecture of how Henryetta was a sinner and what she had done was shameful, but uncharacteristically, Flo didn't.

Instead, in defeated voice she simply said, "Henryetta, go warm up the car."

It took two weeks for Marjorie to fully recover and for Flo to speak directly to Henryetta. Even though there had been money to pay the doctor, buy medicine, buy coal for the furnace and food other than beans and oatmeal, and the occasional ducks or geese Thom brought home from hunting, Flo barely acknowledged Henryetta. Several times, Marjorie asked her mother why she was mad at *Auntie Hen* as she now had taken to calling her, but Flo didn't even respond to that. Henryetta didn't push Florence to reconcile. She simply carried on.

Flo's feelings teeter-tottered. First, Flo blamed Henryetta for Marjorie getting sick. She told herself that God was punishing them for Henryetta's sin. She was angry that Henryetta would allow such a temptation to remain in their home and then to lie about it. Flo prayed earnestly for forgiveness while she ironed and when she made up the cots. Out at the trash barrel, she gazed into the flames and wondered if she was destined for hell. Then several days later, a neighbor lady casually reminded her to count her blessings. Looking at Marjorie as she slept peacefully and fever free, Flo realized God spared Marjorie. God had turned the sin into a blessing. Then Flo grew grateful, but too proud to admit it. Flo felt small, petty, and too embarrassed to admit her fault to Henryetta. It was easier to let Henryetta think Flo was still angry with her.

Flo's silence finally broke when a letter from Walter's parents arrived. Flo was so overjoyed she couldn't help but share her news with Henryetta. Walter was coming home. This was the absolution she had been waiting for. Finally, God had spoken.

"Did they say when he was coming?" asked Henryetta.

"The end of the summer, after the pea-picking season ends."

"Well, that's good news, right? Will he stop here to pick you up on his way back?"

"My mother-in-law didn't say. But no matter! He's coming home. My Walter is coming back to us." Joyful tears welled in her eyes as she reached out to embrace Henryetta. Flo held Henryetta for a long moment, and then, Henryetta knew Flo had finally forgiven her. They pulled apart, both laughing, relieved that the silence was over.

Life went back to normal for a while, but Tommy's dirty money dwindled quicker than what they wanted. Worry caused both women to be less and less talkative, and it was a relief when Gertie and another female hobo appeared at their door in the late afternoon one Sunday in March.

"I'm back!" she said, smiling as Henryetta opened the door.

Henryetta was taken aback by Gertie's sunken cheeks, her patched overalls, and her torn coat. Gertie's appearance had deteriorated in the months since she last saw her. Even though Gertie sounded spunky, Henryetta could tell Gertie was exhausted and hungry. Her mouth said one thing, but her eyes revealed another. Not wanting to let on, Henryetta smiled warmly at her.

"Lands sake, Gertie! Where have you been, girl? We missed you at Christmas!"

"Sorry about that. I meant to get back, but I've been all over! Thank you kindly. This here's Beth. She and I have been traveling together for a while. We got sick of them boys, but that's another story." Gertie gave Beth a knowing look of shared secrets. Henryetta hated to think the worst had happened, but Beth's wide eyes at Gertie's remark told her everything.

"Come in, Gertie," Henryetta invited.

"Where's Miss Flo and the children?"

"Church."

"And your brother?"

"You know Thom."

"Yes, ma'am, I do."

"Are y'all hungry? We don't have much, but I can feed you a plate of beans, if you like. Or maybe y'all want to take a bath first? I can heat some water."

"Oh yes, ma'am, a bath would be fine. Beth, you go first. I'll catch up with Miss Henryetta."

Once Beth was settled in the tub behind the makeshift curtain, they had hung in the kitchen, Gertie and Henryetta went out on the front porch to talk. Tennessee had warmed up considerably. The redbuds, the forsythia, and the crocuses had bloomed filling the once dead brown scenery with color.

"Miss Henryetta, I have to ask you if we can stay with you awhile. Things are . . . well . . . complicated." Gertie was wringing her hands and looking at her feet.

"What's happened Gertie?"

"It's hard out there for anyone, but, Miss Henryetta . . . if I told you some of things I had to do just to stay alive . . . well . . .," her voice trailed off. "Well, you just might think I'm not good enough to be sitting here on your porch with you."

"Gertie, it's not for me judge anyone. Your life is your business. You don't have to answer to me or anyone."

"Just God, right?"

"I suppose, Gertie. If that's what you believe."

"Miss Henryetta, don't you believe in God?"

"I do, Gertie."

"How could he let this happen? All this suffering? You think it's because he's punishing us? You know, for loving money too much or gossiping or fornicating?"

"I don't know, Gertie. Sometimes I ask myself that very same question. It sure seems like the preacher thinks that. Maybe God is just trying to teach us something, like trusting him to get us through it all. Maybe he wants us to understand his suffering. With all these bad people running around in the world, he suffers, don't you think?"

"Well, if he's watching all them men in the hobo jungles, I can guarantee he ain't happy." They sat for a moment just gliding back and forth listening to the squeak of the glider.

"Gertie, you want to talk about it?"

"Which part? The part where I was sent to jail for begging? The part where some thugs beat me up for some bread I nicked from outside a market? Or maybe the part where I figured I could cut some hair in the hobo jungle outside of Atlanta for money, but it turned out real bad?"

Henryetta sat, listening silently.

"That Beth, in there? She saved me. I had only been in the jungle outside of Atlanta a day. Beth had been living there six months. I figured I'd make some money cutting hair and all. I hadn't never had no trouble before, but this jungle, it was different."

"Gertie, what' a hobo jungle?"

"A den of vipers as far as I'm concerned, and I ain't never going back to one as long as I live." Gertie paused a moment. "A jungle's a place where hoboes camp out. Most of the time they are close to the railroad tracks in the woods. It's almost like a little town. You got men who run things, men who sell things, winos, old, young, criminals . . . You see about everything in a jungle . . . and a whole lot you never want to see again." Gertie looked far off in the distance as if in a trance.

"You don't want to hear about all my troubles, Miss Henryetta," Gertie said, looking back and Henryetta smiling. Gertie wrung her hands anxiously as tears seeped from her eyes. Noticing this, Henryetta put her arm around Gertie and pulled her head to her upper chest.

"There, there, Gertie. You are all right, now," she said, trying to comfort her.

Pulling up, Gertie looked at Henryetta directly.

"Miss Henryetta, I'm spoiled. No man will ever want me now. At least not the marrying kind." She began to sob as she laid her head in Henryetta's lap. She stayed there for a good while. Henryetta said nothing, but petted Gertie's hair at her temples like her own mother had done to her when she was young.

"It was awful . . . what that man did to me." Gertie shuddered. "I never knew . . . I never knew. I think he would have killed me if Beth hadn't come in and hit him over the head with a hot cast-iron skillet. She told me the whole jungle heard me screaming, and not one of those men tried to help me. Not one, except Beth. She saved me for sure."

"I'm so sorry, Gertie."

"Me too, me too. Beth says I need to get checked by a doctor for diseases or for a baby."

Henryetta hadn't thought that far ahead.

"You got a good doctor in Brownsville?" Gertie asked.

"We do. I'll take you tomorrow, first thing."

Gertie rose to face Henryetta. "I got money to pay. I guess folks feel sorry for a girl hobo. In lots of places, they walk up to me and just put money in my palm. When I got off the train in Memphis, a real rich-looking couple put five dollars in my hand and told me I was a *child of God*. It made me feel better, you know? Like God was watching out for me. That he wasn't blaming me for what happened back in the jungle. I just pray I don't have a baby growing inside of me or some disease that will make me crazy."

Henryetta nodded and smiled at Gertie reassuringly. "You'll be all right, Gertie. You are one of the toughest people I know."

Gertie wiped her nose and the tears from her cheeks. "You think so, Miss Henryetta?"

"I know so, Gertie." Henryetta smiled, embracing her.

CHAPTER TWENTY-ONE

*E*ven though the seventy-five dollars was used up fairly quickly, Tommy Sylvester's dirty one-hundred-dollar bill had managed to stay tucked between the pages of her father's journal all winter, spring, and into the early summer. Between Gertie's hairdressing, Thom's odd jobs, and Florence and Beth taking in primary school aged children to teach them basic reading and arithmetic, there always seemed to be just enough money. Now, it didn't *hurt* that Henryetta's father's underground photos kept a consistent flow of money coming in.

As Henryetta continued to read her father's journal entries, she discovered that the third key on the ring opened the door to her father's makeshift studio/darkroom in the cellar. Inside, she found roll after roll of film negatives which she sent to Tommy Sylvester. Henryetta was methodical in spacing out mailing them to not draw suspicion to her pocket change and to keep the money coming in steadily. She feared if she sought all the money at once, it would be spent too quickly. If Florence suspected, she never admitted it, but by mid-June, Henryetta had all but exhausted her father's supply of negatives.

There had to be a way to keep her home, to keep her family. But what? What money was to be made? Henryetta had to find a way to support herself.

Then one day, "Out of necessity comes ingenuity" popped into her head and would not leave her. Even some fifty some years later, Henryetta would be able to recall the exact moment her ingenuity sparked that ultimately would be one of her life's greatest mistakes, or triumphs—she wavered depending on her mood. Her inspiration came from a combination of serendipitous moments. Henryetta and Florence were on the front porch snapping green beans to can for winter. Junny was swinging on a tire swing in the front yard, but Marjorie was nowhere to be seen. Florence called for her several times, but there was no answer.

"Let me go in," Henryetta said, putting the newspaper that held the snipped ends of the green beans on the glider cushion.

"I'll find her," she said letting the screen door snap closed behind her. Henryetta got the idea if she changed her voice to sound like they were playing hide-and-seek, she might have a better chance of finding Marjorie, but it didn't work. The house was silent. Henryetta was on her way out, when she noticed several books from the lowest living room shelves on the coffee table. She moved to reshelf them when she saw her art book lying open, fully exposing a painting of three men picnicking with a nude woman. She paused to look at the painting for a moment until a flash of movement behind the arm chair caught her attention. She looked underneath to see the bottom part of Marjorie's squatted bottom.

Smiling, Henryetta remembered how she had tried to conceal this book from her family too, so instead of exposing Marjorie for natural curiosity, she closed the book and returned it to a high shelf. Henryetta said in a loud voice through the screen door that Marjorie must be around back. Sure enough within a few moments, Marjorie appeared in the side yard as if she had come from the back.

"Outhouse," she said and went to pushing Junny in the swing.

Inspired moment number two happened when the circus came to town. The household decided that Junny and Marjorie must go to the circus. They followed the throng of excited circus-goers toward the tent city. Inside the menagerie, elegant tight rope walkers, fire breathing men, daredevil trapeze artists, and elephant riding bejeweled showgirls took their breath away. When the show was over, they wandered with the crowds through the maze of carnival games, food booths, and trinket stands.

For a good while, Thom Jr. and Sy did a good job of entertaining Marjorie and Junny. They cheered when Thom Jr. made the bell clang loudly. They jumped up and down when Sy won a teddy bear at the ring toss. They laughed when the four of them all took one bite of an elephant ear funnel cake at the same time, all emerging with powder sugar moustaches. The men entertaining the children allowed the women to talk, people watch, and revel in all the strange sights and sounds that is the circus. This was such a welcomed diversion from the ordinary.

A caller's voice advertised, "Rare beauties! Leave nothing for the imagination! Exotic ladies from around the globe! Paris, France! Cairo, Egypt! Grecian goddesses! Step right in to see the tantalizing delights! Just a quarter! Step right in!" Sy and Thom stopped mid-laugh when the caller projected his voice their way. In fact, all of them halted and turned toward the caller. Men were lined up to get in, shoving excitedly with their quarters ready to be dropped into a hat before they entered.

Inside, vaudeville music harmonized with lusty cat calls and whistles. Once, when the tent flap flew up to allow a few more patrons inside, Henryetta caught a momentary glance of a buxom blonde, naked head to toe with the exception of her ruby red slippers and the golden tassels attached to her breast nipples that dangled and flipped up and down as she shimmied on the stage above the horny crowd of men. Even though the visual was only three seconds long, the woman's lusty expression stuck with Henryetta for years. She likened this to "the look" her father had written about in his journal and captured in his photographs. She juxtaposed Gertie's face to the show girl's and it baffled her how sex could instill passion or devastation.

"Keep moving!" Florence commanded Thom and Sy as she shooed them forward, but what they ran into next, caused Henryetta's heart to pound with anxiety. Before her was a man with a wooden crate strapped to his body.

"Pictures of exotic ladies! Take home your very own exotic ladies! Photos from around the globe! Get your enchanting beauties here!" Florence shot Henryetta quick glance. Henryetta so wanted to approach the seller to see what he had. Could any of those photographs be her father's? She caught Sy glance at Thom and get a sly grin on his face.

"Y'all go on. We'll catch up to you," Sy said.

Henryetta knew exactly what Sy was up to. Florence put her hands on her hips and scowled at both of them. Gertie rolled her eyes in disgust. Beth was her typical stoic self. She was not talkative until she was teaching. Henryetta just moved forward and away from them, but she couldn't stop herself from looking back at Thom as he stood by Sy who had just paid his money for a few photographs. She would have loved to have seen them. She wondered what the models wore, what the setting was, and the expressions on their faces. How did they compare to her father's photos? *Were they her father's photos?*

Then anxious guilt flooded her body. From time to time, Henryetta worried about the women in the photos and the dire consequences they could face if discovered. She imagined a picture perfect housewife, happily married with three tiny children, but cast out when her husband's buddy informed him that his wife used to be a whore who posed for naked pictures. Henryetta would never want to be that dejected woman. She hated the thought that she was putting each and every woman in that possible situation. With each shipment of negatives, Henryetta prayed for forgiveness and prayed no harm would come to the women in the pictures.

To comfort herself, Henryetta always swallowed remorse back down and told herself they willingly posed. Hadn't her father's journal said so? From that thought she then justified that selling off her father's photos was keeping them in their home and fed. Fear of going hungry and being out on the streets had taken Henryetta's hand and led her willingly down the wide and crooked path.

Surprisingly, serendipity struck a third time one afternoon when she, Florence, Gertie, Beth, and the children had gone to a deep pool in a nearby creek Henryetta happened across while looking for good places to take photographs. None of the women had swimming clothes and since it was just them and the children, they swam in their undergarments. They splashed and cavorted in the muddy water and later sunned themselves on an old tartan plaid blanket Henryetta kept in her car trunk for emergencies.

"I have to tinkle!" Gertie said, gently moving a napping Marjorie's head from her lap to the blanket where Junny also slept soundly.

Henryetta shielded her eyes from the sun. As Henryetta looked at Gertie, she noticed Gertie's nipples through the see through fabric of her brazier. Trying not to look obvious, Henryetta averted her eyes. Gertie didn't seem to notice. As she walked off, Henryetta followed Gertie's figure until it disappeared into the brush. At that very moment, the nude picnicker from the painting and tasseled breasts of the circus performer popped into her head. Even though she had never heard Tommy Sylvester's voice, she could hear him saying, "The more creative a photo is, the better it sells." Words from his letter.

Eureka! She could take photos that mimic art. Her photos could depict scenes from mythology. Her photos would be beautiful, but exotic enough to entice viewers. "Enchanting beauties," she almost said out loud forgetting she was not alone.

"What is it?" Florence asked sitting up, looking at Henryetta. Just three short words from Florence was enough to douse Henryetta's creative flame with the fear of hell, of being ostracized, of being *alone*.

"I just had an idea," Henryetta said, flipping over to lie on her stomach.

Flo joined her. "Well? Are you going to tell me?"

"Tell you what?" Gertie said, joining them.

"No. You'll hate me," said Henryetta.

"Impossible," said Gertie.

"No. This is a bad idea. Probably a sick idea." Florence rolled her eyes and bit her tongue. She didn't doubt the possibility.

"Tell us!" insisted Gertie.

For several moments Henryetta said nothing. She just thought and thought of why her idea had any merit. In her mind, she knew Ezra would support her idea. He believed the human body to be one of the most complex, beautiful subjects of art. But here sharing a blanket with her was a victim of a brutal rape, a moral champion, mother, and wife, and Beth, whom no one knew that well. She decided to put out feelers rather than risk judgment.

"So what do you think about the human body?" Henryetta put forth in a soft voice, not wanting to wake the children.

"It's the Lord's temple, plain and simple," Florence said resolutely in an audible voice.

It figures, Henryetta thought, unsurprised by Flo's matter of fact answer.

"Well, yes, but do you think the human body is beautiful?" Henryetta prodded again.

"Some are and some are just downright disgusting," said Gertie matter-of-factly.

"So is it a sin to paint a picture of a human body for art's sake or to further science?" Henryetta was using a question Ezra had asked her the first summer she studied with him. The women were quiet. She recalled she hadn't answered Ezra right away either.

"Not at all," answered Beth, surprising all of them to the point they all raised up to look at her.

"Well, it's not," she said, not moving from her position.

The other three women moved into sitting positions on the blanket to face one another.

"It is how the viewer responds to the picture. The body is what it is. A painting merely represents what the artist sees. Sin starts in the mind, not in a painting," contributed Beth.

They all sat quietly for a few moments looking at each other, waiting for the next person to speak.

"So is the person who poses for the painting or the painter committing a sin?" Henryetta asked.

"Both!" Florence said, wasting no time. "Henryetta, what's your point? You of all people know what I think about that sort of thing."

Henryetta looked into Flo's eyes only to have Flo stare her down.

"No. I disagree with you, Florence. The body is just a body. A painter has a job to paint what he sees. If he needs a body to paint, then that is just it. The painter is not painting the soul, only the shell that houses it. It is just a body, Florence," challenged Beth.

"What do you think, Henryetta?" Gertie said, turning the tables.

"Well . . . I have this idea. An idea that could make us some money."

"Just don't even start, Henryetta! I already know what you are going to say," Florence jumped in as she folded her arms across her chest in judgment.

Gertie looked to Florence, thinking she would speak her mind, but she just sat like a somber judge.

"You might as well come out with it," said Beth, still lying in the exact same position.

"I want to create photographs, nude or almost nude photographs to sell to Tommy Sylvester in New York," Henryetta confessed.

"What! Oh my god, Henryetta! You are going to burn in hell for using all the money he's been sending you for your daddy's photos. You think I haven't noticed? A letter here, money for extras there? I am on to you, Henryetta Dixon. And now this? I won't have any part of it! You should have known better than to even think of a thing like that!" Flo blasted her.

"Wait! What are you two talking about?" Gertie said.

Even Beth sat up to look at Henryetta.

Flo looked at her sleeping children before she whispered angrily, "Henryetta here has been selling her father's collection of photograph negatives of naked women pictures to a man by the name of Tommy Sylvester in New York," Flo spat just above a whisper.

"Is it true?" Gertie asked, leaning in toward Henryetta, smiling.

She looked at Gertie and then Beth. Henryetta shook her head in agreement.

"I did it because we needed the money. We've already come close to losing everything twice. Once when my mama died, and then when Marjorie got really sick. I didn't want the children to go without. Nobody will buy our house. Nobody has the money."

"But it's illegal," Gertie said.

"Yes, I know it is," conceded Henryetta quietly with tears in her eyes, "but I had to chance it. I didn't want us to end up in the streets. Surely, Gertie, you understand that better than I do. Money from those pictures has made it possible for you and Beth to stay on with us."

Suddenly the crickets' chirping and the kill deer calls were amplified by the silence of the group.

154

"What about all those women? Imagine getting married and then your husband seeing one of these photos of you one day," postulated Gertie. "You'd be ruined."

"And damned. Don't forget that," Florence offered.

Tears flooded Henryetta's eyes, and she got up to run from the group.

"Who would be the models?" Beth called after her, again going against the grain. "For your photographs?"

Florence only glared at her.

"I don't know. I was just thinking I could recreate scenes of art through photographs. I have this book filled with art. Some of the photographs my father took were exquisite, well, the bodies were exquisite. Some reminded me of Greek statues. Many of the models were mesmerizing to look at. Some of the photos didn't even show any female parts. They just hinted, if you understand what I mean."

"I'll do it. I'll pose for you," Beth volunteered, causing immediate uproar from Florence and Gertie. With that, Junny woke up, startled, and began to cry. Flo grabbed him and held him, but she continued with her tirade. Henryetta didn't know on whom to focus, the screaming Florence and Gertie, or stoic Beth who was unfazed. Once Florence and Gertie calmed down to silence, Beth spoke again.

"I have nothing to lose, no one to lose. If the worst I have to do is take off of my clothes and allow Henryetta to take 'exquisite' photographs that men will worship and I will get paid for, then I will do that. I would do that any day over losing my personal dignity—begging like a dog in the street, or being chased away by railroad bulls with clubs aimed for my skull. I'd do *that* before giving my body to some stranger to do his nasty business inside of me, or use me as a punching bag. I'd do that before I broke my back picking peas out in California for a crummy seven cents. If taking those photos keeps me in a home with people who care about me, keeps me fed, and helps me keep my head held high, then that is what I will do. I'm never going back out there, if I don't have to. Never."

CHAPTER TWENTY-TWO

*F*or a week, Flo would only speak to Gertie. She shunned any attempt at conversation with Henryetta and displayed outright contempt for Beth. The children picked up on the rift between their mother and their aunties, but if they asked why their mama was so mad, Florence shot them a look that shut them up.

Meanwhile, Henryetta sold her grandmother's pearl necklace to the peddler man in exchange for film and developing supplies. She and Beth moved her mother's chaise lounge from the living room down to her father's cellar studio one evening after dark to avoid being seen by the neighbors or passersby. Henryetta worried about the lighting, but found the oil sconces that hung on the walls provided subtle, almost sensual lighting. She knew the photos could be exposed longer to lighten them if need be.

In the afternoons, while the children were napping, Henryetta and Beth studied the paintings and the sculptures in her art book, deciding which ones they could best mimic. Gertie pretended not listen, but Henryetta caught Gertie glancing at them with curiosity.

"Gertie," Beth said, "come and look at this painting. Do you think you could arrange my hair like this?"

Gertie looked up from the game of solitaire she was playing, but tried to shy away from her request not wanting to betray her alliance with Flo. Beth held up the book and pointed to a nymph with long wavy tresses, crowned with braids and flowers.

"Not for a million dollars will I do your hair for some naked pictures. No, ma'am," Gertie rejected.

When Gertie wasn't looking, Beth and Henryetta smiled at each other, knowing it was just a matter of time before Gertie caved in. She was a joiner at heart and hated being left out. Florence, however, believed herself to be a staunch moralist who would rather die hungry in the streets than commit some sin. Her faith that she would always be taken care of never wavered. Flo found all sorts of ways to avoid Beth and Henryetta's plotting—washing dishes, cleaning out spotless cupboards, working at the soup kitchen—anything to get away from what she knew was happening. She prayed and prayed for Henryetta to come to her senses or for Walter to return and take them back to Kentucky before this nonsense got much worse. If Flo had money she would have left already, but she didn't dare write Walter's parents for it. She didn't want to put them out or have to explain the circumstances. One night, late, she contemplated hitch hiking back home with the children. When Flo whispered her idea to Gertie the next day, Gertie warned her not to.

When Henryetta had all the props from her studio prepped and the peddler man delivered her film, she and Beth set to work. The cellar was dank and tinges of onion odors hung in the air. When she and Beth stood in the cellar studio together they both paused and looked around until their eyes met.

"I don't know if I can do this," Henryetta whispered to Beth, who appeared serious. Henryetta wondered if Beth was having doubts too.

"I'm not going back out there, Henryetta. There are so many other sins I could commit that are ten times worse."

Henryetta couldn't face Beth. Those sins were for other people, not her.

"Henryetta think of this as art. You are capturing beauty as you see it," Beth convinced.

"Yes, but what if someday you want to marry a wonderful man and then he finds out what you've done? What then?"

"If he's worth anything, that wonderful man will not care about my past. He will love me as I am. If not, well then, he's not worth it." Beth began to unbutton the top of her dress and walked over to the trunk of props.

"Which picture shall we do first?" Beth inquired, but Henryetta stood frozen.

Henryetta wondered if her father ever felt torn the way she did at this moment. The best artists took risks. She knew this, but this was a risk that could cost Henryetta her freedom, her reputation, possibly any chance at a future husband. *Would she ever be good enough again?*

"Henryetta?"

Henryetta turned to see that Beth had stepped out of her dress. Beth stood in only her raggedy underthings.

"Well?" asked Beth.

"You can't have your picture made without hair and makeup," said Gertie's voice from the door, causing Beth and Henryetta to turn around.

"Sit on the stool, Beth, and I'll make you the siren all men dream of," Gertie said with a sigh.

Henryetta and Beth looked at each other smiling.

"Change of heart, Gertie?" chided Beth.

"It is putting food in our stomachs. That is all," Gertie replied.

Gertie outlined Beth's lips in a deep-crimson shade and her eyes with kohl, transforming her into what looked like an actress in a silent picture show. She piled Beth's auburn hair on her head and bobby pinned it in place. When Gertie finished, Beth looked in the mirror to see a woman she didn't recognize. The woman who stared back at her was sophisticated, glamorous, and even beautiful. Beth's mother had told her over and over she was plain and probably would have a hard time capturing a man's heart. *If my mother could see me now.* Beth smiled at this woman in the mirror and secretly relished the fact that her mother would have to eat her words if she were here now. Then her grandmother's voice popped into her head. *Pretty is as pretty does.* Beth had never really realized until that very moment that her grandmother used those words to counteract her own mother's put downs. "How do you want me, Hen?" she asked, putting the mirror in the prop trunk.

"When you are undressed, put on the long strand of pearls and those lacey pumps. I will wrap this shawl around you."

As Beth slipped out of her bra and panties easily, Gertie handed Beth the pumps and then the pearls. Henryetta avoided looking at Beth's body, but like the paintings, the allure was mesmerizing. As her eyes drank in Beth's curves and nipples a surprise twinge of lust ignited deep inside Henryetta. She thought of Gus and what it would be like to stand naked before him. When Beth noticed Henryetta's eyes on her body, Henryetta's cheeks flushed, and she turned away awkwardly.

"Go ahead. Take a good look, Henryetta. It's just my body. I look at it every day. You need to know what it looks like to take the best photograph," Beth said seriously.

Her words snapped Henryetta back into a working mode. *Good old, stoic Beth.*

"Yes," Henryetta replied, looking and thinking about how she would position Beth. Even though they had spent hours picking out paintings, deep within herself, Henryetta wanted to create her own photographs. She wanted to be as tasteful as possible. She imagined there could be much stranger, much more graphic photographs— ones that debase a woman's dignity and self-respect. That was not her goal at all. She wanted to immortalize beauty.

"Gertie, get out the paisley shawl with the yellow fringe. Then find the artist's palette and the paint brush in the trunk," Henryetta directed.

Gertie handed the shawl to Beth.

"Where do you want me?" Beth asked wrapping the shawl around shoulders. Henryetta took the artist's palette and the brush from Gertie.

"Sit on the chaise with your legs crossed like when you wear a skirt. Look down and to the left in a moment." Henryetta handed Beth the palette and the brush, but didn't like the way it looked.

"Beth, sit up tall and arch your back. Put your left arm out straight and then gracefully place your pointer finger on the lounge."

"She needs to sit on the shawl a bit, don't you think? The fringe should hang from her outstretched arm," Gertie suggested.

"Arrange it, Gertie," Henryetta said while she looked through her camera's lens. Gertie motioned for Beth to stand up. She arranged the shawl where the fabric paisley pattern would be seen, then gently put her hands on Beth's shoulders for her to sit down. Still looking through her camera, Henryetta asked Gertie to situate the shawl so that it covered Beth's pubic area and nipples. What remained was the curve of Beth's breasts and hourglass waist. The pearls hung quietly between her breasts that had spread wide with the arch of Beth's back.

The beauty was mystifying, but Henryetta knew the face needed softening. She wanted a quiet, demure feel to the photo. Before her was a shy maiden in the moment just before she looked into the man's eyes. Henryetta believed teasing the viewer to be more erotic than simply bearing all. This she learned from her father's photos. Henryetta wanted the viewer to beg to see Beth's eyes and nipples.

"Look down to your right and barely smile," Henryetta said, trying to capture a sweetness to the photo. She snapped the photograph.

"I never thought . . .," Gertie's voice trailed off.

"What?" Henryetta and Beth questioned simultaneously.

Gertie looked at both of them.

"It's just that you are beautiful, Beth, enchanting. Really, Henryetta, it was like a painting."

"Are you saying you want in?" asked Beth pointedly. "Perhaps Gertie wants to be immortalized as well, Henryetta," Beth teased.

"Gertie?" Henryetta said, looking at her.

Gertie's eyes opened wide with surprise, and then she shook her head no.

"I can't do it. I know you are women and we have the same parts, but I just can't." Gertie couldn't look them in the eye.

"I understand, Gertie. Nobody is forcing you to do anything you don't want to do. In fact, if you want to leave, you can," Henryetta offered.

Gertie just stood very still.

"No, I will help with the props. I just don't want any photographs taken."

"All right then," chimed in Beth. "Let's continue. Can we take the picture of the Venus looking in the mirror with the baby cherub, next? I loved that one."

"No. I want that photograph for myself," came a voice from behind them.

The women turned to see Florence standing in the door of the cellar studio. A cry of disbelief erupted as she stepped through the door.

"You're going to hell for sure, Florence," Beth said, mimicking a preacher's voice.

When their voices calmed, Henryetta spoke. "Florence, I know you. This goes against everything you stand for."

"Yes, it does. So I have some conditions. My photograph doesn't ever get sold. There will be one copy, and that copy is for my eyes only."

"All right, but why did you change your mind?" asked Henryetta, puzzled at Florence's atypical behavior.

"I got to thinking about what Beth said about the sin starting in our minds. I don't want to hurt anybody with this photo. Not me or some random man who buys it for ten cents. I don't want to do that, but I do want something to remember myself by when I'm old and my body is wrinkled. I want to know that for once, I chose what I did with the body God gave me. Lord knows, everyone has been telling me how to dress it, how to give it up when my husband wants it, what makes it beautiful, and what doesn't. I'm tired of all that. I just want to capture it for what it is in this moment in my life. I want to be brave and see my body for what it is. I want to give thanks to God for my body. It has given me two beautiful children and it allows me to take care of them. This is not about sex at all. It is about me and who I am as a woman. Am I making any sense at all?"

The women looked at Florence and then at one another and nodded and smiled understanding.

"But no cherub. This photo is sans cherub, and no one else in the room except Henryetta," commanded Florence, back to her bossy self.

Because Florence's dark hair was bobbed and rather matronly, Gertie suggested Florence wear one of the wigs from the trunk. Gertie carefully tucked Flo's hair into the wig, adjusted it, and then brushed it out until it hung in soft waves all the way down to her hips.

"Can you imagine having all this hair?" Flo said, swinging it back and forth, holding on to the edge of the wig to keep it in place.

"Stop," scolded Gertie, "you are going to mess up your hair! Here, Flo. Let me pull it up into a loose bun, like in Henryetta's painting."

"Are you sure you want to do this, Flo?" Henryetta asked her once more before moving toward her art book that rested on the stool next to her camera tripod.

"Positive. Gertie, it's time for you to go. Watch out for my children. Keep them occupied for a bit," Flo said, moving to the chaise lounge.

Gertie closed the cellar door behind her as she left, leaving Florence and Henryetta alone. Henryetta thumbed through her art book until she found the exact picture of Venus and the cherub. Henryetta liked the thought of photographing this scene because of the challenge it presented for her in developing it. If she would truly emulate the painting she would have to blur Flo's reflection as well as the sides of the photo. Henryetta wanted Florence's body to be clear, but her face could remain a mystery.

Once Henryetta had the camera focused on the lounge, she asked Florence to look at the exact position of Venus in the painting. After several tries of propping up the mirror and it falling, Henryetta almost gave up on the pose altogether. When Henryetta suggested letting Junny pose as Cupid so he could hold the mirror, Florence dismissed her idea with a staunch Baptist no. Henryetta knew better, but she enjoyed pushing Flo's buttons from time to time.

"It's time, Flo. Disrobe please," Henryetta coaxed gently.

Florence had her back turned to Henryetta. She allowed the robe to fall to just above her buttocks, and then she climbed on the lounge. Henryetta took a deep breath before she looked through the lens to capture Flo's curves.

"Do you think you will ever let Walter see this photograph?" Henryetta questioned as Flo allowed the robe to fall from the chaise to the floor.

"I don't know. He might not approve. More than likely this will be my secret. Something that belongs only to me," Flo replied, looking at her face in the mirror.

"Smile," Henryetta directed.

"This isn't a school picture, you know," retorted Flo.

"Look at the painting, Flo," Henryetta justified, pointing out the light smile on Venus's reflection.

"She looks pleased, doesn't she?" observed Flo.

"I imagine that is the same smile you will have the day Walter comes home," Henryetta said, putting her hand on Florence's shoulder.

"I think you are right, Hen. I am going to imagine that very moment."

"Wonderful. Now hold still. I am about to take the photograph."

Flo inhaled deeply and held until she heard camera's shutter click.

"A few more, Flo. I want to have choices. You are doing very well," Henryetta said as she readied her camera for the next few shots. Satisfied, she picked up the robe off the floor and dropped it on Florence who still was lying away from the camera.

"That's it?" Flo asked, a little surprised at how quickly the whole process was.

"That is. Now to find the time to develop them," said Henryetta.

CHAPTER TWENTY-THREE

*S*everal days passed before Henryetta ventured down to the cellar to develop the photographs. There had been plenty of time, and the girls were so excited to see the photos, but a sense of foreboding came over her every time she passed by the cellar doors. Finally, Flo placed the cellar key on the kitchen table, encouraging Henryetta to go ahead and develop the film.

As she passed through the cellar door, she paused to study the bittersweet space. She imagined her father standing at the table coaxing photos to life. *I miss you, Daddy.* Then, she let go of the moment and went to work. Henryetta whistled with the music that flowed from the old Victrola, one luxury Henryetta refused to part with. She and Beth had moved it to the cellar before they began their photo shoot. Anticipation now coursed through her as she coaxed the photos to come alive on the paper as she moved them back and forth in the developing fluid.

As the pictures came to life, Henryetta felt a sense of accomplishment and pride in her willingness to take a risk as an artist. She wished Ezra were there to encourage and coach her. She imagined Ezra's voice in her head, directing her. She was most interested in the photograph of herself, the one photo she couldn't see. She set up the camera and knew how she wanted to pose. Beth helped arrange the shawl around Henryetta's body so that none of her parts were revealed.

Henryetta's photo was the most modest of all. She hadn't smiled, but looked directly into the camera's lens. Despite her directness,

Henryetta appeared as if she were thinking of something far off. She was there in body, but not in mind. Henryetta was truly a beauty, but her photo did not evoke lust. Henryetta was a serious woman, and this side of her was what her picture spoke loudest. She wondered if other people would see the tragedy in her eyes. She could see it so clearly.

She worked the hardest on Flo's portrayal of Venus. She blurred the reflection of Flo's face from the mirror so that no one would know who she was. The likeness to the painting was remarkable the girls all agreed minus the absence of the cherub, of course.

Above ground Sy McGhee pulled into the drive, there to pick up Thom for a night out. It had been several weeks since he and Thom had driven out to the drinking shack for a few rounds of poker. Thom had found fairly steady work with the peddler man, but because the peddler traveled from town to town, Thom had spent many nights on the road or in Memphis in a small room off of the peddler's shop. So Sy was in high spirits, ready for a boys night out, and then there was Henryetta. Even though Henryetta rejected his advances, he would not give up. Sy knew he could make her love him. He *would* have her.

Getting out of the car to head up to the back door, Sy heard faint trumpets and then the crooning of Louis Armstrong. Pausing by the car, he looked around the yard. The skies were orange and brilliant pinks in the backdrop of the quiet oak trees. Lightning bugs flitted and flashed announcing nightfall. Sy turned toward Henryetta's darkroom at the back of the garage, but the music was coming from a different direction. Curiosity drew Sy closer and closer to the cellar doors that were flung wide open.

Sy stepped down into the cellar, his eyes taking a moment to take in the stone walls and dirt floor. A wooden door on the opposite wall was shut tightly. As he stepped in, a string from a single light bulb above tapped his cheek. He pulled the string to illuminate a second wire that had been strung from the socket above to the room on the other side of the door. Clearly hearing Henryetta's whistle, Sy burst in the door, flooding the dark room with unwanted light.

"Sy, what are you doing? Close that door. I am developing, can't you see that?" Henryetta cried out, hoping he would just back right out. But when he shut the door behind him, sudden fear choked her. To be caught would ruin her, ruin all of them.

"Just get out!" she screamed at him unsuccessfully, waving her arms to try to distract him from seeing the photos. Sy stood there frozen, smiling at the collection of half-nude sirens calling to him from the clothesline where they were hung to dry. His white teeth seemed to glow beneath the red bulb that dangled just above their heads.

"Well, well, well. What do we have here, Henryetta?"

She tried to speak, but no sound would emerge from her mouth. Sy moved closer and roughly pulled down a photo of Beth. In a desperate move, Henryetta tried to yank the photograph from Sy's hand, but anticipating her action, Sy held it high above Henryetta's head.

"So is this what you girls do for fun?" Sy taunted as she jumped up trying to reach for it.

"Just give it back, and get out of here," Henryetta said, switching into fight mode. Henryetta planted her feet stalwartly and held out her hand, shaking with anger.

She had never noticed how close in height she was to Sy as she stood almost nose to nose with him. Noticing this made her feel not so small. Then Sy leaned in, his lips almost touching her cheek next to her ear. His breath reeked of stale cigarettes and coffee, causing her to feel a tinge of nausea, remembering the day he had forced a kiss on her in his car. Then he gripped her wrist with his free hand and pulled her into his body. Her breasts flattened against his chest, and she struggled to step back, but could not with his hand locked tightly around her wrist.

"Henryetta, this is quite a secret you have here. Wonder what everyone in town would think if they knew their golden girl was some pervert photographer?" Sy chuckled a moment, nodding.

"Mm . . . mmm . . . mmm! Boy! The apple sure don't fall far from the tree," Sy taunted nastily just above a whisper, allowing his lips to touch her ear. Henryetta shuddered at the goose flesh his chin stubble caused as he slowly backed away from her, not letting his grip loosen. Again, she tried to break free, but Sy roughly pulled her close to him again, this time making sure she could feel the hard mound of his groin against her middle.

"Just like your pervert daddy. Taking naked pictures. That's a crime, Henryetta."

"You don't know what you're talking about, Sy!" She tried to back away from him, but he was too strong and pulled her straight back into his middle that had grown harder.

"Oh, don't I? You might want to ask Thom about what he'd seen your daddy doing on more than one occasion. Right . . . here . . . in this very cellar, too." Sy nuzzled Henryetta and ran his tongue in circles along her neck. Henryetta froze in panic.

"Think about it, Henryetta. Right under y'all's noses, too." Sy smelled Henryetta's fear, and it was intoxicating. He wanted her here. He wanted her now and rubbed himself against her body.

"Don't you worry none, though. I can think of some ways we can keep your secret safe," Sy murmured lustily again, this time flicking his tongue in Henryetta's ear and squeezing her left breast with his free hand.

"Get the hell out, Sy!" Unfrozen and with adrenaline charged strength, Henryetta bit into Sy's shoulder, and when he jerked up, Henryetta shoved Sy away, breaking his grip.

"So that's how you want to play this, Henryetta?" Sy said, straightening back up, rubbing his shoulder. With a sick smile, he stood very still, just looking at Henryetta. Sy seemed barely fazed that she had bitten him.

"All right then. I'll just let you think about it," Sy said, reaching out to touch her cheek. Standing her ground, Henryetta didn't flinch or shy away from his touch.

"But not for long." Sy nodded, pursed his lips, and then put Beth's photo on the table.

With that, Sy turned and walked out of the darkroom. Heart pounding, Henryetta yanked the door shut turning the peg to lock herself in and then collapsed to the dirt floor. Fear gripped her of being exposed. Fear of what Sy could do to her. Now that Beth and Gertie had *educated* Henryetta, she knew there were only two kinds of sex—the kind a woman wanted and the kind she didn't. Sy

McGhee would come for her. He knew it. Henryetta knew it. It was only a matter of time.

Taking a few deep breaths, she felt strong enough to stand. She listened for the loud rumbles of Sy's engine. When she was sure they left, Henryetta let herself out of the darkroom, locked it back, pulled the string light, and allowed the cellar door to fall shut with a loud bang.

As she came into the kitchen, Flo was on her knees next to the water trough tub where she was bathing Junny.

"He knows," Henryetta announced. "Sy knows about the pictures."

Flo's mouth dropped open as Junny continued to splash her.

"Sy walked in on me when I was developing the pictures just now. He saw our pictures on the clothesline."

Flo now placed her hand over her mouth.

"What did he say?"

Henryetta could not speak. She only offered fat tears that streamed down her cheeks.

"Tell me, Henryetta. Did he say he would tell?" Flo insisted emphatically.

"Not if I give him what he wants."

Henryetta looked away from Flo, ashamed of how Sy had made sexual advances on her. At that, Flo stood up and rushed over to Henryetta.

"He's all talk," Flo comforted, reaching out to embrace Henryetta.

"I don't think so, Flo. He touched me . . . in wrong ways. He called me a pervert photographer like my daddy. He said—"

"You are never going to guess who we just saw at the soup kitchen!" Gertie called out bursting into the kitchen breaking off Henryetta midsentence.

"My old gang! The boys are headed to Florida to work on a celery farm and they want us to come with them. They said some Amish people are looking to hire good workers. They need women to do the washing and cooking for the workers. Isn't that exciting news? Florida is so nice. Can't you just see us on the beach on the weekends?"

Henryetta and Flo parted and both just looked at Gertie and Beth with unchanged expression.

"What's wrong?" asked Beth seeing Henryetta's face wet with tears.

"Sy McGhee saw the pictures, and now he's threatened to tell on us if Henryetta doesn't give him what he wants," Flo revealed.

"That's blackmail! He can't do that!" cried Beth.

"Well, he did, and there's nothing I can do about it. If I go to Deputy Stanley, I could get us in big trouble."

"Go ahead and mail the negatives," Beth suggested. "Then you and Flo and the children can come with us to Florida. We can burn the pictures. He won't have any ground to stand on."

"He said that Thom knows about our daddy . . . about his business. What if Sy tells Thom about what he saw?"

"What if? What can he do, Henryetta? What's done is done. We just need to get rid of the pictures, that's all," reasoned Beth.

"I can't lie to Thom. He knows me. Those pictures are beautiful. I can't bear destroying them. I don't even want to send them to Tommy Sylvester."

"So send them to your photography teacher up in New York."

"I don't know. I have to think about it. Are y'all really leaving?" Both Gertie and Beth nodded in unison.

"Come with us, Henryetta!" Gertie pleaded taking hold of Henryetta's hands. "We're leaving tonight. The gang is hopping a late train tonight bound for New Orleans. This time in three days, we'll be sleeping in the land of eternal sunshine," Gertie said excitedly.

Beth remained cool.

"This is all so sudden. Are you sure about this? I thought y'all were happy here. What if there are no jobs when you get there?" Henryetta spoke looking directly at Beth who she figured didn't really want to leave. Gertie was impulsive when it came to change. She acted thinking only of the good, never the reality, but Beth? *Surely Beth didn't want to do this.*

"Miss Henryetta, it's time. We've been here long enough. We don't want to wear out our welcome," Beth lied, averting her eyes away from Henryetta. Beth's loyalty to Gertie ran deep. Beth found something in Gertie she would never have, and Gertie, well, Gertie floated along in life, allowing fate to blow her from one place to the next. Gertie had her heart set on leaving and so, where she went, Beth went.

"You have been no trouble. I'm going to miss you both, but it looks like you've made up your minds."

"Yes, ma'am. We have," Gertie asserted linking arms with Beth.

"Beth, do you want your photos?"

"No. Send the negatives up north and burn the rest. What's done is done."

Within two hours, there was no trace Beth and Gertie had ever stayed with Henryetta. They hugged on the front porch as Henryetta slipped a few dollars in each woman's hand.

"Please write to us, Gertie. Let us know you made it and are safe."

"Will do, Miss Henry and thank you for everything," Gertie said. Henryetta and Flo watched as they started down the steps when Beth stopped and turned back.

"Henryetta, You're good. You're a really good photographer. To hell with Sy. Don't give up."

Henryetta half smiled and nodded thanks to Beth and then watched them walk down the drive until they were out of sight.

CHAPTER TWENTY-FOUR

The lonesome train whistle sounded signaling their departure. Lethargic, the train began to jolt forward filling Flo with a sense of relief. The sooner they were out of Brownsville the better. Henryetta, holding her camera in her lap, sat numbly looking out the window. It was right at suppertime, so the porches and yards sat empty. Inside those sad, dilapidated shotgun houses families gave thanks for what little cornbread, beans, or greens they had to eat. It did not take long for the train to pass out of Brownsville and into the vast expanse of cotton fields, just picked. Miles and miles of spindly, coffee brown stalks and small white tufts of dusty cotton were all that remained. As the train picked up speed, Flo's worries raced in time with the steel wheels that spun round and round on the tracks. This was not supposed to happen.

This day had begun as ordinary as any other. After the children woke from their early afternoon nap, Flo took them with her to volunteer making soup at church. They had been whiny that morning. They missed Gertie and Beth who had entertained them quite often. Florence pulled into the drive and halted the car. Flo stepped out, thinking about what she and Henryetta were cooking for dinner that evening, but as she slammed the car door shut, she thought she heard a female scream. She paused, but heard nothing and figured she must have imagined it, but as she opened the car door to retrieve the children, a distinct, high-pitched wail came from inside the house. She paused dumbfounded, as a second cry sounded.

"Stay in the car. Do you hear me?"

"What's wrong, Mama?"

"I don't know. Whatever you do, don't get out of this car until I come back for you. Understand?"

"Yes, Mama," the children said in unison.

As Florence ran from the car, she caught her heel on the gravel, twisting her foot causing her to stumble. She righted herself, bolted up the stairs, flung open the screen door to find Henryetta lying spread eagle with her dress up around her neck. Henryetta cried desperately as Sy lay atop her, entering Henryetta violently.

"Get off her!" Flo screeched as her eyes scanned the kitchen looking for a frying pan, a rolling pin, a knife, any weapon that would make Sy stop. Spying the rolling pin still dusty with flour from Henryetta's biscuit making, she grabbed it quickly.

"I'm warning you! Get off her!" She screamed once more as Flo hit Sy square on the rump.

"You're next whore!" Sy cried out enraged, thrusting even harder into Henryetta.

"Not if I have anything to do with it!"

In an instant, Flo took hold the rolling pin in both hands. With adrenaline charged force, she swung for the back right side of Sy's head. *Whack!* One full wallop knocked Sy sideways. She watched as Sy's eyes rolled back in his head. In a split second, he fell unconscious. Flo cringed as Sy fell forward, unconscious, on top of Henryetta.

"Get him off! Get him off me!" Henryetta wailed. Flo dropped the rolling pin and pulled Sy by his feet off Henryetta, his left eye taking a direct hit on the corner of the table before his head bounced as it hit the floor with a final thud.

Chest heaving, Flo tightly grasped the rolling pin lying on the linoleum and stood poised, ready to hit Sy again if he came at her, but he wasn't moving. He lay on his stomach with his pants down to his ankles. For several seconds she waited, but he did not stir. Then Marjorie and Junny popped into her mind.

Oh my God, had they seen everything?

Flo went to the screen door to see the tip of the red tassel on Marjorie's hat peeking just above the bottom of the car window. Relief flooded her body. Still gripping the rolling pin tightly, Flo ran back over to where Sy lay corpse like. Carefully, Flo eased up to Sy, and when she was close enough, she jabbed his side with the end of the rolling pin, but his body lay there lifeless. *Thou shalt not kill.* She kicked at his foot only to have nothing happen. *Thou shalt not kill.*

"Oh my God, what have I done?" She whispered, tears smarting in her eyes. *Thou shalt not kill.* She leaned down to listen for breathing. Fear swallowed Florence whole.

"Please, God, don't let him be dead. I didn't mean to! Oh, Lord Jesus! I didn't mean to, Lord. Oh, Lord, please help me! Oh, God, no!" Florence squeezed her eyes shut and clasped her hands in prayer. She began saying the Lord's prayer just above a whisper, not aware that she was rocking back and forth. Tears began streaming down her face.

"Is he dead, Flo?" Henryetta said just above a whisper from the table where she still lay flat on her back, her dress still up to her neck.

"I think he might be," Flo whispered back. She unfolded her hands and stood up to face Henryetta.

"Are you all right?" Streams of mascara ran down Henryetta's crimson cheeks. As Flo drew near, Henryetta broke into sobs. Flo bent down and took Henryetta into her arms. Both sobbed until a calm came over them.

"Can you stand up?"

"I think so." As Henryetta slowly eased herself off the table, her flesh burned and a gush of fluid ran down her legs.

"Oh my, Lord. What are we going to do? What if I've killed him?"

"I don't know, Flo, but I can't be in this place any longer. I don't have the strength. I need a fresh start. Somewhere no one knows me. Somewhere no one knows what has happened to me." Henryetta's voice trailed off, her eyes filling with unhinged rage for her daddy, then her mama, her brother's drinking, and now this. *Why, God?* Henryetta wanted to kick Sy hard, but Minnie's words, "Don't you go stoopin' to his level" came to her, and she looked back into Flo's eyes.

"All right, then, but we've got to go now," Flo agreed.

Upstairs, Florence and Henryetta met in the hall. Florence carried her small, oval-shaped suitcase, but Henryetta gripped only her father's pistol.

"Yes," Flo said after a moment, "Yes, you're right. You never know when we might need it." *Thou shalt not kill.* Flo thought, but a wicked ending followed, *unless you have to.*

Henryetta nodded to her and moved toward her parents' bedroom. She pulled a coat from the closet, retrieved her father's journal from under the mattress, grabbed the last two pieces of her mother's jewelry, and threw them in a small tapestry fabric bag. Next, she packed two clean dresses, a few changes of underclothes, and a bar of soap from the bathroom, rags from the hall linen closet, a brush, other basic essentials she might need. She nestled the pistol between her dresses.

Downstairs, Flo paused to look at Sy once more who had not moved. She thought to wrap up some bread and cheese for later. As Flo approached the car, she rapped on the back rear window.

"Are y'all okay?" Flo asked peering in the back rear window to see both children had fallen asleep in the backseat.

"Thank, God," she said.

Henryetta let the screen door slam. In one hand, she held her camera case, in the other her suitcase and pocketbook. Quickly, Henryetta placed her things in the trunk. "If we hurry we can make the train to Nashville," she suggested as she climbed into the front seat.

After a solid night's rest in a hotel close to the Nashville depot, Flo hugged Henryetta for the last time before she and the children boarded their next train back to the hollers of Eastern Kentucky.

"Where will you go?" Flo asked, but Henryetta put her pointer finger to her lips, nodding toward Marjorie who stood listening, and shook her head no. The less they knew about each other's whereabouts, the safer they would be. Flo tried to smile at Henryetta, but fear shone through her hazel eyes. Flo guessed Henryetta would run south, to Florida, where Gertie and Beth had gone to look for work in the celery fields of Sarasota.

Maybe she would even go as far south as Key West where Gus had gone. Flo had caught Henryetta daydreaming while holding Gus's postcard from Key West on several occasions.

"Write to me. I need to know you are safe. You have my address?" Henryetta nodded and patted her pocketbook in reply.

"Flo, thank you," Henryetta's voice was quiet, and tears welled up in her eyes.

Henryetta gazed deeply into the eyes of the woman who entered her life just a little more than a year ago begging to be saved, and who in return had saved Henryetta. Now, it was up to Henryetta to heal herself. To find a life beyond Brownsville.

"Be careful and find a good doctor to make sure you are healthy," Flo said, touching Henryetta's cheek.

Smiling, they embraced once more. Florence and the children turned to board the passenger car that would separate their lives. Henryetta stood watching them with tears trickling over her cheeks. Once the children were up the steps, Florence felt a pang of bittersweet homesickness for Henryetta. Despite the trouble they were in, there was something so deeply freeing about the photographs Henryetta took of her. Flo would never forget that experience. No one could take it from her.

"Henryetta!"

When Henryetta turned back to face the train, Florence called out, "Henry! That day. That photograph. I never felt so beautiful!"

With that she blew Henryetta a kiss. Henryetta bowed her head in acknowledgment and blew a kiss back to her friend, feeling hopeful and a sense of freedom, even control. They had been in charge of their decisions, hadn't they? Good consequences or bad, they had chosen.

CHAPTER TWENTY-FIVE

The Dixon house sat quietly vacant for two days, but how was Minnie to know this? She had stopped by to bring Henry some rhubarb preserves. She hadn't been over to the Dixon's in some time. Minnie figured Henryetta was doing fine having all those boarders living with her. It had been raining for three days straight because of a tropical storm down south. The rains had traveled north, drenching everything in their path. At least now the dust was washed away. This was the first morning Minnie had been able to go out without an umbrella.

"Miss Henry!" Minnie's voice called through the kitchen door. Hearing no response, she walked into the kitchen like she had for twenty years, placed her handbag on the stool in the corner and walked through the kitchen, noticing the metal watering trough in the opposite corner closest to the stove. She knew Henryetta had been without city water for months and had taken to bathing in a water trough like everyone else. Dried up biscuit dough lay out on the counter, but the rolling pin was across the kitchen floor. The chairs were pushed away from the table as if they had left in a hurry.

"Miss Henryetta! Where you at?" she called out again as she passed into the dining room, but the empty space where the china cabinet once stood stopped Minnie dead. The silver Miss Lucille insisted she polish once a season was gone. Minnie stared, mouth agape at the darker patches of wallpaper where framed paintings had hung since the Dixon's had moved in. The mahogany dining table that was never without a lace table cloth or a vase of fresh flowers in the summer, magnolia stems in the fall, and holly in the winter had vanished. Flashes of happy family gatherings and glitzy parties for Mr. Thomas's theatre friends interrupted the loneliness that met her now. Minnie knew Henryetta had run out of dresses months and months ago, but Henryetta never let on that she was in this poor of shape.

Minnie started for the living room to find it much the same. Miss Lucille's chaise lounge, the table lamps, the sofas, and the knick-knacks that had been on the built-in shelves around the fireplace were all missing. All that remained was one arm chair by the fireplace, and Miss Lucille's secretary that sat quietly in its place. Walking back over to the steps, she called up to Henryetta, but silence replied.

Stumped, Minnie backtracked out of the kitchen and headed toward the garage. Maybe they were out there. Minnie dodged muddy brown puddles that rested in the gravel drive. Standing on tiptoes she peered inside a back window to find it as empty as the dining room. The darkroom she thought. She walked around the right side of the building to find the dark room locked. It appeared that no one was home until a pair of amber colored cat eyes meowed at her from a small hole at the base of the garage. A scrawny gray cat crawled out from under the siding and with what little energy it had rubbed up against Minnie's legs. Minnie was not one for animals and stepped away from the cat who looked up at her with a hollow look that she had seen in so many people's eyes. *Was the whole world hungry?*

Realizing everyone was gone, Minnie turned to fetch her purse and begin her walk home. Then she heard the grumbling of shifting truck gears and screeching breaks down at the end of the drive way. She turned to see a cotton truck pull into the drive way and stop at the front walk. The peddler man exited the truck and disappeared from her sight as the house blocked her view. In a few moments, he reappeared empty handed, his head shaking. He didn't notice her as the truck backed out bouncing and splashing muddy water onto the yard that flanked the drive.

Where were they? Suddenly, Minnie imagined them dead in their beds. With that, she ran back into the house and up the stairs.

She went directly to Miss Henryetta's room. It was emptied out. The guest room-emptied, not a stitch of furniture. Mr Thom's room-unkempt, but all of his belongings were still there. Then she went to Mr. Thomas's and Miss Lucille's room. It was exactly the same as the day she was let go. She noticed blankets neatly folded and a stack of three pillows in Miss Lucille's reading chair in the alcove by the bay windows. Mr. Thomas's closet door was flung open, emptied of suits, shirts and shoes. Inside were four army cots, folded up. What caught Minnie's attention was a lone strongbox that rested on the shelf that had once held Mr. Thomas's hat boxes. She went over and reached up for it. As she pulled it down toward her, a set of three keys on a velvet ribbon fell, striking her on the nose. Not expecting them, Minnie momentarily let go of the box causing her to fumble to catch it. As she righted herself, the strongbox felt light, but clearly there was something inside as whatever it was, made a sound that reminded her of cards being shuffled and tapped on the table.

She put the strongbox on the bed and then reached down to pick up the fallen keys. Minnie went over and sat on the bed, but not before checking to see if someone was watching her. This was something she would have never thought of doing while she was a housemaid. The help didn't sit on the owners' beds. She looked at the two photographs that hung on the walls. One of Mr. Thomas and the other of Miss Lucille.

"Y'all don't mind if I sit a spell, do you, Mr. Thomas? Miss Lucille?" she said out loud, smiling at the thought of Miss Lucille throwing one of her conniption fits if she ever found Minnie sitting on any of their furniture other than the kitchen table or the chairs out on one of the porches.

Returning her attention to the strongbox, she tried opening it to find it locked. She took the smallest key and easily inserted it into the key hole. The box lid easily unlatched itself from the box. What Minnie saw inside rocked her to the core.

"Oh lo' Jesus," she said in shock, looking away and slamming the lid as quickly as she could. She had instantly recognized Miss Lucille's chaise lounge in the photograph, but she didn't want to believe who or what was on the chaise lounge was true. A rush of panic raced from her stomach and got stuck in her throat. Minnie had to look again.

She opened the box again and took a deep breath before she touched the photograph. She stared at the perfectly painted nails and worked her way up the milky white legs to see a magnolia leaf perfectly placed where womanly parts should have appeared. Her eyes followed the curve of the model's hips to her upper waist where a gauzy wedding veil trailed from the beaded crown headpiece that held perfect pin curls in place. One arm rested along the model's waist line comfortably while her head rested gently in her other hand that revealed a wedding ring Minnie had polished on more than one occasion.

Minnie's eyes skipped what she knew were nipples that waited for her gaze. Minnie went directly to the model's eyes, eyes she had looked at many times for many years, Miss Lucille's eyes. Half-open, inviting lust, they were outlined in heavy kohl and framed with wispy feather-like lashes. Lucille's face reminded her of the glamorous silent movie starlet posters she had seen outside the movie theater. The eyebrows were perfectly penciled, and the lips full and glossy. Then Minnie could no longer help herself, she had to study the curve of her employer's breasts that could be seen under a single layer of wedding veil gauze. The photograph captured Lucille's virginal innocence and the thirsty lust of a bride's wedding night.

Then Minnie noticed that the blurred foreground was the backside of a groom in tuxedo tails, clearly Mr. Thomas, gazing at his bride. With closer observation Miss Lucille was not looking into the camera, but into the eyes of her doting husband. Flashes of Minnie's own flesh entangled with her lover's rushed her thoughts and stirred her own desire. Minnie had been powerless against this reckless kind of lust for only one man in her life. She sighed deeply, feeling cavernous emptiness. Maurice was gone. Forever.

She turned over the photograph to see "Wedding Night 1904". Under the title were the words, "Lucille loves Thomas." How young they had been then. It was awkward seeing Miss Lucille's forbidden raw lust and true love for Mr. Thomas. These were emotions Miss Lucille masked so well behind strict manners, fancy dresses, flower arrangements, and church socials. Things were all business, all the time during the daylight hours. She smiled imagining Miss Lucille as a lover after dark. It seemed almost impossible. Miss Lucille was always so curt with Mr. Thomas. Lucille acted exasperated with the strange hours Thomas kept and cavalcade of theater types he brought home for forbidden drinks. But here, now, looking at her photograph, Minnie could see the bliss in her eyes. No wonder Miss Lucille lost her poor mind when he passed. Mr. Thomas had been the love of her life. The person who knew every crevice of Miss Lucille's body, heart, and soul. When he died, she died right alongside him.

Minnie looked back up at their photos on the walls, then back to the photograph. Smiling sadly, she carefully placed it back in the box, shut the lid and placed the strongbox back up on the closet shelf. As she began to place the keys back on top of the box, it dawned on her that she knew where she had seen the other two keys before. One was to the darkroom door down in the cellar.

Minnie recalled going down to the front room of the cellar to bring up some sweet potatoes for Thanksgiving pies. As she walked into the dank cellar, she was greeted by Mr. Thomas placing an envelope into the breast pocket of his suit coat.

"Oh, Minnie," he said, surprised, and then turned to lock the door with one of the keys on the velvet ribbon.

She typically hurried down and back out just for potatoes, onions, and canned goods the family stored down below. It wasn't typical for people to have cellars in West Tennessee. The water table was too high for them, but this was one of the few homes that had one. There had been several instances neighbors had run to their cellar for protection from the tornadoes that could ravish the countryside in the spring. Other than that, no one had reason to go down there except Mr. Dixon.

Mr. Thomas turned and nodded to her and moved past her, up and out. Minnie soon forgot about the encounter with all of Miss Lucille's demands for getting Thanksgiving dinner on the table. Now, alone in the house, she could revisit this door. Anyway, she didn't particularly like going down to the cellar alone. She feared getting locked in, only to suffocate or be overcome by dinner plate sized spiders. She knew it was ridiculous, but the monsters that lived in the cellar still haunted her. Still, she had to know if her hunch about the keys was right.

Minnie opened up the cellar door and walked down the stone steps. She inhaled the putrid smell of rotting onions. Then she waited for her eyes to adjust to the dark and then found the pull string that would turn on the lightbulb that hung from the ceiling. She half expected the light to not turn on. Many folks had given up electricity for the sake of putting food on the table. Even though Mr. Roosevelt had been elected and promised big changes, they hadn't happened yet, at least not in Brownsville.

The light came on and all at once the stone-walled room was illuminated. She went over to the door and inserted the key. She had to force the tight bolt to move out of the door jamb swollen by humidity, and back into the lock. With a little maneuvering, it finally released, and the door popped open. Minnie opened the door wide and again had to let her eyes adjust to look for a light to turn on. From what she could see, it looked like another darkroom. There were waist high tables and the light from the bulb flickered against the brown bottles of developing chemicals. Above them hung a single red bulb. Seeing this makeshift darkroom reminded Minnie of a day in her past.

Sometimes, Henryetta had requested that Minnie help her develop some of her photographs in the garage darkroom. That is how their friendship had woven itself tighter and tighter over the years. Minnie recalled the day Henryetta had gotten permission from Miss Lucille to take the old Victrola out to the darkroom. Henryetta was one who would play records from dawn to dusk if her mother would let her. Henryetta, then sixteen, begged and begged her mother to let her move it out to the darkroom. The answer was always, "No, and that is final."

Later, after the radio started playing what Miss Lucille called her "stories" she relented and allowed Henryetta and Minnie to carry the Victrola out to the darkroom. That was the day Henryetta told Minnie to call her by her given name. No "Miss" was necessary.

Minnie agreed that was all right for the darkroom, but outside she must still be "Miss Henryetta."

Minnie stepped into the darkroom looking for another regular bulb but found only the red one. Then she caught sight of an oil lamp out of the corner of her eye. As she moved toward it, she noticed a large box of matches beside it. Before striking the match in the darkness, Minnie considered the danger of lighting the lamp in a room full of chemicals, but curiosity whispered to her to *take a chance*. As the room lit up, Minnie turned to see the room was in fact much larger than what she originally expected.

Propped up on a tall wooden legged tripod was Henryetta's studio camera. Minnie had seen her use it many times for school class photos, church picnics, and weddings photos. Several more oil sconces sat quietly on the walls that wrapped around this makeshift photo studio. A woven pastoral tapestry backdrop rested quietly behind Miss Lucille's chaise lounge. Under the lounge was the Oriental rug out of Henryetta's room. To the left was Henryetta's vanity table and chair, flanked by her grandmother's full length mirror from out of the attic. Off to the right, just out of the camera's sight was a large traveling trunk.

Minnie could see part of a black feather boa hanging outside of it. Minnie walked over and lifted the lid. As Minnie crouched down, she found ostrich plumes, strands of pearls, a pair of long white gloves, and a pair of low-heeled shoes Miss Lucille had worn in the early years Minnie had worked for them as a housemaid. She remembered they had been dyed rose petal pink to match Miss Lucille's dress she was wearing on a train trip to New York City. As Minnie dug deeper into the trunk, she found several women's wigs and beaded masks like the ones she'd once seen revelers wear at Mardi Gras when Minnie visited a cousin in New Orleans. Then she handled Miss Lucille's hand mirror, the glass gone.

Minnie paused a moment to wish Miss Lucille peace in the great beyond, but then felt puzzled. She didn't understand why all these things were down here when Henryetta had a perfectly good studio off the back of the garage. It had natural light from the windows that faced south. Henryetta had props and accessories she used routinely. This was strange. Minnie turned back toward the dark-room table where she noticed several photos were hanging to dry. The backs of the photos faced her. Minnie placed the costume props back in the trunk and stood up to go over to the photos. She reached up and unclipped the first photo she came to and then turned it over.

"Oh Lo' Jesus," Minnie half whispered, covering her mouth. "What have you gone and done, girl?"

Stretched out on the chaise with her back to the camera was Florence's milky-white nude body. Minnie recognized the gentle slope of Florence's shoulders, but the loose bun and the long tendrils that spilled down her back was one of the wigs from the trunk. She was posed, holding a mirror as if gazing upon her blurred reflection. Minnie closed her eyes to take in the photo, and then it came to her where she had seen an image like this.

After a trip to New York, Henryetta's prized possession was a book of classic paintings she had purchased with money her father had given her. The problem was, the book contained many nude paintings from centuries past, and her parents didn't know this. Miss Lucille would have taken the switch to Henryetta if she had known what the real attraction was. Minnie had entered Henryetta's room to put away some clean clothes in her dresser when she happened upon Henry hiding from sight on the far side of the bed. There was Henryetta, stretched out on the rug, looking at a painting of a nude looking at herself in a mirror held up by a naked baby cherub.

"What you lookin' at?" Minnie said, stepping past her to pull open the dresser drawer. Henryetta instantly slammed the book shut when she heard the first syllable come out of Minnie's mouth.

"Art," Henryetta replied with a know-it-all tone.

"Hmm. Can I see?" Minnie said, shutting the drawer, turning to face Henryetta, who was probably thirteen or fourteen at the time.

"You wouldn't like it."

"Well, how do you knows what I likes and what I don't? Ain't that up to me?" Henryetta considered this for a moment.

"Well, I don't know. You might get mad at me, if you saw some of these paintings."

"What do you mean?" Henryetta turned away from Minnie and didn't answer her.

"Come on, Miss Henryetta. Let me see the book. I promise I won't get mad at you."

"Will you tell Mama and Daddy?"

"Is dey's something I have to tell 'em?" Henryetta rolled her eyes at this.

"Okay. I guess, but you have to have an open mind. This is just art," Henryetta said.

Minnie and Henryetta sat side by side, arms touching as Minnie opened the book and began to look at the paintings page after page. Neither of them spoke a word, but with different paintings they communicated with raised eyebrows, gasps, pointing at different parts of paintings that captured their eyes. At the end, Minnie closed the book and just looked forward for a moment.

"Well, Minnie? Did you like them or not?"

Minnie sat still, thinking. "Some of 'em I did like, but some were real strange like. I don't know what to think about all those paintings of naked women."

"Me either, Minnie. Me either. You gonna to tell on me?"

"Your mama would have herself a fit if she knew you was looking at *art* like this. You best keep this book to yo' ownself," Minnie said with raised, disapproving eyebrows.

Looking at Florence's photo was mesmerizing just like that art book had been all those years ago. When Minnie looked up from the photo she noticed that the very art book from long ago was here, lying on a stool next to Henryetta's camera. An envelope peeked out from the pages. Minnie picked up the book and opened it to where the envelope marked the page. She removed the envelope placing it on the stool. The painting in the book mirrored the photograph she had just seen. Minnie walked over to compare the photo to the painting. The replication was very similar, except for the missing cherub.

Someone would have to know Florence very well to recognize her. It was clear the wig and developing techniques were purposefully hiding her identity. This alone told Minnie something wasn't right about this situation. Several other photos were hanging facing away from Minnie, but fearing what they would reveal, she returned the art book to the stool as she had found it. Then, she rehung the photo on the line with a clothespin, blew out the oil lamp, and locked the door behind her. She put the keys back where she found them and left the house. She would have to think about what to do.

CHAPTER TWENTY-SIX

S ome miles outside of Brownsville, the water tower came into Gus's view. Appearing small on the horizon, it grew larger and larger as the locomotive inched toward the Brownsville depot. It was the first time Gus had climbed up and out of the boxcar in several days of non-stop rain. Gus was already in Tallahassee when he heard the news of a tropical storm making landfall in the Keys. This was atypical for this time of year. Afternoon monsoon rains were to be expected, but a stronger storm that had the power to drench everything north of it was not. Those storms started in the fall. So little did Gus know that leaving when he did, would be a stroke of luck. Gus climbed down the boxcar ladder, preparing to jump off the moving train before rolling into the Brownsville station where he risked being caught by railroad officials.

Even though it was early evening, the sun beat down and the thick, wet air had warmed up to the upper nineties. This was par the weather often for West Tennessee all the way up to late November. After Gus jumped for land, he looked back to see several of the other hoboes jumping like dominoes off of the train. They headed for tree cover, but Gus waited for the train to pass him as he walked over the tracks and toward town. The sun felt good on his still sun-kissed face, but he missed the tropical breezes that made the humidity bearable and the quiet lull of the tides against the shoreline. As much as he hated to leave, he knew it was time to head back out on the rails for more research. Gus decided he would travel west to see some of the wonders from Ernest's great pub tales. He had to see for himself if these great skies existed or if the rum just embellished his adventures. Gus also heard radio reports that the dust bowl in the Midwest was pushing thousands of devastated farming families west for work. He would have more than enough subjects to interview for his dissertation. Admittedly, he knew he would have food, a bath, and a real bed to sleep in for a few days in Brownsville, but all this time he had been thinking of Henryetta more than just a little.

By the time he reached Brownsville on foot, the train he had ridden from New Orleans had already pulled off for Nashville. The depot was almost a mile down from Henryetta's house that stood on Main Street. As he walked up the sidewalk, he noticed several men sitting on benches around the courthouse. One sat with his head in his hands as if praying. The braying of mules from behind him startled Gus as he saw a "Hoover wagon" parading down Main Street. It was not uncommon to see broken down cars being pulled like wagons these days. The first time Gus saw this was in a small town in Georgia. Since then, it was no longer surprising, but just the way it was.

When Gus reached the end of the Dixon driveway, he caught sight of a Negro woman he thought to be Minnie. He had met her a few times during his prior stay in Brownsville and knew she meant a great deal to Henryetta. She was walking down the driveway looking a little bewildered.

"Minnie? Is that you?" he called out to her.

"Yes, suh. Mr. Gus?" she returned as she continued down the drive. He waved in reply.

"Hello. Minnie. Are you well?" Gus asked, always polite.

"Yes, suh. Yoself? I heard you done gone down to Florida or somewheres," Minnie said, shading her eyes from the sun that now shone brightly from the western sky.

"That's right. I'm headed out west now, but I just wanted to stop off and say hello to everyone. Are they home?"

"No, Mr. Gus. Ain't nobody home. In fact, I's a bit worried. This ain't like Miss Henryetta. Dey's dried up biscuits settin' on the counter, and dey's hardly anything left in that house. Miss Henryetta done sold off most everything."

Gus looked at Minnie, puzzled.

"Maybe I ought to go take a closer look."

"I think we might ought to call the police. I'm tellin' you now, Mr. Gus, something jis ain't right."

Minnie didn't want to reveal what she had just found down in the cellar. Henryetta's secret was too big for any of them, but Minnie had begun to assume that maybe these photos were allowing them to stay fed, keep the house, and the appearance that all was well. There were too many women like Henryetta—too proud to ask for help. Just the other day one of her sisters at her Bible group had asked for prayers for her former employer who had locked herself in her house, starving to death, and too proud to march herself down to the church to get a crust of bread with some Hoover stew. The neighbors finally broke into her house when she refused to come to the door.

"What about Thom Jr.? Have you heard from or seen him, Minnie? Maybe they all took a drive since the weather is so fine."

"No, suh. Dey ain't no money for gas, jis food. I's telling you, something jis ain't right."

"Well, Minnie. I'll look in to it and see what I can find out from folks up town," he said, nodding at her.

Gus walked toward the church where he knew warm stew or something close to it waited for him. As he neared the doors he noticed a short line out the fellowship hall door. A woman came out and told those in line to come back tomorrow, that they were out of stew. The protests were minimal because there was no use when there was no stew to be had. The men shuffled past Gus talking about pooling their pennies for a can of beans they could cook and share.

Gus still had money from his work on Patricio's fishing boat, but he had promised himself to use it only in dire circumstances. He followed the crowd down the street toward the diner. As the men entered, a man with a blackened eye and a bandaged head glanced at them and down at the ground.

"Sy McGhee, what happened to you?" One of the men said, recognizing him.

"Don't you worry about it none," he grumbled, bumping into Gus, and looking at him with a scowl. Sy tired of that question long ago with the routine bruises and black eyes he had worn like a regular suit of clothes growing up. Then Sy paused, recognizing Gus. Distaste filled Gus, remembering his first encounter with Sy at the drinking shack.

"She ain't here," Sy announced gruffly to Gus.

"Who you talking about, fella?" Gus said decidedly cool.

"Henryetta, who else," Sy growled. Henryetta's name drew attention from the other men standing at the diner entrance, hoping for a handout from someone's leftovers. She was well known as a prized catch.

"Looks like you've had a bit of trouble," Gus slightly nodded toward Sy's eye attempting placate him.

"You need to mind your own business, bum." Sy stood staring at Gus with bully eyes. Gus didn't shirk. Two could play at this power game. *What happened to this man to make him so crude?* When Sy saw Gus wouldn't back down, Sy's shoulders relaxed and he turned away from Gus looking toward the street.

"So do you know where the Dixons are?" Gus prodded.

"I wouldn't tell you, even if I knew." Sy continued to look out across the street, seeing man after man loafing against buildings. Then without a word, Sy just walked off from Gus, leaving him standing in the diner's door. As Gus watched Sy wander off, he caught sight of the peddler man's truck loaded with furniture and cast-offs secured with ropes. On the tail end of the truck, he caught sight of Thom.

Gus burst into a sprint, waving his hat, calling after Thom, who couldn't hear him over the grumbling of the truck's engine. By the time Thom looked up and caught a glimpse of a man in the middle of the street, Gus had stopped running, breathless. The truck rounded the circle of the court square and out of sight. Gus sighed deeply. Then abruptly, a car horn honked, causing Gus to jump out of the street.

CHAPTER TWENTY-SEVEN

*F*or almost a day, the achiness in Henryetta's groin constantly reminded her of Sy's attack. The trained lulled her in and out of fitful sleep. Lucid dreams caused her to wake-up with tear stained cheeks. Twice, the conductor startled her awake, asking her if she were all right. Finally, sheer exhaustion gave way to several hours of deep sleep. When she awoke, her body felt normal, as if nothing had happened. Feeling physically better, Henryetta was better able to guard her thoughts. If she strayed to memories of the rape or burying each parent, she would take a deep breath and concentrate on the landscape through rain-stained windows. Sometimes she calmed herself by tapping her fingers in time with the chugging of the train.

The rain had finally quit when the train crossed over into Florida. For miles and miles, orange pickers entertained her as she looked out the window. She wondered who they were, where they lived, what their lives must be like. Cattle with white tag-a-long birds perched on their backs grazed in wide-open pastures. *How interesting. The cattle don't even seem to mind.*

Later, though, she grew tired of mile after long mile of dense palmettos and inhospitable foliage that made her wonder how early explorers ever got past any of it. Occasionally, a passenger would excitedly point out a gator sunning itself.

After several hours, she felt the train begin to slow. A few rows up, the conductor explained to a curious passenger that their train was stopping to pick up cattle that would go to market in Miami. The sunny, blue skies beckoned her to come off the train. Weary, stiff passengers meandered down the platform looking for a bathroom or an ice-cold bottle of pop. Noisy balling from distressed cattle, who were crammed into cattle cars echoed in the distance.

"One hour! One hour until departure! That's 10:00 departure time to Miami!" bellowed the conductor.

Uniformed railroad bulls, Billy clubs in hand, were poised to strike any freeloaders hiding out in, on, between, and under boxcars. Henryetta thought of Gus and the difficulty he must face every time a train arrives and departs. It must be hard hiding and running with no idea of where you would end up. She understood it now, now that she was the one who was running. Too bad, she couldn't escape herself. No matter where Henryetta went, she would always be herself. It was inside she had to change, not the scenery.

Slowly, the train lurched forward, beginning the process of linking to the cattle cars. As the line of boxcars moved away from her, she caught sight of a bedraggled family sitting in the shade of a halted caboose on the northbound tracks. She could only see their bodies, but no heads, so she squatted down to her knees to get a better look. Henryetta wondered what circumstances had led them to that very spot. Dusty frowns were upturned when the young couple's baby attempted to steady itself with the help of its mother's outstretched hand. Henryetta couldn't hear the parents' words of encouragement, but she could hear the baby's squeals of delight as it took its first steps to its mother, toppling over into her embrace. Henryetta smiled at this small blessing, causing an idea to spark. She reached into her skirt pocket for change. Pulling it out, she counted fifty cents, enough for the family to purchase a few meals if they spent the money wisely.

Looking for oncoming trains, she stepped down off the platform and out on to the limestone gravel bed that flanked the edges of the tracks. The father was the first to notice her high heels coming toward them.

"Hello," Henryetta called out, stepping out from behind the caboose into full view of the couple. They were younger than her. The mother's hair was dirty and matted to her head in a tight bun. Henryetta had seen poor Negros out where Minnie lived, but never Whites as destitute as these filthy, sad creatures. The patched knees of the father's pants, the soiled fabric of their clothes, and the odor of dirt mingled with sweat met her before the family could reply to her greeting.

"Hello," said the father.

"My name is Henryetta. I was wondering . . .," she hesitated, fearing she might insult their dignity.

"I would like to photograph you," she said, asking with a hopeful smile and holding up her camera that rested at her waistline.

They looked at Henryetta without changing their expressions. It was as if their emotions were flat. Tragic and undeniable defeat. Lost hope, she thought.

"I would pay you of course," she offered.

The mother reached out to her husband's shoulder at this.

"How much?" the father asked tentatively.

"Fifty cents." Henryetta knew it was a long shot, but she gambled that hunger would answer for the man even if he didn't want her to take their pictures.

"All right, but let me see the money first," said the father.

Henryetta smiled and dug into her pocket, pulling out four dimes and two nickels and then stooped down to hand the money to the man.

"What are you going to do with our pictures?" asked the mother.

"Keep them, I suppose. I could send you copies if you like."

"We ain't settled just now. Ain't got no place to send them to," the father said.

"Just the same. I don't want to remember this no how," said the mother.

"But your baby just walked, surely you want to remember that?" Henryetta reminded the mother in whose lap the baby now sat.

"Oh, well, I suppose," she said, snuggling the baby.

"All right then. I will take a few natural shots first and then a few that are posed, if that is fine with you?"

The husband looked at his wife. She nodded. The husband then nodded to Henryetta. She smiled and then unwrapped the camera strap from around her neck.

"Just act natural," Henryetta directed, taking shots from different angles and distances.

"You don't even have to look at me."

In more than one frame the mother hid her face with her hand from the camera, but when Henryetta posed them with the baby standing between the parents, grasping both their pointer fingers for balance, the family genuinely smiled for her camera. In that moment, Henryetta felt purpose beyond survival for the first time in the months. She had captured hope and vowed to herself to never let it go again.

From this day forward, Henryetta was on the lookout for interesting people to photograph. When the train stopped, she got off and searched. She enjoyed photographing the landscapes adorned with tropical flowers and palm trees. They were so foreign looking compared to the forsythia bushes and pecan trees of back home. She thought it a shame that her photos would never fully depict the brilliant colors her eyes feasted upon. People made the best landscapes, even if they were suffering. There was a true story behind each photograph.

In a larger crowd of people, Henryetta would scope out the one individual that stood out from the rest, yet one who spoke for them all. When possible, she wrote down the names of her subjects, but she always recorded the location and the date. The day she photographed the young couple sitting in the shade of the caboose, the only thing she found to write on was her father's journal. In the back of it, around ten pages remained blank. She wrote her name and address back in Brownsville, ripped out the page, and handed it to the father who folded it up and put it in his empty wallet.

It was hard to believe that five days and almost 1800 miles separated Henryetta from all the things and people she was trying to escape as she stepped off the train in Miami. Outside the station, palm trees that lined the streets rustled in the salty breeze. How different it smelled from West Tennessee, and it was warm. So warm, she stopped to remove her coat. It reminded her of Gus's postcard. In the distance, Henryetta could hear drums and brass music, unlike any she had heard before. She passed by a barbershop. Dark skinned men in crisp white shirts sat in barber chairs puffing on Cuban cigars speaking Spanish. The smoke, intertwined with their voices, drifted out into the street. Their staccato intonations sounded aggressive, even angry, making Henryetta wonder what could be wrong. Then laughter erupted just as aggressively. She moved on.

In her peripheral vision, a bright light caught her eye. As she turned right, the street deadended at a beach of white sand, illuminated by the sun's rays and the bluest sparkling water she had ever seen. She couldn't help but wander in the direction of the sea. When she finally reached the sand, she wandered not thirty feet out from the street, her pumps filling with hot sand.

The expanse of it! The birds squawked above her as they dove and whirled in the breeze. She had always wanted to see the ocean like this. She had seen the water off the coast of New York City, but it was nothing like this sea of diamonds that reached beyond the horizon. She dropped her belongings to the ground. She spread her coat out on the sand and in one swift movement dropped to the ground. She removed her pumps, and dug her toes into the hot sand. For an hour she sat. Just still, breathing, not thinking about anything other than what was right in front of her. Could a place heal you? This place surely could she thought as she stood up to leave.

Later, after Henryetta had settled into a boarding house room, had a bath, and a meal, she sheepishly asked the manager for a good ladies' doctor. If the manager was curious, she didn't give it away. Which was a relief to Henryetta. Back home, her affairs were everyone's whether or not she wanted them to be. This boosted Henryetta's confidence all the more that she was doing the right thing.

Henryetta had never been to a ladies' doctor. She never had cause to. The room smelled sterile and white. Everything seemed to be white. She wasn't expecting to completely undress. Her knee jumped nervously as she waited on the examination table.

"Well, now Ms. Dixon, I'm Dr. Rutherford. This is my nurse Vivian. What seems to be the trouble?" Henryetta looked at the doctor and nurse, but didn't know what words to use to explain what had happened to her.

"Cat got your tongue? Maybe you would feel more comfortable talking to Nurse Vivian?" Henryetta drew in a deep breath and as the doctor was just about to turn to leave the room she blurted out, "I was raped."

"What was that?" the doctor asked.

"I…I was raped five days ago." The doctor paused, looked down and shook his head.

"I'm…I'm all right. I just want you to check me. My friend said I could be pregnant or maybe the man had something I could catch…you know." Henryetta's voiced faded as she spoke.

"Well, I'm sorry this has happened to you. You aren't married, you say?"

"No, sir."

"Any family here?"

"No sir."

"Did you tell the police?"

"No sir."

"Well, that's that then. Let me have a look. Now, you know we won't know if you are pregnant until your monthlies come. When was your last period?"

"Three weeks ago. Maybe around the fifteenth."

"All right. Have you ever been examined before like this?"

"No sir."

"Well, relax. It won't be the most comfortable thing, but I assure you, it will be fine."

Henryetta let the door slam behind her as she left the doctor's office. The good news was she was going to be fine. The bad news was the waiting she would have to endure for at least another week to see if she was carrying Sy McGhee's child. That night she screamed into her pillow several times and sobbed and sobbed. The house staff knocked on her door to see what the matter was, but she just said through the door, "Please go away. I will be fine."

The next morning she woke to the hustle and bustle of a typical boarding house. As Henryetta lay in her bed she took in the sounds all around her - the bathroom door squeaking open and clicking shut, the early morning conversations of boarders taking their coffee out on the front porch, just below her window, and the clicking sound of working girl heels on the stairs. A waft of bacon drifted into her room, arousing Henryetta's hunger.

Downstairs, Henryetta ate her fill, but on her way back upstairs to gather her camera, she saw a lone di resting beneath a side table in the living room. She picked it up and decided this lone di would choose where she went each day. One, two, or three said, go. Four, five or six, said, stay. For a week, the moment the sun rose, Henryetta headed out, hopping on and off buses never knowing in what part of the city she might end up, but it was a distraction from waiting for her body to reveal what was next for her.

CHAPTER TWENTY-EIGHT

L aughter and the sound of glasses clinking blended with the musicians in the corner of the drinking shack. Gus entered looking for Thom. It was early evening, but he knew Thom's habits. Moonshine didn't keep a clock. Through the smoke, he spied an empty bar stool. Gus wasn't a drinking man. He didn't believe in wasting money on something that only harmed your body. He'd seen his fair share of drunks while out riding the rails. They were unpredictable and dangerous.

"What'll you have?" the bartender asked Gus, sliding a glass to him.

"Root beer," he said, smiling.

The bartender looked at Gus queerly, but then reached under the bar, popped the cap off of the bottle, and poured root beer in the glass.

"Suit yourself." Then the bartender went back to drying glasses and stacking them on the shelves behind him.

"You see Thom Dixon tonight?" Gus asked the bartender.

"No, sir. He hadn't been here in a few weeks. I heard he got himself a job working for the peddler man out of Memphis."

Gus nodded.

"I thought I saw him today on the back of the truck. Know anything about his sister?" Gus asked casually.

"No, sir."

He looked around at the faces, but there weren't any he recognized. He decided this was probably a dead end, but he would wait another hour for Thom to show up. When Thom didn't, Gus put a few cents down on the counter, thanked the bartender, and started walking back toward town. Worn out from the journey and the long walk to and from the drinking shack, Gus got the notion to head to the depot to rest for the night. He could ask in the morning if the Dixons had taken a train somewhere.

The next morning, Gus sat propped up against the outside of the depot wall under the ticket window, waiting for the clerk to open up. He had found a single boxcar loaded with cotton bales making a good place for a hobo to rest his head. He wasn't alone, but as soon as the sun came up, he crawled from the boxcar and walked toward the depot. The morning was cool. The sun reflected off of dewy leaves and spider webs.

When the clerk finally opened the window, Gus popped up, startling the man who had entered through the office door on the other side of the depot.

"Sorry, sir. Didn't mean to startle you like that." The clerk continued to stack tickets and straighten his work area.

"Aren't you a little early, son? Ain't no train coming for hours."

"No, sir. I need to find someone. Do you know Henryetta Dixon?"

"Henryetta Dixon? Thomas Dixon's daughter? Photographer?"

"Yes. That's her. Do you remember her buying a ticket recently?"

"Let me think a moment . . . As a matter of fact, I do, because she paid with a one-hundred-dollar bill. We don't see many of those."

"Well, do you remember where she went?"

"Nashville, if I recall. She was with that other woman, her boarder, and two small children. They bought round trip tickets. Let me check my register.

"Yes. It says they'll be back tomorrow. Check back here tomorrow at 10:00 am. That's when the train from Nashville arrives."

"Thank you," Gus replied kindly and turned away from the window.

Gus decided to go back to the Dixon house to see if Thom was home.

"Gus? Is that you?" Thom called from just inside the screen door.

"Gus! I thought that was you yesterday when I was on the back of the peddler man's truck. Did you see me?"

Gus smiled and extended his hand to Thom, who took it and patted Gus's shoulder.

"You want to come in for some coffee? I don't have much to eat, but I do have a bit of coffee."

"Sounds fine. How are you Thom? I heard you got a job working for the peddler man."

"That's right, Gus. Just here and there, though. His main hand hurt his back lifting a big mirror down in Memphis. So I've been riding along when he comes into town to help out when I'm needed."

"Well then, that's something, isn't it?"

Thom nodded as he poured coffee for Gus.

"Sure is quiet around here. Where are the ladies? The children?"

"That's a good question. I think they ran off."

"What makes you say that?" Gus, ever so cool, probed.

"Well, about a week ago, I found Sy lying right over there half-dead from blow to the back of his head. He had a real shiner, too. The crazy part was that his pants were down to his ankles."

"What happened?"

"Nobody knows. Sy can't remember a thing. *I think* he tried to rape my sister and Flo knocked him upside the head with a rolling pin."

"My God...I'm sorry Thom."

"Well, I'm not especially surprised. He has wanted my sister for years. I just never thought it would come to this."

"What did you do when you found him?"

"At first, I ran over to him. I couldn't think of anything but helping my friend. But then, when I realized what he did or tried to do, I wanted to kill him myself. I was crazy mad. Madder than I've ever been in my life. I kicked him hard in the ribs, but he didn't even move. That's when I sure he was dead. I called Doc Castellaw and his daddy."

"You didn't call the police?"

"Nah. I was scared out of my mind. What if they accused *me*? What if they wanted to put my sister in jail? Or even Flo? I just couldn't do it."

"I don't believe that." Gus challenged. Thom hung his head in shame.

"Look, it's complicated. Sy's daddy is up for re-election to the city council in the fall. This would cause a big scandal."

"Thom I don't care who Sy's daddy is. You have to report this. What if Sy rapes another woman?"

"We don't even know if he did or didn't."

"You can't be serious, Thom. Report this. If you don't I will." Thom responded with silence, shaking his head.

"She's your sister, for crying out loud!"

Thom's hands shook as he fumbled to pull out a pint of boot-legged whiskey to pour in his coffee.

"Thom, I need you to listen. They are not safe out there. Sy is just the beginning of many men if we don't find them. I know Thom. I've been out there. Women and girls, young *girls,* Thom, offer their bodies just for a scrap of food."

Thom knew this was true. Out at the drinking shack, Thom had seen women, some of them mothers, others just single and out of luck, drunkenly throw themselves at any man in hopes he would give them a little money to put bread on the table. Most of them were women that before the Great Depression would have never even looked in the direction of the drinking shack.

"The police can help us."

Thom couldn't meet Gus's gaze.

CHAPTER TWENTY-NINE

On this particular morning, Henryetta rolled the di one last time in Miami. Go to Key West or stay in Miami. The di directed her to search for Gus in Key West. Henryetta paid her bill, and quietly returned the di to the table where an open backgammon board lay open.

As she boarded the train, she felt a familiar tinge of pain in her lower abdomen. She smiled, relieved there would be no baby. The train ride proved even more spectacular than her first experience at the beach. Henryetta's eyes beheld the turquoise and emerald waters that swam around the base of one of the many bridges that connected the string of keys one to another. The sun reflected off waves, twinkling like millions of tiny stars. *No photograph could ever capture this.*

Within a few hours, the train stopped on a small island. The platform was perched high above the island allowing Henryetta to look down on a small boat dock, where a fishing party of five men were boarding a boat with their poles. She turned to look out the windows on the other side of the train. A parade of wealthy passengers from the luxury cars were being escorted down a steep ramp toward a village of quaint, yellow, seaside cottages.

The conductor was coming her way.

"Excuse me, sir. How long will we be stopped?"

"Not long miss. We will be pulling out as soon as the rest of the luggage is taken off of the train. Five minutes or so, I expect." Disappointing news. Henryetta wanted to explore.

"Sir, may I trouble you again?" she called after the conductor as he moved on past her down the aisle. He turned to her.

"Of course."

"What is this place?"

"Paradise for the rich, my dear." She frowned at the reply.

"Just the wealthy? No one else can stay here?"

"Not typically, Miss. Not unless you are the help."

"Oh. I see. Thank you."

"My pleasure, ma'am."

What a shame she thought. All throughout her trip she had photographed the destitute and the average. So much suffering everywhere, but for the wealthy, it looked as if nothing had changed. Uncomfortable, Henryetta became very aware of the envy she felt and swallowed it back down. *Oh, the silky sheets. The caviar. The fine china.* No longer were these things hers. She wished she'd never known them.

Then, her mind traveled to the loss of her parents. Their absence rode alongside her, sometimes bound and gagged, and other times begging to be heard, constantly pecking at her, tapping her on the shoulder, and other times screaming like the tea kettle for her to take it off the burner. Money was not everything. People were. How ironic the state of humanity is. People break us and people make us all at the same time, but, now, she was alone.

"Next stop, Key West!" the conductor shouted from the front of the car.

For the past thirty miles, Henryetta played the game of looking out the window at the vast aquamarine waters and back down at the palm trees on Gus's postcard she pulled from her pocketbook. She knew it was a long shot, finding Gus here, but she at least wanted to try. In the aftermath of the recent tropical storm, she spied several people cleaning up woody, brown palm fronds and scattered patio chairs as the train made its way over land. The wreckage was minimal, but still there were photographs she wished she could capture if the train would have only stopped for her.

As the train came closer and closer to a complete stop, Henryetta looked out the window, scanning faces, hoping to recognize one of them as Gus, but did not see him. As she disembarked, she asked the conductor for the name of a hotel. He told her the hotels had closed, but if she headed down to Duval Street she might ask around for a boarding house that might take her in. As she walked, she noticed very few women. The streets were flanked with more men out of work, the only difference from home being their tanned skin and salt-bleached hair. Down the street, she spied a boxes of mangoes and oranges displayed outside of a corner market reminding her she hadn't eaten since earlier in the morning.

Inside, she asked the meat counter man to make her a sandwich. She selected an orange and headed out of the store to be met by a gang of bony teenage beggars whose cheeks were sunken in.

"Miss, you need any work done?"

"We'll work for food."

"Please, miss."

Henryetta paused for a moment to look at them, feeling sympathy. They reminded her too much of Gertie, Beth, and the hobo boys that ran with Gus.

"You tramps go on now!" the store owner reprimanded from the front door. "Leave the nice lady alone."

At first, they paid no mind to the man and continued to look at Henryetta hopefully.

"Don't make me call the coppers, boy. You move along now," the grocer threatened a bit stronger.

Henryetta looked at the owner and then back at the boys, who hung their heads and were beginning to scatter.

"Wait!" she called after them.

They stopped and turned. She held up her camera.

"Pictures for a meal?"

They looked puzzled at her.

"You ought not to have done that, miss. They won't leave you alone now. Little buzzards," the storekeeper said, shaking his head as he headed back into the store.

"It's fine. My father always said—" she began only to halt mid-sentence when the store door slammed shut. "If you have money to spare, share it. It always comes back threefold," she whispered to herself.

"You fooling us, miss?" the smallest tramp, who looked to be about twelve, said, coming up close to her. His tanned face made his green eyes sparkle in the sun. She noticed he had a slight scar that ran from his upper lip to his cheekbone.

"Not at all. My name is Henryetta, what's yours?"

"Phillip."

"Well, nice to meet you, Phillip. Do you live around here?"

"Nah, just passing through. I thought I might get hired working in the sponge factory, but they didn't need me. There isn't anything here for me."

"How old are you, Phillip?"

"Twelve, but I can work as hard as any man. Ask my big brother, Frank."

"Hello, ma'am. It's true. He's tough as nails."

"Hello," she said, nodding in greeting.

Frank looked to be about sixteen. He had the same golden blonde hair, but his eyes were lighter, she noted. Almost the color of celery. She could tell they hadn't been on the road for very long. Their denim overalls didn't have holes yet, and their shoes were not worse for the wear. Unlike some of the others in their gang, both boys still had meat on their bones.

"You a tourist? Reporter or something like that?"

"No. I am a photographer, and I suppose a bit of a wanderer, like y'all."

"Where have you been?" Phillip asked.

"I came down from a small town in Tennessee. I'm actually looking for someone. You may have met him. His name is Gus. From Chicago? About six feet one inch, brown hair, talks really educated, and he writes in a journal. Do you know him?" Frank and Phillip shook their heads when a heavily accented voice boomed from behind Henryetta, half startling her.

"I know this Gus!" the voice called out.

Henryetta turned to see a short, balding Cuban balancing a crate of fish against his plump belly making for the store door. His smile, surrounded by white whiskers, was friendly and welcoming. As he waddled toward the store, his fat shoulders rocked side to side. He laboriously sucked in and breathed out air with each step.

"One minute. I tell you later. Now, I do the fish."

"That's some luck, huh, Miss Henryetta," said an optimistic Phillip.

She smiled and nodded at him.

"How's about that picture, now?" Frank pushed.

He was hungry. They hadn't eaten in a day and a half.

"Oh yes, well, I typically like to do several natural poses and then a posed one in case you want me to mail it to you later on."

"And you pay us? You must be rich or something," Phillip commented.

"No, not at all," she said with a tinge of remorse hidden under a smile.

She pulled out her camera from the case. She looked to see how many exposures she had left on this roll of film. Five.

"What' something you typically do down here?" she asked.

Before Phillip could answer, the store door flung open.

"Gus!" the smiling fisherman called to her, raising his arms in excitement.

She looked past Frank to this squat fisherman. His skin was almost the color of black coffee against his white shirt that carried fish blood stains on the sleeves and his wide waistline. He was one of the roundest men she had ever seen. His personality took up the whole sidewalk, and the boys backed away and made room for him to come right up to Henryetta.

"You know Gus? Yes?"

"Yes. I am Henryetta."

"Henryetta? You are a long way from home, senorita."

She nodded.

"I am Patricio. *Encantado*. Pleased to meet you."

"Likewise. How do you know Gus?"

"Fishing! He work the boat with me. A good man, this Gus."

"Does he still work for you?"

"No, senorita. He say it time for him to go. He say he would go to see you before he go to the west. You see him, no?"

West? She thought. West? How would she ever find him, now? "No."

"Ay. No problem. He come back here to work for me again. He have the heart of a *pescador*, a fisherman."

Her smile faded as she turned away from all of them to hide her deep disappointment. She was alone, more alone than she had ever felt in her life. A sob began to form deep in her throat as she looked out toward the sea where gulls screamed. No. She couldn't cry here, not now. She wiped the two tears that had escaped each eye and turned back to face the men who stood in silent respect. Then she had an idea.

"Patricio, this is Frank and his little brother, Phillip. They need work," she said, forthright.

"They are hungry." All eyes turned to Patricio, hopeful.

At first, he looked at Henryetta with a look of discomfort of being put on the spot. He looked down at the ground, frowned, gesturing his hands back and forth as if he were weighing pros and cons. He looked up at Henryetta, whose eyes pleaded with him. Then Patricio looked the two boys up and down.

"Pues . . . well . . . I have two sons in Cuba . . . like you . . . You work hard for me, yes?" he said to little Phillip.

"Yes, sir. I grew up on a tobacco farm in Kentucky. I know hard work," Phillip said.

The mention of Kentucky struck a chord in Henryetta. She said a quick prayer in her head for Florence and the children.

"All right. We see how you work. If you no good, I let you go. Understand?" Patricio said to the excited brothers, who were hugging and congratulating themselves.

"Thank you, mister. You won't be sorry," said Frank, extending his hand to Patricio.

They shook hands heartily. Henryetta smiled at the deal. Her willingness to speak up saved these two boys at least for a time.

"Boys, are you still ready for some food?" Henryetta asked.

"They eat on the boat with me. We have fish. You come and eat with us, yes?" Patricio answered. Henryetta wanted to go with them, but she hesitated.

"Thank you, but no. I have to find a place to stay. Can I see the boat tomorrow? I still want to take your pictures. Working on the boat would make for exciting photographs."

"You sure you no want to eat? Patricio makes the best fish in all of the Key West."

"Tomorrow. I promise. How do I find you?"

"Go to Mallory Harbor and ask for Patricio. We go out at dawn. We back around 11:00. You go with us on the boat tomorrow, yes? I teach you to fish, like I teach Gus. You love it."

Henryetta found Patricio hard to refuse. His passion was magnetic.

"Yes. Yes, I will. But what do I wear? I only have dresses."

"You no worry about this. I give you Gus's fishing clothes. You change on boat. Yes! This is going to be great!" Patricio put his arms around the boys' shoulders, and they walked away from her.

After finding a boarding house a few blocks over from Duval Street, Henryetta slept soundly. She was up before dawn and started the coffee for the house. After a cup, she grabbed her camera case, another roll of film, and began walking toward the harbor. Her nerves were jumpy from walking alone in the dark in a strange place. The whole idea of going out on the ocean in a boat that could sink frightened her. Worries plagued her mind until a singular thought interrupted them. She hadn't thought about her mother, her father, the pictures, or missing Florence and the children for a solid two hours. Drowning, sharks, seasickness, sunburn, the smell of fish—those were her worries today, and what a relief. She smiled and realized this was her life starting over.

CHAPTER THIRTY

*A*fter a night of rest in the bed of Thomas's parents, Gus, together with Thom, walked over to the train depot to wait on the arrival of the ten o'clock train from Nashville. As they walked up to the depot Thom spied the Dixon car parked under a pecan tree at the edge of the depot's lot. Thom opened the driver door to see the ignition without a key. "Well I'll be damned," Thom said. He spied a slip of folded stationery lying on the passenger side floorboard. When he picked it up, he spied the car key under it. He quickly pocketed the key and opened the folded paper to find a note in Florence's hurried, frantic handwriting.

"There's a letter here, Gus!" Thom called out to Gus, who had already claimed a seat on a wooden bench in the shade of the depot's porch.

Gus turned to see Thom waving the note back and forth. Other than the ticket seller, it was just the two of them. Birds chirped their morning songs from branches high atop the oak trees that flanked the depot parking lot. As Thom made his way over to the bench, the bird chorus was interrupted by the loud whistle of the train that was quickly approaching the depot. Black billowy clouds of smoke chugged out from the smoke stack leaving a trail of soot that hung in the air just above the tree line.

Gus covered his ears as the steel giant's breaks screeched to a painful halt. He could hear a conductor call out, "Brownsville!"

When Gus glanced at Thom, he was engrossed in the letter. Gus started toward the passenger cars to wait for Henryetta to disembark.

But other than the train employees who had stepped off the engine, not a soul moved from the train. Gus began to walk the length of the passenger cars looking in the windows to see strangers looking back at him. Some looked curious, others blank as if they weren't looking at him at all, but rather at an alternate world. Some stood stretching. Others were occupied with wiping children's noses or flicking cigarette ashes out of the opened window. The passenger car itself seemed only half full.

"She's not coming back," Thom said as he came up quickly on Gus. "They're gone. Here. Read this," Thom said, handing the folded letter to Gus.

> Thom,
>   I don't have long to write this. The train is boarding soon. Just know this. That lowlife Sy McGhee you call friend, raped your sister. He deserves everything he got. Don't come after us. You'll just be wasting your time.
>
>   Florence
>
> PS. If Walter ever shows up, tell him his wife is gone for good, and to just go on home.

Gus folded the letter back and looked down toward the boxcars and then back to Thom.

"Where do you reckon they went?" Thom asked.

"That's a good question. You think they went up to Kentucky, where Flo's from?"

"Might have, but there's nothing for them up there either. People are starving up there too. I figure they might try their luck in a city. Maybe New York. Henryetta has her photography teacher up there," Thom said, thinking about who Henryetta would turn to if she were in trouble.

Gus wrinkled his brow.

"Thom, did Henryetta ever mention me? You know, maybe talk about me some?" Gus fished.

"I knew it!" Thom burst out, grinning. "You sly devil! You're sweet on Henryetta, aren't you?"

Blood and heat rushed up Gus's neck straight to his cheeks, quickly flushing light crimson. No matter how hard Gus tried, he wouldn't fool Thom.

"Was she sweet on you, too?" Thom wanted to know.

"Well, I suppose, maybe. That's what I was coming to find out. I couldn't get my mind off her. I wanted to see her before I rode the rails out west. How long ago did Gertie leave?" Gus asked, thinking her whereabouts might give him a clue.

"Not long. They were headed south. A few days before Flo and Henry took off. Something about working the celery crops near a place called Sara . . . Sara something. I had never heard of it. Down in Florida somewhere."

"And the other girl, Beth? Anything from her?"

"No. She didn't talk a whole lot. She just left with Gertie is all I know. Those four gals were thick as thieves. Maybe Gertie will know."

"You remember where Florence was from up in Kentucky? I can't imagine them traveling far with Marjorie and June Bug," Gus probed.

"She's from up in the mountains in . . . uh . . . let me think . . . Pike County . . . Pikeville! That's it! I'm positive. She lived in Pike County," Thom answered confidently. "But why would they go there if they thought the police might come looking for them? I don't think Kentucky is it. I think you have a better chance finding her with Gertie and Beth."

"Don't worry, Thom. I'll find them and bring them back," Gus reassured.

Thom half smiled. He wanted to believe Gus, but the world was big.

"All aboard for Memphis, Tennessee!" the conductor called out, looking directly at Gus and Thom.

"You going, Gus?" Thom said, nodding at the conductor.

Gus fingered the cash he had saved from working on Patricio's boat. He was tempted to pay for a ticket, but knew better. Then Thom pulled out his wallet.

"Here. This is Henryetta's school picture," Thom said, handing the photo to Gus.

"Maybe this will help."

At this, Gus nodded and smiled. He looked down, and there she was. Henryetta looked hopeful and eager. There was a sparkle in her eye, the same one he glimpsed while she worked in her darkroom. Her cheeks were fuller and radiated confidence. He would have many hours to study her photo, but this girl in the photo was different. The Henryetta Gus knew was much wiser to the world of suffering. A frown crossed Gus's face when he thought of the terror Henryetta faced when Sy attacked her. He let the thought pass. He was determined to find her before worse happened.

"Promise me you will go to the police." Thom only nodded and smiled. "I'll be seeing you, Thom," Gus said, outstretching his hand to Thom, who took it heartily. Gus dropped his hand and began walking south along the gravel beside the tracks. The conductor eyeballed Gus, but when the departure whistle sounded, he stepped up and into the car. By this time, Gus had disappeared into the tree line.

CHAPTER THIRTY-ONE

$\mathcal{A}$s Gus traveled south, he dodged railroad bulls and slept in empty cattle cars where the breeze would keep him cool. Depot after depot, jungle after jungle he searched and showed Henryetta's picture, hoping for just one lead. Heads nodded "no." Nobody had even heard of celery crops in Florida or a place called Sara-something-or-other. Some faces, so hungry, just stared at Gus, returning nothing but a silent plea for nourishment. Gus noticed as he traveled, the soup lines had gotten longer, the arguments for scraps had turned into wrestling matches, and that there wasn't an empty boxcar to be had. In some towns, people spat at "dirty bums."

Because so many more young unemployed men and homeless boys had taken to riding the rails, Gus could easily tell the green hoboes from the seasoned ones. The clothes were a bit cleaner, the cheeks not sunken in as much, and they were getting younger. When pocket change allowed, Gus would find a coffee shop or a diner where he could sit and write his reflections of his experiences and about the people he was meeting along the way.

November 1933

> I just spent a stretch of rails traveling with two young boys- Randy, sixteen, and Irving fifteen. Both were a little worse for wear. They met back in Pennsylvania and had spent that last six months riding the rails together. Every now and

then they found farm work helping them earn enough pennies to keep a bite of food in their stomachs, but no job seemed to last, and there was never enough money to send home. Their leather shoes were worn and dusty. No amount of washing would rid their pants of the deep dirt stains or the weeks and weeks of sweat stains that peeked out from their underarms. They quickly took to me. Most folks do. I'm not that bad of a sort.

Randy's story was not unlike some of the others I've heard. Day after day, Randy's father joined hundreds of men at sun-up who formed the line outside of the unemployment office only to be turned away. His family was struggling to survive just like many of the other families who lived in his tenement house. He told me of how families often pulled together to share left overs, if there were any. They took care of one another, but it grew harder and harder as the Depression lingered. One day, Randy walked into their home to find his parents at the kitchen table with their heads together praying. When they separated and looked up at Randy, he noticed his mother was crying.

"You have to move out, son. I have too many mouths to feed. You are a man now and it's time for you to look after yourself." His father's words stunned Randy and his mother began to sob. Randy's little sisters sat on the couch with their heads down, not looking at their distressed family members. Randy heard himself saying he understood, but on the inside, fear paralyzed him. Where would he go? What would he do for money? As he began to leave, Randy kissed his crying mother, hugged his sisters, and simply walked away from the tenement house they had lived in their whole lives. That was nine months ago.

Irving came from a middle class family. At first, the Depression caused them to tighten their belts, especially when they reduced his father's hours at work. His mother was an established dressmaker. Before the Depression, her earnings went straight into a savings account for Irving's college fund, but now they used them just to get by. Irving recalled he had been playing baseball in a nearby park the day he left home. His mother had a strict rule that everyone took off their shoes before entering through the backdoor. The front door was for guests and sewing clients, not "ruffians and such," she always said. She was very particular about her house. I smiled at this. It made me think of Aunt Trudy.

As Irving went around back of their house, he spotted his father standing alone near the wood pile. Irving began to call to his father, but halted when he saw his father's shoulders heaving up and down as he sobbed silently. This was the first time he had ever seen a grown man cry.

"That did it for me," Irving explained. "I found out later that day that my pop had been out of work for two weeks and didn't tell any of us, not even my mother. He had been looking for work, but got turned down day after day. He didn't know what to do. He was frustrated and worried that we would lose everything. That made it easy for me to just walk away. I was one less mouth to feed. I couldn't stand to see my Dad cry, so I wrote them a note and left in the middle of night."

I asked the boys if they communicate with their families. Irving replied, "I've sent them a couple of letters letting them know I'm all right."

"No." Randy said unapologetically to me.

I'm not traveling with them now. As it turns out, we separated when I found a sign for Sarasota.

There, up on the destination board was "Sarasota." He never would have noticed it had it not been for a well-to-do couple with two children who were pointing and looking at the board, talking about meeting up with family for a vacation at the beach. They went back and forth about whether or not to just stay in town for a few days until the train to Sarasota arrived or to find a bus station.

"Well, Sara-something-or-other, there you are." Gus smiled triumphantly. Since the next train for Sarasota wouldn't be for two days, Gus wandered into town to a gas station and bummed a map off of an attendant who gave him general walking directions and the names of towns he would pass through on his way. For miles and miles, Gus walked alone on dirt highways surrounded by Palmetto scrub or a random orange grove where he plucked ripe oranges and sucked their tangy juices to quench his thirst. In an afternoon, he had only seen two cars pass him by in a cloud of dust. At dusk, hunger began to gnaw at his stomach. He had eaten six oranges, but his mind kept returning to Aunt Trudy's pot roast with Idaho potatoes, carrots, and celery. His mouth watered remembering the taste of her cooking. For a solid hour he catalogued his Aunt Trudy's cooking in his mind. Then, noticing the sun had disappeared from the horizon, he knew dreaming of home-cooking was not doing him any good. He needed to find somewhere to sleep for the night.

Gus heard hoboes' tales of wild boars and alligators. The worst one was of a fella who was sleeping soundly on the edge of a hobo camp outside of Gainesville who woke up to the excruciating snap of his femur as a fifteen-foot gator took a voracious bite. Most hoboes from other parts of the country never realized that gators were nocturnal predators. Most of the out-of-towners were used to camping by streams and lakes where the biggest threats were mosquitoes. That night those poor hoboes were educated by their traveling companion's near fatal encounter. They agreed that being eaten alive by a hungry alligator who had developed a taste for human flesh was far worse than any railroad bull's club.

Keeping this story at the forefront of his mind, Gus weighed his options—keep moving in hopes of stumbling on a rancher's homestead or a small town, or sleep on the road's edge. He decided to keep walking. Not some two miles down the road a small light flickered in the distance. He couldn't tell if it was from a fire or from a house. The closer he got he saw that it was an oil lantern suspended from a low branch of a tree.

Then Gus noticed a black buggy that reminded him of a picture he had seen of colonial America in one of his text books. The two horses tied to an ancient oak tree quickly lifted their heads looking wide-eyed with their ears perked. A male figure stood and walked over to calm the horses as he looked suspiciously in Gus's direction. Gus continued to slowly advance toward the campsite. The orange coals of a smoldering fire gave almost no light, but Gus made out three more figures—another man, two women—one plump and the other petite, all of them dressed in black, facing the fire. Again, their straw hats and the women's bonnets reminded him of Puritans. Then it occurred to Gus that they must be Amish or Mennonite.

"Hello!" Gus, smiling, called out causing all three figures to rise and face him. In the dim lantern light Gus saw alarm run across their faces. The man who had been comforting the horses marched right up to Gus. Not three feet away, the man was intimidatingly tall. His alabaster beard reached half way down his barreled chest.

"My name is Gus. I'm a friendly traveler looking for a safe spot to rest for the night."

The patriarch did not utter a sound. His stare was stern. Then right behind the old man appeared a younger version of himself, only the beard was shorter and darker from what Gus could tell.

"I don't mean you any harm. I am traveling just like you. I am trying to get to Sarasota to find some friends of mine. I need a safe place to rest. May I rest near you tonight?"

The older man's intimidating gaze never stopped examining Gus. In response, Gus continued to smile.

"Nein!" the younger man said resolutely, shaking his head as he crossed his arms over his chest in disagreement. Then the older man motioned for the other to stop. They spoke to each other in German, debating. The younger of the two protesting, but then the older man posed a question. When the younger man's puffed chest deflated and his shoulders slumped, Gus knew that he had relented. The younger turned to Gus in a calm stance.

"I am Malachi Yoder from Pennsylvania," began the older man.

"We are on our way to Sarasota as well. My brother bought land to raise celery. He needs our help. This is my wife, Ruth, and my son, Michael, and his wife, Faith."

Gus's heart leapt at this stroke of luck. How many celery farms could there be? This would certainly make his search a bit easier. Something deep inside told him that he would find them, find Henryetta.

CHAPTER THIRTY-TWO

*F*rom a distance Gus heard the whistle of the train before he saw anything other than scrub. Then around a bend he was greeted by acres of celery for as wide as the eye could see. Stooped over bodies, black, white, male and female, hoed weeds from between the rows. When he reached a person he inquired about where to find the migrant tenants' camp. Gus explained he was looking for two, maybe four women with two small children. The man directed Gus to travel down the road a few more miles and then he would see the farm office. He could ask if they were on the payroll.

By lunchtime, hunger gnawed at Gus's stomach, reminding him he hadn't eaten anything since sharing a breakfast with the Amish family. He considered breaking off a few stalks of celery that had a few more weeks of growing before it would be harvested. Gus realized he wasn't even sure what day it was. He had been walking for so long. He counted out the days and then knew it was Sunday. In about an hour, a tent village, a few houses and barns flanked by railroad tracks came into view. He set his mark on a pale yellow Florida style clapboard house with a peacock blue tin roof and hurricane shutters. As he drew closer he could see its siding was beginning to peel here and there from the salty humidity. A sign with OFFICE next to the front door calmed him. Gus believed he was going to find something.

"Can help you?" boomed a baritone voice rounding the corner.

Gus waited for the older gentleman still outfitted in his Sunday best come up closer.

"Hello. Yes, sir. I am looking for two women with two small children that may have tried to get work here. Well, actually it might be a group of four women and two children."

The man was not taller than Gus, but his pot belly, moustache, and steely stare intimidated Gus, and he was not one easily shook.

"Well, which is it? Two or four women?" he trumpeted.

"It's a long story. I am looking for two women and two children, but they may have come here looking for two of their friends who came to Sarasota to harvest celery."

"Is that so? They running from the law? We don't house criminals 'round here."

"No, sir," Gus replied. They were just looking for honest work like everyone else. The man measured Gus and just stared at him making Gus uncomfortable.

"Harvest isn't for a few weeks. Most everyone working here is settled in Sarasota. If they were looking for work, we'd have turned them down and told them to come back later in the season," the man replied loudly as if he were giving a speech.

Gus backed away from the man a few steps.

"I'm afraid I can't help you, young man," he continued.

Gus looked down at his feet and then off in the distance. He noticed sheets on a clothesline blowing in the wind. Beyond them, off in the distance, loomed great walls of dark clouds that were making their way from the sea to the shore. Looking back at the man, Gus nodded in thanks and walked off toward the road. It would be a rainy walk to town.

"Son!" the man bellowed, causing Gus to turn back.

When he looked back, he noticed two feminine figures in the distance. They were unclipping the sheets from the clothesline. Together they were folding the sheets and laying them in a clothes basket. Seeing Gus's eyes looking at them, the gentleman turned toward the line, too, but quickly returned his attention to Gus.

"You hungry?" Gus's mouth watered at the question. Silently he thanked God.

"Yes sir, but I can pay for a meal. I don't need charity," Gus responded, thinking this man might be more likely to not only feed him, but respect him.

Something about this man commanded respect. Gus imagined him to be the owner, or the foreman at least.

"Well, consider yourself lucky. I'm feeling Christian today. Wash up good over there at the pump, then come in the side door." The man gestured to the red water pump that was situated atop a well to the side of the house. Gus figured the door was around the corner.

Gus removed his knapsack where he kept a change or two of clothes and his journals. As he pumped water into a bucket, he smelled the ripe tang of his body mixed with sulfur from the water. If he thought no one were looking out the windows, Gus would have stripped to bare flesh to wash his whole body. Instead, he removed his shirt and then doused it in the water. Twice he plunged it in the bucket and wrung it out. Rooting in his knapsack, he found a half-gone bar of soap. He lathered his unshaven face, neck, torso, and armpits with the soap and water from the bucket. After refreshing the water in the bucket, Gus bent over and rinsed his head and upper body. At least he was half clean.

He hung his wet shirt over the wrought iron banister on the steps that led to the side door. Gus donned a clean short-sleeved shirt, and when the last button was fastened, he knocked on the screen door.

"You don't have to knock! Come on in!" the man called from somewhere inside.

Many times Gus had imposed on families when he sometimes traveled on foot. Some were happy to have Gus eat with the family. Some made him eat out in the yard. Others stood firm on their porches with a gun. No words were necessary. He was not the only man walking the highways and riding the rails.

Gus opened the door and placed his knapsack on the floor next to the door. The man appeared now in a work shirt and pants.

"Come in and eat a plate," the man said, leading Gus to a dining room.

As Gus entered, the man motioned for him to sit. Across the hall, Gus could see an office desk and filing cabinets that lined the walls.

"Where is that girl?" the man thundered. "Get that food on out here, would you!" The man shook his head in frustration. He started for the kitchen but almost collided with a plate of meatloaf, mashed potatoes, and peas that appeared before its porter.

"Sorry, sir." The voice was unmistakable. Gertie! Gus's heart began to race with anticipation. Shock, followed by gleeful surprise, came across Gertie's face.

"Gus!" Gertie exclaimed. Gus got up from his chair and came to hug Gertie, who balanced the plate with her right hand and a glass of iced tea in the left.

"What are you doing here, Gus?" she asked, disbelieving he was right here with her.

"Now hold on just a minute. What is this?" the man interrupted before Gus could even respond to Gertie.

"This is one of the women I was looking for," Gus said excitedly.

"Well, I'll be. Is that right? And how do you know each other?" the man asked.

Gus started to talk, but Gertie rushed to put the food and the glass of tea on the table. She motioned for Gus to sit down.

"Gus, you eat," Gertie turned to the man. "We met riding the rails up near Chicago." The man had not moved. When Gus had shoveled and swallowed two forkfuls of mashed potatoes, he extended his hand in greeting.

"Gus, sir. Nice to meet you."

The man looked at Gus as if he were an insect, not a man.

"This is Mr. Culpepper, Gus. He hired me to cook and clean for him, isn't that right Mr. Culpepper?"

"I found this whippersnapper and that crazy Beth sleeping in one of my boxcars after I'd run them off once. I had a good mind to haul them straight to the Sarasota jail, but I hired Gertie here instead. I haven't had a decent meal ever since," he said, frowning at Gertie, who just rolled her eyes at him and smiled at Gus.

"You look good, Gertie. Are you . . . good, Gertie?"

Gertie glanced at the man and smiled back at Gus.

"I am Gus. And yourself?"

"Gertie, that's a tale. I'm fine, despite your poor cooking," Gus joked.

Gertie lightly smacked Gus's arm. It was good to see Gus after all this time. They had experienced so much out there together. It would be so good to catch up.

"Let the man eat, Gertie. You've got dishes to wash," Mr. Culpepper barked from the sofa in the next room, where he had settled to read the Sunday paper.

"Yes, sir, Mr. Culpepper. Gus, if you want seconds . . ." but Gertie was interrupted by Mr. Culpepper with the exact same offer. Gus smiled at her, and she left the dining room. All bark, no bite, Gus surmised of Mr. Culpepper.

Later that same evening, after Gertie had finished her chores and Mr. Culpepper said she was free to do as she pleased, Gertie met Gus at the train platform where he imagined celery was loaded and shipped up north and east. The train yard felt abandoned and was quiet. He figured there were hoboes camping out in some of the boxcars, but Gertie convinced Gus there were not because Mr. Culpepper made sure of it.

"I've been saving and saving, Gus. I'm going to be a real beauty operator. I found a little shop in town that will let me rent a chair so I can build up clients. Mr. Culpepper set it up for me."

"That's swell, Gertie. He's good to you, isn't he?" Gertie nodded.

"He is. I know he seems mean and all that, but really, he's just a lonely widower. He treats me better than my own daddy did for the most part."

Gus wanted to believe Gertie and, for the most part, felt she was being truthful about the relationship.

"Where's Beth?"

"She ran off with the circus," Gertie said, trying not to laugh.

"Circus?" Gus said, confounded.

"Yes, a trapeze artist, a real heartbreaker. He fell and broke his leg in the middle of the season. He had just had his cast removed and was headed to meet up with the circus to finish out the season before they return to Sarasota for the winter. He asked Beth to go with him, and she did. She ran off with the circus," Gertie's voice trailed off as Gus laughed at the story.

"I guess Mr. Culpepper was right. That was pretty crazy," mused Gus.

After a moment, Gus knew he had to be direct.

"Gertie." Instantly, Gus could read the anxiety in her eyes at the change of his tone. "It's Henryetta and Flo. Something bad has happened. They've run away and I'm looking for them."

Gertie's eyes widened at this. Her first thought was their photos.

"Gertie, I think Sy McGhee raped Henryetta."

Gus's words stung, but relief flooded her mind. This was not what she expected to hear.

"The best Thom and I can figure, Flo must have caught Sy in the act and hit him over the head with a rolling pin. She almost killed him, and I'm betting she thinks she left him for dead. Sy's not talking. He has amnesia."

Gertie gasped and covered her open mouth with the back of her hand. Then she wondered what business Gus had in all of it.

"I thought they might have come to find you and Beth. Gertie, can you think of any place they might have gone?"

"Other than Kentucky? New York, maybe?" Gertie paused and thought. Then she knew.

"Gus, the Keys, to find you. Henryetta carried around the post-card that you sent her like a preacher carries his Bible. Gus, did you have something going with her?"

"I didn't make her any promises, if that's what you mean."

"Come on, Gus! You know what I mean. Were you two sweet on each other?"

Gus averted his eyes from Gertie, and his face flushed.

"Yep. You're sweet on her. Why else would you be chasing after her? Go to the Keys, Gus. I'll bet you five dollars that's where they've gone."

"But there's nothing there for her. I don't know how she'll make it," Gus said.

"I don't think you need to worry about Henryetta and Flo. Those ladies are resourceful."

"Agreed," Gus said as he sighed, thinking of the many hours of travel he had ahead of him. Then he slowly stood up from the edge of the train platform.

"Well, then. I'm heading to Key West. Thank you, Gertie. I wish you well."

"If you wait a day, there's a truck to Miami in the afternoon. I bet you could hitch a ride if you help unload crates. I can talk to the boss, if you like. I know him personally, after all."

Gus wasn't happy about the prospect of wasting time waiting, but not having to hop into a boxcar and risk the wrath of the train yard bulls outweighed the day's wait.

* * *

"Gus, before you go, I have something for you," revealed Gertie the next morning.

In her hand she held three bacon and egg sandwiches wrapped in wax paper. On top of them was a piece of folded stationery.

"Lunch and a letter," Gus announced, taking them gently from Gertie's hand.

"Yes. The letter is from Henryetta. She said that if I ever ran into you, to give it to you."

"Why did you wait so long, Gertie?" Gus asked.

"Because I wanted to make sure you were worthy of it. I like you and all, Gus, but Henryetta is no ordinary woman. She's been through a lot and she doesn't need her heart broken further."

"I agree, Gertie. I would never do that. I just want to find her and Flo and the children. I want to make sure they are safe. That's all. I appreciate what you've done for me. I'll write you when I've found them. Best of luck to you Gertie," Gus said, extending his free hand to shake Gertie's.

CHAPTER THIRTY-THREE

*T*he endless scrub that carpeted the interior of Florida made the drive monotonous. The only excitement was the occasional gator sunning itself at the side of the road. Gus and the driver, also a Chicago native, shared lively conversation about baseball and local politics. It turned out they had a common acquaintance and then the story telling ensued. At a filling station, Gus shared one of the bacon and egg sandwiches Gertie had packed for him and bought the driver a soda. By the end of the drive, they had exchanged addresses back home in Chicago and agreed that when the Depression was over they would reconnect up north. Certainly, the ride was better than a musty, damp boxcar. The Florida sun was often too strong to sit atop a car for very long for fear of sunburn, so riding below with a host of foul smelling hoboes and pesky mosquitoes was the only other option.

In Miami, Gus took advantage of the one-day pass for migrants and headed to a local shelter for a shower, a bed and a meal. The air was humid, despite the ceiling fans. Once the weary travelers had settled into their bunks and the room quieted, Gus pulled out Henryetta's letter.

> Dear Lead Goose,
>
> I hope that if you are reading this letter, it finds you in good health and fortune. Life, like time, has marched on in Brownsville as I imagine it has for you on your travels. Mama's passing was

a relief, but it all but broke us. Still, we have been making do. Gertie and another girl named Beth have been staying here some months now, but I imagine if you are reading this you have crossed paths with our Gertie, another traveling soul.

Marjorie, June Bug, and Florence are also still here with me, and I am grateful. Florence received word from Walter's parents that he is saving enough money to come home. We have all been blessed with little odd jobs here and there— Thom with the peddler man, Flo and Beth teaching, Gertie doing hair, and me with photography.

So, Gus, I am really writing to tell you that I have been thinking about you. Sometimes I look up at the moon and wonder if you are seeing it as I am. There are so many things I want to say to you, more than would ever fit in this letter. I do hope that our paths will cross again, that you will find your way back to Brownsville so that I can express them to you in person.

For now, I send you my sincerest thanks. Just know that I consider you a miracle that I didn't even have to pray for. I do not know if I could have made it through that day with Mama had you not been there. Until we meet again.

Yours,
Henryetta

Gus lay back on his cot resting the letter above his heart. He thought back to the night he and Henryetta danced under the oak tree in her side yard. Pulling out her photograph from his wallet, he caressed her hair and prayed he would find her.

The next morning, Gus boarded a train headed for Key West, this time using money to pay for a passenger seat. When Gus arrived in Key West, he headed straight for the marina where he knew he would find Patricio unloading his daily catch as he did every day at this time. Patricio caught a peripheral glance of Gus and kept working, but then it registered that he had just seen Gus. He looked back up to see Gus coming toward him.

Between them with her back to Gus stood Henryetta with her camera. Gus smiled at the sight of her in men's cutoff pants, barefooted, and her long tanned arms that gracefully held her camera aimed at Patricio and some young boys who were carrying fish from the boat to the dock. Patricio happily called out to Gus. At the sound of his name, Henryetta turned around, but she only saw worn men's shoes and tweed pants up to the knees due to the blinding sun. She shaded her eyes with her hand, not believing the feet belonged to the man. But it was him! Gus was not fifteen feet from her.

Gus was elated to find her, yet he stood perfectly still, just smiling at her. He thanked God she was safe and appeared healthy. Henryetta drank in all of Gus. For months she had dreamt of this moment and now here he was with that same genuine smile, the same one since the moment she met him in front of the lawyer's office. Henryetta's heart revved up and she just knew it was going to explode out of her chest. No one had ever had this power over her. She felt quite sure it was beating so loudly Gus and all the other fisherman could hear it. Her impulse was to rush him and fall into his arms, but they were not on those terms. What if he had just come back to the Keys with no intentions of finding her here?

For a brief moment, they just stood looking at each other, saying nothing. Their obvious attraction mesmerized everyone. Just as they were frozen in this moment, so were all others around them. All stopped what they were doing to see what would happen next.

"Miss Dixon, you're a long way from home."

She smiled at Gus's greeting and began to inch toward him only to be bulldozed to the right by Patricio, who did everything in a big, dramatic manner, including greeting Gus with waving arms and happy greetings.

"Gus! You return! I tell this to Henryetta. You have a heart of fisherman, I say to her. And now, here you are!" Almost a head taller than Patricio, Gus embraced him heartily, slapping him on the back.

"Just as I remembered, you old sea dog," Gus greeted. Patricio reeked of fish, onions, and cigars, smells that when Gus first met Patricio were repugnant. Now they were familiar and comforting. Patricio let go of Gus and gestured to Henryetta who was now flanked by Phillip and Frank. Even Ernest who had just returned from a morning fishing trip walked up to shake hands with the man who borrowed his typewriter from time to time.

"Look, Gus! It is her. It is *your* Henryetta!"

Back and forth went Patricio's eyes from Gus to Henryetta, waiting for Gus to say something. Both of them had gone red from the neck up at Patricio's comment. Then something curious happened. Gus and Henryetta both awkwardly began to fumble in their pants pockets, and simultaneously began to say, "I got your . . ."

Both of them stopped and smiled again when they realized that in Henryetta's hand was a well-worn postcard from the Keys and in Gus's hand was the letter still crisp from having received it only a few days earlier from Gertie. Again they blushed, but did not look away from each other.

"Gus, it is good to see you," Henryetta offered, attempting to sound friendly and casual. Gus's smile grew stronger. Did she detect he felt equally happy to see her?

"How are you, Henryetta?" Gus too, tried to sound normal. He knew she had been through so much trauma, but he didn't want her to think he was taking pity on her. He would get the real story another time.

"Oh fine, Gus. The boys and I have been having a grand time. It turns out, I am pretty good at fishing. Aren't I Patricio?" Henryetta said gesturing back to him.

"The best woman fisherman in Key West," Patricio wholeheartedly agreed.

"You mean, the only woman fisherman in Key West," Henryetta corrected. Brief laughter broke out among the group.

"And Flo and the children? How are they?" Gus prodded naturally assuming they would be together.

"I hope fine. They aren't with me," Henryetta revealed, surprising Gus.

"So you traveled all the way down here by yourself? How long have you been here?"

"Not long actually. I came by train, but I wasn't brave enough to ride the rails like you and Gertie."

"Well, I'm glad you didn't. You were much safer that way. I see you have your camera. Did you take any photos on your way down?"

"Dozens. I am in need of a dark room, but I was told I will have to go to Miami for that."

"Hmm. Well, sounds like an adventure to me."

Gus turned to Phillip and Frank and held out his hand in greeting.

"Gus is the name. Nice to meet you."

Both boys firmly shook Gus's hand.

"Well, what are you standing around for? Let's get back to work! You too, Gus!" commanded Patricio in his thick Cuban accent.

Gus smiled at Henryetta, wanting nothing more than to be alone with her. Though she smiled, Gus could see the pain in her eyes, just simmering below the surface.

"See you later then?" Gus asked Henryetta before walking onto Patricio's boat.

"I'd like that. Perhaps some supper? I could tell the boarding house that you are coming. I don't think they would mind," offered Henryetta, hoping Gus would say yes.

"If it is no trouble, I would be delighted. What time is supper?"

"Six o'clock sharp. Just don't come smelling like fish," Henryetta joked.

"I'll be there."

CHAPTER THIRTY-FOUR

S upper was filled with small talk as were the next several days fishing out on Patricio's boat. When either one of them was about to bring up what happened in Brownsville, one of the boys would interrupt them or Henryetta would think of something funny someone said or did. Gus assuredly wasn't going to pressure her, but it worried him that she wouldn't talk about what happened to her. The last thing he wanted to do was reveal he knew everything, including the fact that Sy was still alive. Gus didn't want to betray Henryetta's trust.

Then a moment came, at sunset, one evening. The western sky was painted tangerine and flamingo pink while the sun slowly made its exit behind billowy, gray cloud silhouettes. Gus and Henryetta walked down a lone dock toward the sea. Located on the north side of the key, they had spotted it from the water several days earlier while out fishing. Determined to find it on land, after supper, they walked the whole of Key West until they found the street that led straight to the dock.

"We found it!" Henryetta cheered taking in the wide expanse of golden capped waves.

"Isn't it marvelous, Gus?" she exclaimed.

"I'll say. I bet you wish you had your camera, now."

"True, but who could ever capture all this?" she questioned dramatically, throwing out her arms and whirling around in a large circle. The more Gus was around Henryetta, the more he thought he was beginning to know her. She was the embodiment of an analogy one of his psychology professors had made. He said people were like onions. To get to the heart of a person, you had to peel away the layers. When Gus first met Henryetta, despite the fact she was confronting enormous tragedy, Gus very much liked her pensive, quiet, introspective personality. He understood she was silenced by grief to a certain extent, but suspected she was like him, a person who needed alone time-him to think and write and her to think and create. They were both artists of sorts. Here, in the Keys, Henryetta acted and sounded different. He found her gregarious, energetic, enthusiastic, easy to laugh, and even a prankster at times. Gus wondered if this was an act to hide the deep rooted pain or this was how she was before Gus met her on the fated day Henryetta's mother tried to take her own life.

Somewhere he read that avoidance was a coping mechanism, but knew that repressing those emotions was not healthy. Some way or another the fury and the pain would come out. He just hoped it would be in a healthy way rather than in a self-destructive one. He thought about Sy McGhee and Henryetta's mother. They were both prime examples of repressed emotions gone bad, really bad.

"Let's swim, Gus!" Henryetta called out, galloping toward the end of the dock. Gus jogged to catch up with her.

"We're not dressed for swimming," Gus reminded Henryetta as she unlaced her shoes and took them and her ankle socks off.

Winded, Gus bent over at the waist, looking through the slats at the sea water lapping against the barnacle crusted posts. Turning away from Gus, Henryetta began to unbutton her blouse. She realized this was the same blouse she was wearing the afternoon she posed for the camera. She marveled how clothes could remind you of your past.

"Gus, where is your sense of adventure?" Henryetta said, pulling off her blouse revealing her lace trimmed, cream-colored, silk camisole. Gus rose to see Henryetta's shoulders now tan from the days she had spent on Patricio's boat. Henryetta's A-line skirt parachuted down her legs to land with a poof of wind.

"Henryetta, this is not appropriate. What if someone were to see us?" Gus reprimanded, reaching for her forearm, hoping to make her pause and think. She turned to face Gus and smiled coyly at him.

"And just who would that be, Gus? Just look around. There is nobody. Just you and me and this big old ocean calling our names. Just begging for us to jump in. Now, please let go of me."

True. He looked all around. There was no one. No houses, no boats. Nothing, just the two of them, the water and the painted sky. Before Gus had finished looking back at the palm dotted coast line, Henryetta, clad only in her undergarments, had taken a running start for the end of the dock. By the time he saw her, only the tips of her fingers could be seen disappearing below the wooden dock. Then he heard her splash.

"Come on, Gus!" she called from below the dock. "The water feels great!"

He watched her dive back into the water and resurface smiling. Down below was the girl from Thom's photo. Henryetta looked deeply content for the first time since he met her. In that moment, Gus knew he wanted this woman to be his wife. Helpless, Gus couldn't fight his yearning for Henryetta and losing control frightened him.

"Come on, you slow poke!" Henryetta called out again. He gave in and he shyly disrobed with his back to her on the dock above. Henryetta tried not to watch, but Gus's body was more toned and muscular than she had expected. She imagined what it would feel like touching his back, tracing her fingers over his chest. Down to only his skivvies, Gus turned and beat his hands on his chest calling out like Tarzan causing Henryetta to giggle and splash the surface of the water in response. Gus then backed up and ran along the dock aiming to jump right beside her, hoping to cause a Titanic splash. They swam, splashing one another, and tried dunking each other until they became exhausted.

The tip of the sun was all that remained in the now purple and green stained sky. The full moon had risen in the east. Gus and Henryetta sat side by side with their feet dangling over the edge of the dock. They both were very aware that their knees and shoulders were touching. The rest of their bodies were cold and covered in goose flesh, but where their flesh met, heat blazed.

"Gus, I have something I need to tell you," Henryetta said just above a whisper. Gus heaved a sigh and looked at her without saying anything.

"Gus, something bad happened in Brownsville. Something really bad."

Gus reached over and took Henryetta's hand and held it between both of his. They looked at one another very seriously without speaking. As Henryetta looked deeply into Gus's eyes, she sensed Gus already knew what she was about to recall.

"Tell me," was all Gus said.

"It was awful, Gus. He . . . Sy was awful." Tears began to stream down her face.

"Well, Sy . . . he always wanted me, you know, romantically, but I rejected him. At first he just ignored me, then he started being rude. I never thought he would turn on me like he did because he spent a lot of time at our house growing up. He was like a brother, so when he got nasty, I told him to leave me be. After a while, he got to drinking real bad—all hours of the day, and Sy McGhee is a mean drunk."

Gus nodded in understanding.

"Sy walked in the kitchen that afternoon, just drunk enough to do and say the kinds of things a man never should. He was taunting me and calling me ugly names, and threatening me if I didn't give him sex. I just ignored him and kept on making biscuits like he wasn't even there. I knew Sy hated to be ignored, and most times he just would leave if he didn't get the attention he was seeking, but not that time.

"Sy grabbed me from behind. I remember fighting him off. I even bit his shoulder which caused him to let go of me, but he caught me again and slapped me hard across the face and bloodied my nose. I was stunned just enough for him to wrestle me to the kitchen table where he forced me on my back. I remember his breath right in my face. He stank of cigarettes and moonshine so I closed my eyes and turned my head away from him. He was bearing down on me with all his weight while his hand went up under my skirt and tore at my panties." Henryetta paused and closed her eyes. She shook her head and held up her hand. She couldn't speak the rest, but after a moment of reliving the worst of it, Henryetta continued.

"And then Flo came in. She saved me, Gus." Tears turned into a sob. Gus wrapped his arm around her shoulder allowing Henryetta lay her head against his chest and just cry. After a few moments, she paused and looked up at Gus.

"Gus, I probably shouldn't tell you this, but I think Flo may have killed Sy. I was in shock and don't really remember it all very clearly. I got some money, Thom's Colt pistol that belonged to my daddy, and my camera. It's strange, I wasn't thinking about anything, but getting my camera for the trip. Flo was rushing about and telling me to hurry up and what to bring. I remember seeing Sy lying on the kitchen floor. It crossed my mind to shoot him myself, but I just didn't have the energy, you know? I felt like a dish rag. Shock maybe? Then I remember that I just stepped over him like he was a toy that one of the children left on the kitchen floor, and walked out the back door. It seems like a dream now, but I know it was real. I do remember sitting on the train feeling like I had been split in two."

Again, Henryetta paused looking at the last slivers of light on the horizon. Somewhere in the distance she heard the canon blast signaling the sun had officially retired for day. When Henryetta turned to look at Gus's reaction, he gently wiped her tears from her sun kissed cheeks. She wished Gus could just take the pain from her. She half smiled at him knowing that could never happen, but she was just grateful he was there with her listening.

"You know something, Gus? I don't even know your last name. After everything we've been through, and I have never thought to ask you your last name."

Gus smiled at the timing of this peculiar remark.

"Truly. What is it?" she inquired.

Gus smiled at her and gestured toward the full moon.

"Moon. My last name is Moon."

Henryetta smiled, but Gus detected disbelief in her eyes when he told her, but she didn't challenge it. He was, after all, a drifter. Henryetta just wondered if maybe he had taken on an alias because he didn't want to be found. It occurred to Henryetta, she really knew very little about Gus's life, who he was before he left to ride the rails. It's not that she wasn't interested. Gus seemed to appear just when she needed someone the most to support her and listen. She smiled at her silly notion that perhaps he was her guardian angel, but then the slow dance came back to her, reminding her he was the closest thing to a love interest she had ever had.

"Gus, do you think any man will ever want me now that I am damaged goods? Gertie used to talk about that a lot after what happened to her in a jungle outside of Atlanta."

"I would say the fellow who wins your heart someday will be the lucky one."

"I was saving myself, and now I don't have that gift to give to my future husband. Gus? Have you ever been with a woman? I mean all the way?"

"No. I can't say that I have, Henryetta. I am waiting for the right one. Don't get me wrong, I've had opportunities, but no, Henryetta."

She blushed.

"I have to tell myself that someday another person will show me the whole other side of what it means to be intimate. I wish I could forget it all ever happened. You know what I worry about, Gus?"

"What's that?"

"I worry that every time I am with my husband, you know, in our marriage bed, that Sy McGhee's face will pop in my mind and ruin it for both of us. I just don't know how I am ever going to forget about what happened."

"Henryetta, it will fade with time, but whoever you marry, you have to tell him, so he can help you work through it. That is what marriage is about, and when the time comes if you love and desire one another, Sy McGhee will be the furthest person from your mind."

"Yes, but when do I tell him? I'm afraid if I told him before we married, he'd call it off. You know, some men are funny like that. They want virgins, not a girl whose flower is forever spoiled."

"Listen to me, Henry. Marriage is much bigger than the marriage bed. Any man who choses you, will go to the ends of the earth for you."

"You really think so, Gus?"

"There's no one like you, Henryetta Dixon," Gus said and then, feeling bold, whispered in her ear, "I know that I would, if I were him."

CHAPTER THIRTY-FIVE

*T*hom roused from a hazy afternoon nap to the sound of light footsteps coming up the front porch stairs. Out on the glider sofa, Thom had dozed off reading a two-week-old newspaper from Memphis. Thom's brain lingered between sleep and alertness. As he came to, before him stood an unshaven scrawny scarecrow of a man. Seeing Thom had awakened, the stranger removed his crumpled felt hat and grasped it firmly in both hands as if that were all he had to hold on to. The bedraggled man's clothes were worn and stained by dirt of a different color from that of Tennessee soil. Small hints of clean pink thread peeked in and out of the patch over the left knee of the man's worn, pin-striped pants. The stranger's face and hands echoed his tired and weathered clothes.

Thom's first impulse was to expel this hobo from his property. Thom was used to seeing men down on their luck. As much as Thom hated to admit it to himself, he had hardened to the sight of them. He rationalized it quite simply. There were more of them than him. If Thom stopped to empathize with every poor man he met, he would surely dry up and disappear himself. He recalled the pastor's words, "The poor will always be with us." Thom figured it was hard enough to keep food in his own belly, let alone worry about another man or another or another. If Thom were to survive, he would have to live by his own wits. Every other man had to do the same. He couldn't do it for them. Sensing Thom's distaste, the stranger spoke first.

"I'm looking for my wife, Florence Bell. My name's Walter. I heard it from the grocer that she was living here."

Surprised, Thom's eyebrows raised at the reappearance of Flo's Walter. Though Thom never said anything to Flo, he never believed this man in front of him would ever come back for her, but this wasn't the first time Thom had been a poor judge of character.

"You're too late, Walter. She and the children are gone," Thom said matter-of-factly, watching disappointment dawn in Walter's eyes.

"I don't reckon you know where they went off to?" Walter asked, still hopeful.

"Can't say that I do," Thom answered. "They've been gone for a little over three weeks now. You see, Walter, Flo got herself into some trouble."

"What sort of trouble?"

"Rape . . . murder," Thom said without flinching.

Thom wanted to watch Walter squirm with worry. No real man just up and left his family behind in a strange place, especially a family like theirs. Thom had considered that if Walter never came back, he might be inclined to court Flo in the future. After all, Thom thought Flo had a good head on her shoulders, was born to mother, and was more than easy on the eyes.

Consumed by guilt, Walter slumped over, crumpling the edge of his hat.

"The children?" Walter asked, looking up into Thom's face, hoping for good news.

"Gone with her and my sister. Like I said before, I don't know where they are. They bought four round-trip tickets for Nashville but never came back. That is all I know."

"The police out looking for them?" Walter wondered.

"No. None of us reported what happened because the fact is, we really don't know who did what, and the man who supposedly raped my sister has amnesia. One of them—Flo or Henryetta—took a rolling pin to his head and liked to kill him. He says he can't remember, but I don't know if that's the whole truth or not."

"I see," said Walter. "Can I ask one more thing of you before I am on my way? Did Flo ever say anything about me?"

Again, Thom felt the inclination to lie to Walter. He wanted to tell him that Flo had disowned him for abandoning her and the children, but Thom could see the near hopeless man had already tortured himself enough. Plus, Thom knew that was all Florence had ever wished for—Walter's return. Flo was one of the lucky ones. The papers and radios reported hundreds of thousands of wives and children abandoned and destitute.

But looking into Walter's eyes, Thom found only longsuffering.

"Flo loved you. She always believed you would come back for her and the children," Thom revealed.

Walter smiled, but it was only a half grin. He wondered if Thom was being honest or telling him exactly what he wanted to hear so he'd let him get back to napping.

"Thank you kindly." Walter tipped his head, put his hat back on, and turned to walk down the front porch steps. Thom figured that would be the last he would see of Walter Bell. Thom silently wished the man well, and hoped he would be reunited with Florence and the children. Thom understood the emptiness of losing one's family. There were moments Thom would have given his right foot or any another appendage just to eat a family dinner with his parents and sister. But that could never be again. At least Walter and Flo might have a chance at it if he ever found her. Thom supposed it was all right to go a little soft. He could hear Henryetta chastising him if he didn't.

Walter roamed the court square until he found the police station. As he entered, a deputy stood up from behind a desk and came over to the front counter.

"What can I do for you?" the deputy asked.

"I want to report a missing person, my wife, Florence Bell," Walter said.

Two hours later, Thom hadn't moved from the glider other than to refill his tea glass and turn up the radio so he could hear it out on the porch. Thom's eyes were closed as he reclined the length of the glider. He smiled, thinking about how his mama would have corrected him for his posture. She would have made him sit up properly. Thom loved the freedom to lie in whatever manner he felt like, but then a pang of longing for her crept in. The sweet melody that came from the radio only exacerbated her absence. What he would have given for her to come out on the porch, pick up his newspaper, and swat him for reclining in the glider. He could hear her, "On the front porch of all places!"

Eyes closed and deep in memories, Thom was caught off guard by the sudden sound of heavy boots that marched up the wooden front porch steps. He sat up to see Deputy Stanley standing tall with a straight expression Thom couldn't quite read. The idea that Walter might go to the police had never really crossed Thom's mind. He had underestimated the man. Thom just pictured Walter moving along, heading for Kentucky. Thom knew this could mean trouble for all of them. Serious trouble.

Deputy Stanley had the reputation for being a straight arrow when other officers tended to look the other way if the mayor's son got into a little trouble or one of their friends partook of a little southern comfort every now and again. Thom had several run-ins with Deputy Stanley out at the drinking shack, none of them pleasant.

No, Deputy Stanley followed the law to the tee and didn't care who it embarrassed. The law was the law and he was there to enforce it. He was praised by some who felt the same way, but for those in high places who did less than high things, Deputy Stanley was seen as a nuisance. It was rumored the KKK paid Deputy Stanley a visit one night just because he "needed a little reminding of who was really the law in Brownsville." If it happened, Deputy Stanley never spoke of it to anyone and he didn't change his tactics.

"Hello Jr.," Deputy Stanley greeted, purposely trying to irritate Thom.

Everyone who knew Thom, knew he loathed the nickname Jr. Deputy Stanley didn't really dislike Thom, but he had witnessed Thom at his worst—inebriated almost to the point of passing out, or deep in a hand of cards, and even once, groping a "bad girl" out behind the drinking shack. He wondered what had changed Thom. At one time, Thom had been a well-respected student and young man. He never figured Thom for a drunk, but he seriously had lost his way.

"This must be visiting day at the Dixon's. I haven't had this much company in months!" Thom exclaimed, not offering his hand to the deputy, a clear snub.

"Thom, I won't mince words. A man by the name of Walter Bell came by the station and reported his wife, their children, and your sister missing for three weeks. He said he learned this from you. Is that right?"

"About," Thom said coolly.

"So tell me about the rape and attempted murder," the officer said.

"I told Walter there's nothing to tell. Nobody really knows *exactly* what happened anyway. The girls and the children were long gone by the time I got home."

"Did you see the perpetrator, Thom?" asked the deputy as he pulled out a notepad.

"Supposedly."

"Well? Who was it?"

Thom paused for a moment because he knew this was going to open a big can of scandal. It was hard for him to say Sy's name out loud, but there were too many witnesses that had been at the scene of the crime.

"Thom, not reporting this is serious. There can be real repercussions for you and anyone else that may have concealed evidence in this crime. I advise you to cooperate fully to avoid any charges yourself. The courts might view you as an accessory, if you don't."

Thom never took his eyes from the deputy. He was in a corner now.

"It was Sy McGhee. I found him, knocked out cold, lying on our kitchen floor. His pants and underwear were down around his ankles. The back of his head had a huge goose-egg from where he had been hit. I suspect it was by way of a rolling pin. There were unfinished biscuits on the counter, and Sy had flour in his hair. At first, I thought he was dead, but when I leaned in, real close-like, he was breathing and had a steady heartbeat. I called Doc Castellaw and Sy's daddy. Doc Castellaw took care of him. When I found out he was going to be fine with the exception of slight amnesia, I just let it go. You know how people talk in this town. I figured when the ladies came back, we'd sort it all out privately. How was I to know they weren't coming back?"

"Didn't you find it strange that they just disappeared after all this happened?" reprimanded the deputy. "Most women would have called the police themselves." Deputy Stanley pushed.

"I don't know, Deputy. Maybe they thought they killed Sy? Maybe they were embarrassed? Who knows? They are women. Who understands why women do anything?" Thom said as he shrugged his shoulders, feigning ignorance to protect his sister.

"So who do you suspect was raped?" Thom remained silent then resigned himself to giving the deputy what he needed.

"There is something I need to give you, Deputy. Flo, Mrs. Bell, left a note. I found it a week after they went missing. Our car was gone out of the garage. I figured they'd run off in it, but then I walked down to the train depot to meet them after I heard they were due back from Nashville. When I got there, I found our car parked at the train depot, and inside it was a note from Mrs. Bell. Give me a minute, and I'll get if for you. It's in the secretary." Thom returned to the porch and handed over the note. Sy's fate was surely sealed now.

"Do you know where I can find Sy McGhee right now?"

"Try the court square or out in front of the barber shop. He tends to hang with the men down on that corner."

"Just for your information, Thom, I will be speaking to the other witnesses. If I need more evidence, I will be in touch. Do you have any questions?"

"No, sir."

"If you have any contact with your sister or Mrs. Bell, please notify me immediately. It will be important for us to bring them into the station for questioning. I'll call around and see if we can't get some other police departments on the lookout for them."

"Yes, sir. I will do that." Thom nodded to the officer and then watched as his police car backed down the driveway. In this moment, Thom's heart ached for his mother. She would have advised him what to do. He tried to imagine her voice and recall her reassuring touch, but there was nothing and it only left a deep ache in his chest.

Flickers of camera flashes, supple nudes, his mother's grave, and seeing Sy laying unconscious on his kitchen floor pushed themselves to his sober mind. As much as he tried, Thom couldn't control his thoughts. Cruel memories he had routinely swallowed back down with a swig of whiskey or moonshine battled to be dealt with, but Thom couldn't stand the deep, fatigued aching in his bones. He just wanted to pass out and not have to think anymore.

Thom headed up the stairs toward his dresser that held bootlegged corn whiskey. As he passed his parents' bedroom door, the longing for his mother overtook his need for oblivion. As Thom opened the door, traces of his mother's perfume took him back to the safety of childhood. Thom deeply inhaled hoping somehow to connect with his mother, but then his father's portrait grabbed his attention, robbing him of any relief. Thom stood there just looking at this much younger version of his father. Thom could see himself and Henryetta in his father's features.

"Why did you do this to us?" he whispered, the urge to sob mounting in his throat.

Memories of the first night he discovered his father's secret flooded his brain.

Thom and Sy had been in the bottoms frog-gigging. It was almost midnight when they reached the court square. Thom figured his father would still be at the opera house partying with the company that had come in to do a big production. He told Sy that he would catch a ride with his daddy. Upon entering the opera house, Thom found it deserted, at least he thought so, until he heard singular, female laughter coming from a prop closet. Then his father spoke. Thom was ready to open the door wide, but through the tiniest sliver of opening bare breasts flashed. Thom froze. His heart raced in panic and fear. He instantly suspected to see his father engaged in sex with one of the actresses. Slowly, Thom backed up behind a stage curtain and continued to watch his father who was not near the actress but behind his camera gently directing the actress to move into different poses. At times, his father would approach the actress to move a prop to reveal a nipple, or move a shoulder back to create a wanton pose that would evoke arousal. Thom couldn't stand to watch another second so silently he crept out of the opera house. Once outside, the adrenaline coursed through his body urging him to sprint all the way home.

For the next few days, Thom avoided his father altogether, fearing he would lose control of his anger and expose his father to his mother and sister, but he didn't want to break up their family. He knew this would devastate his mother. Thom couldn't do that. This was one secret he would keep.

Later, when the opera house burned, Thom Jr. figured that would end his father's pastime, but he was mistaken. Three days before his father shot himself, Thom caught his father still at it. It was two in the morning. Sy had dropped him off at the end of their drive way not to wake the Dixons with the rumbling of his engine. Thom, fairly drunk, haphazardly sauntered toward the back door as he fumbled for his house key. A light beamed out into the yard from the open cellar doors. Puzzled, Thom wandered down into the cellar to see one of his prettiest classmates, nude, lying on her side on a velvet covered platform. Filled with fury, Thom stepped into his father's cellar studio. His father was peering through the camera lens when Matilde suddenly sat up, covered her lady parts, and cried out Thom's name.

Thom shook his head again, allowing himself to feel the same deep betrayal from that night.

Why did you do this to us? A deluge of unbridled tears flowed down Thom's cheeks, now flushed with growing anger. The urge to throw something, anything, compelled him to scan the room for his mother's hairbrush or any trinket, but nothing remained. Henryetta had pawned everything.

"Damn it!" Thom cried out in frustration as he charged the portrait and yanked it violently from the wall. Dust particles flew from the frame and tumbled and danced in the rush of air as Thom bashed the portrait's glass cover against the bedpost.

"You bastard!" Smash! More shards littered the bedspread and floor.

"You whore . . ." *Whack!* "Chasing . . ." *Smash!* "Bastard!" His anger now released, Thom looked down at the broken frame and bent portrait. Thom somehow thought his parents' expressions might have changed after his assault on them. He hoped his father felt pain, and he yearned to see gratefulness in his mother's expression. Thom hoped his mother felt vindication for what his father had done to her, but there they sat upon a couch with the same smiling, youthful expressions of hope. He realized he could do nothing and allowed the portrait to fall to the floor.

Closing their bedroom door behind him, Thom went to his dresser. From it he took out the Mason jar, screwed off the lid, and guzzled half of the corn whiskey without taking a breath. Thom sat on his bed waiting for numbness to comfort him. It couldn't come fast enough, so Thom guzzled again, this time taking in another fourth of the jar. He sat the Mason jar on his bedside table and laid back on his pillows. Soon the ache was fading and that old familiar buzz calmed his raw emotions. Slowly his thoughts turned away from his father and back to this mess with Henryetta and Sy. Flo's note could be enough to convict Sy as Henryetta's attacker, but not without testimony to back it up. And what was he going to do about Sy? This was unforgivable. He hadn't really spoken to Sy since that night. Thom had found ways to avoid him, mostly working out of town with the peddler man.

Then Thom's thoughts returned to Walter. He had underestimated the man's grit because of his raggedy appearance. Thom bet this was only the beginning.

CHAPTER THIRTY-SIX

*I*t took Walter around a week to traverse the rail roads, highways, and dirt roads until he reached his parents' homestead that sat nestled at the base of a short valley between the mountains. As he traveled, he dreamt of holding Florence and the children in his arms. That longing is what drove him home, despite his hunger, his aching body, and the filthy state he was in.

When Walter reached the wooden fence that surrounded his parents' property, he paused just at the end of the gravel lane to watch Marjorie pushing Junny on the tire swing that had been attached to the old maple tree since he was a boy. *My, how they have grown.* They almost looked like completely different children. Junny had lost his baby pudge and looked tall for a four-year-old. Marjorie's long straight hair had turned from a platinum blonde to silvery ash color. Her hair had grown out from the short bob she had when Walter last saw her. Marjorie looked thick like most kids her age right before they shoot up in puberty.

Back and forth, Marjorie pushed Junny as he cried out in glee. Then, Marjory looked up to see Walter. She halted the swing, helped Junny out, and they ran into the house allowing the screen door to slam. Their behavior disappointed him. He expected them to run to him and happily fall into his arms. A few moments later, Florence came out, wiping her hands on her apron. She stood looking at the solitary stranger just standing down at the end of the lane.

Walter waved, but his family just looked at him in strange curiosity. Could it be they didn't recognize him, he wondered. He started up the lane which sparked Florence to move. The children started to follow her, but she motioned for them to get back up on the porch. As Florence approached, she realized that the scruffy hobo was her Walter. He looked so old and thin as if he were wasting away.

"Walter?" Florence cried out to him. "Walter? Is that you?" her pitch rising in excitement. Walter continued to walk as fast as he could, but his lack of energy kept his pace sluggish. He fought it to move faster, but Florence who had begun to run, reached him quickly. She jerked to a halt and stood just looking at what was left of her husband. Clearly, Walter was not healthy.

"Walter," Florence whispered, causing Walter to drop to his knees in front of her. He looked up at Florence with tears in his eyes and begged her forgiveness. Florence just gazed upon her pitiful husband. Walter dropped his head as if he were bowing to royalty. Gently, Florence reached down and lifted Walter's chin up.

"There's nothing to forgive, Walter," Flo said just above a whisper.

Walter threw his arms around her legs and sobbed into Flo's body. Flo caressed Walter's matted, oily hair the best she could until he was spent. She didn't care that he was all but dust in the ground. Walter had come home. He had come back to her. Now, everything would be all right. She said a silent prayer of gratitude.

It took several weeks for Florence and Walter's mother to fatten him back up. His strength came back, and Walter was able to resume working alongside his family on the farm. During his recovery, Walter hadn't brought up what happened in Brownsville, nor did Flo. One Sunday afternoon though, Walter planned an afternoon of picnicking and love making in their favorite spot deep in the forest of hardwoods near a rushing creek. It would be the first time they had been intimate since he returned. They had no privacy with the children and Walter's parents in the next room, and honestly he hadn't the strength, but he was well now.

Anticipation made them walk quicker down the path to their sacred spot. They had been coming here since they first met when they were young. Florence fondly recalled the first time she and Walter had lain together on their wedding night. They were both nineteen and inexperienced in the ways of love. Walter fumbled everything and was awkward and quick. This first experience left Florence to believe that love making was not as beautiful as she had imagined, but over time, that changed. Walter began to linger in his foreplay, enticing Florence, driving her closer and closer to climax, and making her beg for him to enter her. Florence flushed thinking of this intimate side of herself that only Walter knew. What an incredible gift to be totally free with another human who loved the soul inside of the body.

Florence knew they were close to their special place because of the carvings on the trees. After four or five times of coming here, Walter had carved their initials into the maple tree that shaded their blanket. Later, he carved, "Will you marry me?" word by word in the trees that led up to their spot.

Seeing the first word, Florence turned back and smiled at Walter. She reached for his hand, which he squeezed in return. They continued up the trail until they reached their spot. The mossy forest floor welcomed them like an old friend with its arms open wide. Together Florence and Walter, spread out an old quilt they used just for picnicking, church socials, and the like. Florence noticed Walter was a much quieter man since his return. She didn't know if he hadn't the energy or if something bad had happened to Walter out in California or on the road. She wondered if Walter felt too ashamed.

The one thing Florence was sure of was that she had become bolder. She was always strong and confident, but being on her own without a man, Florence had discovered a strength deep inside she never knew she possessed. It was a strength she knew she could call on in times of trouble or when tragedy struck. If she survived the last year and a half, she felt sure she could survive anything. Florence felt that somehow she and Walter had almost switched roles. Before he was in charge and the family followed Walter's wishes, but now he wasn't asserting anything. Florence was in charge.

"Walter," Florence began in between bites of an egg salad sandwich. "You are so different now. Did something bad happen to you? Do you feel bad that you left us for so long?"

"Yes and no, Florence. Nothing really bad happened to me other than being half starved. No one did anything wrong to me, if that's what you mean," Walter replied.

"Do you regret leaving us in Brownsville?" Flo asked, getting right to the point.

"Sometimes, because I couldn't be there to take care of you . . . California is overrun with Oakies looking for work. California even started sending Mexicans back home by the thousands, and don't you know that most of them were born right here in the USA? They said they were making room for all the Oakies. It was still a miserable life. It was a miracle that I was able to make it back to you. I saw children from our camp die from hunger or diseases almost every day. Every time I heard a mother sob for her poor dead child, I thanked God that you were safe. When I look at it that way, I know it was a blessing for us to get stuck in Brownsville and you to find Miss Dixon."

"I'm not going to lie to you, Walter, she was good to us, but times became desperate," Florence hinted. She wanted to tell Walter what Henryetta did, what they all did, but she couldn't. She caught herself thinking about the photographs Henryetta took of her and smiled. Such beautiful photographs.

"Flo, what happened in Brownsville?" Walter finally asked. He wanted to ask her not ten minutes after he saw her and figured that Florence would tell him, but she hadn't.

At first Flo feigned ignorance, "I don't know what you mean, Walter." But she couldn't look Walter in the eye for thinking back to that night that Sy attacked Henryetta. Despite the heaviness of the wooden rolling pin, despite Flo's typical sense of morality, she marveled at how in the moment, she easily, without forethought, pummeled Sy's head. There was a deep instinctual, carnal satisfaction knocking him off of Henryetta and down to the linoleum. Flo peered down at Sy's unmoving body, posed ready to strike him again should he retaliate, but nothing. His body lie like a corpse, then the terror hit Flo. She remembered whispering to God, "Did I kill him?"

"I can't lie to you, Florence, I called Deputy Stanley down in Brownsville to let him know you were here."

Flo's mind jumped, hopped, and skipped to an image of her being locked up in a barred jail cell, her children screaming after her. Walter sensed Flo's fear and reached out to take her hand.

"It's all right, Flo. That man . . . he's alive," Walter gave her a moment to let this fact sink in.

After she took a deep, long breath and released it in relief, Walter figured he could tell her the rest. "Deputy Stanley needs you to come back to Brownsville to testify about what happened that night."

A sense of flight overcame Flo. She had been telling herself that this whole nasty business was behind her, but Walter had changed all that with one phone call. Surely, the photographs had been found by now and she and Henryetta would go to jail anyway for their own crimes.

"Funny thing is the man has amnesia. He can't remember a single thing about the night," Walter revealed.

"How convenient." Florence smirked but then realized that if Sy had amnesia, he might not remember finding Henryetta's photographs.

"Have you heard from Henryetta? The police want her to come home, too. Deputy Stanley said Thom found the note you left in the floorboard." Flo had never lied to Walter or really anyone for that matter, but she didn't want to reveal she received a letter from Henryetta the day before Walter's return. It was postmarked Key West, Florida. She immediately burned it in the trash barrel that same evening, smiling, knowing Henryetta was safe and sound.

"She didn't tell me where she was headed," which was true, but Flo rationalized not telling all of what she knew was not as sinful as telling an outright lie. All these little sins. They were starting to pile up she thought. A tarnished woman. A sinner after all. No amount of prayer or church going was going to get her out of explaining herself to Peter at the pearly gates.

"Well, if you do, you need to convince her to head home. That man that hurt her needs to be locked up and it won't happen unless y'all testify against him. You don't want him hurting anyone else do you?" Flo contemplated the risk of returning to Brownsville, of being outed. She stood to lose everything, but in her heart, Flo knew going back was the right thing to do.

CHAPTER THIRTY-SEVEN

"All aboard! Last call for Miami," the conductor called out as Gus and Henryetta boarded the train. They settled quickly into their seats, saying their secret farewells to the palm trees and hibiscus shrubs that lined the streets and dotted the gardens to the ripples of the turquoise waters just off to the west, to the noisy squawking of greedy seagulls, even to the rank smell of Patricio's fishing boat. Yes, both of them paid silent tribute to all the sights and sounds that would be treasured in their memories of Key West. They had said their farewells to Patricio and the boys the evening before, knowing they would be out fishing when the train pulled out of the station. As the train crossed over water, both Henryetta and Gus hoped they would catch a glimpse of Patricio's boat tilting back and forth in the waves, but only, wide empty waters greeted them.

Within several hours Henryetta and Gus found themselves in Miami. Henryetta couldn't hide her excitement of developing her photographs she had captured during her trip south and of her stay in Key West. It took some asking around to find a studio where she could work, but finally she happened on the Miami Herald newspaper office who agreed to let her use their darkroom. Once Henryetta was fully engrossed in her work and out of sight, Gus took full advantage of a room of typewriters to write up his field notes. By the time Henryetta emerged from the darkroom smiling, but tired, Gus had already finished his notes and returned from a walk down the street where he sipped a soda as he read a little of the day's paper.

In her hand, Henryetta held a stack of five by seven photographs. She started for Gus who was seated in an empty chair next to an empty reporter's desk, but was intercepted by a taller, middle aged man who balanced a cigar between his teeth.

"Young lady!" he called out, startling Henryetta.

"If you use my darkroom, I insist that you show me your work," the newspaper man almost badgered.

At first she was taken aback, but then just smiled. She was pleased with her work. It was some of her best, and Henryetta was proud to show it off.

"Mister...?" she inquired, handing him the stack of photographs.

"Mr. Editor to you," he teased.

Henryetta had a hard time reading his neutral facial expressions as he gingerly inspected each photo, puffing out cigar smoke each time he looked at a new one.

"What do you think, Mr. Editor?" Henryetta asked.

"Hmm," he responded and then handed the photos back to her. He just eyeballed her up and down, almost as if he were sizing her up. Then he pulled the cigar from his mouth.

"Fine photographs. You ever want a job working at the *Herald*, you come and see me," he said directly.

Henryetta's face lit up at the compliment. She had never considered working as a photojournalist.

"Thank you, sir. I just might do that," she replied, smiling and offering her hand.

Not expecting her hand, the editor awkwardly gave her hand one quick firm shake and nodded. Then he disappeared as quickly as he had appeared. Meanwhile, Gus had watched the entire exchange. He stood up once the editor had turned and left.

"Did you hear that, Gus?" she beamed, walking over to where Gus was waiting.

"Sure did. That a girl!" Gus encouraged. "If we hurry, we can catch an overnighter headed north."

Just north of the Miami station, Gus sensed Henryetta's uneasiness about hopping on a boxcar. Even though he had told her story after story about riding the rails and she had practiced hopping into parked boxcars in Key West, he could see the worry in her eyes.

"Do you remember how we are going to do this? I go first, then you come right behind me and I'll hoist you up," he tried to reassure her as the train whistle blew, signaling the train's exit. Soon the clattering of the wheels on the tracks grew louder and louder. As she looked for the train, shadowy male figures emerged out of the brush, braced as if ready to run a race. Soon the noise of the engine blasted and blared.

"Ready?" Gus yelled out. "This is it. When I say run, you run. Got it?"

Henryetta nodded.

"Now!" Gus called out, running beside the train. When he was close enough, he flung Henryetta's small suitcase into the boxcar. Had Henryetta not been so focused on keeping up with the train, she might have worried that she would never see her belongings again. In a wink, Gus grabbed hold of the ladder bar on the side of the train and hoisted himself up and into the car. He turned quickly and held out his hand to Henryetta as she ran.

"Come on, Henry! Faster! You can do this!" Gus encouraged. His outstretched hand was just centimeters from her face when another hobo appeared from the shadows of the boxcar. In sync, Gus and the hobo grabbed Henryetta under the arms and hoisted her up and in. She landed on her knees and toppled over on to her back. For a moment Henryetta lay with her eyes shut, her chest heaving up and down, trying to recover. When she finally opened them, Gus and the hobo stood above her, just smiling. In that moment, she became very self-conscious of how she must look lying on the ground. As she sat up quickly, Gus extended his hand to pull her up.

"You did it. You're officially a hobo," Gus congratulated.

The hobo clapped, exposing his gummy smile. Henryetta smiled back and nodded.

"Can't say I would want to do that all the time, but this is quite the adventure, isn't it?" Henryetta said.

Then she noticed the sun setting in the distance over the Florida scrub.

"Want to see something?" Gus asked, taking her hand and leading her toward the door.

"What are we doing, Gus?" she hesitated.

"Are you scared of heights?" Gus asked.

Henryetta shook her head no, but she knew where this was going.

"Trust me, Henryetta. You will never forget this," he convinced, pulling her toward the door. Gus let go of her hand and reached out for the ladder. "Watch me. It is easy. Just don't look down or behind you." Gus confidently climbed up the side of the boxcar. He made it look so easy. He climbed back down to her. "Look, I'll go first, and I'll be at the top to help you on the roof."

"But I am scared, Gus," she revealed.

"Shoot, girl, what you just did was two times scarier than climbing up this ladder. I promise. Don't you trust me Henryetta?"

"I do, Gus. It's just . . ." Henryetta couldn't finish. She swallowed and took a deep breath. "All right. I'm coming now. Go on up," she said, resolved to climb up the side of the boxcar. Her heart racing, and her knees knocking together, she stepped out on to the ladder only to freeze in place. The wind blew her hair in her face and her palms were sweaty. What if she lost her grip? Then there were the slippery soles of her shoes. What if she stumbled and fell to her death? She was paralyzed.

"Come on up, Henryetta!" Gus called down to her from the top of the car. "One foot at a time!" Henryetta looked down and behind her. "Don't look down!" Gus corrected. She looked up at Gus who was motioning for her to begin climbing up the ladder. One foot at a time, she began her ascent. When she reached the top Gus pulled her to him on the boxcar. Once she found her balance, Gus let go of her and stepped back a moment to allow her to acclimate to the train's motion.

She couldn't believe it! There she was, Henryetta Dixon, standing upright on the roof of a moving boxcar in the middle of Florida. She smiled at her bravery—at never feeling so alive. Thrusting her arms up toward the heavens, she cried out, "I forgive you!" and let the southern winds carry her words away. Letting her arms drop, she turned to Gus who pulled her to him. Clinging to Gus in a tight embrace, Henryetta felt deep joy for the first time in a very long time.

Gus and Henryetta traveled atop the boxcar watching the sunset usher in the universe's symphony of stars. Sometimes they talked of little things, and other times they just sat looking out into the night skies. As the hours passed, Henryetta began to feel the chill of the humid night air causing them to take shelter in the boxcar below. A hobo never knew what he was going to find in a boxcar. In this case, there were a few crates on one end and on the other end were bales of hay. A stroke of luck for a tired wanderer.

The hobo from earlier, his hat covering his face, was snoring peacefully as he reclined on a bale that had been untied and spread out for sleeping. Gus pulled out a pocket knife and undid a second bale of hay and spread it out for them to lie down. Henryetta opened her suitcase to pull out a sweater. Gus sat down in the hay and Henryetta joined him pulling her sweater over her chest and arms. At first, they sat shoulder to shoulder, both with their eyes closed, but when Henryetta started to nod off, Gus rearranged the bale so that they could actually lie down to sleep. Gus laid down on his back with one arm positioned behind his head. Henryetta looked at Gus for a moment pondering how she would sleep beside him, but in the most natural movement, Henryetta snuggled up to his body, resting her head on his chest being lulled to sleep by the quiet rhythm of Gus's heart.

Gus smiled wondering if this peaceful contentment he felt from being so close to Henryetta was what kept that spark between older married couples. Had the fates brought them together through a chance encounter? The more he knew Henryetta the more he believed that God had fashioned them for one another. Gus released his arm out from under his head and placed it on Henryetta's arm.

"Good night, Gus," Henryetta whispered.

Gus kissed her forehead and lingered there a few moments before wishing her goodnight. By then, Henryetta had already fallen into a deep sleep.

CHAPTER THIRTY-EIGHT

*M*innie balanced a quarter of a jam cake in her arms as she walked up the Dixon's driveway. She had heard the talk in town about what had happened to Henryetta and how she and her boarder had run off to God only knows where. She figured she'd get the real story out of Thom with a little cake bribery. Since he was a little boy, Thom had loved Minnie's jam cake. She didn't make these for just anyone, but the money she saved from selling off clothes she put toward a baking business. The grocer and the diner paid her a fair price for her pecan pies, jam cakes, and fruit tarts. She baked according to the season. Peaches and blackberries were easy to come by in the summer. Pecans and persimmons in the fall. She spent a fair amount of time canning fruit when it was in season.

Minnie had been thinking on what to do about the photos she found in the cellar. She wondered if Thom Jr. knew anything about them. She doubted it. He had no reason to go down there, but they were pretty damning as far as Minnie was concerned. Since she discovered them, Minnie oscillated between shock and anger and then understanding why Henryetta would have taken those kinds of pictures. *If Henryetta were just here.* She could get the truth out of her. Of that, Minnie was sure. She and Henryetta had never had secrets between them.

The family car was parked just outside the garage. Maybe Thom Jr. was home. Moving the cake to one hand, she pulled open the screen door and rapped on the back door, trying to see through the break in the curtains of the glass pane. She waited a few moments, but Thom didn't appear at the door. So Minnie turned the doorknob as she had done for twenty years and called out, "Hello? Thom? You home?"

As Minnie stepped into the kitchen, she heard heavy quick footsteps coming down the staircase. "Minnie? Is that you?" Thom called out as he walked toward the kitchen.

"Yes, suh! I brought you, yo' favorite!" Minnie called back, smiling.

As Thom appeared, Minnie noticed a bit of shaving soap on his cheek beside his right ear. Minnie pointed at her own cheek and nodded at him. He smiled and took the towel in his hand and wiped away the remnants of shaving.

"How are you, Minnie?" he greeted with a friendly, familiar smile.

"Hello, Mr. Thom. Blessed. How about yoself?"

"I can't complain, Minnie. I can't complain."

Minnie wanted to ask after Henryetta, but instead, she just smiled at Thom.

"I brought you some jam cake. It's extra good this time. I used my very own blackberry jam. Canned it myself this past summer, I did," Minnie offered, handing Thom the cake on a hand-me-down plate Miss Lucille had given her several years back. He took it gladly and walked straight to the drawer to pull out a fork.

"I am looking forward to this, Minnie. Thank you. Come on over and sit down," Thom invited, putting the cake on the table, pulling out a chair for Minnie.

"You know about Henryetta?" Thom asked between mouthfuls of jam cake. Minnie just nodded.

"I've heard talk, but you know how people is. Deys always tellin' it wrong," Minnie played dumb, as she watched Thom devour the cake forkful after forkful.

"What happened, Mr. Thom? I heard she done run off with Miss Florence and her chillins. Is it true?"

"I'm afraid it is," Thom said after swallowing the last bite of cake.

"Lo'. I don't know what that girl be thinkin'. Is the rest of it true too? You know, about what Sy McGhee done to 'er?"

"Well, Minnie, there was a note that sounded like it, but Sy has amnesia and supposedly can't remember anything about that night. So he says."

"Amnesia, you say?"

"Yes'm. I think Miss Flo cracked him over the head with a rolling pin trying to get him off of my sister. At least, that's what it looks like. Nobody really knows except them three. Nobody's heard a word from Henry or Flo."

"Do you think they went to Miss Flo's people up in Kentucky?" Minnie inquired, but before he could answer, the front doorbell rang, followed by loud knocking.

Thom looked puzzled, stood up, and went to the door. Deputy Stanley stood waiting.

"Deputy Stanley. Come in, sir," Thom said, ushering him into the front hall. Minnie sat at the kitchen table, but curiosity got the best of her and she walked through the dining room to the front hall entrance. If Deputy Stanley noticed that the living room was virtually emptied of furnishings, he didn't let on.

"Deputy Stanley, this is Minnie. She took care of me growing up," Thom introduced.

The Deputy acknowledged her with a slight nod.

"I have had word from Walter Bell. He made it back up to Kentucky. Mrs. Bell and the children are there with Walter's family."

Thom's face lit up, hoping Henryetta was with them.

"Henryetta? Is she there?"

"No, I'm afraid not, Thom, and Mrs. Bell told Walter she didn't know where Henryetta went off to. They separated in Nashville, and she hasn't heard from her since."

Thom's face dropped at the sour news. "Did he say anything else?" prodded Thom.

"Not much. Mr. Bell reported he was trying to convince his wife to come down to serve as a witness against Sy McGhee, but Mrs. Bell wasn't agreeable to that," Deputy Stanley replied. Thom frowned in frustration. He knew how stubborn Florence could be.

"You're the law. Can't you make her . . . ? Subpoena her? I think the term is."

"Well, yes, in fact we can, but we would like her to come forward of her own volition. She may be more willing to testify than if we don't give her a choice."

"Any word about Sy's amnesia?" Thom asked, wondering if Sy had remembered anything, not that he would admit to any wrongdoing, but still, Thom wondered. He hadn't talked to Sy since Henryetta's disappearance. Deputy Stanley shook his head.

"Well," said Thom with a sigh. Heavy, empty silence hung between them until Deputy Stanley excused himself and told Thom he'd let him know if anything had changed. Thom wondered if Gus had found Henryetta. He figured it was a long shot, but something told Thom that Henryetta was fine. No news was good news, right? Thom closed and locked the front door and then turned to face Minnie.

"Well, Mr. Thom, I'm glad you enjoyed yo' cake. I'm off. If you hear from Miss Henry, you send word," Minnie said, picking up her plate and walking toward the backdoor, "And Mr. Thom, you know she be all right. Miss Henryetta is strong. You'll see. She'll be back. Don't you fret none," Minnie said trying to reassure Thom, but really Minnie felt sorry for Thom. He was alone in the world. She knew the bitter pain of losing your family.

"Thank you, Minnie. That means a lot to me," he said, watching her head down the steps. She waved one hand up and kept walking off.

"Minnie!" Thom called out to her. Minnie turned around.

"You are the closest thing I have to family," he said to her.

Even though there was a man before her, Minnie saw Thom as that little boy who had been introspective, who spent more time out of doors than in, who when he spoke, spoke with quiet sincerity. She believed him and returned a smile. As she turned to go, in her peripheral vision, Minnie spied the closed cellar doors. Another day, she thought to herself. Another day.

A week later, Minnie couldn't live with this secret another moment, so she rode to town by way of a wagon from a neighbor man who had come to sell the pecans he had harvested. A day earlier, she bought pecans from him in order to make several pies the grocer had ordered. In their conversation, he mentioned coming to town and Minnie politely bartered a pie for a ride.

It was early morning, and Minnie was relieved that the usual men that crowded the sidewalks with nothing better to do hadn't yet gathered just outside hoping for a handout from shoppers. Since Maurice's death, she was wary of any white man—poor or not. She forgave Maurice's killers, like the good Lord commanded, and she was glad for it. That burden would have been too hard for her heart to carry around day after day. Still, Minnie never forgot. She knew the evil the white devils were capable of, and all just because of her caramel colored skin. Not having to face possible degrading name-calling or innuendos just walking into the grocer's was a blessing.

Her neighbor pulled the wagon up to the sidewalk in front of the grocer's store. He helped Minnie down from the wagon and handed her the picnic basket she used to carry her pies. Minnie thanked him kindly as he held the grocer's door open for her. The neighbor told her he would be around back unloading the pecans and for her to come out the back way for a ride home. He would be waiting for her.

Inside, the grocer was happy to see her. They had always had good rapport. From time to time, he would send groceries out to her with his delivery boy free of charge because Minnie's pastries made him consistent money. Even though the Depression lingered, folks still scraped together enough pennies to share a slice of pie, even if they only got one bite. One taste reminded them of better times, made them count their blessings, and most of all reminded them that this Depression could not last forever. Already, Roosevelt was enacting legislation to put Americans back to work. Able bodies were being hired to build schools, roads, dams, and bridges.

After Minnie collected her money for the pies, she turned to go, but Thom Jr. called her name. He had come into the store for sandwiches for him and the peddler man. They were headed to Jackson today and then back to Memphis as they had all but exhausted Brownsville's cast offs. Thom wouldn't be home for several days.

"Say, Minnie, would you be willing to give the old house a once-over while I'm gone? I was never much for cleaning, and with me living alone, I've let it go. I'll pay you right now, and if you need more, I'll have it for you when I get back to town." Thom wanted to take care of Minnie, but he really did need help.

"The good news is that there's hardly anything to dust any-more," Thom joked.

Minnie smiled at this and accepted his offer. Her neighbor dropped her off at the Dixon place, and she got right to work, like no time had passed. When she was over last week, Minnie noticed the house was unkempt, but nothing that she couldn't take care of in a day or two. She knew every nook and cranny of this place.

Minnie easily walked right in through the back door. Minnie decided she would start with stripping the bedding and washing it first. It would take a while to dry in the cool November air.

When Minnie entered Thomas and Lucille's room, the first thing she noticed was Thomas's missing portrait. Then she saw the broken glass on the floor. The frame was intact as was the portrait other than a small wrinkled dent right between Thomas's eyes from where Thom had slammed it against the bed post. She wondered, but then returned the portrait to its spot on the wall, but it didn't look right without the glass, so Minnie took it down and walked to the closet where she intended to store it faced toward the back wall.

The strongbox was still on the top shelf and the tip of the velvet ribbon that secured the three keys was barely visible. It didn't appear that it had been moved. She was relieved and continued to work. It didn't sit well with Minnie that she hadn't destroyed the photos that sat like a hidden trap in the Dixon's cellar. For weeks, Minnie's sleep had been restless and fitful since she first found them. She should have burned them right away.

It was obvious Thom Jr. didn't know a thing about what Henryetta had been up to. It surely explained how Henryetta was able to keep the place going and feed her boarders, too. How Minnie wished she could talk to Henryetta. *If only she hadn't run off.*

Standing on her tiptoes she was able to reach the end of velvet ribbon that held three keys. Minnie pulled down the metal strongbox and placed it on her former employers' bed. It easily sprang open and Minnie pulled out the single photo that remained. Without looking at the photo, Minnie slid it into her hand-me-down pocketbook.

After quickly replacing the strongbox on the closet shelf, Minnie headed directly for the cellar.

The cellar door to the makeshift darkroom was starting to swell. She easily turned the lock, but the door itself was stuck. She yanked and yanked at it, but it wouldn't budge.

"Want some help?" said a voice startling her from behind. She knew that voice and it caused her heart to beat wildly.

"You ain't 'posed to be here, Mr. Sy," Minnie said before turning around to face him. At the top of the cellar stairs, he sauntered down to where she stood.

"You ain't either, Minnie. What are you doing down here anyway?"

"Not that it is any of yo' business, Mr. Thom has me workin' some for 'im," Minnie said, boldly putting her hands on her hips.

"Well aren't you a little high and mighty? Careful there, Minnie. You know what we do to niggras that get a little too big for their britches." Minnie just frowned at Sy.

"I ain't scared of you, so jis go on and let me be! I's got work to do."

Sy responded with sharp, angry slap to Minnie's left cheek, turning her entire head right.

"Scared yet?" Sy taunted as a tear ran down Minnie's defiant cheek.

"My Lo' tells me to turn the other cheek, so I reckon, Sy, that's what I's gonna do." Very slowly, not taking her eyes from Sy, Minnie turned her other cheek to him. For several moments she stood there expecting a second blow, but it never came. Instead, Sy stood still, as if he were in a trance of some sort. Minnie turned back to face him, looking him straight in the eye with no emotion on her face. It was just a simple, calm stare. Still it was as if he were looking off into the distance even though he was looking directly at her. Minnie looked at him quizzically. Then he snapped back to the present.

"You ain't worth another slap!" Sy turned away from her muttering obscenities the devil himself couldn't repeat.

Coward.

Minnie followed Sy out of the cellar. He walked on ahead of her toward the driveway, so she turned and slammed the cellar doors for effect. He turned and glanced at the sound, but didn't stop. Minnie walked over to the driveway, her eyes following him down the drive.

Poor, pitiful wretch.

With Sy gone now, Minnie hurried back to the cellar.

"Now, Lo' if yous could jis open this door, now. I'd be ever so grateful." Then quite easily, it occurred to her to lift and tug. Finally, the door began to budge and she was able to open it enough to slip through. She allowed her eyes to adjust just enough to go over to where she knew the photographs were hanging on the drying line. One by one she pulled them from the clothespins. Once she had every photo, she straightened them and then placed them in her pocketbook.

Then, Minnie quickly turned to go, but stopped when she noticed the light from the doorway illuminating the art book that lay open on the stool beside the portrait camera. Just as the book came into view, Minnie was simultaneously reaching in her coat pocket for her gloves, where the tips of her fingers grazed the small slip of paper with her daily Bible verse. Minnie pulled out Matthew 7:7 and inserted it between the pages of the art book. If Henryetta ever came back and found her photographs gone, she would be beside herself with worry. Minnie hoped Henryetta would know she was the one who had saved her when she discovered the verse.

CHAPTER THIRTY-NINE

The water tower with "Brownsville: A Good Place to Live" came into view from the train window. Florence's heart began to beat frantically. Walter had arranged for Deputy Stanley to meet her at the station. Florence was alone. It was already a financial hardship sending her by train, even with the Brownsville Police Department paying part of her ticket. Having Walter come down with her was out of the question. They discussed him bumming rides and walking, but Florence figured it would all be over before Walter could even make it to her.

The night before she left, Walter was restless and didn't fall asleep until almost dawn. He felt so helpless in all of this, a feeling he couldn't seem to shake since living out in California. Not being able to go with Florence nagged at his inadequacies as a husband. Would he ever redeem himself? Florence never made Walter feel small, rather it was Walter who refused to forgive himself for abandoning his family in Brownsville.

Florence held her children like she would never see them again before she boarded the train, and perhaps, she would not see them for a long time. As the train screeched to a slow halt, Florence caught sight of a tall, serious looking deputy standing with his arms crossed as if he were watching prisoners in the yard. She wondered if this was a premonition. She slowly got up from her seat and gathered her small suitcase. She was one of the three people who stepped off of the train.

"Mrs. Bell?" he said uncrossing his arms walking toward her. What a formidable man she thought. He had to be one of the tallest men she had ever seen, well over six feet tall and built solidly with squared shoulders. He didn't smile at her, nor did he frown. He was just there to bring her to the station for questioning. She followed him to the police car.

At the station, Deputy Stanley opened the back door of the car for Florence. As she entered the station she saw Thom Jr. there waiting for her.

"Florence," Thom greeted almost anxiously.

"Hello, Thom," Florence replied with equaled nerves.

"Mrs. Bell, this way, please. Thom you can listen in, but you are not allowed to talk."

The one-room station was cramped with three desks, filing cabinets, and chairs. The creamy beige walls were sparse minus a small bank calendar pinned to one wall and wanted posters on another. No one else was in the office. The secretary had been let go two years ago, so it was up to Deputy Stanley and the Chief to keep up with their paperwork. It wasn't hard in sleepy Brownsville. The worst they typically dealt with drunks or folks dying. This was definitely the biggest "situation" they had encountered in a year or so.

"Mrs. Bell, are you ready to start?"

"Yes, sir."

"Can you identify this letter?" Deputy Stanley pulled Florence's letter from the case file and handed it to her.

"Yes, sir. I wrote this," Florence said, handing it back to him.

"Mrs. Bell, what happened that night?" Deputy Stanley began. Florence gripped the handles of her pocketbook that rested in her lap.

"I had been out with the children. I worked at the soup kitchen that afternoon. When I pulled up in the yard, I noticed Sy McGhee's car, which wasn't unusual. He would come over and pick up Thom, and they would go out together, but on this day, Thom was out of town working with the peddler man. Isn't that right, Thom?"

Thom nodded.

"I got out of the car and was going to open the back doors for the children to get out, but I heard a scream from inside the house. I told my children to stay put. I rushed into the kitchen. That's when I saw them on the kitchen table. Henryetta was struggling and crying, but Sy had her pinned down. His trousers were down . . . he was forcing himself into her. I think I yelled for him to stop, but he didn't. So I looked for whatever I could find to make him get off of her. That's when I saw the rolling pin. I reached for it and hit Sy on his backside thinking I could get him to stop, but he just kept on. He told me I was next. That is when I hit Sy's head. He stopped, looked around at me, but then his eyes rolled back in his head and he fell unconscious, on top of Henryetta. She started screaming for me to get him off her. So, when I pulled him by his feet, his eye hit the corner of table. He landed on the floor pretty hard. At first, I thought he might get up, but he just laid there, not moving." Florence paused.

"So what made you run, Mrs. Bell?" asked Deputy Stanley.

"Henryetta said she had to get away from Brownsville. She said she couldn't face folks knowing what had happened to her. We were both in shock. I was scared. I thought I might have killed him. I'm scared now." Florence admitted.

"Well, he didn't die, but he does have amnesia. Did you take Miss Dixon to any sort of doctor who could confirm the rape?"

"No. We just gathered our things and left. I made her promise to go to a doctor to make sure she was all right."

"Do you know where Miss Dixon went?" asked the deputy, not looking up from the notes he was scribbling. Florence looked at Thom and argued with herself about telling the truth. Thom nodded at her that it was all right.

"Henryetta went to Florida. I got word from her about a month ago," Florence revealed. Deputy Stanley stopped writing and looked up at Florence who looked fearful of her admission.

"Whereabouts in Florida?" he asked.

"Key West, Florida, but I don't know if she's even still there. Like I said, that was a month ago."

"Any idea why she'd go down to Florida, Mrs. Bell?"

"Gus, I suppose."

"And who is he, ma'am?"

"A man, well, a drifter, but he helped us out—he helped Henryetta out when her mama . . .," Florence's voice trailed off as she looked at Thom's pained face, knowing she should not utter those words.

"Were they involved, Mrs. Bell? Romantically, I mean?"

"Not really, no. We all suspected they were sweet on each other, but no, they hadn't made any promises or commitments to each other."

"And the man's last name?"

"You know, I'm not really sure, to tell you the truth. Thom, do you know it?"

Thom shrugged his shoulders, indicating he did not.

"Gus was in and out. He stopped over to rest, bathe, and eat a few meals with us."

"Where was he going that he needed to stop over?"

"All over, I reckon. He was one of those hoboes that was riding the rails. I don't know, not really. He seemed too educated for that life, but there he was. I guess we all have changed since times got hard." Florence stopped talking and Deputy Stanley put down his pen.

"Well, now Mrs. Bell, that's about all I need from you. You'll have to stay here, in Brownsville, I mean, just in case I need more information. More than likely there will be a court case, sooner rather than later, I suppose. I'll be needing you to testify. Do I need to find you a place to stay, Mrs. Bell?"

"Thom?" Florence asked with just his name.

"Of course, Florence. You are family. You can have mama and daddy's room. Besides, I'll be getting back to Memphis to work in the morning. Well, that is, if you don't need me for anything, Deputy," Thom said.

"I should have a court date later this afternoon, so it should be all right."

The three nodded in understanding.

"Well, then, it is settled. Mrs. Bell do you need to contact your family to let them know you will be staying on for a time? You are welcome to use our phone or you can send a telegraph."

"Well, that would be nice, but my Wal . . . my husband has to walk to town to make a call. I'll just post him a letter. Thank you."

"All right then. Stay put at the Dixon's, and I'll let you know when I need something more from you," Deputy Stanley directed as he stood up from behind the desk. Florence stood up, but staying seated, Thom asked, "What's going to happen to Sy?"

"He'll be arrested and locked up until the trial or until bail is met. Y'all need to talk to a lawyer. Henryetta will need one to represent her case," Deputy Stanley explained. Thom got up from his chair.

"How are y'all going to find her?" asked Thom.

"We'll make some phone calls down to Florida and get police departments looking for her. If you should hear from her, y'all need to tell her to come home."

The Deputy moved out from behind his maple wood desk and paused to hold open the swinging gate that separated the office space from the reception area of the station. Thom returned the deputy's nod as he passed by. Florence said nothing, and continued to the door. Just as the tips of her fingers met the brass door knob, Thom's hand covered hers, turned it, and pulled the door open. An unexpected gusty north wind blasted through the door. The seven months of summer had finally made room for winter. Florence shuddered at the cold and shoved her hands deep into the pockets of her coat.

CHAPTER FORTY

*H*enryetta woke up to numbingly cold feet and hands. Her body hurt from sleeping in one position on the boxcar's unforgiving wooden floor. Gus's body was warm and she nestled closer to him. The early embers of sunrise shone through the slats of the boxcar as it rattled along past frosted over cotton fields of the upper Mississippi Delta. The air was crisp and she could see her breath just above Gus's chest that moved up and down in deep, slow breaths. Florida's warmth was now miles and miles away.

Despite her aches, the lulling motion of the train combined with Gus's warm body filled Henryetta with comfort. This was the third night she had slept in Gus's arms. Henryetta smiled. She didn't want this moment to end. She would gladly suffer cold and soreness if she could lie with Gus like this forever. Not wanting to wake Gus, she laid very still and passed in and out of wakeful sleep. Finally, she gave up. She was awake.

As she lay there trying not to fidget, Henryetta's thoughts turned. She became keenly aware of Gus's body beside her own. Her arm was draped across his chest where she could feel the curve of his taut stomach muscles just below his rib cage. Reeling in nets and hauling crates of fish for Patricio had bulked up Gus's upper body that Henryetta secretly admired as she watched him work shirtless on the boat.

She moved her hand to Gus's chest. Drowsily, Gus caressed her shoulder. Henryetta noticed that her hands were no longer cold. An urge to know every inch of Gus's body overpowered her mind.

She wanted nothing more than for Gus to kiss her deeply, to put his hands on her body. This profound longing took her by surprise. Then like an unexpected slap, thoughts of Sy holding her down as he rammed himself into her body tried to push themselves into her thinking mind, but she told herself to block them out. That was done. Over. Past.

Henryetta was here, now, with Gus. It was just the two of them in this particular boxcar they had caught just outside of New Orleans late last night. The wanton lust she felt now took her back to the afternoon Gus showed up on her porch. What was just a twinge, was this time, powerful, magnetic, and it willed her to drink. She wanted Gus, all of Gus, forever. She wanted to be his first and his last.

Just then, the train whistle trumpeted startling Gus from his half drowsy state and breaking lust's hold on Henryetta. Gus pulled Henryetta closer to him. She responded by holding him tighter. How she wanted to tell him how she really felt. Henryetta's heart silently cried out, "I love you, Gus."

She feared she had nothing to give Gus. She didn't know what awaited her in Brownsville. If Gus knew what she had done, selling off her father's pictures, taking nude photographs herself, would he ever accept her? Henryetta felt dirty, so dirty. She heard her mother's voice condemning her to a life of loneliness for what she had done. She imagined people would whisper that she wasn't worthy of any man, wasn't worthy of Gus and this silenced her poor heart. She pulled away from Gus and sat up.

As Gus rolled onto his side placing his arm under his head, he groaned from the mangled aches his back felt from sleeping in one position for such a long time. Henryetta looked back at Gus, but then put her head on her knees and tears flooded her eyes. Gus opened one eye.

"You all right, chick?" Gus said reaching for her and caressing her back, but Henryetta did not reply.

"Hen?" Gus asked sitting up, putting his arm around her shoulders. "What is it? He whispered. Henryetta raised up to face Gus. Tears streamed from her bloodshot eyes, the morning sun turning them greenish blue. Gus took his thumb and tenderly wiped the tears from her face and caressed her cheek.

"What is it, Hen?" Gus whispered again. She gazed back at Gus in sorrow and laid her head on her knees, still looking up at Gus.

"I can't have you Gus." Gus looked at her confused. "I don't understand, Hen."

"I want *you*, Gus. I love you. But . . . I've lost so much. So . . . much," she sobbed. "I don't think . . . I can lose you. I don't even know if I have anything left to give you." Henryetta waited for Gus to react, but he was so overcome with her admission of love he didn't comprehend the last two sentences. His heart raced. His mouth felt cotton dry. His head was woozy.

"Gus?"

He shook his head to regain his senses. "What? You love me? What was the last part? I'm sorry, Henryetta. It's just that, I wasn't expecting you to say that to me." What was wrong with him? He never fumbled for words and here he was acting like a bumbling idiot. This girl, *the* girl, had professed her love for him and he had asked her questions? He read disappointment and fear all over Henryetta's face, and she turned her head away from Gus.

"I'm so sorry, Henryetta. I didn't mean to hurt your feelings. Tell me, please." Gus coaxed, but Henryetta did not turn to face him.

"Gus, I've done something awful. Something unforgivable," she cried into her knees. Gus took several deep breaths to help him focus.

"It can't be that bad," Gus encouraged.

"Oh yes, it can, and yes, it is," she responded, sitting up, looking straight ahead.

"Whatever it is . . ." Gus began, but paused.

"Gus, if I tell you, will you promise not to hate me? I couldn't bare it. You don't have to love me back, but I can't bare having you hate me."

"I could never hate you, Henryetta, not in a million years. Never," Gus promised. "I—"

"Wait, Gus," Henryetta interrupted, holding her hands up to his lips to silence him. "Before you say anything, just listen, then you can make up your mind about me."

"When I was cleaning out our attic to sell dresses to Minnie, I found a strongbox full of photographs . . . photographs of nude women."

Gus tried not to appear shocked or judgmental.

"They belonged to my father. He took them, you see." Henryetta paused and took a deep breath before continuing. "There was a letter in the bottom of the box from a man in New York City. It asked my father to send more photographs . . . that there were buyers who wanted that sort of thing . . . They would pay good money for them." Henryetta stopped talking. She was overcome with this impossible thing she had to tell Gus. As she searched his face for rejection, she found none, only his steadfast, open expression.

"I sold the photos, Gus . . . for money. I was afraid we were going to starve if I didn't. Flo was so mad at me when she found out what I'd been doing. When I first found them, I showed them to Flo, but she told me to burn them. She said they were filthy and that we could get arrested with that sort of thing being in the house and all. At the time, Thom wasn't any help with his drinking and running around. I knew there was only so much furniture I could pawn off to the peddler man. So I started mailing them a few at a time so it wouldn't look suspicious. Then I found Daddy's journal under the mattress in their bedroom. Gus, the things he wrote." Henryetta paused and shook her head in disbelief.

"My daddy became a desperate man after he lost my mother's inheritance in '29 and then the theater. I didn't know the man who wrote those entries. It was like my daddy was this whole other person. He wasn't the daddy that raised me." Henryetta sat silently for a few moments.

"You know something, Gus? I often wonder if Mama knew all along and said nothing. Or, Gus, if maybe she found Daddy's journal after he died and that's what made her crazy. I noticed the pages right after his last entry had been torn out."

Gus wanted to respond, but knew it was always better to simply listen.

"Anyway, when I read it, one of his entries led me to find more of his negatives in the cellar where he had his darkroom . . . I sold those too." Again Henryetta paused to remember, but to also let it sink in. This was the first time she had spoken her secrets aloud. The earth did not cease to spin. God did not command deathly lightning strikes to aim for her. Henryetta was just here, sitting in a freezing cold boxcar that jostled her back and forth as it clanged and clacked its way closer and closer to home.

"You did what you had to do, Henryetta. There are things ten times worse you could have done or might have been forced to do."

"But the lies, Gus. Flo didn't even know what I'd done because I had been hiding it from her. At least until Marjorie got real sick. We were petrified she was going to die. We were down to literally pennies after mama's funeral. There was no money for Doc Castellaw. We barely had enough for canned beans. So Florence was on her knees praying for God to give us a miracle. He did all right. The very next day, the postman delivered an envelope fat with money from the pictures I sold. Florence was hopping mad at me, but when things with Marjorie got worse she gave in and agreed to let me use the "dirty money" to pay the doctor, and not too soon. Doc Castellaw said had we not gotten Marjorie the proper treatment she might have gone blind from the fever."

"I see that God turned my sins to a blessing, but Gus, I think about all those women. What if I ruined someone's life by selling those pictures?"

"Henryetta, those women knew exactly what they were doing when they posed for those pictures. They knew the risks."

"Did they, Gus? Did they really think about the consequences? I think they were just trying to survive like me. My Daddy talked about that in his journal. As the Depression went on, Daddy said he had a hard time finding women to pose who weren't half starved."

"These are hard times. I've run across all sorts of people doing things they claimed they'd never do just to fill their bellies with a bit of food." Gus pulled Henryetta to him.

"That's in the past. Take the albatross from around your neck. We all make foolish mistakes, Henryetta. If we didn't, we wouldn't learn, and that's why we're here, to learn." Gus kissed Henryetta's forehead and then her lips very tenderly. Gus didn't understand why

Henryetta still felt tense and was not comforted. Reading his confusion, Henryetta knew she had to confess all of it. These sins would haunt her the rest of her days if she didn't.

"There's more Gus."

"More?" This baffled Gus. Henryetta winced as she revealed her next set of secrets.

"I had mailed off the last set of Daddy's negatives. Beth and Gertie were living with us at the time. I feared for us. One day, I posed the idea of us photographing ourselves in the nude and selling the photos for money."

"And did you?" Henryetta bit her lip at his question.

"Yes, Gus. All of us except Gertie."

"Did you sell them?"

"I didn't have a chance to. Sy caught me developing them." Her voice trailed off. Gus knew what she would say without her even uttering a single syllable.

"Sy threatened to expose me if I didn't give him what he wanted."

"And did you? Did you give your body to him, Henryetta?"

"No, Gus. I wouldn't lie about that. He raped me because I refused him."

"And the photographs? Where are they now?"

"I hope they're still in the darkroom in the cellar, but there's no guarantee. If Sy told the police, I'll be going to jail right alongside him. I just pray I can get to them before someone else does. The worst part is they actually turned out really beautiful," Henryetta said wistfully. "They looked like paintings."

Henryetta smiled for a moment, feeling triumph for her work. Ezra would have praised her bravery as an artist. Henryetta smiled sadly at Gus, who appeared indifferent. When his expression did not change, nor did he speak, Henryetta feared that any love Gus may have felt for her had just dried up and blown away, making its home with the dust of Oklahoma and Texas. Not able to bear it, Henryetta turned away from him.

"Henryetta, I have my own confessions to make." Gus placed his hand gently on her shoulder, asking her to face him.

"There is something you need to know. Sy has amnesia. At least he did when I saw him last."

Henryetta's mouth dropped open.

"You were in Brownsville?"

"I was on my way out to Montana. Ernest's stories were too much. I had to go see it for myself, but not without stopping to see you. I thought about you every day. I must have written you a thousand letters."

Henryetta smiled as she pictured him writing letters on the dock, or under a palm tree.

"But when I got there, you had just vanished. Nobody knew where you had run off to, but Thom told me he suspected you had been raped by Sy. He sent me to bring you home, but honestly, wild horses couldn't have kept me from looking for you."

"You knew? The whole time? And you didn't tell me?"

"I didn't want you to run away from me. I just wanted to know you were safe. I traveled all over the darn place trying to find you. I walked halfway across Florida looking. It was Gertie that told me where you'd be. I didn't know if you'd tell me what happened, but I wanted things to be as normal as they could be. I wanted you to tell me in your own time. What happened to you Henryetta, nobody should have to carry that alone. Despite your actions Henryetta, Sy needs to pay for what he did to you."

Henryetta didn't respond, but rather, stood up and walked away from Gus over to the opening of the boxcar. Outside, the countryside was bathed in early orange light. Frost sparkled on the grass and wilting wildflowers. Henryetta, holding fast to a bar at the edge of the door, stood for a long while just looking out until Gus got up and walked over to her. Henryetta looked at him and gave him a smile of regret. Her eyes watered from the cold wind, and her nose shone bright red. Gus reflected the same smile as he pulled his hands from his pants pockets.

"Henryetta Dixon, nothing has changed the way I feel about you," Gus said in a regular tone, but Henryetta didn't hear him over the wind and the raucous of the iron wheels rolling down the tracks.

"What?" Henryetta asked.

Gus turned her to face him. Leaving his hands on her arms, he leaned in close. "Nothing has changed about the way I feel about you!"

Henryetta shook her head no.

"Listen to me, Henryetta. There is no one like you. No one. I don't care what you did. All I know is that I want you. I love you, Henryetta Dixon." That was not what Henryetta expected, not what she felt she deserved.

"Did you hear me?" Gus said and pulled her to him and held her in his arms. Her body was tense and straight, one hand at her side and the other hand still on the door handle. Gus whispered he loved her in her ear over and over. Would she ever relent and love herself? That is what it was going to take for her to let Gus love her. She would have to forgive herself to make space for love.

Suddenly the train jolted causing Henryetta to lose her balance. She lost her grip on the handle and wrapped her arms around Gus for balance. He felt like home, and she couldn't fight the comfort she felt there so, she let her body relax into his, lying her head on his chest with her eyes closed. As Gus held Henryetta in his embrace, she recalled something Minnie said to her one morning at breakfast when Thom Jr. came down, still drunk and out of sorts with himself. He had cursed Minnie for the bacon being too crisp, Henry for being a "prude," and the "damned Depression." His words were altogether uncalled for at the beginning of a fresh morning. Other than his coarse words, it was only the clinking of their forks against the plates in the kitchen that morning. Then, unexpectedly, Thom threw his fork on his unfinished plate and abruptly pushed away from the table. Henryetta winced and Minnie just turned to look at him.

"Damn you all!" and he stormed out of the kitchen, allowing the screen door to slam shut. Henryetta looked down at her plate and continued to eat as if nothing had happened, but sick sorrow settled right into her gut, making Minnie's breakfast sour. Minnie could see it all over Henryetta's face. Minnie put the skillet on the counter and threw the tea towel over her shoulder and walked over to stand right behind Henry.

"Child," Minnie began, "deys a lot things in this life we gots to bear. Deys crosses you know, like the good Lo's. Yo' brother's one of dem. Ain't nobody got a choice about whose dey brother is or ain't. I seen lots of folks dat gots crazy families, you hear me? But do it stop 'em? No. Now you listen to Minnie. Deys gonna be people in your life who's no blood kin to you, but dem da ones who's gonna be yo' real family. Understand?" Minnie said, patting Henryetta's shoulders.

"Yes, Minnie," she lied.

Now, standing there enveloped by Gus's arms as he stroked her hair, she understood Minnie's words. Gus was her family, and it was going to be all right. It just had to be.

CHAPTER FORTY-ONE

*T*his morning was nothing special. No morning was really that special when Sy came to think about it. He felt flat. As he lay in his bed, looking up at the ceiling, he wondered why he was on this earth. Things never changed. For years, his mornings had started the same. He heard the kitchen cabinet doors opening and shutting, followed by the clinking of the silverware on the plates. Aromas of breakfast tempted him to get up and join his parents for breakfast, but Sy waited. He waited for the sound of his father's car to rumble off and for the house to grow quiet before he crept downstairs for coffee.

His mama, Dovie McGhee, was usually already about the business of cleaning or laundry. Sometimes she left early to go to the grocer. When Sy crossed paths with his mama, he spoke to her, but rarely more than a few words. If Sy was flat, Dovie was a plane that dropped off into a sphere of nothingness. Luther McGhee made sure he kept them down, hollow, and muted except when he no longer could stand their silence and he entreated them to scream. Sy clung tightly to memories of his mama before she began to pass through life in numb sadness.

He was very young, maybe three. It was Dovie's custom to read him bedtime stories in her lap. She cuddled Sy closely to her as she made the voices and the faces to match the characters. Together, Sy and his mama would huff and puff and laughing, blow the house down. Sy clapped and told her to do it again. Then the cuddling went away. Sy couldn't remember when exactly his mama retreated from loving him, retreated from being his mama. His childhood was a blur of nights he spent hiding in closets or under beds while his father rampaged until he was big enough to run away from the house.

Sy and Dovie never knew what would trigger Luther McGhee's temper flares, but something always did. It could be that the potatoes were too lumpy or Sy had left a toy in the living room. It was always random, but there was always something that discontented Luther. Dovie worked all day at making sure everything was the way Luther wanted it. She had to anticipate what might make Luther furious that led to badgering, slaps across the face, dumping a full plate of food on the kitchen floor, or worse.

Dovie never left though. During the daylight hours, Luther was a good provider and a stand-up citizen in the eyes of the town. What went on after nightfall, behind closed doors, was their business. Outwardly, they looked like the model family. The McGhees always had the best. Ironically, for as mean as Luther was, he was just as generous. Whatever Luther gave, good or bad, he gave big. Luther never made promises to stop his angry heart from hurting them or apologized for his beastly behavior. He simply showed up with gifts for Dovie and Sy. In those moments, Luther seemed genuinely content with himself, but Dovie and Sy knew that when Luther bestowed a gift that a fit of rage was right on its heels. They came to dread Luther's gifts.

As Sy grew older, he came to hate his father, but even stronger, he resented his mama's inertia. When Sy was fourteen, he begged his mama to leave, but Dovie looked blankly at Sy and said, "I can't." She didn't explain herself, leaving Sy to exercise his frustrations on his classmates. Dovie knew the kind of boy Sy had turned out to be, but never took it upon herself to correct Sy for his misbehavior. She waited for Luther to come home to give him the teacher's note or to tell him about the telephone call from the school. Luther did the correcting, and after all, Dovie wouldn't have punished him properly anyway. Still, Luther blamed Dovie for Sy's behavior. Neither escaped and both paid. So it was best for Sy to avoid his father as much as possible.

Today, Sy didn't wake to a pounding headache as he had for several weeks since the night of his "accident." He touched the part of his head where the goose egg had been. He still couldn't remember what happened that night or the days that led up to that night. Dreams rattled his mind in and out of sleep, but every time he woke, thinking he would recapture what he lost, the dream images disappeared, leaving him foggy. His parents wouldn't talk to him about that night. Doc Castellaw was just as tight lipped, keeping his comments focused only on Sy's injury.

Sy wanted to ask Thom, but he was scarce these days. Sy shirked off the inkling that Thom was avoiding him on purpose. Why would he? Thom was his only steadfast friend, his blood brother. No, Sy rationalized. Thom was just working with the peddler man. That was all it was. Sy wondered if Henryetta had done this to him. She had run off after all—her and that Florence, but that was as far as his mind would let him go. All he knew is that the moment his thoughts went to Henryetta, a consuming wrath came with them causing his head to pound with pain.

After Sy had washed and dressed, he made his way to the kitchen. Looking up at the clock, he realized it was much later than what he originally thought. Almost half the day was gone. Outside, the day was grey and windy. He watched the assortment of crimson and sunshine colored leaves fly and tumble across the lawn that was beginning to turn brown and crispy. Then quite unexpectedly the town police car pulled up. Sy frowned, but got up from the table to open the door for Deputy Stanley. He had been out twice to see if Sy could remember what happened the night of his head injury. He would disappoint Deputy Stanley again.

Deputy Stanley sauntered to the door where Sy held open the screen door. Sy looked quizzically at the slip of paper Deputy Stanley waved as he approached the door.

"Sy McGhee, you are under arrest for the rape of Henryetta Dixon," the Deputy announced firmly, voice booming, holding up the paper not six inches from Sy's face. Sy's heart began to race and then suddenly, a sharp pain struck his head at the deputy's words. Sy bent at his knees when a flash of the Dixon's kitchen floor came into his memory. It was sudden and quick, but Sy remembered the momentary pain of the blow to his head before his body made contact with the Dixon's linoleum floor. Sy didn't notice, but inside, the staccato sound of Dovie's heels rushing to the screen door where Sy stood with the Deputy, echoed in the kitchen. Dovie's face looked slightly confused and pained. It was almost as if her face said, "What is it now?" She wasn't scared for Sy, but simply wondered what she would have to endure next.

"What's this about, Deputy Stanley?" Dovie inquired flatly, sounding tired.

"I have a warrant for the arrest of your son, ma'am," Deputy Stanley said, holding up the warrant.

"What's he gone and done?" she said, again devoid of any emotion.

"He's under arrest for the rape of Henryetta Dixon."

At this, Dovie gasped and covered her mouth with the back of her hand. Luther hadn't mentioned one word to Dovie about why Sy was in such poor shape, and she sure wasn't going to ask.

"We have a witness. I have to take him to jail."

Dovie began to cry, but she wasn't sure for whom she was crying. She hadn't cried in years. It was just a waste anyway. No, it was better to just be numb. But here were these surprise tears running down her face. Was she crying for Sy? His life was a mess. Was it Henryetta? She was such a good girl. Or was it herself? What would Luther do? Would he take out Sy's arrest on her flesh? Or was it her whole cursed life? Would Sy have turned out differently if she had just left Luther? Self-condemnation filled her heart. It was the first time she had allowed herself to feel in a very long time. How she wanted to drop to the floor and wallow in years of pent up grief and frustration.

Sy stood back up, his hand still on the back of his head. He looked at his mother, who was dabbing her eyes with an embroidered handkerchief and the deputy who had folded the warrant and put it in his uniform pocket.

"Sy, I have to cuff you now," the deputy said as he unlatched the cuffs from his belt.

"I didn't do this!" Sy started to holler, but stopped midsentence. He didn't know what he did or didn't do.

"All right, then," Sy complied, holding out his hands.

"I'll call your father. He'll get you out," Dovie thought to say as Deputy Stanley escorted Sy to the police car. "Appearances matter," her inner voice reminded, but Dovie had no real intentions of calling Luther. Let Luther find out on his own. He would in due time anyway.

"Don't bother, Mama. Daddy's help is the kind I can do without," Sy said before slipping into the backseat.

Dust and leaves billowed down the drive as Deputy Stanley drove off with Sy.

Behind bars at the Brownsville Jail, Sy sat on a lumpy cot. Its navy blue and white ticking was stained from who knew what. Passersby had stopped to look as a handcuffed Sy McGhee stepped out of the car and was led by the arm into the station. Not twenty minutes later, Luther appeared entering the police station like a raging tornado.

"What's the meaning of arresting my son!" he bellowed. Had Luther forgotten it was daytime? That he was wearing his white medical jacket from the pharmacy? Deputy Stanley calmly looked up from his paperwork at Luther, who had stormed through the gate that led to the desk area. Over to the left, Luther spotted Sy, who had stood up from his cot.

"Well, Deputy?"

"Calm down, Mr. McGhee. Your son is under arrest for the rape of Henryetta Dixon," Deputy Stanley said, not moving from his chair.

"What's the bail? I'll pay it, whatever it is. My son must be released," Luther demanded, thinking that if he got him out quickly enough, the rumor mill would die down before it ever got revved up.

"That's up to the judge. We'll know on Tuesday. For now, you need to go on, Mr. McGhee. Sy is staying put."

Luther panicked at this bad turn of events. It was Friday. He turned to Sy, who was listening to the exchange.

"Sy, you best not talk right now," Deputy Stanley cautioned. "Mr. McGhee, Sy is going to need a lawyer."

"You just stay put, Sy. I'll call in a favor from one of my college buddies. He's a criminal lawyer down in Memphis," Luther reassured.

Sy said nothing and went back to his cot to lie down. Now, all Sy had to do was wait.

A day later, the criminal lawyer from Memphis showed up early in the morning to question Sy, but it was rather pointless seeing as how he couldn't remember anything. The morning Sy had to appear before the judge, a crowd had gathered at the courthouse steps. Brownsville was a small town and Sy's misdeeds were on everyone's lips. As he walked up the steps, a reporter stepped out from the crowd at the top of the steps and pointed his camera at Sy. The day was overcast and the camera's flash blinded Sy momentarily.

As Sy shut his eyes tightly, a memory of Henryetta hanging up a nude photograph of Beth came to him. At first, Sy thought he was imagining it, but as he entered the courthouse, the familiar scent of Henryetta's perfume wafted in the air as a courthouse secretary passed by him. In that moment, the floodgate of memory was sprung wide open. It all came back to him.

He remembered pressing up against Henryetta in the cellar darkroom where she was developing nude photographs of her borders and of herself. That day, her lithe body in the photograph was branded in his memory, driving his lust to a frenzy. Sy fixated on the curve of her waist and the suppleness of her thighs until he couldn't help but relieve himself of the hunger he felt for her body.

Twice, he brought himself to climax imagining himself a participant in Henryetta's photo. Sy imagined himself walking to where Henryetta sat perched on stacked crates that had been draped in rich, hunter green, velvet cloth. An antique tapestry, patterned with primordial quests, hung as the backdrop. Her legs crossed, Henryetta sat poised with a fringed shawl covering her shoulders and nipples. The visible curves of her breasts and waistline lured Sy to her. Not losing eye contact with Henryetta, Sy ran the tips of his fingers on her bare outer thigh where it met her buttocks. Henryetta's lips, stained crimson, beguiled Sy, drawing his mouth to her own where she willingly accepted his tongue and returned his kiss with equal wanting.

When they separated, Henryetta smiled at Sy enticing him to gently push the shawl off her shoulders one by one, exposing her nipples. As Sy drank in the visage of her bare breasts, Henryetta reached for him where she undid his belt, unzipped his trousers, and easily enveloped his pulsing penis with her hand, easing his foreskin up and back. Sy moaned and pushed Henryetta's legs apart. Sy easily entered Henryetta's body plunging himself into the caverns of her sex until, together, they cried out in ecstasy.

But the fantasy wasn't enough. Satisfying his lust only drew attention to the surmounting emptiness he felt. He was alone and longed to be held, longed to be loved by Henryetta. For every hurt he had borne, he sought healing, healing that he determined could only come from her. Sy had to have Henryetta Dixon, all of her. He would make her his once and for all.

Later, after Sy had drunk the emptiness away, he convinced himself that he was worthy of Henryetta, and that this was the night he would make Henryetta understand this. She was his, and only his. She always had been. So Sy got into his car to drive over to the Dixon's house where he found Henryetta alone. She was in the kitchen rolling out biscuits.

When he approached her, she paid him no attention and was intent on pressing the biscuit cutter into the dough.

"Damn it, Henryetta! Look at me! Don't act like I'm not here!" Sy yelled, his voice growing angrier. Sy realized that he sounded like his father and became even angrier with himself. Henryetta stopped and looked directly into Sy's livid eyes.

"Sy, you need to go on. I've told you, I don't want you like that. When are you going to accept it? Do you hear me Sy?" Henryetta said firmly. "Sy, it is never going to happen between us. Never."

Sy stood, trying hard not to hear Henryetta's words. Henryetta just didn't know that she loved Sy. He would show her. Henryetta moved past Sy to put the biscuits in the wood burning oven. As she closed the oven door Sy came up behind her and put his arms around her waist and hugged her tightly laying his head on her back.

"Henryetta, give me a chance. I know I can make you love me." Henryetta startled, stood up and froze, until angry fear coursed through her.

"Get off me, Sy!" Henryetta insisted as she fought to free herself from his hold, but Sy was too strong.

"Let me show you . . . why are you fighting me? I've seen the way you look at me."

Henryetta responded by kicking his shins and digging her fingernails into his arms.

"We both know what kind of a woman you are," he said winded from wrestling Henryetta who pounded his chest.

"You're just making it hard for yourself . . . why . . . won't . . . you . . . cooperate!" Sy growled fighting her hands that tried to scratch and gouge out his eyes.

"Sy! You're hurting me! Stop!"

But Sy ignored Henryetta's pleas. Instead he wrestled her to the kitchen table and forced her to lie down on her back. He lay on top of her, holding her down with his weight. She was crying now, but had stopped trying to fight him. Sy stopped for a moment and looked at her wet closed eyes, swollen lips, and red pocked face. He tried to kiss her, but her mouth would not to allow in his probing tongue. She only sobbed.

Sy stood up, looking down at Henryetta who had turned her head away from Sy and held her eyes tightly shut. Smiling, he quickly undid his pants, allowing them to fall to his knees. He had waited for this moment for so long and now he would have Henryetta. Sy reached down and roughly pulled Henryetta's skirt up, exposing her thighs that shook with terror. Stroking and squeezing them shot currents of electric lust straight to his loins. He coarsely yanked at her panties, pulling them down around her legs and off, where he dropped them to the floor. Sy spread her legs wide and groaned as he penetrated Henryetta's sex. She was tight and hard to enter. Over and over Sy thrust himself into Henryetta until he broke through to fill her body with his.

Sy didn't hear Henryetta's screams. Sy didn't hear Flo's car pull up. He didn't hear the screen door slam, nor Flo scream to get off

Henryetta. He was to the point of climax inside of Henryetta Dixon and that was all he knew, felt, tasted, touched, and heard. Nothing would stop him. Nothing but a blow to his buttocks with something hard.

His thrusting stopped long enough to see Florence with a bat. "You're next!" Then he felt his brains rattle in with the crack to his skull. His eyes filled with stars before all went dark. When Sy woke, he was lying in his bed, his head pounding. Doc Castellaw and his mother stood over him, but he had no recollection of what had happened. Not until this very moment as he walked into the courtroom with his lawyer and Deputy Stanley.

His mother and father sat just behind the lawyer's bench. Both of them stoic. His father nodded his head at Sy's lawyer, but wouldn't look at Sy. Sy's mother stared blankly ahead. She too couldn't make eye contact with him. Sy scanned the other side of the room for Henryetta, but she wasn't there. Only Thom and Florence who glared at Sy disgustedly.

Sy smiled at her deviously, nodding his head back and forth at her. Thom looked at Florence whose expression did not falter, even though, her heart was racing with fear. In one look from Sy, she knew he had regained his memory. How long would it be before she was exposed?

"All rise. The honorable judge Harold Cox, presiding. The court is now in session." After the judge sat, the audience sat in unison. The judge read over the papers in front of him.

"Sy McGhee, you are charged with the aggravated rape of Henryetta Dixon. You will be held in custody until the hearing December 15 at nine o'clock or until bail is posted. Bail is set at $500." The judge matter-of-factly banged the gavel against the podium and rose to walk out.

CHAPTER FORTY-TWO

A s the train slowed, Henryetta's nerves teeter-tottered. Gus explained to her how to jump from the boxcar to the ground. Henryetta fretted she would tumble from the train to crack open her skull on the pumpkin sized limestone nuggets that lined the tracks, or stumble only to be mangled by the train. In the end, though, the station was virtually empty, and they literally stepped off the boxcar ladder onto the ground. When the caboose passed by them, they jogged behind the depot until they reached the parking lot where they slowed to walking.

As they walked along the sidewalk, across the street from the court square, Henryetta noticed a noisy crowd had gathered at the base of the courthouse steps. Engrossed in their own conversations, the crowd didn't seem to notice two travelers, lugging a suitcase up the sidewalk. All eyes were focused on those doors. Henryetta didn't want people to recognize her, so she kept her head down and tucked into her coat. Tempted, Henryetta briefly scanned the crowd for faces she recognized. Seeing several she knew, she pulled her hat down over her eyes, turned her head away from them and kept heading toward her home.

The porches of the grocer's, the diner, and the barbershop were emptied of the regulars that begged a bite to eat or bummed a ciga-rette. Henryetta expected to be stopped by at least one person, but thankfully, she and Gus made it all the way to her home without a single encounter. As Henryetta walked up her drive, she noticed the formerly manicured yard was grown up, and the bushes' lanky branches grew in willy-nilly directions up against the exterior walls. Her home looked empty and lonely. How long had it looked like that and she just never noticed? Her first instinct was to enter through the back door, but then she thought about the last time she was there and veered right, toward the front porch. She tilted up one of the emptied urns that her mother had used for ferns in the summer to find the spare house key. Unlocking the door and entering, that familiar scent of home welcomed her like an old friend. Funny thing to never notice the smell of a place until you were gone from it for any length of time. Henryetta felt momentary contentment, like being wrapped up in her grandmother's quilt when she was small. Then, her mother's words popped into her head, "There's no place like home." Her slight smile faded from her lips. Despite the familiarity, she could not erase the painful memories that hung on the walls, lurked in the cellar, or crept in the shadows. Though the hallway and the living room appeared stark, minus a chair by the fireplace and the secretary, the house seemed crowded with ghost memories. Henryetta felt she might be sick and bolted back out the front door to the yard. Sensing her distress, Gus followed right behind finding her bent over at the waist. Walking over to her he gently laid his hand on her shoulder.

"Home sweet home," Gus offered, smiling at Henryetta.

"Is it?" This was only a structure, four walls emptied of almost all its contents and certainly the family who once occupied it was gone forever. No, this looked nothing like the home where Henryetta had grown up.

A pang of urgency overtook Henryetta. Was Thom still living here? Without warning, she sprinted back into the house and up the stairs to Thom's room. The door stood open. To her relief, everything was there and surprisingly straightened up. It reminded her of Minnie's work. There was no dust that clung to the curtains, the dresser, or Thom's trinkets he had collected over the years. The bedsheets were tightly tucked and the bedspread smooth. Minnie fought to teach Thom how to make his bed like she did, but try as he might, Thom never really mastered the art of a tidy bed. He must not live here anymore Henryetta surmised noticing the emptied ashtray and no pint bottles of liquor. She was let down to find Thom absent, but then who could blame him? Life had gone on while she was away. Henryetta assumed Thom had moved to Memphis. Being closer to the peddler man meant more work. It made sense she reasoned.

"Everything all right up there?" Gus called to her from the base of the staircase.

"Thom's gone," she called back. The sound of Gus's footsteps echoed as he traipsed up the stairs. Henryetta backed out of Thom's room to be met by Gus.

"His room is perfect. Like when we were children."

Gus peeked in and nodded.

"Looks that way, doesn't it?" Gus remarked.

Henryetta turned and went back down the hall to her parents' room, whose door was closed just as it always was. Even when she was growing up, her parents had always kept the door closed. She never questioned it, but now it did seem a peculiarity. Had she and Florence kept the door shut when they stayed in it with the children? She supposed they did.

The door squeaked in greeting as she opened it. The room was unchanged other than her father's portrait was missing from the wall. The closet door stood wide open just as it had the last time she was there. The strongbox rested on the top shelf of her father's closet, seemingly untouched, with the strands of velvet ribbon barely peeking over the edge. Then she spotted the picture that had been placed against the back wall of the closet.

Henryetta rushed for the metal box whose corners had rusted over the years due to heavy humidity. Hopping on one foot, Henryetta pulled down the velvet ribbon of keys.

"The keys," she said to Gus as she moved past him and out of the bedroom. Gus simply followed her downstairs to the secretary in the living room. Would there be any letters or envelopes from Tommy Sylvester? If there were, had Thom opened them and figured it all out? Before she had run off, Henryetta had been careful to burn any envelopes after she was sent payment for her father's photos. As she bounded down the stairs, Henryetta kept her eyes toward the secretary looking for mail on the corner of it. Growing up, anyone who collected the mail put it there for her father to read. No envelopes waited there. So she pulled down the secretary door that converted into a writing surface. She quickly pulled out all the envelopes from the slots, only to find nothing.

"Everything all right, chick?" Not responding, Henryetta sped past Gus, through the empty dining room to the kitchen. As she passed through, Henryetta put up her hands as blinders and focused on the back door.

"Hen?" Gus began to follow Henryetta, who was already half-way down the stoop steps. When Gus caught up with Henryetta, she had just flung open the cellar door.

"Henryetta!"

But she didn't pay Gus any mind. She opened the second door and continued down the steps. When her eyes adjusted, Henryetta unlocked the cellar door, hoping she could rid herself of all evidence of the photos she had taken. When she pulled at the cellar door, it wouldn't budge. Henryetta's shoulders slumped, and she groaned in frustration.

"Let me help you." Gus motioned for her to move out of the way. He gripped the door, but it had swollen at the bottom causing it to get hung up, so he tried lifting up under the knob expecting to free it from the jam.

"Eureka!" Gus called out. The door opened just enough for a thin person to slip through.

"Gus, I need you to gather wood for the stove and fireplace. Will you? Please?" Henryetta didn't want Gus to see the photos. He looked at Henryetta, stroked her cheek, and smiled reassuringly at her.

When Gus had cleared the cellar steps, Henryetta slipped into her father's darkroom and waited for her eyes to adjust to the dark. Henryetta carefully stepped over to the table where she knew she would find an oil lamp. Illuminating the room, it looked as Henryetta had left it until her eyes darted to the table where she had hung the photos to dry, but as she approached, the clothes line was empty. Setting the lamp on the table, she ran her hands over the table searching for negatives, and gathered them up. The developing pans stood empty. Henryetta looked under the table, on the floor, across the room, but no photos were to be found.

Who had them? Her heart began to pound and a pang of nausea swept over her. Thom? Sy? The police? Then she spotted her art book on the stool. She went over and picked it up. Venus's bare buttocks, covered in a thin film of dust, greeted her. Henryetta blew the dust away, slipped the negatives between some pages, closed her book, and knew there was nothing she could do at this point. Someone else knew.

Outside, as Gus gathered wood he wondered if Thom had truly moved to Memphis. The place felt all but abandoned. It would have been much easier for Thom's work, but then the rumblings of a car engine coming up the drive distracted Gus from gathering firewood.

Henryetta had just emerged from the cellar, toting her art book. She had just let the exterior cellar door slam shut, when a shiny, pine green Plymouth rolled to a stop just short of the garage. Soon after, a police car squeaked to a halt not six feet to the left of the unknown vehicle. She heard a man's voice call out to her, "You best leave them doors open, missy!"

Henryetta turned around to see Luther McGhee emerging from the passenger side of the car. The driver, a man she didn't recognize, paused at the tail end of his car to allow Deputy Stanley to walk around the back end his car to take the lead. Henryetta froze, but Gus went directly toward the three men as they approached Henryetta.

"Can we help you, gentlemen?" Gus was always amiable.

"Police business."

Gus blocked their path.

"You best move on out of the way. I need to speak with Miss Dixon," the stranger warned.

"It's all right, Gus," Henryetta said, moving from out behind him.

"Henryetta, you don't have to say anything to these men."

"Miss Dixon, I see you've returned," Deputy Stanley greeted, tapping his hat at her.

Luther and the stranger were not as friendly. Their gaze was quite the opposite.

"Miss Dixon, let me get right at it," began Deputy Stanley. "I am here for two reasons. First, you are summoned by the court to testify in the case of the *People vs. Sy McGhee* December 15, at nine o'clock in the morning." Deputy Stanley handed her the summons papers.

"Who are these men?" Gus inquired.

"That is none of your concern, now is it, boy?" Luther McGhee bullied.

"Miss Dixon, I also have a search warrant. Sy McGhee claims that you were running an illegal pornography business. I'm here to search the premises."

"Sy said the photographs were in the cellar, Deputy," the stranger chimed in as Deputy Stanley held up the warrant. Gus took two steps up to block Luther from coming any closer.

"These men can't be here!" protested a booming voice from the corner of the house.

Everyone turned to see Thom with Florence in tow. When Henryetta connected with Florence's face, tears flooded her eyes. Florence shook her head no and motioned for Henryetta to hold up her chin.

"Deputy Stanley, these men are trespassing on my property, and either you make them leave or I will," Thom commanded, not changing his confident saunter to where they all stood. Thom joined Gus and placed his hand on the back of his shoulder. When Flo reached Henryetta, she put her arm around her shoulders and looked directly at Luther McGhee. Flo was not afraid of him.

"We aren't going anywhere!" Luther shouted, shoving Gus back a step as he attempted to stare him down, but Gus replied with a glare with equal steel. Luther backed down but turned to Henryetta, who wasn't looking at any of them, but only at the ground directly in front of her. She held the book with the negatives behind her back, her palms sweaty.

"This little tramp wants to accuse my son of raping her while she and this no-good, two-bit whore were taking naked pictures for money. I'd say she asked for anything she got," Luther spat.

"You miserable son of . . . !" Thom said, stepping in front of Henryetta, blocking her from Luther's line of sight.

"Boy!" Luther began to rage, holding up his fist as if he were about to strike Thom.

"Enough!" Deputy Stanley shouted as he placed his hand on Luther's fist to halt him.

"Mr. McGhee, he's right. Y'all can't be here. You're going to have to be moving on . . . Now!"

"But!"

"Mr. McGhee!" Deputy Stanley shouted to get his attention. "We can do this the easy way or the hard way, but either way ends with y'all leaving the premises. Go on now."

"This ain't the end of this!" Luther stormed off with the stranger in tow. Henryetta didn't watch after them but rather kept her eyes down.

Once the stranger's car had rolled down and out of the driveway, Thom and Florence both reached to embrace Henryetta.

"Thank God, Henryetta. Are you all right? Where have you been?" Thom questioned.

"I'm fine, Thom, just a little tired. We rode the rails all the way up from Key West. It took us several days."

"Thank God you are safe," Thom said, hugging her close to his body once more. Allowing them a moment more, Deputy Stanley waited before speaking.

"Thom, I have a warrant to search the place for pornography. I'll be needing you to let me into the cellar, the garage, pretty much everywhere. Miss Dixon, Mrs. Bell, I'll need to question y'all if I find evidence, so don't go nowhere."

They nodded at the deputy.

"Y'all have a key to the cellar?"

"It's not locked." Thom followed Deputy Stanley down into the cellar.

"I'm sorry, Thom, you'll have to wait here. If you could, go ahead and open up any locked doors. I will be checking everywhere."

"Yes, sir."

Inside the house, a damp chill hung in the air. Henryetta could see her breath, so she went straight to the fireplace to kindle a fire. Suddenly, she thought of her father's journal and quickly tiptoed upstairs to pull it from her suitcase. Downstairs, Florence got the wood burning stove going, claiming she would make coffee for everyone. Checking to make sure the main hall was clear, Henryetta rushed to the fireplace and tossed in the negatives and her father's journal. She watched the flames mercilessly consume her family's secrets. *Ashes, ashes, we all fall down.* Within minutes all evidence was gone, so Henryetta placed her art book back on the book shelf that flanked the fireplace. Florence entered the room carrying two cups of coffee.

"Florence, what is going on?" Henryetta whispered emphatically.

"I have no idea. Deputy Stanley sent for me to testify in the case against Sy. I'm the leading witness."

"Gus told me that Sy has amnesia. Is it true?"

"It was until this morning when he went in front of the judge for bail to be set."

"Did Thom say anything to you about our pictures?"

"Nothing. I decided it was best to keep him out of our mess. He's been trying so hard to turn around."

"Who could have them?" Henryetta continued to wonder.

"I don't know, but this could be really bad for us. I may never see Walter and the children again, or at least for a very long time." Florence's eyes were pained, but not teary. Henryetta marveled at Flo's strength. She was never one for crying over spilt milk.

"Before we left, I was expecting one last payment from Tommy Sylvester. I feel almost certain Thom would have received it by now."

"I don't know. He hasn't said anything, and I don't want to bring it up," Florence replied as she shrugged her shoulders and shook her head no.

They stopped their conversation when they heard the deputy's boots coming into the kitchen. He stopped long enough for him to refuse Florence's offer of a cup of chicory coffee. Deputy Stanley went to work.

For several hours, he delved under mattresses, rifled through correspondence in the secretary, open and shut closets, the attic, the garage, and her darkroom. Not one inch of their property went untouched. Deputy Stanley was so thorough he combed through their suitcases and rummaged through the kitchen cupboards and bathroom medicine cabinet. Deputy Stanley scoured every bookshelf, flipping open every book one by one, looking for the photographs in question. The more he looked, the less he found.

Outside, echoes of lonely crow calls floating in the dull winter sky entertained Thom and Gus as they sat out on the back stoop waiting for the search to end. After sitting a few moments, Thom broke the silence.

"This is all my fault," Thom announced, fighting a strong craving for a drink to numb his remorse. Instead, he pulled out a pack of Lucky's and lit his last one in the pack.

"No, Thom. You're wrong," Gus consoled.

"No, Gus. You don't know the half of it. Not too long after Henryetta and Flo ran off, an envelope from New York, addressed to my father, arrived full of money. I thought that maybe the man just owed Daddy some money and didn't know he had passed. I didn't think about it anymore. I was just grateful and counted it as a blessing. In fact, I took it as kind of a message from God that I needed to straighten up. You know?" Gus nodded.

"But, Gus, just now, when Sy's daddy and his lawyer accused Henryetta and Flo of pornography, I had a terrible thought about where that money came from."

"What do you mean, Thom?"

"For years, my daddy took photographs of naked women and sold them. You know, for those *exotic ladies* postcards like the ones at the circus? That could have been dirty money from those pictures."

Gus acted surprised.

"What makes you say that, Thom?"

"I don't know, Gus, but my gut is telling me that Henryetta might have found some of Daddy's photographs when she was selling off everything. She could have sold them. Things were getting desperate after Mama's funeral."

"Do you really think Henryetta would do something like that?"

"I don't know," Thom thought for a moment. "Maybe Sy is trying to frame her for something my daddy did. He knew all about my daddy's side business."

"It's possible, I guess. How did you find out about your father?"

"I caught him. Twice. The first time, Daddy didn't know I was watching him. He had a big show in from New York. I was almost twenty-two. Sy and I had been out frog-gigging late one night, and I knew my daddy was probably still at the opera house. He normally didn't leave until after midnight on show nights. So I told Sy to drop me off and I would catch a ride home with Daddy.

"When I entered the opera house, everything was quiet, like it was deserted, but then I heard a woman's laughter and my father's voice. I followed the sounds until I saw a light coming out from a door that was left open less than an inch. For all the times I had been in the theater, I just thought this was a prop closet. I was just about to open the door, but a flash of bare breasts caught my eye, and I froze. My heart began to race. You know, what I mean?"

Gus nodded, fully engrossed in Thom's story.

"I was afraid they would know I was there, so I moved away from the door into the shadows of the stage curtain, but I could still see what was happening. My daddy was putting his hands on her body, posing her in different positions and maneuvering her props. In some of the photos, you couldn't see anything private, but in others, you could see everything."

"Did . . . they?"

"No, at least not while I was there. She acted willing enough. I don't know how my father resisted her. I couldn't have. She was a doll—one of the actresses from the show. I had just met her the day before. She didn't strike me as a girl who would do that sort of thing."

"So what did you do?"

"I froze. I didn't know what to do. I was in shock, so I just ran home. I was shaken up, really shaken up. Then, I got really angry with him. My daddy had been everything to me. I felt so betrayed. I couldn't figure out how he could do that to all of us, especially my mother. He made me sick. That's when we fell out.

"Then awhile later, the circus came to town. There was a man selling postcards in the cooch tent. I couldn't help myself. From the night I caught my Daddy, I wondered what he did with the photos. It struck me he might be selling them, so I wanted to see if I recognized any of the women from daddy's shows."

"And?"

"Well, I thumbed through the postcards. I remember the other men in line got real impatient with me, but I just gave them dirty looks. I was almost to the end of the stack, when I saw her, the girl my Daddy had photographed at the theater. I recognized the actress's face and the furniture she was sitting on. My daddy had lots of prop furniture at the theater that had been around for years.

"I put the picture in back in the stack and just walked off. I remember the men cursing me for not buying anything, but I didn't care because I was blinded with anger and shock. I felt like I would vomit right there in the cooch tent. I grabbed Sy from the audience and told him I'd had enough of the circus. Sy knew something was wrong with me, but he said it wasn't anything a bottle couldn't cure, so we headed out to the drinking shack. I got rip-roaring drunk and finally told Sy my Daddy's secret. It had just been festering inside of me. Gus, I admit it, finding out about my daddy . . . it changed me for the worse. That's when I got to drinking so bad."

"That was a lot to carry around," said Gus, trying to comfort him.

"I don't understand how your mother didn't know. Married people know these kinds of things," Gus responded.

"Well, I don't think Mama did, or if she did, she turned a blind eye. Everything seemed normal. Besides, she was used to my Daddy being out late when theater troupes came to town. Actors are famous for partying well into the night after a show. Other times, Daddy would be gone from home for weeks at a time for theater business. Mama never seemed to mind. She had all her friends, church, and her clubs to occupy her time. When the opera house burned down, I figured Daddy would stop for good, but I was wrong. He just brought it home, to our cellar, right under our noses."

"The cellar? It would have been so easy to catch him. And the guilt? How did he hide it from her?"

"He was an actor, Gus. He knew how to play the part. He was clever too. When Henryetta started her photography business, my Daddy moved his dark room down to the cellar so they wouldn't get in each other's way. He always kept his darkroom locked."

"Why didn't you tell him you knew? You must have wanted to?"

"It was eating me alive, but, Gus, I just couldn't. We were the *Dixons*. We were royalty in this town. I didn't want to tear apart my family. Plus, if it got out about what my daddy was doing, the shame would have killed my mama."

"I imagine that was a lot of pressure for your father to maintain appearances," said Gus.

"Maybe that's why he did it. He lost all of mama's inheritance in the Crash, but we didn't know it then. Life went on as usual. Maybe it was those pictures that kept us afloat. When he died the only thing we owned outright was this house."

"So you said you caught him twice. Was he in the cellar the second time?" Thom nodded and put out his cigarette.

"That time, I let him know I was there. It was late, maybe two in the morning. I'd been out with Sy and the fellas, when I saw the light coming from our cellar. At first, I wasn't going to even go down there, but I heard my father's voice. I wondered who in the world he could be talking to, so I walked down the cellar stairs. Through the dark room door, I saw my father bent over looking through his camera. My heart started beating real fast. I already knew what he was doing and this time, I wanted him to know that I was on to him. So I crept forward, but he didn't notice me. When I stepped in the doorway of his makeshift studio, there sat Matilda, the prettiest girl from school, stark naked on a red velvet bench. My father was telling her to arch her back and cross her legs. She had this gypsy looking head wrap on," Thom described pantomiming wrapping his head.

"I remember she was wearing fancy women's shoes, pink satin with pearl beads. She had this white scarf draped over her lap. Her head was turned toward me. She startled real bad when she saw me. I remembered she screamed my name and put her hands over her breasts real quick. If you could have seen the look on my father's face when he looked up from his camera at me," Thom paused and shook his head.

"What did you do, Thom?" asked Gus.

"I started to storm off, but Daddy called after me. He said he could explain, but when I wouldn't stop to listen, we got into a shouting match. I really just wanted to hit him . . . just hurt him. Then, he turned the blame on me and started telling me how shiftless *I* was and how *I* should be doing my part to help the family so he wouldn't have to take these kinds of pictures." Gus shook his head in utter disbelief.

"Why didn't you stand up to him, Thom? Tell him that you knew he had been at it a lot longer than what he let on?"

Thom shook his head and turned away from Gus for a moment.

"It was just easier for me to play the shiftless son than to admit to the whole world my father was the complete opposite of a hero. This town would have strung him up if his secret got out. I guess though, in the end, they didn't have to. Daddy did it for them. He shot himself three days later on the ground where the opera house used to stand. The police said when they found him it looked like he was sleeping on his side. The crazy part is that he shot himself right where the stage would have been."

Gus studied Thom's forlorn eyes. In them, he saw Henryetta. He had seen that very same expression on her face the day he helped her take her mother to the asylum. Gazing on Thom's raw pain felt awkward, even paralyzing.

"It's not your fault, Thom. You are not responsible for your father's actions, any of them," Gus said patting Thom on the upper arm.

"Yes, but Henryetta. What if she has gotten herself mixed up in my father's mess? Or worse? What if what Sy is claiming is true? She'll be locked up for sure. I don't want that for my sister."

"That's not your fault either. You can't control what other people do, Thom. Henryetta is an adult. She has to face the consequences of her actions good or bad.

"Have you found anything that links her to selling off the pictures?"

"No, not really," Thom admitted. "I never suspected anything."

"Let's go in. It's getting cold out here," Gus suggested as he stood up and opened the back door. Setting their empty coffee cups in the sink, Gus and Thom joined the women who sat at the kitchen table.

"It feels much better in here!" Gus exclaimed as he walked over to warm himself by the stove. Just then, Deputy Stanley appeared. In his hands was the strongbox from the closet.

"I need the key for this," he announced.

Act natural, Henryetta told herself as she walked calmly to the secretary in the living room. Earlier, before lighting the fires, she thought to deposit the keys there, getting them out of her hands. *Would Deputy Stanley believe this is where she ordinarily kept them?* Still, Henryetta fought off nervousness. She wasn't sure what Deputy Stanley would find in the box. She hoped nothing more than her mother's nude photograph, but with the disappearance of her photographs, she couldn't be sure. She held out the key to the deputy who then carried the strongbox to the secretary that was still open. At that moment, Gus and Thom entered the living room.

Henryetta held her breath, just waiting to see him pull out her mother's wedding-night photograph. The deputy sighed and then closed the lid.

"Nothing," Deputy Stanley announced. He closed the box and handed it to Henryetta.

"Do you mind putting it back for me?"

"That's fine, Deputy," Henryetta replied, trying to smile.

"I didn't find any evidence, but do you mind telling me about the room in the cellar?"

"That was my father's studio. He moved down there when I took over the garage studio for my business."

"I see. Well, don't plan on leaving town in case something turns up." Deputy Stanley's tone was firm and matter-of-fact.

"I'll be going now." He tipped his hat at the ladies and nodded at Thom and Gus and then let himself out the back door.

Relief rushed through Henryetta, relaxing her body that had tensed up the moment Deputy Stanley began to open the strongbox. Flo clasped her hands together, looked upward, and whispered gratitude to God.

Gus pulled Henryetta to him and held her for a long time, standing in front of the fire. Thom and Florence excused themselves to the kitchen. Thom needed to talk to Florence.

"Flo, is it true?" Thom asked, pouring himself another cup of coffee.

"Thom, I can't say."

"I have to know, Florence. Tell me the truth. Please."

"Thom, I told you, I can't say. Now leave it at that. Be grateful your sister is home and in one piece. This trial is not going to be easy for her, and now with what Sy has accused her of, it's going to be ten times worse. We need to support Henryetta."

CHAPTER FORTY-THREE

*G*us planned to slip out of the house just after breakfast. His ploy was that he wanted to catch up on the news, which was partly true. He wanted to map out the next part of his journey using the library's atlases. He figured as soon as the trial was over, he would winter in Nevada where the weather was sunny and warm. He imagined he could get work building the Hoover Dam, and then make his way up to Montana for the summer. Moreover, Gus wanted to use the librarian's typewriter to catch up on his dissertation. Gus made a habit of mailing notes he had turned into chapters back home to Aunt Trudy for safe keeping. He learned early on that life on the rails was precarious. Rain, sweat, altercations, theft, all these posed threats to his research.

When Gus was green, he had spent the better part of a morning filling the last pages of his first journal while traveling in a boxcar he had caught in Muncie, Indiana. Satisfied, he placed his journal in his knapsack and leisurely took in the sprawling acres of dried up Midwestern farmland. In the shadows of the boxcar was a hobo, asleep on his side, facing the wall. Gus hadn't had any trouble and figured the man was either sick or sleeping off last night's liquor. Many of the older hobos tended to be drunkards or crazy. If you left them alone, they'd leave you alone is what Gus reckoned.

But he reckoned wrong. When the hobo woke, he became territorial, threatening Gus to get out of his boxcar. Gus figured he could reason with the man. Again, wrong.

"You won't leave? Well, then you have to pay up. Hand over the knapsack," the hobo swindled.

"Can't do that, friend. I'm willing to share, but I need my knapsack. Surely you know that."

"I ain't going to tell you again. Hand over the knapsack." The hobo reached behind his filthy coat to pull out a deer-gutting knife. He approached Gus step by step.

"You are going to give me that knapsack, boy."

"I have a few coins. You can have those."

"I'll have those and the knapsack!"

Gus held up his hands.

"Put down the knife, mister, and I'll give you the coins. You'll be able to get a few meals." The man was now only two feet from where Gus sat. The hobo stood for a moment. He wobbled back and forth as if he were still drunk. Still holding the knife up, the hobo held out his hand. Gus slowly put his hands down and dug for the coins. He placed them in the man's hand.

"Now the knapsack," he said, motioning for Gus to hand it to him. Gus sat still.

"Damn it! I said give me your knapsack!" the hobo roared as he waved the knife at Gus. Without taking his eyes from the hobo, Gus picked up his knapsack and then slung it over to the right, away from the hobo.

"Ain't you a smart one?" The hobo began to sidestep over to the knapsack, eyeballing Gus, his knife still up.

"Put your knife away, mister. You've got what you want." Gus knew the only real valuables in the knapsack were his pencils and journal. The rest was all replaceable and wasn't worth his life. Gus figured what the hobo didn't want, he'd toss out or leave. Besides, the bulk of Gus's cash was safely hidden in his sock under the arch of his foot.

"You stay put, you hear?" the hobo said as he moved closer to the boxcar door where he could see what was inside the knapsack.

Gus watched as the hobo rifled through his knapsack, tossing his belongings on to the boxcar floor. When the man got to the journal, he paused and looked at Gus. Could he read Gus's anxiety? He saw that Gus valued that little book. It meant nothing to the hobo. He couldn't read and had no interest in the journal at all. He just liked watching Gus squirm.

"What do we got here?"

"My journal. It's got all my notes on my travels. I really want to keep it. Please, just give it to me. You can have the rest."

"Well, is that so?" Without much effort, the hobo grinned crookedly and meanly pitched it out the boxcar door. Gus watched a month's worth of notes roll down the tracks. Lesson learned. From there on out, Gus typed up notes and mailed them home as soon as he could find a typewriter.

As Gus hop-skipped down the Dixon's back stoop steps, he decided to act on an idea that sparked back in Miami when the editor offered Henryetta a job. He thought the editor was only half serious, but it got Gus thinking. Gus had been keeping up with the news and learned that Roosevelt's New Deal was employing thousands of people—artists, builders, craftsmen, seamstresses, and the like. Only recently he'd read the Farm Security Administration was hiring field photographers.

Gus knew it was a stretch, but one of Gus's advising professors hobnobbed in political circles. Gus hoped that if he sent Henryetta's photos to this professor, he would push them to someone working for the FSA. Gus believed Henryetta's photographs had the power to tell the truth, but if he revealed his plan to her, he would have to reveal his true identity. He wasn't ready. He had more work to do. He needed to leave and it was going to be hard enough.

It was easier to allow Henryetta to believe he was just a drifter who had stopped for a meal at a soup kitchen, but now? He knew he needed to tell Henryetta the truth, but he wasn't ready. His ruse had allowed people to accept that he needed to be free to go. Gus convinced himself that the people who had helped him or with whom he'd shared miles of stories were more forgiving when he simply disappeared or said he needed to get back on the road. But now? Gus couldn't run from fate. His life was deeply intertwined with Henryetta's. The more time he spent with her, the more he knew he loved her, and the harder it would be to leave her.

Gus came up with all sorts of justifications for leaving even though he knew it could crush Henryetta. But, there were more untold stories to be recorded. After all, his work was unique. It gave a voice to those marginalized and often misunderstood vagabonds that called the rails home. He had to finish. Henryetta would be fine, especially if she had a job. She wouldn't have to make more unthinkable choices to keep from going hungry. Henryetta traveling and getting out of Brownsville would be a good thing. It would give her time and space to heal. It would take her mind off his absence.

Finding the door unlocked, Gus entered Henryetta's darkroom. Only last night Henryetta had been working on redeveloping some of the negatives from her travels to Florida. Gus looked at the photographs that she had hung to dry. The exposure on several photos was more toned down than the originals she developed in Miami. Several, she had enlarged to focus on just the feet. He smiled when he recognized his own bare feet in a row fishermen lined up on a dock in Key West. One of Gus's favorites was of baby booties taking their first steps by the tracks. He scanned the table and the shelves until he found the envelope containing her original photos.

"Life on the rails," he smiled, thumbing through the pictures she'd shot down in Key West. Several photographs of traveling families and young vagabonds followed. He wondered if she'd let him use any of them for his dissertation. He chose ten of her best photos, including one of himself she had snapped while traveling between Key West and Miami. It served as his own record. Gus had no sooner stashed the photos in the breast pocket of his jacket when he heard the door open with a rusty squeak.

"Well, well, well. What have we got here?" Sy McGhee leaned against the door, an unlit cigarette hanging from his lips, blocking Gus's path out.

"You can't be here," Gus said with a steely tone.

"Who says? I'm here, ain't I, and you can't do nothing about it."

"Is that right?" Gus challenged. "Leave, Sy. There is nothing here for you."

"Aw, now. I think there is. Henryetta has done got herself in a mess of trouble, and I'm willing to bet you know exactly what I am talking about." Gus didn't take his eyes from Sy as he struck a match to light his cigarette. Sy took in a long drag as he put out the match and threw it to the floor.

"I'm calling the deputy, Sy. You'll leave now if you know what is good for you."

"I'd like to see you try," he laughed, standing up to block the door completely.

"We can do this the hard way or not, Sy."

"I like hard and your little whore . . ." Sy inhaled smoke and held it there. Then as he exhaled taunted, "Henryetta, she likes it hard too." Furious now, Gus allowed all his pent-up anger for Sy to power a two-handed shove to Sy's chest that sent him flying backward three steps. Sy recovered quickly and came at Gus, but he was ready for Sy. Gus grabbed his arms and hurled Sy, knocking his head against a shelf full of brown glass bottles that clinked as they knocked into one another. The blow was directly to the area where Florence had whacked him with the rolling pin, causing him to fall unconscious to the floor. Wobbly bottles fell to the floor only to break into jagged fragments and splatter chemicals on Sy's shoes and clothes. Sy's cigarette dropped from his lips directly into the chemicals that pooled and ran across the floor in different directions.

Instantly, the toxic combination burst into flames. Gus watched as the fire ran across the floor following the trails of liquid. Then the room erupted into flames. It all happened so fast. Gus tried to pull up Sy from the floor, but the sleeve of Sy's shirt ignited, breaking Gus's grip on Sy. Wet with chemicals, the fire, voracious and hungry, devoured Sy's whole body. Instinct took over. Gus had to flee. Turning away from Sy, he shoved open the darkroom door. As the rush of cool air hit Gus's face, Sy came to. His tortured cries for help from within the burning dark room compelled Gus to go back in. He couldn't leave Sy to burn alive.

CHAPTER FORTY-FOUR

The first Sunday after Henryetta returned, Florence convinced her to go to church. At first, Henryetta flat out rejected the idea. Ironically, it wasn't God she was afraid of. She wasn't sure she even believed in God anymore. Where was he? Why had he allowed all this to happen? Yes, she and God had been at odds for a long time. Before all this, she remembered how she could see God in all things—the blessings in all circumstances. The joy, the peace, all of it. She understood it. She claimed it. She believed it, but now she felt so detached from God. It was easier to accept suffering without having to consider the idea of God allowing it to happen.

What Henryetta truly feared was responding to underlying judgment and the false pity she would see in people's eyes once again. It had been bad enough with her parents, and now this? It was one more thing for the people she grew up with to know about her. It was one more thing that they would talk about whenever the Dixon family name was brought up in conversation. She didn't blame them because she grew up here. She knew how people were. Gossip kept boredom at bay. It would be hard enough when she was on the stand. At church, people had open access to her. They could pelt her with questions and sentimental comments that only reminded her of who she used to be—who the Dixons used to be. It was all just too much. Being away from people was easier.

Then, Minnie's voice popped into her head. "You've got to put on God's armor. Nothing can get at you then." Minnie said this to Henryetta right around the time Maurice had been strung up. These words, maybe more than any others she had learned from Minnie, stuck, especially these past few years. When things got difficult, good old Minnie would pop into her head showering her with wisdom.

"I know what you're doing," she whispered to God. "It's not going to work."

Then, Henryetta thought back to the evening she and Gus had gone to the top of the train taking in the glorious colors of the sunset over the Florida scrub. Maybe not at the time, but now that she was home, Henryetta felt God used that sunset, that moment, to prompt her to let go of her pain and to allow forgiveness to flood her soul.

Suddenly, Henryetta felt clarity. Free will caused suffering, not God. He was there to pick up the poor sinner when all else had failed. Facing God meant facing the truth. Henryetta had to own her choices in private and in public. Then Henryetta felt a rush of righteousness. She had taken in boarders and kept them fed and warm, hadn't she? Henryetta had kept more than just herself alive when whole families were losing their homes, starving, and burying their loved ones. They were alive now, but had she sold her soul to the devil to do it? Would God ever take her back? Then the words, "Lo, thou art with me," came to her.

If she could survive all that, the least of her worries should be people's scorn, and even jail if the photographs surfaced. She would simply put on God's armor. In the end, it was just between her and God anyway. What people thought didn't matter. She alone would stand before God to account for her life.

Thom and Gus joined them for church and as the four of them entered the sanctuary, people appeared pleasantly surprised to see all of them. They were all smiles, handshakes, and slight hugs. One of the men in the pew behind them put his hand on Thom's shoulder and told him it was good to see that pew full again. It had been empty for too long. Henryetta wanted to believe their gestures to be of genuine concern. Maybe, she thought, people were not as bad as she had imagined them to be. It didn't matter either way. In three days' time, her truth would be told—all of it, if need be.

CHAPTER FORTY-FIVE

The next day, Henryetta was alone in the house for the first time since she had returned to Brownsville. With only two days left before the trial, it loomed in all their minds. At breakfast, the atmosphere was tense and quiet. Florence volunteered to help Thom with chopping firewood out in the woods of their grandfather's old farm. She "needed to be useful." Gus bowed out of wood cutting, claiming he wanted to wander down to the library to get caught up on the news.

After they all left, Henryetta checked every door to make sure they were all locked. She was admittedly frightened when Thom told them that Luther had paid Sy's bail and he was out in less than three hours after court. Still, she needed to be alone to sort out her thoughts, and if the truth be told, she wanted to bathe in peace, and wash and set her hair. It always made her feel better. She had to make her home hers again. Sy had stolen that from her, but Henryetta was determined to restore what he took.

After she finished the breakfast dishes, Henryetta pulled back the curtain that hid the horse trough bath tub. She was thankful that the kitchen was nice and warm from cooking biscuits in the oven. The stove was still hot and it wouldn't take long for the water to heat for her bath. Henryetta looked forward to the day hot water would flow from the faucet into her bathtub upstairs and she could soak neck deep. She placed a few more pieces of chopped pecan wood into the stove. Earlier, Thom and Gus had filled enormous soup kettles with well water. Henryetta placed them on the stove to heat up for her bath. For her hair, she would use her grandmother's copper tea kettle.

Once the kettles were heating on the stove, Henryetta allowed herself to look, really look at the kitchen for the first time since Sy's attack. For three days, she refused to eat at the kitchen table and took her meals to the secretary in the living room. Finally, she couldn't resist the lively conversations she strained to hear Flo, Gus, and Thom having. She got tired of yelling answers to their crazy questions. She knew they were trying to lure her back into the kitchen. So with plate in hand, Henryetta came to the kitchen and sat down. "Welcome back," Gus said. Thom, Florence, and Gus all smiled at one another. Henryetta rolled her eyes at them, and faked a smile as she put a forkful of lima beans in her mouth.

She didn't linger in the kitchen this morning. Instead, Henryetta went upstairs to bring down a fresh set of clothing while the water heated. Henryetta had just reached the top of the stairs when she smelled a faint scent of smoke. At first, she didn't think anything of it. Wood stoves meant wood smoke. She was used to smelling wood smoke in the house. So she went into her parents' bedroom and pulled out clothes from the dresser. When she peeked out the side yard window, she saw a smoky haze lingering in the air. Oh my god, she thought. Was the kitchen on fire?

Henryetta dashed down the stairs, but there was no sign of thick smoke. Where was it coming from? Henryetta peered out the front door but saw nothing except a slow moving man shuffling down the sidewalk toward the court square. As she turned to go, in her peripheral vision she saw the man stop at the base of her driveway. His mouth was agape and he took off his hat as if awestruck. Then she saw several people running up her driveway with buckets.

In her bare feet and nothing but her housecoat, Henryetta ran for the kitchen. Light smoke was illuminated by the sun's rays that came through the kitchen windows. As Henryetta pulled the kettles off of the stove to prevent them from boiling over, she heard agonized screams coming from the yard. Through the window sheers, she saw the men who were at the water pump, furiously working to fill bucket after bucket of water suddenly stop. Everyone's attention was on a male figure wearing a suit of tormenting flames that scorched his flesh head to toe. Wildly he ran helter-skelter and then hurled himself to the ground of the yard. He rolled, but the flames kept at him until two neighbors braved the heat, and dashed up to douse the man with buckets of well water. Onlookers, helpless against the heat from the inferno that threatened to melt them whole continued to back away from the body that lay on the ground, black, bloody, and roasting alive.

Henryetta burst through the back door to see thick, swollen charcoal colored clouds filling the air just above the back of the garage where her photo studio had been. Frozen by the overpowering blaze, Henryetta could only watch as the angry flames quickly swallowed the entire garage and even threatened to catch the hundred-year-old oak tree on fire under which she and Gus had shared their first dance.

Looking back, Henryetta would not be able to remember if she called out for help or if she cried or if she just stood there. She would only remember the numbing sensation of helplessness, but then remember an idle observation she made that day. All things mimic nature. Fire was no different. It was simply a reflection of life, good or bad. Whether it was trouble, love, a new venture, a loved one's death, the emotions were all consuming at first, but with time, dwindled to nothing, just chunks of charred wood and ashes, remnants of what was before.

More neighbors and townspeople came running into the yard, each with buckets in hand, from all directions, some barking orders about how to best put out the fire. Their efforts would not matter. The garage was lost. Her props, the backdrops, her developing materials, gone, forever. Two of her favorite cameras melted in the heat of the flames. Years of school pictures, church picnics, weddings, anniversary portraits, records of people's lives—all were lost.

In the middle of the chaos in her yard, the train whistle blew in the distance, reminding her that all the photos she had taken while riding the rails were in her studio. Her best work, burning. They were good too. That's what the *Miami Herald* editor said, wasn't it? For a moment that day, the editor's words planted a seed of hope in her wounded heart. She wanted her photos to tell the story of everyday people just trying to survive one more day. Memories fade, but her pictures wouldn't. With each address she collected, she prayed happier days would come for all of them. Would the people in the photographs find gratitude for survival? Would they find remorse and regret in some of their choices? Would they be reminded that life is not always fair? Now their stories were gone, burned up. It was as if their struggle never existed.

"Miss Henryetta, you all right?" a voice said to her.

Then someone touched her forearm.

"Miss Henryetta?" the voice said again. "Miss Henryetta," the voice said one more time, gently shaking her arm, but she wasn't hearing or seeing. More men arrived quickly and seeing that the garage was too far gone, began to drench the bushes and the side of the house closest to the garage with bucket after bucket of water in hopes of saving them from the flames. After about twenty minutes, the fire had died down enough for the onlookers to form a line to pass buckets from the water pump to the flames.

By this time, Doc Castellaw had arrived to tend to the unrecognizable victim by whom a woman sat. The woman couldn't do anything to nurse him. He was too badly burned. Somehow she figured sitting beside him, reassuring him that he was not alone would have to be enough. Then Henryetta registered that the woman who sat beside the body was Florence. *When did she appear?* If Florence were here, Thom would be too. Henryetta scanned the yard and sure enough Thom was at the front of the line pitching water on the now steaming wood that hadn't completely burned.

"Thom!" Henryetta called out, but he didn't hear her above the noise.

Henryetta scanned the yard wondering if Gus had made it back. He was nowhere. Panic riddled her body. Was that Gus's body, lying dead in her yard?

"Oh, please, God. Not him! Not Gus!" Henryetta whispered. She was not hysterical, but rather grew silent and braced herself, a way of being she learned after her mother's breakdown. If this were Gus, she had to know. She walked slowly across the yard to where the body lay. Doc Castellaw was pronouncing the time of death. As

Henryetta peered down, she began at the man's feet and worked her way up the body. Would she be able to recognize him? Then she saw it. His ring. It was black, but she recognized its shape. She remembered the feel of it on her jaw.

"Sy," Henryetta said just above a whisper.

CHAPTER FORTY-SIX

*H*enryetta sat alone on the cot in the living room waiting for Thom to come home from Memphis for Christmas. They had planned to attend a typically joyous Christmas Eve service, but a somber quiet blanketed the whole town. Brownsville didn't feel festive. Villain or not, Sy's death twisted fate and reminded the townspeople that life could end at any moment. With no evidence of the *photos*, the case was thrown out, and the accusations against Henryetta forgotten. The autopsy revealed that Sy's head had been reinjured, but other than that, what he was doing in Henryetta's darkroom and how it caught on fire was a mystery. Some people said it was suicide. Some said it was justice. Some whispered Sy was "done in" but nobody could prove a thing. So they were left with mystery.

Once Flo was sure she could leave Henryetta alone, she returned to Walter and the children. Florence invited Henryetta to spend Christmas in Kentucky with her, but Henryetta declined saying Thom needed her. But it wasn't true. Thom lived in Memphis now. He was only coming home for Henryetta. After all, they only had each other. Family should be together on Christmas.

The truth was Henryetta was waiting for Gus to return to her. He vanished the morning of the fire. Although there was no real evidence that Gus had perished in the garage fire, it was suggested that his ashes slept with those of the photographs, props, and wood all blanketed by the winter's first snowfall. No one saw him that day. He never made it to the library. Gus was gone. He was a ghost that haunted her heart.

Henryetta got up to look out the front windows. Outside, silent snow flurries gently floated to rest on bare branches, the frozen grass, and bushes that slept for the winter. She wished she knew more about Gus's past, his family, anything, but it had always been about her, hadn't it? Henryetta wanted to cry because her front walk was empty. She hoped to see Gus coming home. Henryetta supposed she should be grateful for divine justice. Sy was out of her life forever. The photographs had disappeared, saving her from jail. At least for now. What was next for her?

She turned away from the window and went over to the secretary where her camera rested on the art book. Picking up the camera, she thought of the editor in Miami. Maybe she would write to him asking for a job. She couldn't just sit here. She'd lose her mind. She set the camera aside and picked up her art book to return it to the built in bookshelf next to the fireplace.

Henryetta held the book by its spine and carried it over. As she began to put it on the shelf, a tiny slip of paper fell from the book. Henryetta bent down to pick it up. On it was written, "Seek and ye shall find." Henryetta looked at the slip, puzzled, but then it came to her. Minnie. Rereading the verse, Henryetta prayed to find out the truth about Gus. Not for a second did she understand Minnie's verse contained a totally different message.

CHAPTER FORTY-SEVEN

*W*inter passed, and there were signs that spring was coming. Robins foraged for worms, and the jonquils her mother had planted in front of the porch surprised her with early blooms. Henryetta had written to the editor of the Miami Herald, but he promptly sent a letter of apology. He couldn't hire her. The Depression lingered and was dipping deeply into the newspaper's pockets. So Henryetta busied herself with charity work down at the church. It was as if she stepped right into her mother's shoes. The ladies were friendly and chatty as if nothing had ever changed. Henryetta smiled and listened, but she was quiet and never really had much to offer them in terms of conversation. If the ladies noticed how morose she felt, they didn't let on.

Henryetta looked forward to receiving letters from Florence and Gertie even though they were sometimes painful to read. They had corresponded faithfully to one another. Gertie had finally saved enough to become a beauty operator and Flo had been given a job as a pack horse librarian. Henryetta laughed to think of Florence traversing the hollers of Kentucky on a mule loaded down with saddle bags filled with children's books. Henryetta could tell Flo was happy from the way she described her work. Flo even talked of her and Walter trying for a third baby. For a brief moment, Henryetta felt real joy for Florence, but also a twinge of envy that nagged at her. Henryetta fought it by surrounding herself with people and serving others, but even so, Henryetta had never felt so alone and she didn't want to be. Just when Henryetta thought she was finally moving forward, accepting that Gus was gone from her life, Flo's good news pulled her back to that place of loss.

One Saturday in April, Thom had come home for the weekend. It was early morning and he was still sleeping comfortably in his own bed. As Henryetta looked outdoors, she was compelled to cut some of her mother's jonquils and drive them out to where her parents now rested. It wasn't often that she could use the car, but with Thom sleeping soundly, she took advantage of it. She hadn't been out to the cemetery since they buried her mother.

She stood looking down at their graves, thinking about what she would say to them, but in the end, the only words that came to her were, "Rest easy now. Rest easy." Henryetta stooped over to lay the flowers between her parents' graves when she felt a hand on her shoulder.

"Hello, Miss Henryetta."

"Minnie? What are you doing out here?"

"I jis came to pay my respects same as you." For a moment Henryetta just stood trying to read Minnie's expression.

"Henryetta, you find my verse in yo' art book?"

Henryetta's face changed from surprise to sudden realization. Minnie! Minnie had the photos! Henryetta rushed to Minnie where she collapsed into her arms, weeping.

"There now, Miss Henry. There now. Everything's gonna be all right. This is gonna pass, and it's all gonna be all right." When Henryetta was cried out she pulled away from Minnie.

"Thank you."

"Hush now. God's gots plans for you. Plans to prosper you."

"You think so, Minnie?"

"I know so, child. He done told us so in Jeremiah. Look here. God keeps his promises."

"Oh, Minnie. I've done so many bad things. Do you think God is punishing me?"

"No'm, I don't. Dey's not a one of us that's been born righteous. We's all sinners from the moment we's born. Grace is the only thing a savin' us. You sorry for what you did?" Henryetta nodded.

"Well then, that's all it takes. God can take the ugliest thing and turn it into something good. The ways I sees it, you's jis punishin' yoself a whole lot harder than the good Lord is. You got to forgive yoself and move on."

"But, Minnie, how? You know, don't you? What I did? What we did?"

"Listen to me. It's over. You did what you did, but it's over. You can't live in the past. You have to live for today."

"Do you think I'm horrible, Minnie?"

"No'm, I don't. It's not for me to judge anyways. That's between you and the Lo'. Besides, we's all made mistakes." Minnie pulled Henryetta to her again.

"Let it go now, or it will eat you up." Minnie stood, holding Henryetta for a long time. When they separated, Henryetta wiped the tears from her face. She couldn't explain the peace she felt, but it was there inside of her telling her it was going to be all right.

"Thank you, Minnie. Thank you for getting rid of the photographs."

"Oh, I still have them."

"What? Why?"

"Henryetta, dey's beautiful. Now, I can't say it was right, what you did, but God gave you a talent. Miss Henryetta, you's a storyteller. You and that camera of yours capture life—good and bad. That camera don't lie. Someday, those pictures you took, they'll remind you of what you went through and who you was at that time in yo' life. Nah, I's keepin' 'em safe. When the time's right, I'll give 'em back. For now, they's jis disappeared." Henryetta didn't know what to say.

"Jis trust me. I's never gonna let you down, Miss Henryetta."

Henryetta smiled and hugged Minnie tightly.

"Minnie, you are an angel. I just know it. God sent you to watch over me. Thank you, Minnie. Thank you."

CHAPTER FORTY-EIGHT

S pring turned into a sweltering summer. Henryetta went out on the front porch. The postman was just walking up the porch steps. She hadn't had any letters recently so she hoped to hear from Florence who had discovered she was pregnant in her last letter. They had been talking of Henryetta coming to Kentucky for a visit right around the time the baby was due, but it had been several weeks since Florence had sent word to her.

"Got some mail for you today, Miss Dixon. All the way from Washington, DC, it seems," the mailman said, reading the post mark.

"Washington, DC? That's strange. I don't know anyone there. You sure?"

"Yes, ma'am. It says DC right here."

Surprised and curious, she took the letter, thanking the postman. Instantly, she recognized the envelope contained photographs. Her heart started to race. Had the photos she sold come back to haunt her? Surely not. In the months since she had returned to Brownsville, there had been one final letter from Tommy Sylvester. He wanted more photographs; however, Henryetta replied, this time as herself. She explained her father had passed and all business would cease.

Henryetta took a deep breath before she opened the envelope. She pulled out a letter on parchment. It looked formal, not at all like Tommy Sylvester's letters. As she opened the letter, a gold embossed American eagle seal centered at the top of the letter grabbed her attention. Under it read, "United States Department of Agriculture." Henryetta began to read the typed letter.

Dear Miss Dixon,

Allow me to introduce myself. My name is Roy Stryker. I am the director in the Farm Security Administration (FSA). I suppose you have heard of it in the papers and on the radio news. I would like to offer you a job working for us as a field photographer. The FSA is dedicated to photographing our American farmers during the Great Depression. It is the aim of our department to use your photographs to inform our federal government of the state of our people—progress or otherwise.

Because of your talent, location, and the fact that you are unmarried, we would like for you to photograph farmers and their families in Tennessee, Arkansas, and Mississippi.

Typically, the FSA will send its photographers a list of places and topics to be photographed. Once an assignment is complete, the film is sent directly to our department for developing. You would receive credit for the photographs you take and would be provided copies for your own personal collection; however, the negatives would be property of the US Library of Congress.

It is my sincere hope you will accept this offer and be able to begin work as a staff photographer for the FSA as soon as possible. I look forward to hearing from you.

Sincerely,
Roy Stryker,
Sr. Director
Farm Security Administration

Henryetta calmly placed the letter in her lap and looked out into the yard, grinning ear to ear as she glided back and forth in the in the shade of the front porch.

"But how?" Henryetta said out loud, confused and thrilled all at the same time. Quickly, she pulled the photographs from the envelope. They were hers! They were the photographs she had taken on her travels to Key West. At the bottom of the stack nestled between the last two pictures, both facedown from the rest, was a small folded sheet of stationery. She picked it up and opened it.

Dear Miss Dixon,

I know you are wondering how I came to have your photographs. Forgive me, but I was not permitted to tell you how I came to have your photographs in the formal letter. Allow me to explain now.

A young professor, a Dr. August Moon, from the University of Chicago, claims to have met you while out riding the rails conducting his own research for his dissertation. Apparently, Dr. Moon mailed your photographs to a dear friend of mine, who is also a professor at the University of Chicago. My colleague was so intrigued by your work that he made sure they got to my desk.

Miss Dixon, your photographs are marvelous. If you do decide to join us, I will make sure you are well cared for while on the road. I have been in contact with Dr. Moon several times recently, and he asked me to send you his warmest regards.

Roy Stryker

"Gus! Thank you, God!" Henryetta cried out in joy. Gus was alive! That was all this letter meant to her at this moment. Aware that her hand was quivering uncontrollably, she laid the letter on the seat cushion. Then she turned over one of the last two photographs. The first one was of her with Gus. Patricio snapped a candid photo of them on the boat after a morning of fishing. Grinning ear to ear, both she and Gus held four oversized Bonita fish by the tails. Their shoulders were touching, as were their bare feet. Henryetta smiled, fondly remembering that day.

Since the garage burned, besides Gus, her greatest loss was this very set of photographs. They represented so many things to Henryetta—flight, bravery, redemption, love . . . She hoped the last photograph that remained facedown would be the one she took of Gus on the train the day they left Key West to return to Brownsville. They had only been on the train for a short time. Henryetta was sitting in the shade of the boxcar, but Gus wanted to see and feel the sun's warmth one last time. He knew it might be a long time before he would return. They didn't talk, so Henryetta just sat admiring the curve of his shoulders and the strength of his back. Gus sat in the door of the boxcar with his feet hanging over the edge. Behind him, there was nothing but azure water, dotted with whitewashed fishing boats. Knotted in the back, a red bandana encircled Gus's head, like a crown. "King of the Road," Henryetta thought to herself and smiled. Out on Patricio's sloop, she had teased Gus about how ridiculous it looked, but Gus protested that it kept the sweat out of his eyes. Something about it didn't match his personality, but in this moment, Henryetta accepted it and smiled. It was a part of who Gus was and she never wanted to forget him or who he was to her. That's when it struck her to photograph him.

With camera in hand, she stood up to move out of the shade and into a position that would allow her to capture Gus from the side. She positioned herself so that if Gus turned to look at her, the sun's rays would illuminate one side of his face. Henryetta adjusted her camera settings and readied herself to snap his picture. She waited patiently. Was he aware that she was about to take his picture and was playing dumb or was Gus just caught up in the waterscape?

Finally, Gus glanced back at Henryetta. In a millisecond she had done it. She encapsulated all that was Gus—relaxed face and an ocean of wanderlust reflected in his eyes. She had seen that very same face each and every time he left for his next adventure—just happy to be free to roam. He only half grinned at her and didn't seem caught off guard by the camera. Henryetta decided that, whether or not Gus remained a fixture in her life, she never wanted to forget the young drifter who had saved her in every way she could be saved. This picture would be one of her most prized possessions.

Later, when it was suggested that Gus had perished in the fire, Henryetta grew more and more distraught about losing this particular photograph. How would she remember what Gus looked like after so many years of separation? Would she be able to recollect how his voice sounded? That photograph suddenly became something she wasn't sure she could live without.

"Please God, let this be Gus's photo," she prayed, closing her eyes tightly and then turning it over. There in the palm of her hand, Gus looked straight at her as if he were right there. Henryetta smiled and could hear Minnie's voice in her head, "Seek and ye shall find."

Seeing the photo rekindled a pang of such longing for Gus her chest hurt. Now she understood why they called it a broken heart. She was grateful he was somewhere out there, but it was so much more painful than if Gus had died in the fire. If Gus was alive, why did he simply disappear? He said he loved her, but why did he leave her without telling her who he was? Maybe his need to be free was bigger than his love for her? Maybe Gus was not meant to be hers for the rest of her life?

Henryetta looked at the photo and decided that maybe him leaving was how it should be. Letting him go *was* loving him. Still, what she wouldn't have given to have him be sitting beside her at that very moment. She shook her head at all her unanswered questions.

"Why, Gus?" Henryetta wondered out loud.

"Why what, chick?" a voice said, approaching the front porch from the brick path that led from the driveway. Henryetta looked up to see Gus standing there, but not hobo Gus, but Professor August Moon. His gray three-piece suit was properly fitted, his hair trimmed smartly and oiled in place, and his shoes perfectly shined. She started to laugh and cry all at the same time at the sight of him. She wanted to be mad, but couldn't muster it. She was just so happy to see him standing there in front of her.

"You have a lot of explaining to do mister, I mean, *Dr.* Moon," Henryetta half-heartedly scolded as she stood up and laid his photo with the others that rested on the glider.

"I just gave you a nudge, Henry," Gus said, gingerly walking up the front steps, not taking his eyes from her. Gus came very close to her, taking her right hand in his to caress it gently.

"That's not what I mean, Gus."

"Another day, Miss Dixon." Gus whispered into her ear, causing gooseflesh to explode across her body. Happily, she threw her arms around his neck and pressed her body into his causing them both to burst into laughter.

"Yes, Gus, another day."

POSTLUDE 1978

*M*y children are sending me to a home now that my Walter is dead. Fifty years and one day we were married when God decided to take him home. Now, I have two weeks to rifle through sixty-five years of collecting a life time of memories. I have a neighbor boy who comes and mows the yard for me, so I've asked him to come and help pull down boxes from closet shelves and the attic so that I can choose what to hold on to, what to sell, and what to give away.

Time is a funny thing. It sews bits of memories to other memories, creating a tapestry that changes every time you look at it. That is, you look at it and you see something new or a scene you had forgotten. I was reminded of this when the neighbor boy remarked on the "funny shape" of my oval suitcase I hadn't looked at for years and years. It was quite heavy, and I asked him to put it on my bed.

That oval suitcase took me back to a time in my life I remembered with fond bitterness.

"That's all for today," I told my neighbor and shooed him right out the front door.

"Come back tomorrow at nine, and we'll start again."

"Yes, Mrs. Bell."

As the front screen door slammed, he called out to me, "Sorry, Mrs. Bell. I forgot!"

The brass latch in the middle of the suitcase was worn, and the suitcase itself was scuffed on the bottom, and the yellow covering aged and faded with time. My hands shook as I pressed the button to release the latch, but my hands always shook no matter what I did. The top of the suitcase popped open, and I folded it back to rest on the chenille bedspread to see photographs, letters, magazine covers, and articles lying any which way inside. The most recent were at the top, and they all centered around one person—Henryetta Dixon.

After Sy's death, I returned to Kentucky to my Walter, June Bug, and Marjorie and got on with life. Walter and I had another little girl, Amanda Rose, I called her, but she didn't make it past six months, so I took to the hills carrying books to families all up and down the hollers until the war started and the Depression ended. As the years unfolded, Henryetta sent me photographs and letters from "the field," as she called it. In the latter part of her career, she became quite the celebrated photo journalist for several popular women's magazines, but I always thought she did her best work during the Depression when she had the freedom to photograph what her own eye willed.

As best my hands would let me, I carefully lifted my collection out of the suitcase and placed them on the bed. I wanted to see my photograph one last time. The first time I discovered the Venus photograph Henryetta took of me in the cellar, I had just returned from Brownsville. I was unpacking my things for washing when I noticed the inner panel of my suitcase was pulling away. When I tried to push it back, I noticed just the tiniest tip of a photograph peeking out. It struck me as strange, and I pulled the suitcase panel back easy enough, and there it was. That was actually the first time I'd ever seen it. I was alone in our bedroom. The children were outside playing and Walter was hoeing the tobacco patch on the north end of the farm.

My mouth must have dropped open for even there alone, I felt a sharp sense of embarrassment that I'd posed for this photograph. I looked around to make sure no one was watching me even when I knew I was alone.

"Forgive me," I whispered, looking at the picture of Jesus on the wall between our two closets. Then, I remembered my words from the day Henryetta took this picture. I wanted to see who God had made me to be and be able to remember her when I was old.

Now, here I was. Old! My reflection didn't lie. Cavernous wrinkles lined my still rosy cheeks, and my tightly curled hair was the color of billowy, white clouds on a summer day. You wouldn't recognize me if you held this photograph next to my face. Henryetta had worked and worked to develop this photo so my face was just a blur in the mirror that I held in my hand. I can't say my curvaceous hips and fleshy bottom matched my now saggy buttocks and bony seventy-one-year-old hips either.

This very day, this very moment was the one I had used to justify why I wanted my picture taken. How far off it seemed back then—a lifetime away, and indeed, it was—a whole lifetime. I never showed the photograph to Walter. I didn't want to explain how or why it came to be. This photograph was only seen by four people that I know of. I discovered the identity of the fourth person the day I found the photo stashed in my suitcase. There was a tiny slip of paper that came out with the photograph. On it were words printed as if by one of my younger pupils.

> I expect you'll be wanting this photograph, Miss Flo. Miss Henry sure done a fine job on it. Don't you think? It really looked like the picture in her art book. You's a beauty, Miss Flo.
>
> Every blessing,
> Minnie

How in the world? I wrote Henryetta to ask what she knew about it, and the reply didn't come until many years later when Minnie was older and dying of ovarian cancer. From Minnie's deathbed, she told the story to Henryetta. I put down my photograph and dug through the stack of photos and letters until I found the pink stationery with roses on each corner. I had to reread the words one last time. It's sad for me to say those words "one last time," but honest.

My dear friend Flo,

I hope life finds you well. We are fine, but I have some sad news to relate. Minnie passed away not two weeks ago. I was on assignment when it happened, but I was able to see her a month ago while she was still alive. She had called me to come home and said it was important.

When I arrived, she was very ill. The doctors were trying to make her as comfortable as possible, but you remember how strong Minnie always was. As it turns out, when you and I ran off, Minnie found our pictures on accident. She told me it took her awhile before she decided to take them out of the cellar, but she did. Minnie hid them under a loose floorboard for years and years. When I got them out, they looked the same as the day I developed them. Yours was the only one missing. Minnie explained that the day after the fire when she came to visit, she placed yours in your suitcase where you would find it. The rest she decided to hold onto until the right time. She didn't know how to get Beth's to her, and for my sake, she just kept mine hidden.

I never told you this, but after you returned home to Kentucky, I saw Minnie one afternoon at the cemetery where Mama and Daddy are buried. For months, I had wondered whatever happened to those photographs, but when I saw Minnie, I put two and two together. I don't know why I never picked up on her clue for me. She left me the Bible verse: "Seek and ye shall find." I asked her for them that day, but she thought it best that she hold on to them. Florence, I have something I want you to think about.

A book company has approached me about doing a biography of my life. They would like to include private photos taken that I have never released to the public. I have thought about using our photographs. They would make for a wonderful story, don't you think? Let me know. I have tracked down Beth and sent her a letter requesting the same.

Well, dearest Flo, I must close this letter as I am running out of space. Much love to you, Walter, and the children. I look forward to hearing from you.

With Love,
Henryetta Dixon-Moon

I never responded to her request. Let lying dogs alone is what my mama always told me. In fact, I responded only twice more in our lives—once when Marjorie married and then when Junie graduated from medical school. It wasn't Henryetta's fault. I just was never a big letter writer. My life was simple and mundane, quite the opposite of Henryetta's. What was I going to tell her? I canned some green beans? I taught Vacation Bible School? Even so, that didn't stop Henryetta from writing to me throughout our lives. Not one time did Henryetta ever bring back up the idea of using the photographs.

What am I going to do with my naked picture now? I considered just tossing it into the trash barrel with everything else, but I just can't. Henryetta was right. It *was* a good story-our story. I slid my photograph back into where it lived in the suitcase along with all the old photographs and letters. A few weeks later when Marjorie flew in from Texas to help me have a yard sale, a young history professor bought the whole suitcase full for twenty-five dollars. He was thrilled to find all these "primary sources," whatever that meant. He went on and on about his excellent find. Marjorie paid him little attention. She just wanted all my things sold as quickly as possible so she could take me back to Texas with her and settle me in the old folks home. As I watched him happily tote off my suitcase of memories and put it in the back seat of his Plymouth station wagon, Marjorie caught me grinning mischievously.

"What is it, Mama? Why are you looking at that man that way?" I just kept on smiling.

"Oh, nothing," but I knew better. If that professor was smart, he'd find a whole lot more than he bargained for.

BIBLIOGRAPHY

Freedman, Russell. *Children of the Great Depression*. New York, NY: Clarion Books, 2005.

Green, Elna C. *Looking for the New Deal: Florida Womens Letters during the Great Depression*. Columbia: University of South Carolina Press, 2007.

Hapke, Laura. *Daughters of the Great Depression: Women, Work, and Fiction in the American 1930s*. Athens: Univ Of Georgia Press, 1997.

Literature, Amusement, and Technology in the Great Depression. Cambridge University Press, 2009.

Nardo, Don. *Migrant Mother: How a Photograph Defined the Great Depression*. Mankato, MN: Compass Point Books, 2011.

Partridge, Elizabeth, and Dorothea Lange. *Restless Spirit: The Life and Work of Dorothea Lange*. New York: Scholastic, 2002.

Partridge, Elizabeth. *Dorothea Lange, Grab a Hunk of Lightning: Her Lifetime in Photography*. San Francisco: Chronicle Books, 2013.

PBS. "Riding the Rails." Accessed April 15, 2018. http://www.pbs.org/video/american-experience-riding-the-rails/.

Sandler, Martin W. *The Dust Bowl through the Lens: How Photography Revealed and Helped Remedy a National Disaster*. New York: Walker & Company, 2009.

State Library and Archives of Florida. "Florida Memory." Accessed April 15, 2018. https://www.floridamemory.com/.

UKnowledge. Accessed May 05, 2018. https://uknowledge.uky.edu/wpa_packhorse_librarians/.

"The Pack Horse Librarians of Eastern Kentucky." 2015. *Horse Canada*. June 2. https://horse-canada.com/horses-and-history/the-pack-horse-librarians-of-eastern-kentucky/.

Welty, Eudora, and Reynolds Price. *Eudora Welty: Photographs*. Jackson, MS: University Press of Mississippi, 1989.

AUTHOR'S NOTES

*A*llow me to start by saying I have notepads full of stories I have started. *Enchanting Beauties* is the first one I finished. *Oh what a feeling!*

About four years ago, this story came to me serendipitously much like Henryetta's ideas. It came from my passion for Dorothea Lange's photography and the scene in *The Color Purple* when Miss Celie and Shug Avery find Nettie's hidden letters in Mr.'s strongbox under the floorboards. Also, inside this box were nude photographs. From the two, I got to thinking about a rich white woman who has lost her parents, has a drunkard for a brother, and is on the verge of becoming destitute and homeless. Desperate, she resorts to starting a pornography business to keep her afloat during the Great Depression. The first title was *Antique Porn*, which I couldn't even say aloud at the time, because it was so heinous. Now I just laugh given how the story actually unfolds. I've seen Instagram photos that show more skin than Henryetta's. I settled on the title *Enchanting Beauties* as a tribute to Ziegfeld Follies photographer Alfred Cheney Johnston who in the 1930s published a then-scandalous book entitled *Enchanted Beauty*. Truly his photographs are works of art.

Still, at first, I thought there was no way I was writing her story. She engaged in pornography, for goodness sakes! What will people think of me if I write her story? But the story would not let go of me, so I began reading everything I could about the Great Depression and female photographers of the 1930s. In doing so, I discovered photographer Marion Post Wolcott, the music of Louis Armstrong, and countless other 1930s photographs, trivia, and inventions. I read fascinating stories of real people—packhorse librarians, hoboes, and even an incognito sociologist who rode the rails to research hoboes' lives. While this book is fiction, I wanted weave in bits and pieces of what I learned about the people and life during that time into the fabric of the story. I became a total fan of Eleanor Roosevelt's advocacy for women, and Eudora Welty's realistic photographs of life in Mississippi. I revere the women of that time in history—their bravery, their perseverance.

It was five of Eudora Welty's photographs that inspired my most beloved character Minnie. I have always been fascinated by the complex relationships between African American women and their employers' children in literature and film. I knew early on that I wanted Henryetta to have a strong relationship with Minnie. It was important to me to communicate that love doesn't see color or social status. While researching, my dear friend, Marshetta, traveled to Africa. Upon her return she said, "I realized that I can survive anything because I come from a long line of survivors. My ancestors survived the slave fortresses, the Middle Passage, two hundred years of slavery, the Jim Crow Laws, and marching for civil rights. They are in me." Her powerful words stuck. I wanted Minnie to embody that same strength, ingenuity, and wisdom that flows through my friend.

Having lived in West Tennessee for sixteen years now, I admire the deep spirituality, devotion to family, and the strength to carry on—to survive no matter what—that ties our communities together. At first, I toyed with creating a fictional town, but after researching my former town, Brownsville, it quickly became the perfect backdrop for the story. I was happy to be able to weave its history into Dixon's story. Knowing Brownsville helped me picture the Dixon house, the court square, the landscape, and the culture. While Henryetta's experience was not a positive one, Brownsville is truly one of the best places I have lived. Some of the best people on the planet live there. I am indebted to them.

Also, while researching, I figured out that my grandparents and my dear neighbor Miss Elizabeth had been the same ages as my characters. When they were alive, I relished their stories, but I couldn't recall any from the Great Depression. Still, I wanted to pay tribute to the two women who I consider the most supportive of me to this day. I loved that I could weave in one of my favorite Miss Elizabeth stories—her wearing a red dress the day she got married. For my Granny, I gave Gertie the aspiration to be a beauty operator—the job my Granny worked when she met my grandfather who stopped in to get a haircut while traveling for work. How I wished they were alive to answer my questions about their lives during the 1930s. I consulted the next best source, my mother, who said, "They did not talk about those times." I found her response interesting.

I won't lie. This story was hard for me to write because the main character made difficult choices, very different from my personal beliefs. There were moments my characters did totally unexpected things. However, when I found myself at the end of their story, I felt homesick for my characters for weeks. Gus and Henryetta made me weep. Sy made me cringe. Minnie healed me. I found myself daydreaming about them like you do a friend that has moved away. That was unexpected.

Finally, the defining experience that encouraged me to work toward publication was the night my beta readers (thank you, ladies) came over to dinner to do a book talk on my first draft. My book made them think. My book connected with each person at the table in some deep way. My characters' story meant something to them like it did to me. For me, it was the best book club ever, and it was the book I wrote. It was a surreal moment, and now here I am truly at the end. The last edit. It is finished.

BOOK CLUB QUESTIONS

1. What are the recurring themes of the book? Which one resonated most with you? Why is that?

2. Why did Thom remain friends with Sy despite his shortcomings?

3. What would you have done if you were in Henryetta's position? Why is that?

4. How have women changed since the 1930s? Which ways are better? Worse?

5. With which character do you most identify? Why is that?

6. Would you pose for Henryetta? Why or why not?

ABOUT THE AUTHOR

*H*annah Horch is a passionate educator who has devoted her life to serving children and teachers. Ms. Horch currently serves as the founding Program Advisor for the Newcomer International Center in Memphis, Tennessee. This is Ms. Horch's debut novel.

CPSIA information can be obtained
at www.ICGtesting.com
Printed in the USA
LVHW090015200619
621749LV00001B/1/P

9 781643 505596